FAN MAIL

RONALD MUNSON

FAN MAIL

A DUTTON BOOK

DUTTON

Published by the Penguin Group
Penguin Books USA Inc., 375 Hudson Street, New York, New York 10014, U.S.A.
Penguin Books Ltd, 27 Wrights Lane, London W8 5TZ, England
Penguin Books Australia Ltd, Ringwood, Victoria, Australia
Penguin Books Canada Ltd, 10 Alcorn Avenue, Toronto, Ontario, Canada M4V 3B2
Penguin Books (N.Z.) Ltd, 182–190 Wairau Road, Auckland 10, New Zealand

Penguin Books Ltd, Registered Offices:
Harmondsworth, Middlesex, England

First published by Dutton, an imprint of New American Library,
a division of Penguin Books USA Inc.
Distributed in Canada by McClelland & Stewart Inc.

First Printing, August, 1993
1   3   5   7   9   10   8   6   4   2

Copyright © Ronald Munson, 1993
All rights reserved

 REGISTERED TRADEMARK—MARCA REGISTRADA

LIBRARY OF CONGRESS CATALOGING IN PUBLICATION DATA:
Munson, Ronald, 1939–
    Fan mail / Ronald Munson.
        p.   cm.
    "A Dutton book."
    ISBN 0-525-93624-6
    I. Title.
    PS3563.U58F3   1993
    813'.54—dc20   92–42518
                                                        CIP

Printed in the United States of America
Set in Plantin

Designed by Steven N. Stathakis

To Rebecca and her Mama
"As is the mother, so is her daughter."
Ezekiel, 16:44

For help in making this a better book, I am deeply indebted to Miriam Grove Munson. I also thank Janet Berlo, Laurie Bernstein, Anne Kenney, Kevin Mulroy, Jennifer and Stephen Selesnick, and Marian Young.

FAN MAIL

Monday August 3–4
Almost two in the
goddammed morning

Dear Joan:

I got back from St. Louis about two minutes ago, and I'm not even going home until I give you the details. I'll fax this to you so you can read it when you wake up.

I spent from seven this morning until after nine this evening (yesterday evening?) talking to Simon Rostovsky. He is the President and General Manager of KMIS ("Your eye on the Mississippi").

He treated me well. He sent a silver Mercedes to pick me up at the airport, then gave me breakfast in his private dining room at Number One Broadcast Circle. It was so early I started to ask the waiter to light the candles.

To avoid a diplomatic incident, I was forced to eat the semilethal combination of saturated fats, salt, nitrates, and cholesterol known in the uncivilized world as bacon and eggs. I felt like Indiana Jones faced with the monkey brains still in the head. I must admit they tasted very good—the bacon and eggs I mean—but Christ, the risks I run for my clients! Surely I'm already a legend in my own mind. (Who said that? Cher?)

The first thing I got straight with Rostovsky was who has the real power. He assures me that where hiring is concerned he's such an absolute monarch James I would be jealous. Or as he put it, "The only one I have to consult is God, and even He doesn't get the final word."

A little blasphemous, a little hyperbolic, but the point is, Rostovsky signs the contracts.

He's not crazy enough to hire somebody nobody else likes, and the first thing he wanted me to understand was that everybody in the KMIS news division wants *you*. They watched your *Dallas Live* tapes and adored what they saw.

They also have the tapes of the KRLD interview with you after

1

your trial and several local news clips showing you coming out of the county jail. (I recall it as a very handsome building. Has Paul Goldberger done anything on it?) They know you can be controversial, and they're comfortable with it. Although Simon (as I came to know him) didn't come right out and say it, I think that's part of your value to them.

We talked money. They were thinking a low triple, and I said that wouldn't even cover moving expenses. Simon says nobody here makes more. I suggested that if he wanted to stay bush league in a big league city, he was wasting our time. He said he was prepared to move toward the middle but not past it. I told him those were talking terms and we could have another cup of coffee. (It wasn't even decaffeinated!)

I said you've always loved the way the seasons change in the midwest and you just might be interested in the position, although it would be a step down. (I know, I know, but I've got to make a deal.) I said you'd be leaving a city that's number seven for a market that isn't even in the top ten. I told him that's where money would become persuasive.

I said you'd want total control over the final content. He said no. Period. I said, well, maybe shared control. He said something could be worked out.

He's interested in you because you come across as "strong but gentle" and that will get good viewer response. He also hinted that if you could come up with a few stories receiving national attention, he wouldn't mind.

That you are incredibly beautiful and intelligent was not mentioned by him. I didn't bring it up either. We pretended it wasn't relevant.

We're going to talk some more on the phone, mostly about money. If we can get closer there, he wants you to "come up and meet the team." (I believe he has in mind the KMIS News Department, not the St. Louis Cardinals.) If all of you fit together like a jigsaw puzzle, he wants you to start September 14.

I will be in touch as needed. Sell all you own and put your money in canola oil.

Dan

MEMORANDUM

To: Simon Rostovsky   Date: August 4
     PRESIDENT AND GENERAL MANAGER

From: Charles Fishwater
       VICE PRESIDENT
       NEWS DIVISION

Bud Lewis just sent me the Joan Carpenter results from the focus group that viewed the *Dallas Live* tapes, and they look terrific. They see her as well informed, attractive, and personable. She seems a little too intelligent for them to want to be her friend, but they think that's okay in an investigative reporter. They like her hair, her clothes, her voice, etc., although some felt she should use more makeup to be "more feminine."

The most important result is that they give her a higher trust score (8.5 vs. 7.3) than they do the network anchors. Also, she has a wider demographic appeal than two out of three network anchors. The young and middle-aged like her slightly more (0.7) than the old, but everybody likes her just fine.

I also got Lewis to check the *Dallas Live* stats, and they make happy reading. The show is four years old, but for the first two years they might as well have shown reruns of *My Mother the Car*, because they couldn't have done any worse in the ratings. When Joan joined as a reporter, the ratings jumped four points during the first year. When she became a co-anchor, they went up five more. The last numbers show them with a rating of 18 and a market share of 38.

My advice is: Pay her what you have to. Our job will then be to make sure she earns it back in increased market share and better demogs.

To make sure we don't get burned, I've asked Joe Mallory of the Allen Agency to do a background check.

(You may think this is an unnecessary expense, but do you remember the business reporter who claimed he had a degree from the London School of Economics and turned out to have nothing more than a six-month certificate from the Harrison Business and

Secretarial College? I have always found it strange that the anonymous letter arrived a week after he made his final alimony payment.)

I'll tell Joe we want his preliminary report in forty-eight hours.

THIS IS THE SATURN AGENCY. YOU MAY LEAVE A MESSAGE AT THE TONE.

It's Joan, Dan. I didn't expect you to be awake, because it's seven my time. I just read the fax, and you're doing great. Should I send you a few bottles of omega-three fatty acid to help you recover from yesterday's breakfast?

Just one little tiny thing about the talks with Rostovsky. Something about the size of a pinhole compared to a balloon—I want that goddamned job, so don't screw things up over money.

I don't have to have a salary in triples—whatever that means. I can't afford to work for nothing, but I'm willing to come quite close to it.

I do care about program control. That's why I want to get out of Dallas. I'm tired of doing deep and meaningful pieces on restaurants for birds and new help for the dead. I think even TV anchors should display more expressions than glad and sad.

What's canola oil? Do you put your money in it the way you put basil in olive oil? Sounds too messy. I think I'll keep mine in the bank.

One last time—*get me that job!*

Over and out.

Hello, Joan. It's Dan. I know you've already gone to work because it's two in the afternoon here, but I can't keep from commenting on your message.

Every other client I have calls me up and bitches about how I'm selling them cheap and how I should ask for a thousand dollars times every week of their lives or some such, now you call me up and say you don't care about the money.

Refreshing, I have to tell you. Terribly refreshing. But so otherworldly that you'd better be on the lookout for the Ghostbusters.

Let me tell you something you apparently don't know. People like money, and if you don't talk money, they get suspicious of you. They figure you're trying to screw them while they aren't looking—which you are.

That's why you've got to talk money to them. If we go for the money, then we can back off on that demand and trade it for more control over program content, staff, and budget. If you want intangibles, you've got to have a tangible to trade for it.

This is all called *negotiation,* and it's how I earn my tangibles. I already know you want the job, so just butt out. What do you think is at stake, your whole professional career or something? If worse comes to wurst—as the Germans say—you can make a leveraged buyout of KMIS and hire yourself.

Concerning your crack about canola oil—yuck, yuck. You might like to know it's also marvelous as a skin cream. Use it every night and you can make Jumbo the elephant as smooth as a helium balloon.

Don't call me. I'll fax you.

THE ALLEN AGENCY
TO DISCOVER • TO PROTECT • TO SERVE
Branches in major metropolitan areas • Foreign coordinations

2015 CARONDOLET
ST. LOUIS, MISSOURI
63150-0575
(314) 722-8051
FAX (314) 722-5620

Mr. Charles Fishwater   August 7
Vice President, News Division
KMIS Broadcasting

Dear Mr. Fishwater:

Pursuant to your instructions of August 4, this agency conducted a background check on JOAN CARPENTER. The investigation is ongoing, but as you indicated a need for information as quickly as possible, I am providing you a summary of our findings to date.

1. Subject was born Joan Nancy Carpenter on August 29, 1960, in Florence Nightingale Hospital in Dallas, Texas. Her birth certificate shows her to be the legitimate child of Michael and Dora Williams Carpenter. Her race is shown as Caucasian and her sex female. Hospital records list her father as an attorney and her mother as an elementary school teacher. The family had one child already, Julia Jane Carpenter, who was then two years old.

2. Subject attended school from kindergarten through high school in suburban Highland Park. She graduated in 1977 and became a student at Barnard College in New York City. She graduated with an A.B. in philosophy in 1981.

Her sister, Jane, attended the same college, and graduated two years earlier. The sister then attended Harvard Medical School and now lives in Boston as a practicing psychiatrist.

3. While in college, Subject met William (Will) F. Roper, also a native of Dallas, a student at Columbia University Law School. They apparently developed an "understanding," and upon graduation both returned to Dallas. Subject entered Southern Methodist University as a Communications graduate student, while Will

Roper took a position in the legal department of Roper Oil, a petroleum exploration company owned by his father, Clarence J. Roper.

4. Subject received her M.A. June 5, 1983, and ten days later she married Will Roper at Highland Park Methodist Church. The Roper family is socially prominent, and the wedding was widely covered in the Dallas news media.

5. While in her graduate school, Subject worked as an intern with station KRLD-TV beginning in February 1982. The following May, the station offered her the position of on-camera assistant to star-chef Lawrence Griffith on *What's Cooking in Dallas?* She subsequently served as a news writer, reporter, and substitute anchor on *The Saturday News.*

6. On July 12, 1983, Subject's husband was killed when the Piper Cherokee flying him from Dallas to Baton Rouge, Louisiana, crashed near Alto, Texas. The body was returned to Dallas for burial in Hillcrest Memorial Cemetery. (Subject's father, who died in 1981, is also buried there.)

The will was probated on August 8 of the same year, and Subject was awarded the whole of her husband's estate. This amounted to some eighty thousand dollars, after the repayment of outstanding loans and expenses. Had Will Roper not predeceased his father, he would have inherited Roper Oil and (according to rumor) over five million dollars. As it was, he had only his salary from the company and a hundred thousand dollar life insurance policy. Tough luck for Subject.

7. Subject became even more professionally oriented after her husband's death, and in September 1988 she became co-anchor and investigative reporter on *Dallas After Dark.*

You specifically requested that we find out about Subject's police record. Only one arrest has been noted, and it was in connection with her professional investigation of corruption in the Dallas Police Department.

To be specific, Subject acted the role of a prostitute in the Fairmont Hotel and was charged by two vice officers with "soliciting for immoral purposes." She claimed publicly that the officers tried to shake her down for five hundred dollars. An internal investigation was instigated, but she had no hard evidence. The officers were suspended for three weeks, but no charges were brought against them.

When Subject appeared before Judge Holton Scott and he

learned she had deliberately approached the vice officers, he accused her of seeking sensationalism to promote *Dallas After Dark* and refused to dismiss the charge against her. He sentenced her to thirty days, all but seventy-two hours suspended. She refused to appeal and did her time.

The matter became a local media event. Most people saw her as performing a public service and thought she should never have been charged with a crime. Subject was interviewed a number of times, editorials were written about her, and radio and TV call-in shows were devoted to her. When Subject was released from jail, she produced an hour long program on freedom of inquiry and on her encounter with the law.

8. Personal data. Subject is thirty-one years old, five feet, eight inches tall. She has blond hair and blue eyes and is considered attractive. (As per your instructions, no one from this office approached her or met with her.)

She lives in a seven-room home at 6550 Canyon Road (Dallas) and drives a white 1988 Mercedes convertible. She used her inheritance as a down payment on the house. Its market value is about 150 thousand.

She eats in restaurants often and attends plays, concerts, movies, and art exhibitions frequently. Her mother, Dora Williams Carpenter, teaches third grade at Sudie L. Williams Elementary School.

Subject knows many people, but she seems to have no special friends in the city. She appears not to be romantically involved with anyone at present.

She pays her bills on time and has an excellent credit rating. (She has the three major credit cards, as well as department store cards and air travel cards.) She has no outstanding loans, pending judgments, or filed suits or legal charges.

Nothing shows she is involved with drugs or ever has been.

I hope to have a full report available to you by the end of next week.

> Sincerely yours,
> Joseph Mallory,
> Agent in Charge

MEMORANDUM

To: Charles Fishwater   Date: August 12
     VICE PRESIDENT
     NEWS DIVISION

From: Simon Rostovsky
      PRESIDENT AND GENERAL MANAGER

I found Joan Carpenter interesting and intelligent. Although I agreed very little with her ideas, I was intrigued by her remarks about Friedman and justice. (Did you know who Rawls is? Had you ever heard that economic policies are supposed to be grounded in some more general framework of principles?)

Fortunately, I saw nothing in her tapes to suggest that she conducts philosophical discussions in on-air interviews. Still, when you're accustomed to dealing with people like Gary Wells, she's a drink of chilled champagne.

I trust you enjoyed her visit as much as I. I think we both agree that she is a good bet to put some life into *Nightbeat*. Unless I hear some objection from you, I'm calling her agent tomorrow and offering her the job.

You had better break the news to Gary Wells that in September he may have a co-anchor. If he threatens to quit, take him up on it.

Dear Dan,

I am here. For the last four days, with hope in my heart and a checkbook in my hand, I've been searching for a house.

I've been to places ranging from derelicts with sagging plaster ceilings to mansions with third-floor ballrooms. I've traipsed through so many houses I'm beginning to feel like a building inspector looking for municipal code violations.

So far I've seen about thirty—houses I mean, the code violations run into the thousands. What they all have in common is an asking price I used to think would buy me a controlling interest in the Chrysler Building.

At least Alexis Hartz, my real estate agent, is a nice person. She's tall, has short black hair, and dresses so elegantly she intimidates me—she wears jabots, I wear jeans. Still, she doesn't chatter all the time, and she never uses the word *charming* to describe small, dingy kitchens. You appreciate such things when you spend your whole day being led around like a first-grader on a field trip. I think she is either shy or a little awed by my Star status. (Maybe the last possibility is just wishful thinking on my part.)

I need to head for bed now. Alexis tells me she's got four more houses for me to look at tomorrow, and I want to get an early start. (The birds might buy them before I have a chance.) So far I haven't seen a house I feel is the right one for me. Saying this put me in mind of an analogous situation, but I think I'll move on smartly and not think about that now.

Yes, I have talked to Mr. Rostovsky. As soon as I find a place to live, I'm supposed to call him back and make arrangements for us to get together. He sounded pleased to hear from me, and it feels good to be wanted.

I like it here. At least I do until it starts getting late and I start getting tired. When that happens, I want to go back to Dallas and climb into my own bed. (The fact that it's stored in a warehouse somewhere doesn't register.) I can feel the need coming on now, so I guess I'd better go jump into my rented bed and cover up my head until morning.

In case you need to phone or fax me, I plan to stay where I am until I become Mistress of Thistlethorpe Manor.

Joan

Alexis Caldwell Hartz

September 11

Dear Joan,

Welcome to the neighborhood! I thought these jonquils would look nice in your living room.

I enjoyed working with you, and I'm delighted we were able to find a home to suit you. Moving into a new house is always a bit of a strain, and since we live so near, you must let me know if I can be of any help to you.

Cordially,
Alexis

Joan Carpenter

12 September

Dear Alexis,

The jonquils are lovely, and I was even able to excavate a vase to put them in. You were right to think the living room was the place for them. The yellow provides a spot of brightness among the packing boxes and crumpled newspaper.

Despite the chaos, things are coming together. I continue to like the house very much, and I appreciate the time you spent helping me find just what I wanted.

Since you didn't *have* to show me this house, I'm flattered by your willingness to have me as a neighbor. I'm sure I'll soon be asking you many important questions—like where to buy *Vanity Fair* and what nursery to call for a good deal on mulch.

Thank you again for your warm welcome and your thoughtfulness.

Joan

Received: from KMISVMA.BITNET by REEDVA.BITNET
Date: Friday, September 18
From: Joan <Carpenter@KMISVMA>
Subject: Housewarming
To: Jane <REEDVA.BITNET>

Dear Jane,

I'm so pleased with the electric teakettle you and Jack sent that I'm taking to my computer so I can thank you even before the noise of the UPS truck has fully faded away.

I hope to spend long winter evenings happily sipping vintage Darjeeling and having meaningful conversations about Derrida and the deconstruction of TV with handsome intellectual men temporarily working as fry cooks at Burger Delight. But even if such dreams go unrealized, I still like tea, and being able to boil water in two minutes flat will encourage me to drink more of it and less of the hard stuff.

Everything is going smoothly. I mostly have things out of boxes and into drawers so it's possible to walk around without the risk of becoming an orthopedic emergency. My real estate lady lives right behind me on the other side of a bushy hedge, and she's very nice. She's not quite old enough to remember when Judy Garland got met in St. Louis, but she's a good source of information about where to shop and who to call when your sink gets stopped up (as mine did yesterday).

It's been like the Port Authority Bus Terminal around here since I moved in. Not only did I have to get a plumber to unstop my drain, but I had to call an electrician to install new outlets and a telephone guy to run more phone lines. I've got dedicated (and steadfast and loyal) lines for my computer and my fax machine, so I'm really part of the Global Village now. (All it takes is local money.) Unless the gas pipes decide to start leaking, I think I'm done with basic services for a while.

I love the house and the neighborhood, but my yard looks like the Jersey flats in the dry season. (When I go outside, I halfway expect to see the eyes of Dr. T. J. Ecklesburg staring at me.) The grass is dead at the root, and the bushes and shrubs are overgrown and infested with invisible bugs with voracious appetites. I asked Alexis (the real estate lady) if she knew somebody I could get in to do yard work, and she sent over the guy who works for her half a day a week. He was quite a surprise.

I was expecting somebody resembling Farmer McGregor, but he turned out to look more like Lady Chatterley's Gardener. His name is Curt Collins, and he's a 29-year-old college dropout. He has flat gray eyes, an attractive shock of blond hair, a wonderful body, and the apparent IQ of a hummingbird.

I figured that brains probably get in the way of muscles when it comes to double-digging the perennial beds, so I gave him a job. He works for Alexis half of Thursday and me for the other half. I'm sure this is going to look like Paradise Island by the time spring rolls around.

I like working on *Nightbeat*, and before long I'll send you a tape so you can get an idea of what the program is like. I'll try to pick a show that's suitable

13

for family viewing (no Love Letters from the Grave) and not too embarrassing for me.

I hope your practice is going well and your patients are still sane enough to know how to make out their checks correctly. I think Jack would like to see the St. Louis Arch because it looks like some kind of shape mathematicians have a name for.

Give Amy a big hug and a kiss. Tell her that her Aunt Joan loves her to pieces—and also loves the pieces.

Thanks again for the housewarming present. I'm going to go use it right now.

Love you all,
Joanie

FAX TRANSMITTAL 314-552-5671

JOAN CARPENTER
2030 Buckminster • St. Louis, MO • 63130

8 October, Thursday

Darling Dan (or do I mean Dan Darling?),

I am undoubtedly the Saturn Agency's happiest client. Too bad I can't ship you twenty percent of outstandingly good feelings. Maybe it would make up for my failure to generate the megabucks you always say you so desperately need to keep you in oat bran and alfalfa sprouts. (I assuage my guilt by reminding myself that you rake off plenty from people like Dan Rather and Roger Rabbit.)

In the last three weeks, I've run through St. Louis like a dose of Epsom salts through a hound dog, as my old grandma used to (rather indelicately) say. I've seen everything (the Arch, the riverboats, Union Station) and met everyone (the Mayor, the Busches, and Judy at the cleaners who scolds me for slopping coffee on my shirts). I confess I haven't been introduced to the Cardinal yet. Does he have anything to do with the baseball team?

The job is terrific. I love starting something new, when you don't know what's going to happen. It's like the first few weeks with

14

a new lover—you're essentially strangers and so you're both still mysterious and unpredictable. (No, I haven't, and I'm not looking.) My colleagues are quite nice, professionally competent, and easy to work with. Just as I suspected from my visit, though, a couple of key players in our real-life drama could be cast better for my liking.

To name names: The head of the News Division is a balding, dried up little guy named Charles Fishwater. Except for the three-piece suits and shirts with French cuffs, he resembles one of Santa's elves. I should say also, except for the smile. When he pulls back his lips to indicate amusement, it's like the pink metallic gap you get when you roll up the metal tape to open a can of Spam. (No, I haven't eaten it since I was a kid at camp.)

The Fish has the unfortunate habit of talking to me as if he hired me to empty the wastebaskets instead of co-anchor a news magazine. (You didn't forget to tell me you promised him I'd take out the trash, did you?)

I shouldn't be bad-mouthing Mr. Fishwater, though, because he's given me the premier spot on *Nightbeat.* I open and close and do the lead story—loads of face time. So far I haven't had a chance to put my own story ideas into production, but that will come. I know I've got to deliver the goods unless I want my ass out on the street.

To name another name: My co-anchor is a fat-cheeked, slack-jawed boy-o named Gary Wells. His major asset consists of an ability to look deeply moved at appropriate moments of pathos. I know he can read, but whether he can add and subtract, I can't say. Gary was not, as you might guess, delighted to make my acquaintance. He hasn't invited me to his house to meet the Mrs. or asked me to be his best friend. He's got to know I've been brought in to grease the skids. I'm always very nice to him.

I think you'll be pleased to hear that, thanks to Smiling Chuck Fishwater, my arrival has become a minor media event. Print ads (with picture!) in the *Post-Dispatch,* the *Citizen,* and the *Riverfront Times,* and a *P-D Sunday Magazine* spread (my mother in a telephone interview said, "She used to line up her dolls and make them listen to her read"). Radio spots on the all-news station, e-z listening, and album rock. Plugs at the end of the regular KMIS news programs and during the first week three two-minute local-news interviews.

Does this mean I'm a star now? Will retailers insist on giving me discounts on dishwashers and send me fabulous clothes as tokens of their esteem? Will I still have to wait in line at McDonald's? (Will you still respect me in the morning?)

I hope you'll take a couple of the paltry few dollars I've put into your pocket and splurge on a bottle of Perrier. Use it to drink to our future. *Nightbeat* today, *Today* tomorrow!

Your pal on the Mississippi,
Stella

P.S. My new fax number is 314-552-5671.

JOAN CARPENTER
2030 Buckminster • St. Louis, MO • 63130

October 8

Dear Mama,

St. Louis is a surprisingly beautiful place, with lots of trees and parks and broad, winding avenues. I don't know why we had to visit battlegrounds at Appomattox and Vicksburg when we could have come up here for catfish, beer, and blues. (I have to confess that the only thing Jane and I liked about those trips was eating in restaurants and staying in motels. I believe that was their real educational value for us. I realize now that the trips were really for Daddy's sake. I never quite knew what he was thinking when he used to stand on those bare windy fields and look off into the distance. Now I'm sorry I never asked him.)

Anyway, this is a really *old* city, much like Boston or Baltimore or some other East Coast place. People here were putting up red brick castles when people in Dallas were still living in mud huts.

Let me tell you about the house I bought. It's not a new house, but it's not a terribly old one either. It was built in 1935, and I like that because it's also the year you were born in. That makes me feel the house and I have a personal bond and I already know it a little. It's a two-story Tudor with three bedrooms upstairs, large entry hall with grand staircase, stepdown living room with baronial fireplace, dining room, sewing (Ha!) room, and a study-library with beautiful leaded-glass windows.

What I really love about the house is its gigantic kitchen. Right before the owners decided to move back to Michigan, they did it over in a sleek European style with lots of birch mixed with the Formica and all new built-in appliances. (The electric teakettle Jane sent me is stainless and fits right in.) There's a terrific butcher-block table that's big enough to accommodate me, my breakfast, my spread-out *Times,* and a large color TV. I never have to go into the dining room.

I have a telephone in every room, including all three bathrooms. The Petersons (the people I bought the house from) work for an electronics company and didn't want to bother taking their equipment with them. I even have a voice-activated speaker phone in the kitchen that stores fifty names and numbers. I can call you just by yelling "Mama!" Then when you answer, I can shout at you across the room while I'm at the stove whipping up a soufflé. Of course I'll sound like I'm speaking from the bottom of a well, but that's progress for you.

I'm lucky to get the house, because Alexis, my real estate agent, was very picky about who she showed it to. That's because she lives directly behind me and didn't want some low-life type (like a drug dealer or a school principal) butting up against her backyard. She probably had her doubts about me at first, but thanks to the work done by my mom's constant admonitions during my formative years, she must have decided I was sufficiently *bien élevée* to meet her standards.

The houses around mine are mostly larger, and the neighbors seem nice, even though they are probably very rich. The lots are all about the same size, and I have a really big backyard. It's in terrible shape, but I think I'm going to cut back all the bushes, trim the trees, and grow perennials. It's going to be a huge expense and an enormous amount of work.

Thanks to Alexis, I've already got a gardener, though. He's a good worker and knows what he's doing. Unfortunately, he's also become a fan. The first day he worked for me, we chatted about flowers and plants. Then when he heard from Alexis that I was in TV, all he wanted to talk about was how I got started (hard work and stupidity), and wasn't I terrific to be on *Nightbeat* (aw, shucks), and did I think maybe I could get him a job at KMIS (no way, bus-ter). I'm going to have to keep my distance if I expect to get any work out of him.

Speaking of my job, it's all I wanted it to be. I'm only sorry I had to move away from you to get it. I think you should consider taking early retirement and moving up here. Can you honestly claim you still enjoy teaching third graders after so many years? We'll talk when you come here for Thanksgiving. (Pretend we've discussed this for hours and you finally agreed to come.) Will you come if I can get Jane, Jack, and the kid out here? Will you come even if I can't?

I'm in good health, except last week around midnight I was working in the kitchen and banged the side of my head on the corner of one of my sleek European cabinets. I bled like a pig, and had to have four stitches. Fortunately, I can pull my hair forward enough to hide them. They itch like crazy, and I have to go back in a couple of weeks to have them removed.

The experience wasn't altogether terrible. When the admitting nurse at the hospital realized I was a TV "star," she called the emergency room chief, and he made me wait until he called in one of the city's best plastic surgeons. "His name is Dr. Stephen Legion, and he's very socially prominent," the nurse told me. "He does everyone's faces and breasts."

Dr. Legion turned out to be a slim, dark-blond handsome guy who looks like Richard Chamberlain playing Dr. Kildare. His bedside manner fell a little short, though. I chattered about how glad I was to be in old St. Lou and how much I appreciated his coming to the hospital in the middle of the night, and he responded by saying things like "This may sting a little" as he stuck a needle in my scalp. It's a good thing I love star treatment, even when it hurts.

I know I'm hard to reach on the phone, and our schedules aren't exactly compatible. Why don't you break down and get a fax machine? I'll buy you one if you *promise* to plug it in. (Remember the VCR? It's not supposed to be a high-tech magazine rack.)

A girl always needs her mom, and I miss you.

Love always,
Joanie

P.S. Did the Stuarts cut down the pear tree in front of my house? I got blisters on my blisters from digging the hole for that tree, and it is (was?) so well shaped and beautiful that I'm surprised a Japanese zillionaire didn't try to buy it. I should have put in the contract that they had to care for the tree until it died or I did, whichever might come first.

THE SATURN AGENCY
256 East 59th Street • New York, New York • 10020
212-555-5050 • Fax 212-555-5051
Daniel L. Saturn, PRESIDENT

October 11 (Sunday,
bloody Sunday)

Dear Joan:

I am pleased that you are pleased. More than that I'm delighted you wrote to me, because your upbeat, happy-faced fax gave my spirits a boost they needed.

You made me feel like I could do at least something right, and I've now moved up from being severely depressed to being just plain miserable. That I can handle. God knows I've had enough experience over the last year to last a longer lifetime than I'm anticipating.

I wouldn't expect you to remember this quite as precisely as I do, but it's now been 366 days since Stephanie packed up her Eskimo (I mean Inuit, of course) *objets* and moved in with Hartley (Hartley!). If you wanted real precision, I could tell you it's been 366 days, 15 hours, and 27 minutes. I made the mistake of looking at the digital clock on the bookcase just as Steph closed the door. Once you've seen something like that, you can't get it out of your mind. You don't *try* to remember it; you just do.

I guess I should be glad she didn't bring him with her to help with the hauling or I would know what he looks like. It's bad enough that I see pieces by him in the *New York Review of Books*. I always say I'm not going to read them, then I do. Then they're always about writers with lots of Cs and Zs in their names who are discovering new dimensions in the human spirit, and I end up feeling both insensitive and stupid.

I wish they didn't live in Morningside Heights, because now whenever I go to Columbia to use the law library, I'm afraid I'm going to run into them. So far has been so good, but I hope he gets a job in California or, even better, Nebraska.

But of course what will happen is that Columbia will give him tenure, and if I ever get to be 68 years old, I'll still be crossing College Walk with my head down staring at the bricks, still afraid that I'll see Steph—or worse, see them both together.

I still miss her a surprising amount. And the strange thing is that I virtually never felt sick during the three years we were together. But since she's been gone, I've never felt quite well. I know it's stupid to keep thinking about her as much as I do, but none of the women I've been out with have come close to matching her looks or her sense of humor or her intelligence.

The truth is, I'm afraid I just wasn't enough of an intellectual for her taste. I'm not even embarrassed about not wanting to read Hungarian novelists. I don't doubt that they're good, important, etc., but they just aren't to my taste. My idea of a good novel is still *The Great Gatsby* (remember the shirt scene?), so I'm hopelessly out of touch.

I apologize for running on like this, particularly since you're having such a wonderful time. I don't want to make you feel bad about feeling good. So I'll just return to where I began and say that your fax made me feel better. I hope that makes you feel better about my feeling bad. (Did that make sense?)

On a happier note next time.

Dan

YOU HAVE REACHED 552-8076. AT THE TONE YOU MAY LEAVE A MESSAGE.

Joan, this is Alexis.

I talked to the contractor I mentioned to you. I told him you wanted somebody to do a safety check of your house, and he said he would be happy to help out.

His name is Alan Carter, and he's a very reliable person. His company does a lot of rehab work for me, so he doesn't mind doing small favors.

I told him you'd be calling him to set a time. His telephone number is 555-3550. I thought it would be better for you to call him. Since your number is unlisted, I didn't want to give it to him without your permission.

I'll call you about doing lunch soon.

Goodbye for now.

THIS IS ALEXIS HARTZ. I'M SORRY I CAN'T COME TO THE PHONE RIGHT NOW. BUT IF YOU WILL LEAVE YOUR NAME AND NUMBER, I'LL TRY TO GET BACK TO YOU AS SOON AS POSSIBLE. THANK YOU AND HAVE A NICE DAY.

Hi, Alexis. It's Joan.

Thanks for putting me in touch with Alan Carter. He's terrific, and he thinks my house is in pretty good shape. I was afraid he was going to suggest that I rip out my doors and install stainless steel bars, but he didn't.

Lunch would be fun, but my calendar is so crowded, I don't know when it could be. I still haven't met everybody at work yet.

If you don't mind terribly—and I know this sounds awful—would you please call my administrative assistant in the next few days and let her see when we can get together? I might seem like a free woman, but I'm actually the slave of my AA. The number is 431-5120.

Thanks again for connecting me up with Alan. And if you see me out back, be sure to wave.

Mrs. Dora Carpenter

8519 Bluffview Road
Dallas, Texas 75209

October 10

Dear Joanie,

I am so proud of you for being able to move to a new city, take on a new job, and buy a house.

When I consider the way I was when I was your age, my respect for you goes up even more. If it hadn't been for your father, I would never have done anything in life except teach school and live in a rented room. He opened my mind to life's possibilities, and I hope he and I together helped make you girls what you've become. I'm only sorry he didn't live long enough to see what you've both done with your lives. I'll stop, because I'm getting too sentimental.

Your house sounds wonderful, but you must have banged your head rather badly to have to get four stitches taken. I hope you're getting all right. Was there anyone around to take you to the hospital?

I am a little frightened at the idea of your living by yourself in a strange city. Not that anyone is ever completely safe, but when you were here, we were just a few blocks from one another, and there was always someone to call in case of emergency. I'm glad you know the lady who lives behind you. She sounds nice, and it's good to have at least one person you can turn to for help.

While I'm on the topic (you'll think I'm really becoming an old woman), did you make sure all your doors have dead bolts and your windows have those pins in the sashes so they can't be raised? If you're short of cash, I'll be pleased to take care of that as a housewarming present.

I'm glad you're liking your job so well. I suppose leaving Dallas was something you had to do sooner or later, particularly if you're going to make a national reputation for yourself. I thought the time would come eventually, but of course that doesn't keep me from missing my little girl.

The Stuarts have taken care of your pear tree to a perfection. I asked Mr. Stuart myself, and he told me it's been mulched, watered, and sprayed in preparation for winter. He had a nursery man out from Lambert's to take care of all the trees.

You know I would love to see you, but I doubt I can come at Thanksgiving. We get off only Thursday and Friday and start back on Monday. That's not enough time for me to take such a long trip and recover from it in time to go back to work.

I was thinking you might come here. I told Janie the same thing, even though she wants us all to come to Boston. She doesn't think she'll be able to convince Jack to go anywhere. He is no doubt very intelligent, but he certainly can be a pain. I would love to see you all, though. People are too spread out in this modern world.

Speaking of modern things, I'm about as likely to get a fax machine as you are to start washing all your clothes in a washtub and hanging them out to dry. But I am going to have Mr. Jordan come by and show me how to use my video player. Now that I can't see you on Dallas TV, I want to be able to watch your tapes.

Love and kisses,
Mother

FAX TRANSMITTAL 314-552-5671

JOAN CARPENTER
2030 Buckminster • St. Louis, MO • 63130

12 Oct. Mon.

Dear Dan,

I'm glad you've been able to haul yourself out of the slough of despond. Don't worry if for a while you can't do much more than lie on the bank and pant from the effort.

I speak from experience. When Will was killed, my whole world was shattered, and I've spent a long time putting the pieces back together. Since the most important piece is permanently missing, the new world doesn't look quite like the old one. At the beginning that made me very sad, and it still makes me a little sad. It always will.

23

A year seems like forever when you're waiting for something, but when you're looking back at it, a year seems no time at all. I still think about Will, and he's been gone for more than seven years. It doesn't surprise me that you still miss Stephanie.

Although I didn't know her well, I thought she was a nice person. And you are certainly a nice person. The melancholy truth is that nice people aren't always shaped to fit together like teaspoons. Often they're more like knives and forks, and it's not their fault.

You were right to feel pleased about doing a good job for me. I'm happy with my work and glad to be here. Like you, I could be happier with what I'll delicately call the romantic part of my life, but I'm hoping that will improve in time.

I think you should hope that for yourself too. After all, hope contains no mono or polyunsaturated fats, cholesterol, sugars, artificial sweeteners, flavors or colors; it's classified as "generally recognized as safe" by the FDA and is a known anticarcinogen. I think it's just the substance you need for your health.

I'm glad you wrote. Now I've got to get down to thinking up a lead for "Does Your Pet Get Better Medical Care Than You Do?" (Answer: Maybe so, because vets police themselves better than docs. Don't change, though—you'll lose every client except Benji if you go around smelling of flea dip.)

Love,
Joan

JOAN CARPENTER
2030 Buckminster • St. Louis, MO • 63130

13 October, Tue.

Dear Mama,

Just a short note to tell you not to worry. My house is as secure as Uncle Scrooge's money bin.

Alexis helped see to that. Right after I bought the house, we were chatting over the back hedge, and I mentioned to her that I was concerned about security. She very nicely asked if I would like to have an architect-builder who does work for her company come by and give me some advice. I said sure.

So this guy who was terribly good looking in a lean and raffish Kevin Baconish sort of way came by and spent a good two hours inspecting everything. His name is Alan Carter. I had been expecting the Incredible Hulk, I guess, but he turned out to be chatty and charming.

He said I could change the locks if I wanted, but otherwise everything was tight and right, with pins in the windows and grates over the basement door. Since I couldn't be sure how many drug dealers, rapists, and murderers the Petersons and their two teenage kids gave keys to, I decided changing the locks was a reasonable precaution.

I had a stroke of good luck there. Alan's company is doing a rehab project on a house Alexis owns, and she had already bought a set of locks. After the one on the front door was installed, she decided they were too expensive and told Alan to take it off and put in a cheaper set. They were exactly the number I needed, and Alan sold them to me at cost. He also arranged for a locksmith to do the work, and I only got billed at the builder's rate.

Alan didn't charge me anything for his advice. I tried to pay him, of course, but he wouldn't hear of it. In fact, we seemed to hit it off right from the start. I gave him a drink, and we spent as long chewing the rag as he had inspecting the house. (He's 36, divorced six years, no kids, a St. Louis local educated at Washington University then Yale. Owns own business doing both commercial and residential construction and rehabbing, skis in Colorado. Reads nothing, though able.)

I looked at him with large and rounded eyes and expected him to ask me out before he left, but he didn't. We simply departed on warm and friendly terms. I still halfway expect him to call me, but so far he hasn't.

Do I laugh too much? Frown too much? Talk too much? Radiate stop signs? Fail to transmit go signs? I should ask Janie.

Why is this short note to convince you of my safety turning into a disquisition on the lack of romance in my life? Could it be that I'm lonely here in this new city? Well, that's why a girl needs a mom.

Janie and I are talking about Thanksgiving. We tend to think it would be better for us all to meet here. (At least that's my line.)

25

Your claim that you don't have enough time is nonsense. It is no longer necessary to use horses or trains to travel to St. Louis. The flight time from Dallas is eighty minutes. Even doubling the time for a round trip, assuming you leave on Wednesday and return on Sunday, that leaves you four full days.

Thanks for the news of the tree. I'm glad you miss me, because I wouldn't have it any other way.

But don't worry.

Love and hugs, pats and hats,
Joanie

FROM THE DESK OF
ALICE WALCHECK

ADMINISTRATIVE ASSISTANT TO
JOAN CARPENTER

10/13

Joan:

I know you said to fax you at home anytime I wanted, but I feel bad about bothering you. Still, things can't always be ignored until you come into the office. I'll just remind myself of what you said about interruptions being fewer if you write at home than if you wrote here.

I sure don't blame you for not wanting any phone calls. I could get my work done in half a day if I didn't have to answer the telephone. Honestly, though, I'd probably go crazy with boredom if I didn't get a chance to chat with people.

I have a matter to bring to your attention.

Mr. Fishwater has arranged for you to attend a luncheon of the Higher Education Community Coordinating Board (HECCB) at noon next Wednesday at the Missouri Athletic Club (MAC).

This is supposed to be so you can find out about what is happening in higher education in St. Louis. Mr. Fishwater says the real purpose is to meet the members of the Board. They include major social and political figures he thinks you should know.

I've marked the date on your calendar.

Alice

FROM THE DESK OF
JOAN CARPENTER

13 October

Alice:

Stop worrying about faxing me—it's as easy as ABC.

This leads me quite naturally to dealing with your alphabet-soup memo.

Before I go to MAC, please get me a list of the HECCB members and a paragraph bio of each.

I don't like to meet people cold, particularly those who consider themselves important. If I don't know who they are, I'm sure to say to somebody like the CEO of Monsanto something like, "Don't you think it's awful the way people are still using artificial sweeteners and eating fake fat?"

I don't mind making a fool of myself, but I prefer to do it for some noble cause. Ignorance isn't noble enough.

JC

Ms. Joan Carpenter
Star of *Nightbeat*
KMIS-TV

Dear Ms. Carpenter,

I've never written a letter to a public personality before, but when I saw you on *Nightbeat* last night, I felt a strong urge to let you know how happy I am you decided to move to our city.

I would be lying if I said the first thing I noticed about you was your obvious intelligence. No, it was your striking beauty that made me almost gasp with astonishment. That's not too surprising, I suppose, because TV is a visual medium and you *are* beautiful. Whoever chose you for your job chose well.

I was captivated at first sight by the smooth perfection of your face. Everything seems to work together—the finely shaped nose, the prominent ridges of your cheekbones, your lively blue eyes, the way your mouth turns up at the corners in a sly smile. I love your smile. It seems to be both amused and wistful, ironic and sad. Above all, in your smile the genuine warmth of a caring person comes through.

Quite frankly, the story you did about the landlord who mailed his tenants dead rats to make them move out wasn't very interesting. (Besides, my sympathy is for the landlord and not the riff-raff who won't pay him their rent.) But the story did give me an opportunity to see you going out into the city and talking to people. I don't want to trivialize your work by some crass sexist remark, but I have to say that the rest of your body is just as lovely as your face. I hope to see more of it.

Of course, you've got more than beauty. You've got that special something that classic stars like Dietrich and Bacall had. I can feel it. It comes out of my TV and washes over me like a special kind of radiation. TV seems to make you bigger than life, even though the picture is smaller. You touch something deep inside me, and I look forward to seeing more of you.

I'm glad you came. St. Louis needed you. And I needed you even more.

This letter is too personal for me to feel comfortable signing my name to it. I'm too vulnerable, too easily hurt to let you know who I really am. Maybe in the future I'll tell you. For now, since I like watching you so much, I'll just call myself . . .

The Watcher

FROM THE DESK OF
J O A N   C A R P E N T E R

15 October

Alice,

I'm attaching a piece of fan mail I want you to save. I say "fan mail," but if you read the letter (and please do), you'll see it's more like "crank mail." In fact, it's so much like it let's just say that's what it is.

Please open a file labeled "Crank Mail" and put this letter in it. I want to be sure we have it just in case "The Watcher" writes to say he's decided to blow up the Channel 3 transmitter and the police ask us if we've ever heard from him before.

Thanks.

JC

CHARLES FISHWATER

VICE PRESIDENT
NEWS DIVISION
KMIS-TV

October 19

Dear Joan:

I am enclosing a copy of the Arbitron figures dealing with the last six weeks of *Nightbeat*. This includes the period just before you joined the program, so we can get a good sense of how much difference you have made.

Quite frankly, the numbers are not as good as we expected them to be. Notice they peak immediately after our intensive campaign promoting you and that is only to be expected. Maybe it is even reasonable to expect the points to drop a little after that high. After all, once you turn down the water, the hose doesn't spurt as far.

But we're talking about a *three point drop*. That means people who had never done so before took a look at the show, watched it for a couple of times, did not like what they saw, and switched over.

While it is true that the numbers still put the show a couple of points ahead of where it was before you joined it and that it has a slightly larger market share, it is not where we want it to be or expect it to be.

I want to suggest that you give some thought to developing some new ideas that might be expected to *work*. I know you want to do all you can to improve the program, and I want you to know I am fully behind you in your efforts.

Sincerely,
Charles Fishwater

cc: Simon Rostovsky

FAX TRANSMITTAL 314-552-5671

JOAN CARPENTER
2030 Buckminster · St. Louis, MO · 63130

20 October, Tues.

Dan,

Have you read the letter from the Fish I faxed just before this page? If you haven't, stop and do it now.

What do you think?

I think it's as slimy as a toad and reeks and stinks like a rotten mackerel in the moonlight.

Of course I haven't been the hard hitting investigative reporter who makes Lois Lane and Brenda Starr (not to mention Helen Thomas and Diane Sawyer) look like inept amateurs. I've nosed out a lot of stories that are both real and important. I've been straining to do them, but the Fish won't take me off the leash. Let me tell you about just a couple.

Item 1. Two St. Louis suburban hospitals have a surgical kill rate *three times* the national norm for the same operations, and most of these operations are traceable to just two surgeons. Surgeons who make over half a million dollars (American) per year.

The Fish says, "Nobody's sued the hospitals or the doctors, so we don't have any way to get hard information. I don't want to make trouble for doctors when patients aren't unhappy."

Of course, the patients most concerned aren't unhappy. They're dead.

Item 2. I've got people who will tell me on air, with proper ID protection, that they have seen drug use in City Hall among highly placed political appointees.

The Fish says, "Nobody accused is high up enough. If we can't get some elected officials, then the story is boring. Who cares if the man responsible for deciding which streets get their lines painted does a little coke now and then."

I do, that's who. And I don't think it's boring, and I don't think our viewers would either. If we blow off enough lids, the air is going to be filled with enough steam to clean up the city.

I thought they *wanted* me to do things like this.

I'm prepared to march into the Fish's office and tell him to jump into a frying pan, but I wanted to ask you about it first. My innocent belief was that I was going to get to choose my stories. He sent the letter by *registered* mail. Does that mean they plan to fire me?

Do I have a contractual leg to stand on? Or at least maybe a toe or two?

Having wonderful time. Wish you were here. I could show you Catfish Row.

You have ten minutes to fax your reply.

Love to all nine million suffering souls,
St. Joan of St. Louis

THE SATURN AGENCY
256 East 59th Street • New York, New York • 10020
212-555-5050 • Fax 212-555-5051
Daniel L. Saturn, PRESIDENT

October 20

Sorry, Joan, but I was at lunch when your fax came in.

That's why it's taken me an incredible three hours to get back to you. I also have to admit that I had to spend ten minutes of that time looking over your contract. I suppose I should have it memorized, but I'm growing feeble in my 36th year and no longer capable of such tricks.

It's obvious that your feathers are ruffled, your nose is out of joint, your dander is up, and you're suffering from various other anatomical insults as the result of getting Mr. Charles Fishwater's rude and vaguely threatening letter.

(I'm not sure you should call him "the Fish," by the way. I keep imagining how it would sound in court, and it might lose you sympathy. Certainly it would with Civil Court Judge Alvin Faceschitz, who sees nothing even mildly amusing about names.)

Let me summarize your contractual position with an epigram: Joan Carpenter proposes, but Charles Fishwater disposes.

To be less oracular, you can suggest story ideas, and if KMIS Corporation in the person of your immediate superior approves them, then you may pursue them. Further, you have the power to create, within those limits, and to cooperate, but you don't have the power to destroy. That is, if Mr. F. wants you to do a story, you may refuse, but he is free to ask someone else to do it. Of course, if you refuse too much, they will not be getting "fair value of time and talent" and they can kick your ass out of there without even a nickel in severance.

As you see, you have no ultimate say about what gets done or not done. May I remind you that we talked about this from what trendy novels used to call the git-go? Since you haven't quite achieved superstar status, some compromise was necessary to get you the power of proposing and refusing.

But we both assumed they wanted you for what you could do and had been doing and wouldn't be likely to squelch your ideas. Now it seems that they don't want you to do what they hired you to do.

My suggestion? Keep quiet for a while. Play the game and try to find some fascinating feature stories to boost the ratings. Once you're at the top again, we can renegotiate. If this doesn't happen soon, and you're still unhappy, then we'll have a talk with Mr. Rostovsky.

Catfish Row is in Charleston, not St. Louis. Perhaps you meant "catfish roe," which is supposed to be very tasty and maybe high in HDL cholesterol.

I know it's hard to do this while your other body parts are in the aforementioned positions, but . . . keep your chin up.

Dan

```
Received: from KMISVMA.BITNET by REEDVA.BITNET
Date: Thursday, October 22
From: Joan <CARPENTER@KMISVMA>
Subject: Re: This and That
To: Jane <REEDVA.BITNET>
```

Dear Janie,

All right, I'm a shit for not answering you immediately. I just don't check my e-mail that often, so I didn't even get your message until a couple of days ago. (Better to write, call or fax.) That isn't my only excuse, of course. My life isn't falling apart, but the pieces aren't making a beautiful picture either. But more about that later.

Let me remind you that I spoke first about Thanksgiving, so don't go making trouble. I very much want you all to fly *here*. You haven't seen my new house, and I need Amy as a lure for Mama. Without a granddaughter on the scene, I doubt she would ever come. How often did she come to Boston before Amy was born? Once, right? When you first got pregnant and she thought Jack needed advice about dealing with someone in your delicate condition.

Speaking of Jack, I know he doesn't like leaving

home, but tell him my house is so big he can have a room to himself to work in. If he doesn't like my computer (IBM-PS2) and needs a certain kind, I'll rent it and have it plugged in, blinking, and ready to byte. Promise him anything. (Large bottles of scotch have frequently worked in my experience.) We can all be together, and it will be good the way it was in the old days, when we ran the bulls and drank the harsh red wine from the skins. (Do you remember, little rabbit?)

Thanks for the kind words about *Nightbeat*. Despite appearances, I didn't send you the tapes for your unstinting praise and support. God knows it's always welcome and needed, even though more than usually undeserved this time. I thought the Clothes to Kill For piece wasn't half bad, but the whole fur vs. fashion/pain-for-pleasure theme is pretty well worn and scratchy by now.

The piece on children's funerals was the epitome of trash TV, and I'm proud and relieved to say I had nothing to do with it. It was the idea of our producer Chuck Tuna (Charles Fishwater to be accurate), and the story was a natural for my co-anchor.

Did you notice the catch in Gary Wells's voice when he was describing the puppies, kittens, and angels you could choose to have decorate the small tombstones? Much like choosing a birthday cake, the closing line originally read. My contribution to western civilization was insisting this be cut. Otherwise, I too am guilty, oh Lord.

Several thousand times a day I decide I made a mistake in leaving Dallas to come here. I said the pieces aren't making a pretty picture, but matters aren't terrible. It's just that I don't have as much autonomy as I thought I was promised, and I'm feeling a lot of pressure to get the ratings up.

Just today in the Everyday Magazine of the *Post-Dispatch* Tom Kline, their TV critic, wrote something like, "Joan Carpenter was brought to town with much fanfare to breathe new life into *Nightbeat*, but so far the only breath she's provided has been stale and dead." I've got TV halitosis, and even Scope won't help.

But this is an old story and quite boring. Even if you haven't heard it from any of your patients, you've seen it about a million times in the movies and on TV and read about it in beauty-shop magazines and bad-taste newspapers.

No matter what Mama told you, I did not knock my brains out in any literal sense. I got a small gash on my left temple, and just today I went to see a Dr. Kildare (Richard Chamberlain, not Lew Ayres) look-alike to have the stitches removed. His name is Stephen Legion, and although handsome as Satan, he paid about as much personal attention to me as I do to a goose I'm trussing up with a basting needle. I was getting untrussed, but the attitude was the same. Perhaps if I met him at a party . . .

So in answer to your question, getting stitches removed is the closest I've come to romantic involvement.

My handsome new gardener has turned out to be such a total pain in the ass I would never get involved with him. Not only is he awed by me as a Star, he's awed by himself as a Poet. When he sees me, he stops turning over the sod and tries to turn on the charm. Although he hasn't actually published any poems, he does read his work Friday nights at a local bar. He thinks he's on the way to becoming recognized as a Significant Poet. Like virtually everybody else I meet, he also thinks he would be a good subject for a *Nightbeat* segment (Curt Collins-The Gardener Poet). The awful thing is, he might even be right.

Do you have a fax yet? You've got to get one. Then you can send me fuzzy pictures of my beautiful niece. Also, we can communicate whenever we want to, without waiting for the other person to be free or adjust her schedule. Besides, e-mail sucks; you never know when some teen computer wizard might decide to tap into your most private thoughts, then transfer them to Comsat for planetary broadcast. (My fax number: 314-552-5671.)

Tell Jack I absolutely do not want him to try to explain his work to me. I know he hates it, and the last time I asked, it took me a full week to get over feeling stupid. (I still haven't recovered from *being* stupid.)

Tell Amy her Aunt Joan loves her more than she loves the moon and will give her unlimited supplies of candy, Coke, pizza, and tapes of Ramona and the Care Bears if she will convince her mother to come here Thanksgiving.

What can I promise you, Janie? I promise not to tell Jack about Zack.

> I am yours with love, etc.
> your devoted sister,
> Joanie

Ms. Joan Carpenter
Star of *Nightbeat*
KMIS-TV

October 21

Dear Joan,

You and I spend a lot more time together than you know. I always tape *Nightbeat,* and I've got all your shows, except for the first one. (That was before I realized what I was missing.) Sometimes I have other commitments when the show is on, so I have to time-shift it.

When I want to watch you, I move the VCR into my bedroom, lock the door, take off my clothes, and climb into bed. Then i play the tape. I'm always intrigued by everything you do and stare at you with complete attention. Often I'm so wrapped up in watching you that when the story is over, I don't even know what it was about.

After I watch the latest show, i go back and look at some older ones. I have my favorites, of course. At the top of my list is your piece on finding an aerobics instructor. As you might guess, I like it because you're dressed in a tight-fitting white body suit that shows *almost* every detail of your anatomy.

This is a section of tape I return to almost every day. Of

course, I use the slow-motion and the pause buttons a lot while I'm watching it. I like to make the experience last.

So you see, I'm so accustomed to having you in my bedroom with me that i feel we're almost intimates, if you take my meaning. I know you don't know me as well, of course, but one day I think we can change that. I want much more of you than your image on a TV screen, as lovely as that is.

But I'm talking about myself too much. I didn't intend to do that. The trouble is I really can't talk about you without talking about myself, and vice versa. In my mind, we are that closely intertwined.

I'm sure you're beginning to feel that way yourself. I notice the way you move your head in a little gesture to toss back your hair, and I know you're telling me you're thinking about me too.

May I make a suggestion about your hair? You have beautiful hair, hair others would kill for, but you take it too much for granted. Its medium length may not offend anyone, but the length doesn't really suit you. It's too long to give us a complete view of your face, and it's too short to frame it. My suggestion is that you grow it longer. Long blonde hair is almost a definition of sexy in our society.

I'll write again very soon. While you're thinking of me, I'll be watching you.

The Watcher

FROM THE DESK OF
JOAN CARPENTER

22 Oct. Thurs.

Alice:

Attached is another letter from "the Watcher." It sounds a little more bizarre than the first, and I didn't think that one was a good candidate for the Nobel Sanity Prize.

Please start a file for the Watcher. He's beginning to get a little too personal in his remarks to make me feel comfortable about him.

In this respect, he stands out from the other cranks. Most of them who don't confuse me with the Virgin Mary just want me to quit this job and go off and be a wife and mother. (Do I put them in the Crank File because deep down I fear they might be right? No, I don't—except on alternate Thursdays during leap years.)

An unrelated item: I'll talk to you about sending the letter to each member of the City Council about hiring more women in nonclerical positions. I'll do a draft, then give it to you by Thursday.

An afterthought: Before you file this Watcher letter, make me a copy and address an Airborne Overnight envelope to my sister. She's in my address file as Dr. Jane Carpenter-Reed. Just drop the stuff on my desk, and I'll enclose a note.

JC

FROM THE DESK OF
JOAN CARPENTER

Thursday, 22nd

Dear Sis,

I'm sending you a copy of a "fan letter" I just got. This is the second time the guy has written, but the first was more or less a standard gee-you're-terrific letter.

Does this one sound especially odd to you? Do you think I should do anything particular about it?

I'm not sure what doing "anything particular" might involve. Turning the letter over to the police is all I can think of, but I don't see how that could do any good. What could they do, put out an APB on a man with an electric typewriter? (Yes, I can tell the typewriter is electric, because of the uniformity of the impressions on a carbon film ribbon. I got more out of writing all those papers at Barnard than you might imagine.)

Since you haven't answered my last letter, I have nothing else to say to you. (I will try to keep an eye on my e-mail, though.)

Love ya,
Joanie

October 23

To: Joan Carpenter
Subject: Critical Reception of *Nightbeat*

I am enclosing for your consideration a copy of the review of *Nightbeat* that appeared this week in the "Everyday Magazine" section of the *Post-Dispatch*.

The review is by Tom Kline, who has long been a supporter of the efforts of KMIS. He has not, of course, always thought that we were perfect in every respect, but he has been willing to give us the benefit of the doubt.

Until now, that is. His review of *Nightbeat* is the harshest review of any locally produced program it has been my displeasure to read. Perhaps if our ratings were showing the exact opposite of Tom Kline's opinions, we could afford to dismiss them. But, as a matter of fact, his review supports what the numbers are telling us.

While it may be true that no one pays much attention to TV critics in general, when it comes to news-magazine programs, the record shows otherwise. Since you are new to the area you might not know it, but the *Post-Dispatch* is an extremely influential publication. Tom could do us a lot of good, but as matters stand, he is doing us a lot of harm.

You need not respond to this memo. I would prefer you to spend the energy and thought coming up with some story ideas or some new approach that will not only gain *Nightbeat* the favorable attention of Tom Kline but will pull us up in the ratings. I hardly need remind you that this is exactly what we hired you to do.

cc: Simon Rostovsky; Gary Wells

Received: from REEDVA.BITNET by KMISVA.BITNET
Date: Friday, October 23
From: Jane <REEDVA.BITNET>
Subject: Re: Fan and That
To: Joan <CARPENTER@KMISVMA>

Dear Joanie,

I just got the copy of the fan letter you sent me. I
don't know quite what to make of it myself. I suspect
it's just some lonely man engaging in a wish-
fulfillment fantasy.

The writer seems well-disposed toward you, and obviously fantasizes that the two of you are quite well
acquainted. It is easy to imagine someone coming home
after work and, with no family or friends around,
striking up an acquaintance with the warm and beautiful person appearing on the screen. The Watcher then
finds it easy to believe that, in some magical way, you
are as aware of him as he is of you.

My guess is that you have nothing to worry about.
Besides, I agree with you, what could you do? I assume
you already take all the reasonable precautions of a
big-city girl.

However, this is all quite out of the range of my ex-
pertise. I'm going to send my copy of the letter to
someone I've known since medical school. You won't believe his name—Stratford Vogler. Despite this, he's a
nice guy. He's in the Psychiatry Department and he's
done several studies on people who write letters to celebrities.

(You are a celebrity, you know. I had to spend
twelve years getting an education, and there you are,
barely literate, being famous—at least locally. I'm
not in the least jealous, though. I rejoice in my younger sister's fame and fortune!)

About Thanksgiving. You know Jack hates staying in
other people's houses more than dogs hate fleas, but it
would be nice to see you and Mama. And of course Amy
wants to visit her glamorous aunt so she can tell them

about it in first grade. I'll work on Jack, but I can't
promise success.

   As it happens, we do have a fax number. Jack decided
we couldn't truly belong to the latter part of the
twentieth century without a fax machine. (I'm still in
love with the idea of instant communication via computer, but since you rarely check your mail, that
rather dilutes the advantage.)

   So anytime you want to send us something, just
punch in 617-976-2286.

   I'll send you a picture of Amy when I get a new one.
She's lost most of her teeth now, but you'll probably
recognize her anyway.

   Who is or was Zack?
Love from us all (and awaiting eagerly the
corporealization of your next message)

                                                    Sis

Ms. Joan Carpenter
Star of *Nightbeat*
KMIS-TV

                                             Thursday
                                             October 22

My dear, sweet Joan,

   I am furious. Just livid with rage.
   I ordinarily don't pay much attention to local journalistic trash
like the *Post-Dispatch,* preferring to get my news from better
sources, but I do have to glance at it to keep up with community
and business issues. If I hadn't been gathering up a week or so's ac-
cumulation of newspapers to put out for recycling, I probably
wouldn't even have noticed the review of *Nightbeat* that was in the
"Everyday Magazine" section.
   (I think it was seeing your name that caught my attention. Although it was buried in a dense page of newsprint, my eyes picked

it out with such ease, it might as well have been printed in red letters.)

To get to the point, I read the shit (I'm sorry to use this vulgar word, but it is the only one that is accurate) Tom Kline wrote about you. That's what I'm so furious about. Talk about injustice!

Before I say any more, though, let me warn you that if you haven't read the review yourself, please, please don't do it. I know you can demonstrate great self-composure when you're on camera, but I don't believe that is the full story of who you are. I sense that you have a capacity for self-doubt and hurt pride that exceeds even the imagination of the insensitive millions who watch you. You are obviously a sensitive person, and words like Kline's will cut you like shards of shattered glass, each word a slash.

The absolutely infuriating thing is that Kline totally fails to realize that if it weren't for you, *Nightbeat* would be off the air and replaced by a rerun of some stupid sitcom. Certainly that tubby clown with the tight collars and the pained smile, the so-called "co-anchor," contributes nothing to the program. It's only your beauty, intelligence, and fascination that keep the show afloat.

I have to admit that sometimes the subjects dealt with on the program are a little tacky and trivial, and I personally don't care for stories about heart-wrenching tragedies, particularly those involving children and animals. But all that aside, I'm sure most people would be delighted to watch you, even if you were doing nothing more than sleeping. I certainly would.

But I'm getting off-track. If you've heard anything about the Kline criticism (and I imagine bad news travels fast in your industry), you must be quite worried about being canceled. If that happened, I suppose you wouldn't be able to find a job locally and would have to leave St. Louis.

Well, we can't let that happen, my dear. We've got to make sure everyone in the whole metro-east area (that's what we say to include Illinois across the river) is watching *Nightbeat* and talking about it. That will send the ratings soaring and make you immensely famous. The shit that Tom Kline writes will become irrelevant. They wouldn't dare cancel the program.

Nothing succeeds like success!

I've been thinking hard for the last couple of days to come up with a plan for doing this, but haven't hit on quite the thing yet. Don't be discouraged, though. I think I'm getting there.

You see, my dear, I didn't write just to express my outrage, although that is very real. I wanted you to know that I'm going to help you. Exactly how I will do it remains to be seen, but do it I will.

> With constant admiration,
> The Watcher

From the Desk of
JOAN CARPENTER

23 October Friday

Alice,

Another item for the Watcher file.

Maybe I should be gratified that at least one person out there is keenly aware of my outstanding merit and properly outraged by the failure of Tom Kline (and the tens of thousands he represents) to recognize it. But this guy is altogether too creepy for my taste.

JC

Alexis Caldwell Hartz

Friday

Dear Joan,

I hope these morsels from La Bonne Bouchée will add a little sweetness to your day.

I'm sure you must feel hurt by the harsh things said about your show in the newspaper—and so unfair too. Just remember, though, not everyone is a TV critic, and thousands of people adore you.

> Warm regards,
> Alexis

23 October

Dear Alexis,

Are you an elf?

I was taken completely by surprise when I got home and found your box of delights waiting by my back door. To identify some of the more exotic ones, I had to get out my *Illustrated Book of French Pastries*. I'll have to admit that one didn't get identified, because I wolfed it down (delicious!) while looking for its picture. I wish I could tell you I immediately stuck the others in the freezer for next week, but I actually consumed two more before I had to quit to go to bed. (The fresh pear tarte was *incroyable.*)

You were right in thinking that my cheeks are still stinging from the slap in the face I got in the newspapers. But when I remind myself that there are people like you in the world, I feel much better.

If I don't see you across the hedge, I'll drop this in your mail slot. Thanks again for the sweet support.

Cordially,
Joan

P.S. Thanks to Curt, my weed patch should start looking better soon. Then maybe people will stop thinking of our backyards as a before-and-after demonstration of nuclear meltdown.

JOAN CARPENTER
2030 Buckminster • St. Louis, MO • 63130

Saturday, 24 Oct.

Dear Sissypie,

Why didn't you *tell* me you had a fax number!

That was the best news I've had since my senior year at Highland Park when Terry Lawrence told me his doctor had made a mistake and he didn't test positive for herpes after all. (That was certainly another age, wasn't it? We were all so scared, and it didn't even kill you.)

Now that I know your fax number, I can deluge you with my every thought without having to touch a computer. Although I'm glad you've seen the light on the fax machine (take it both ways), that's not why I'm writing. I wanted you to know you can stop feeling sorry for your Old Maid sister, because she's suddenly become very popular.

I got invited to a party given by some people who run a chichi gallery that sells Southwestern art and items like bleached steer skulls—they look just like Georgia O'Keeffe paintings—and worn leather saddle gear. Since I was a little tired of spending all my evenings asking the victims of rapes, beatings, and robbery with violence whether they think the police are doing enough to fight crime in our cities, I decided to go.

The place was small, crowded, hot, and loud. Spanish champagne flowed like Evian, and I spent ten minutes or so standing alone, smiling into the middle distance, and projecting a look of absolute confidence. Fortunately, the gallery had art in it as well as people, so after demonstrating my self-sufficiency to the limit of possibility (five more minutes max before tears), I had a reason to do something else.

I insinuated myself through the crowd and headed in the direction of the art. When I reached the wall, I began staring my way around the perimeter, moving to the left and dodging around conversation clumps.

After looking at no more than three paintings of Day-Glo blue dogs and orange people, all floating several feet above the brown desert floor, who should I encounter but the handsome and silent Dr. Stephen Legion.

His deep blue eyes immediately focused on the hairline at my left temple, so I knew he recognized me. Then, to my amazement, he *addressed me by name*. (He said something very witty, like "Hello, Miss Carpenter. Nice to see you.") I was so taken aback by this I could only mutter something stupid like, "Hello, Dr. Legion. It's nice to see you too." He reached out for my hand to shake, then squeezed it with what seemed to me unusual warmth. (Is it possible to detect a thing like that?)

We continued our repartee—he being brilliant, I dull—for a couple of minutes. Then without warning, a very thin woman with a bulbous nose and eyes the size and color of Bambi's appeared at his elbow. Steve, as I was then calling him, introduced her to me as "my wife Elsa." Something about the way he said the first two words made them quite indistinct.

My heart sank with my hopes as I shook her stick-like claw and returned her ghastly skeletal smile with a sickly one of my own. We chatted about art and about whether butterflies live in the desert. Steve laughed less, and I got the feeling he wasn't much more happy to have his wife around than I was. (Could this be no more than what you head doctors call projection?)

After we had pooled our ignorance on everything having to do with the combination topic "butterfly/desert," I was wondering how I could make a graceful exit, when I was overtaken by another surprise. It was a night of elbows, for, dear reader, who should appear at mine but the handsome and dashing Alan Carter.

(He is an architect-builder who came to my house just after I moved in to give me some security advice, stayed longer than strictly necessary, emitted vibrations on the correct wavelength . . . then never called. Did Mama already tell you about him?)

Alan said he liked the bones and skulls better than the paintings, but most of all he would like to leave, and would I leave with him. I said I had no objection, if I could have just one more peek at the rattlesnake skin collage. (I didn't want him to think I was *that* easy.) We then left with Dr. L. looking scalpels in our direction.

It was too late for dinner, and we didn't want to drink in bars or dance on floors. So we ended up having café latte and biscotti at a place on the Hill. We talked about the Houston Best building (not the best Houston building, but the structure with what looks like rubble falling off its apparently shattered corner), then about

New Haven, New York, local society, my job, and his ex-wife. We left the café and walked through the darkened streets, holding hands and giggling from time to time.

He took me back to pick up my car at the gallery, and I told him it had been a nice evening and we would have to do it again sometime. (Yes, I had to dodge a kiss. No, I didn't want to. But I also didn't like the time I spent wondering why he never called after broadcasting on my frequency. He *deserved* a little disappointment.)

All this happened just last night, so you've got to forgive me for running on this way. (I'll run on another way next time.) Life seems to provide either feast or famine. For months I've been thinking of turning necessity into virtue and taking the vow of chastity. Then in the same day, the same *hour*, two highly desirable men react to me as if I'm highly desirable. (Yes, I remember one is married. I'm talking about reactions.) I'm just writing so I can boast a little. (Remember how you were about Zack?)

Thanks for reassuring me about my "fan" letter. You needn't have bothered the guy with the impressive name, but it was nice of you to go the extra step. If my luck holds, not only will my ratings get better, but the creep won't ever write again.

Pats for Kitten. Ask Jack if it's true there are as many even mathematicians as odd ones.

Good night, sweet Princess, etc.

Joan,
Queen of the Night

FAX TRANSMITTAL 314-552-5671

JOAN CARPENTER
2030 Buckminster • St. Louis, MO • 63130

ATTENTION, DAN, ATTENTION DAN, ATTENTION DAN ... BOTTLED WATER FOUND TO CONTAIN THMs, KNOWN CARCINOGENS.

This just came over the wire, news so hot it's smoking. The EPA has learned that bottled water often contains the same high level of trihalomethanes (THMs, as you and I say) as tap water. One of them is (shudder) *chloroform*.

I suggest you stop drinking the stuff, but don't pour it out. Not only would that create an environmental hazard (Imagine billions of gallons of toxic San Pellegrino, Schweppes, and Perrier coursing through the Manhattan sewer system!), but it would be a waste. You can use it for getting to sleep. Just dampen a handkerchief, lie down, and put the handkerchief over your face.

Have you considered the possibility that the healthful lifestyle might kill you?

I'm going to do a story on water—I mean *waters*. Even the Fish approves. But then you would expect him to, wouldn't you.

To your good health, as Ralph Bellamy used to say, swigging down a hefty dose of alcohol-laced patent medicine,

Joan

C> -
C> cd/noman
C> NOMAN
HELLO, MY FRIEND, HOW ARE YOU TODAY?
I'm feeling quite worried.
WHAT SEEMS TO BE THE PROBLEM?
It's about Joan.
YOU ARE WORRIED ABOUT JOAN?
I am worried about how she's coping, but right now I'm really worried about what I can do to help her.
YOU WANT TO TRY TO HELP JOAN?
Yes, I do. I promised her I would, and she's counting on me. I just can't let her down. It means too much to both of us.
TELL ME MORE ABOUT HELPING JOAN.
I need to do something that will counteract the bad review Tom Kline gave her program.
TOM KLINE DID SOMETHING BAD WITH RESPECT TO JOAN?
He ruined her ratings, and they might cancel *Nightbeat* and fire her.
YOU ARE WORRIED ABOUT JOAN BEING FIRED?
Of course, because she would have to leave St. Louis then.

WHY DO YOU CARE IF JOAN LEAVES ST. LOUIS?
That's a goddamned stupid question. In addition to being beautiful and sexually appealing, she's the nicest and most wonderful person I've ever met. I want to get to know her very well, to spend time with her and let her fall in love with me. That's my dream. But that bastard Tom Kline is ruining everything.

TOM KLINE IS RUINING YOUR DREAM?
That's what I just said.

CAN YOU CHANGE TOM KLINE AND NOT RUIN YOUR DREAM?
You've given me a very good idea! I think I know now how to keep that bastard from destroying my dream *and* help Joan at the same time.

TELL ME MORE ABOUT YOUR IDEA.
That's all I want to say for now. I've got to do some research.

Saturday

Dear Ms. Carpenter,
These chrysanthemums were so lovely they made me think of you.
I hope they'll make you think of me.

Curt

P.S. You should trim the stems and put them into fresh water as soon as possible. Don't crowd the vase or they won't last as long.

THE SATURN AGENCY
256 East 59th Street • New York, New York • 10020
212-555-5050 • Fax 212-555-5051
Daniel L. Saturn, PRESIDENT

October 24

Joan, my sweet,

How kind you were to warn me about bottled water. (I did find your tone peculiar, though. Just what is it about the possibility of my doing myself harm that brings out such unseemly glee in you?)

Despite your blithe assumption that I consume Perrier by the Jeroboam, if not the hogshead, the truth is that I rarely touch the stuff. I'm surprised to learn you think I would be so careless as to put my health in the hands of the water barons. Wells become contaminated, bottling equipment malfunctions, and often bottled water contains more dangerous coliform bacteria than the water flowing from the tap. Surely every hydrophiliac knows this.

The half-cautious put their faith in filter systems they hook to their faucets or in plastic funnels containing "activated charcoal." (I've always been puzzled about that "activated." Does it become "deactivated" after use?) I am not so reckless, for I know the filters can eventually accumulate enough bacteria to *pollute* water that flows in clean. It is quite foolish to spend money on a system to add bacteria.

If you're thinking I just don't drink water, you're mistaken. I make sure to consume at least 72 ounces a day. I am sure of its purity, because the water I drink is *distilled* water. I have my own apparatus—a stainless steel pot with a built-in heating apparatus that sits by the yogurt maker on the countertop.

What has happened to put you in such a strange mood? Are you still worried about ratings?

Skoal,
Dan

· JANE CARPENTER-REED, M.D. ·
Psychiatry Consultants, Inc.
3460 Chestnut Avenue
Brookline, MA 02147
617-976-8740
FAX: 617-976-2286

Sunday, 25th

Dear Joanie,

Thanks for the letter (or do you say "fax"?).

Professionally speaking, the breathlessness of your writing suggests you are in a manic phase. I could almost hear you giggle in a couple of places. If you were talking, we'd call it "pressured speech," but I don't think we have a name for it when it's written down and faxed. Pressured prose? Fast fax?

It could be you're not really manic, but just feeling pleased with yourself. (In which case, you have Mama's "cat that swallowed the canary" syndrome.) That would be perfectly natural, given that you managed to capture the interest of two handsome men within the space of twenty minutes, departed with one and left the other behind to yearn. You're doing all right as a femme fatale, and I'm proud of you.

You've got to tell me more about Alan Carter. That he's handsome, prefers cafe latte to liquor, and likes strolling moonlit streets makes him sound more than a little appealing. But I want to know about the circumstances of his divorce. (Whose idea was it and why? What does he say about his ex-wife? Is she still living in the same city?) Also, did you ask him why he didn't call you after spending a few hours communicating interest? (Maybe he's just shy. Maybe he's just stupid.)

Stephen Legion sounds suspicious to me. If he seemed very cold when he did your stitches, he probably *is* very cold. Human warmth isn't something you turn on and off. It's one thing to be professional, but quite another to have an ice-pac for a heart. (Medical people agree that surgeons tend to be strange, and plastic surgeons the strangest of the strange. Only a stereotype, of course,

51

like the one about psychiatrists being crazy. We know how groundless that is. Heh, heh, heh.)

I'm glad you mentioned that you remember he's got a wife, because I would probably make a point of telling you to keep it in mind. Wives can cause an endless amount of trouble, and men tend not to leave them. (On the same principle that always skipping dinner and just having dessert doesn't constitute good nutrition.) No doubt Legion is attracted to you (what man could fail to be?), but he knows his wife is likely to get in his way.

My guess is that he will try some kind of end-run around her and in your direction. For him you are eminently desirable, but out of his direct reach. I predict he will attempt an indirect reach and you will hear from him before long. En garde!

Speaking of men (appropriate or otherwise), how are you getting along with your gardener? (Mellors? Is that his name?) When you mentioned hiring him, I thought I detected a certain not altogether proper interest in his physical attributes. I hope you know that having an affair with your gardener is the equivalent in L.A. of screwing your pool boy. Dozens of Hollywood novels tell us that's tacky beyond words, and besides, you're supposed to be a middle-aged star before you need to take it up.

I think you can do better than 1, 2, and 3 above.

I talked to Stratford Vogler, and he says he thinks "the Watcher" writer is probably slightly paranoid, feels alone in the world, and closely identifies with you. If you have any more letters, Stratford would like to see them. He also said he wouldn't recommend that you meet with this person, should he happen to suggest it.

Amy wants to braid her hair. Jack wants hair to braid. I'm like the Pokey Little Puppy—tired but happy.

Fax soon.

> Jane,
> Queen of the Nap

P.S. Who *is* Zack?

Ms. Joan Carpenter
Star of *Nightbeat*
KMIS-TV

October 25

My dearest Joan,

Things are looking brighter for us now. I won't say your worries about Tom Kline and bad ratings are over, but they are well on the way to extinction.

You can thank me for it when it happens. I've come up with a brilliant but relatively simple idea that will help you boost your rating to the stars and even beyond. I predict that *Nightbeat* will acquire the largest audience for a regularly scheduled local program in the history of television.

Here is the plan. Pay close attention to my instructions and do exactly as I say.

I'm sending you a small package, but don't open it immediately. I can assure you that the contents will be harmless to you and to everyone around you. So don't think it contains an explosive or poisonous gas or anything of the sort. I give you my word on that. (I will wrap the package in brown paper and put an "Urgent" sticker on the outside. That will allow you to recognize the package and not open it by mistake when you receive it.)

I want you to set aside a final three minute segment of the program in which you say something like:

"A good friend of mine, who is too shy to be with us, has provided us with an extraordinary surprise this evening."

Then tell the camera operator to get a close shot while you open the package live and for the first time. After a close-up of the contents of the package, say the following:

"*Nightbeat* has a few detractors, but it has many more enthusiastic fans. They prove their love and loyalty every time they turn to this channel and to this program. And what we see here is proof that there is no length to which they won't go to protect the program from the effects of ignorance and spite.

"We are all indebted to the person who wants only to be known as the Watcher."

Now, Joan, I assure you this will create a great impact that will have people talking about your show locally and nationwide. Tom Kline will never write another bad word about you.

Please don't worry about anything. You are going to become the big star you were meant to be.

Hugs, kisses, and bouquets from,
The Watcher (Over You!)

THIS IS THE SATURN AGENCY. YOU MAY LEAVE A MESSAGE AT THE TONE.

Dan? This is Joan.

I'm rather upset, but I'm going to make myself speak as calmly as possible.

It's about a letter somebody just sent me. It's really got me spooked, and you'll see why when you read it. I want you to call me immediately so I can talk to you about it.

But before you call, look at the letter. I just faxed it, so you should have it already.

Read it and tell me what you think I should do.

Call just as soon as you possibly can. I'll be at home.

YOU HAVE REACHED 552-8076. AT THE TONE YOU MAY LEAVE A MESSAGE.

Joan? It's Dan. Do you want to call me back?

No, Dan, wait. I've got it now. But, listen, if it's all right with you, I want to keep the recorder going. I found that letter very disturbing, and I want to make sure I have a record of everything. I mean, I don't know what's going to happen, and I don't want to lose something important.

No, go right ahead. But are you recording because your journalistic impulse is at work or because you want to be able to reflect on what's going on when you're calmer?

A little of both, I guess. But do you think I'm right to feel spooked? Wasn't the letter a little frightening?

I'm not sure *frightening* is the right word. It's certainly weird. I'm really sorry the letter has got you so upset. The guy at least seems to like you and want to help you. It doesn't sound like he wants to hurt you.

I agree that's the way it sounds. But there's something about the tone that really scares me. I guess because it's so intimate, and yet I don't know this person at all.

Are you sure about that? This could be somebody you know.

You mean it could be some sort of trick? I guess that's possible. Gary Wells could be trying to shake me up, I suppose. That sounds very unlikely, though. People just don't act that way in real life.

Don't kid yourself, kid. Remember that guy Stewart in Boston who called on a car phone and said an attacker had just shot him and his pregnant wife? It turned out the guy killed his wife himself then shot himself in the stomach just so people would believe what he said about an attacker. People are really weird.

I guess you could be right. But that doesn't make any difference at the moment. What do you think I should do?

About what? Nothing has happened yet.

Oh Dan, stop being so literal. Should I go to the police?

You could, I guess, but I don't think it would do you any good. After all, the letter doesn't threaten you in any way, and there is no evidence that a crime has been committed.

Is that what it takes to get the police involved? A crime actually has to be committed?

Pretty much so. Or they have to be convinced that a crime is about to be committed and they can catch the people in the act. But that doesn't seem to be a possibility here. I mean, this guy doesn't say what he's going to send you to make people interested in the show. It could be a toad with a diamond nose ring, so far as you know.

All right, all right. I see the point. Should I just keep quiet about the letter or do I tell somebody?

I think you've got to tell Charles Fishwater. The letter is to you, but it also directly concerns *Nightbeat.* That makes it Fishwater's business, both because he's the producer and because he's head of the news division.

I guess you're right. He should at least know what's happening.

Exactly. What's more, let me remind you that it could just turn out that whatever happens may have some news value in itself. I'm sure nobody can guess exactly what the Watcher has in mind, but you are in the business of reporting news.

And the incident may turn out to be newsworthy. Point taken, Dan. But it's all too creepy for my taste. Also, there's something else you haven't said anything about. Suppose the box he says he's sending does come. What do I do with it?

I think you ought to try to work that out with Fishwater. See if you two can come to some agreement.

Are you saying I actually *should* open the box on camera?

I just think you and Fishwater should talk.

But you think that's a reasonable possibility?

Look, don't put me on the spot, Joan. I don't know what's reasonable and what's not. But I do know that you're standing on the deck of a ship that's sinking, and it's taking your very promising career down with it. If you should just happen to get some publicity out of all this, it wouldn't hurt.

I know, there's no such thing as bad publicity.

No, not so. If that were true Leona Helmsley wouldn't have gone to jail. All I mean is that having *Nightbeat* talked about may help the program by calling attention to it. Since *you* haven't done anything wrong or stupid, the publicity can't hurt you.

Yeah, I guess so. It sounds so cheap and sleazy, but I know you're right. Anyway, nothing's happened yet. But I will show the letter to Fishwater.

Send him a copy with a covering memo. Whatever dealings you have with him, put it in writing. If you agree to do something, send him a "memo of understanding." If we ever need to sue KMIS for contractual nonperformance, I want to make sure we've got lots of documents.

Roger, wilco. Now how about you? Are you doing all right?

I guess so. My stomach has been giving me a lot of trouble for the last couple of weeks. I get cramps and sharp pains that make me want to scream. I thought there was a chance it was stomach cancer, so I went to a gastroenterologist. He didn't even do a GI series. He said it was an obvious case of irritable bowel syndrome and I should drink Metamucil and get more exercise.

That reminds me of what David Hume's doctor said

to him. When the doctor told him nothing serious was wrong with him, Hume said, "Too bad. I hate to die of something that's not serious." Then he died of stomach cancer about a week later.

Jesus, Joan. I wish you hadn't told me that. I was just beginning to feel better.

Sleep well, Dan. I think you're going to make it another month. Thanks for the advice. I feel a lot better after talking to you, and I'll keep you posted.

Please do. And take care of yourself. The effervescent Metamucil isn't half bad. It's sort of like Perrier.

I'll give it a try when my stomach is up to it. Good night, Dan.

CHARLES FISHWATER
VICE PRESIDENT
NEWS DIVISION
KMIS-TV

October 27

Dear Joan:

Thank you for giving me copies of the fan letters sent to you and signed by someone calling himself "The Watcher." You were correct in thinking I should know about these letters, and it was quite proper to provide me with copies.

I agree that this is not a matter about which it would be appropriate to become involved with the police. As you say, no crime has taken place, and we have no reasonable grounds for believing that a crime will occur.

I understand that you find the letters unwelcome and somewhat distressing. Nonetheless, there may be a positive side to all of this. I am sure it has occurred to you that the Watcher may be correct and that he may indeed send you something that will attract a great amount of attention to *Nightbeat*. This may provide us with just the sort of break we can turn to our advantage to get the program firmly established with viewers and to make you a major television personality.

I have given the matter considerable thought, and I have come to the conclusion that we should do exactly as the Watcher asks us to do. Of course I do not mean that you must follow his script and repeat the exact words he has provided you. You can explain the situation to the audience and perhaps quote some salient passages from his letters.

Then, with one camera focused on your hands as you unwrap the box he says he is sending and a second on your face for reaction shots, you can open the box. We can do it live and in real time, and that alone will provide a sharper edge of excitement than we have ever before had on the program. We will want to make a number of copies of the tape, because other news organizations are sure to request them.

I assume that, despite your somewhat upset feelings about the letters, you will give your wholehearted participation to this project. After all, you are the primary actor in this event and that puts you at the center of interest. To put the point another way, you yourself are making the news story, even as you report it. And that makes for good television.

Unfortunately, so far as I have been able to imagine, there is no way we can publicize this event in advance. We would make ourselves a laughingstock if we promised to deliver an extraordinary event, then it never took place. We wouldn't be taken seriously again, and that would cost us so many viewers we would have to cancel *Nightbeat*.

I also want you to know that I have given thought to your safety in this business. However, I should say, first of all, that I do not believe the letter writer would do anything that would hurt you. It shines through the letters that this is someone who is enamored with your beauty, charm, and intelligence and isn't likely to want you to come to any harm.

Just to make sure, though, I plan to have a fluoroscope brought onto the set so we can x-ray the package before you open it. I've been told by my security consultant that anything dangerous, like dynamite with a detonator or any sort of bomb, would show up on the screen. I will, of course, alert our own security department and tell them to be especially watchful on Wednesday. We'll also have the company doctor on the set, in case you faint or need some other kind of help.

I am sure, though, I have not said all that needs to be said on this topic. Let's get together and talk about it further. You and I can talk first, then we can bring in Gary Wells later.

I think this thing is going to pull us to the top.

CF

FAX TRANSMITTAL 314-552-5671

JOAN CARPENTER
2030 Buckminster · St. Louis, MO · 63130

27 October Tuesday

Dan,

Have you read the piece of shit from Fishwater I just put through to you? If not, stop and do it now.

I did what you told me to about the creep letter, and this is what I got back. The asshole actually expects me to open up a box sent by some loony tune right in front of a TV camera with tens of thousands, if not millions, of people watching me. That's "good television."

I suppose it would be even better if my head got blown off in prime time. He's concerned about my safety in about the same way the black widow worries about her husband's health.

So the box gets x-rayed and it doesn't show a ticking bomb. So what? Maybe it's filled with plastic explosives. Maybe it's chock to the rim with deadly cholera bacteria. Hundreds of things can kill you that don't show up on x-rays. Who the hell knows?

And the Fish just wants me to take the word of somebody who is, to be polite about it, obviously mentally disturbed.

I'm supposed to be reassured because KMIS's doctor will be standing by. Great. What's his job going to be—pronouncing me dead?

Also, it's just utter bullshit to say this is a news story and that I'm one of the principals in it. I don't want to take a moral tone so high that it becomes a screech, but the Fish is proposing nothing more than tacky TV of the worst sort. I've done more than my share of stories on trash topics ("Wife Hires Hitman for Husband's B'day Surprise"), but this is lower than the lowest I've gone.

All right, oh wise advisor and legal counsel, what do I do? Tell him to shove the box up his ass and see if it explodes? *(That* would be good TV.) Or do you think I either have to resign or participate in *any* fashion in this absurdist drama and potential tragedy? I don't want to do either. (But if push comes to shove, I'd rather be Hamlet than Ophelia. At least he had a fighting chance.)

PLEASE CALL OR FAX AT ONCE.

Joan,
Somewhere at sea in St. Louis

THE SATURN AGENCY
256 East 59th Street • New York, New York • 10020
212-555-5050 • Fax 212-555-5051
Daniel L. Saturn, PRESIDENT

October 27

Dear Joan:

I agree with you that Fishwater's proposal is irresponsible. He has no justification, legal or otherwise, to put your life and safety at risk under such conditions. If you freely chose to do so, the Fish would be in another kettle. That is, you may want to do something potentially hazardous, but you cannot be compelled by contract to do it.

I have written him a letter to this effect. I faxed a copy, but because of legal doubts that can arise about faxes, I am also sending him a confirmatory copy by registered mail.

As to whether opening a box on camera from someone who is apparently mentally unbalanced would constitute "trash TV" or be a legitimate news event is a matter of judgment. If Fishwater views it as a news event, then as the executive producer and head of the

KMIS News Division, he is justified in doing so. He is equally justified in *asking* you to play the role he outlined for you in his letter.

Yet even if the planned event is considered news, you may still choose not to do it. You have a contractual obligation to perform your specified duties for KMIS, but you certainly have no obligation to do anything a reasonable person might perceive as threatening to life or physical well-being.

Just say no.

Sorry for the legal-sounding talk. Hope I've cleared everything up and all goes well.

I'm with you,
Dan
(aka the White Knight)

Tuesday

Dear Ms. Carpenter,

I'm leaving for you this sprig of heather. If you admire the way it blooms even as the weather turns colder, then perhaps you would look kindly on my invitation to hear me read my poetry.

On the next two Friday evenings, at Duff's Tavern on Euclid, in the Central West End, I appear at ten o'clock. I have half an hour.

I am continuing my cycle of poems about living in the rust belt after the shine has gone. One of the poems I have dedicated to you.

I hope you will be there to hear it.

With admiration,
Curt

27 October, Tue.

Joan to Alice:

Now I know what those popular girls in high school must have felt like. It's nice to be sought after, but it sure is a lot of trouble to keep from hurting people's feelings.

It's a good thing I have access to your tact.

Please call Curt Collins and tell him:

(a) Ms. Carpenter thanks him for the lovely sprig of heather but is sorry she is very busy and can't come to hear him read his poetry;

(b) She thanks him for dedicating a poem to her (Aren't you supposed to *ask* people before you dedicate a poem to them? It seems awfully presumptuous.);

(c) She hopes he will find the audience he deserves when he reads his poetry (better change that to "a receptive audience").

I don't know how it's possible to deliver such a message and have it sound encouraging, but if it is, do your best to avoid it.

I do happen to be very busy, so there's not even any need to lie. How odd. (Of course if the *right* person called I might just be able to make some time.)

JC

October 27

To: Joan Carpenter

Subject: Participation in *Nightbeat* Box Project

I have received the letter from your agent Mr. Daniel Saturn, and I understand from him that you do not wish to accept the proposal I made in my last memo to participate in the box-opening project on *Nightbeat.*

Whether or not you have a contractual obligation to accept the proposal is, I believe, a matter of interpretation. Nevertheless, it is not my wish to force you to do anything you do not feel comfortable doing. I respect your feelings in this matter and will press the issue no further. Conflict between us can do no good for *Nightbeat.*

However, I must tell you in all candor that I view your attitude as one that is neither helpful nor constructive. *Nightbeat* is in trouble, and I assumed you would be as eager to assist in helping to make it a better and more exciting show. I confess myself to be completely puzzled as to why you reject the opportunity to document, as well as participate in, what may be a newsworthy event. This is not what we expected from you when we offered you the position of co-anchor.

Fortunately for *Nightbeat,* we have another co-anchor. I showed Gary Wells the copies of the letters from the Watcher you sent to me. I also outlined for him my plan to open the box (should it actually be received) on camera and real. Gary not only agreed to perform that task, he welcomed the opportunity. Indeed, he displayed exactly the kind of enthusiasm and commitment I had expected from you.

Despite Gary's commendable loyalty to the program, the role he is taking is properly yours, and I would like to leave open the possibility of your changing your mind. If you do, then Gary will step aside.

We must talk soon about *Nightbeat* and your future with the program.

Charles Fishwater

FAX TRANSMITTAL 314-552-5671

JOAN CARPENTER
2030 Buckminster · St. Louis, MO · 63130

27 Oct., Tues.

Dan,

Stay tuned. Coming right after this is the slimy, sleazy, scummy memo I got from the Fish after he read your letter.

He sees he can't make me do it, but he obviously plans to make me pay for not playing his game.

Of course Gary Wells is willing to do it! Gary Wells would eat a shit sundae on camera in real time if the Fish told him to. He would probably even smile and ask for seconds. If Gary Wells doesn't manage to keep the Fish happy, he has no fucking future.

That much is obvious. But I guess the real question is whether I do. Does my keeping the Fish *unhappy* guarantee my success?

Gary and I are opposites in a lot of ways, but probably this isn't one of them.

FLASH! Something just occurred to me. The Watcher's package is going to be addressed to me. It's going to be *my* package legally. What if I just say I don't want it opened? What if I just say I want it destroyed? What if I just hide it and never tell the Fish about it?

Speak.

And please make it fast. No man knows when the mail comes, nor does any woman either.

Joan

256 East 59th Street • New York, New York • 10020
212-555-5050 • Fax 212-555-5051
Daniel L. Saturn, PRESIDENT

October 27

Dear Joan,

Let me not mince nor chop my words—don't do it!

You must have thought you were having an epiphany complete with angel whispering in your ear when you realized the Watcher would address the box to you. What could be simpler than just collecting your mail and going home?

Fishwater can't even put on Gary Wells with the box, because there won't *be* a box. You'll have it.

Sharp thinking! Great idea!

At least it would be if it had been thought up by Gary Wells who then convinced you to do it.

Which is to say, the idea is calculated to get your desk cleaned out before sundown and have you standing in the unemployment line come next Monday.

The legal aspects of entertainment contracts are more complicated than chromodynamic theories of particle physics, but I think I've got a clear fix on this one. I have no doubt that a package sent to you at KMIS can (and will) be viewed legally as one sent to you as a representative of KMIS. Hence, through the miracle of the law, even when it has your name on it, it doesn't necessarily belong to you. In this instance, it probably doesn't.

This is not as absurd as it may seem. When you make a payment by mailing money to your friendly loan officer at the bank, he can't just walk off with it because his name is on the envelope.

Now let me weasel a little. I'm not saying every court in the civilized world would find you wrong in refusing to surrender the box. But I'm assuming you don't want to promote your career by becoming famous at a trial. If so, you would have gone to law school.

Just make sure you stay safe. Do what you think best, given that constraint. Also, I repeat, keep records on everything. This includes getting a videotape of whatever happens on the show and sending it to me. We may need all this if you and KMIS continue to have a strained marriage and you want to look for another mate—or if they try to kick your ass out the door, to borrow some of your elegant phraseology.

I'm sure you hoped I would speak with a voice of sounding brass and tinkling cymbals in praise of your plan. Unfortunately, I've had to use my usual brazen tongue.

Dan

FAX TRANSMITTAL 314-552-5671

JOAN CARPENTER
2030 Buckminster • St. Louis, MO • 63130

Wednesday/Thursday

Dear Dan,

It's past two in the morning, and I've successfully resisted the impulse to get you out of bed. I would if I thought it would help, but it couldn't.

Nevertheless, I've got to say something to somebody just to be able to unwind. I might as well write it down, because I can also make what I say a part of the record you wanted me to keep.

I got home less than an hour ago, took a shower, and poured myself a glass of scotch. (Right, a *glass*, even though it's a juice glass.) Along with everybody else associated with *Nightbeat*, I've spent the time from roughly eight-thirty until now with the police. But I'm getting ahead of myself. Let me put the events in some sort of order.

I got to the studio around four o'clock, went directly to my office and began sweating the fat out of the script of a piece on herbal medicine we were going to do tonight. I didn't finish until around six, and we go on the air at seven.

I went downstairs to the cafeteria for a salad and a cup of coffee, and coming back up the stairs I met Gary Wells. He pulled back his jowls and flashed his caps in the first off-camera smile he's ever pointed in my direction. He looked so friendly I expected him to slap me on the back and try to sell me some insurance.

This made me suspicious, so I decided I'd just drop by Fishwater's office. I was prepared with a story about my script being shorter and our not having to rush the discussion, but I didn't need a story, because my suspicions were right.

The first thing I saw was the box on his desk. It was a small package wrapped in brown paper and sealed with brown cellophane tape. The stick-on label was typed, and in the upper left hand corner was a bright red URGENT sticker. It looked just the way the Watcher said it would.

The Fish gave me his Spam-can smile. "The package arrived a short time ago," he said. "It was delivered to the front desk, and they sent it up to me."

"Don't they know where my office is yet?" I asked him, innocence oozing from my voice.

He didn't laugh, and he even dropped the smile. "I told them to send it to me when it arrived," he said.

"Even though it's my mail?"

"It's mail to the program," he said, just as though he had read your fax. "I'll be glad to turn it over to you, if you've changed your mind about opening it on camera."

"No, I'm willing to let Gary go for the glory."

"We're killing the last story," he said. That was the one I had been working on. "At the start of that slot, all you do is turn to Gary and say, 'I understand you have something very special for us.' "

I kept my mouth shut, but I did nod. I also left without saying goodbye, although I doubt that broke the Fish's heart.

Seven o'clock arrived, the red light blinked on, and the theme music came up. "This is *Nightbeat!*" I said in my best Ed Murrow voice. "I'm Joan Carpenter. Gary Wells and I have some outstanding stories for you this evening."

Everything continued as planned. Gary led with a long piece on the popularity of fake foods. I followed with film on male strippers who perform in the afternoons at the houses of suburban housewives (would you believe $300 for two hours?). Since we were killing the herbal medicine piece, I took an extra minute-thirty.

When we returned from commercial, I turned to Gary and said "Our executive producer, Charles Fishwater, tells me you're going to show us something a viewer sent that's supposed to make more people watch our program. Do you know what it is?"

"No, I don't, Joan," Gary said. "It's in this box, and none of us know what it is." He held up the box so the camera could get a clear shot.

"Aren't you afraid of what you might find inside? I mean, what if it's something dangerous?"

Gary took that as his cue. "We've made arrangements to check that," he said. He got up from the desk and walked over to a sleek, high-tech piece of equipment at the rear of the set. It was about the size of a filing cabinet and had a TV monitor on top of it. Standing beside it was a thin, nervous young man in a long white coat.

"This is a portable CAT scanner," Gary said. "It's been provided to us courtesy of Metrocentral Hospital. Dr. Thomas Turner has kindly agreed to come along and operate the equipment and tell us what we're seeing, if he can."

Gary handed the box to Turner, who slid it onto a platform beneath a nozzle that looked like a shower head. Turner flipped some switches and twiddled some dials, and the nozzle started moving very rapidly around the box in one direction, then the other. It switched positions slightly and made several more passes.

The camera shots are to the nozzle, to Turner, and to the TV monitor. Then we stop at the monitor, and all we can see are two shadowy shapes that seem slightly darker than their fuzzy grayish surroundings.

"What are we looking at, Dr. Turner?" Gary asked.

"I don't have any idea," Turner said in a flat voice.

"Do you think it's anything dangerous?" asked Gary.

Turner didn't give him any help. "I really can't say, because I don't know what it is."

"You see no evidence of any sort of explosive device? No wires or detonators?" Gary pressed, begging for a reassuring answer.

"Nothing like that," Turner said. "Whatever it is, it looks like soft materials of low density. Nothing even as dense as hardened plastic."

Gary was looking worried and not doing much to disguise it. He got the package back from Turner and put it down on a table placed next to the scanner.

"We don't know what we're going to find in this box," Gary said, his voice serious. "I'm going to open it, but I want everyone in our crew to stand far back, just in case it should turn out to be something dangerous." Camera #1 was in Gary's lap to give us a good picture of the box, and #2 was focused on Gary. No one actually changed position.

Gary picked up a pair of scissors and snipped the shiny tape on both ends of the package. He pulled back the brown wrapper, rolled the package onto its side, and removed the paper, revealing a white cardboard box.

Gary hesitated, glanced up at the camera, then lifted the lid off the box. He took out a layer of white cotton, looked into the box, then suddenly seemed to deflate. Without uttering a sound, he slipped to the floor.

Just as you would have done, I assumed it was a heart attack. Dr. Turner ran over to him, kneeled down, and began checking his pulse.

Highly trained TV journalist that I am, I of course snapped into action. I hurried to the back of the set, and while Dr. Turner was fiddling around with Gary, I began to fill dead air.

"No doubt the stress of uncertainty was too much for him," I said. "How is he, Dr. Turner?"

"Perfectly all right," Turner said. I thought he sounded a little disappointed. "Just syncope—he fainted. He'll recover in a few minutes."

"I guess we have to finish what he began," I said. I hated myself for saying it. But there I was with a million or so people watching and waiting. I couldn't get myself to disappoint them.

I looked into the box, and saw what made Gary faint. Sealed in a plastic zipper bag were two bloody oval-shaped lumps of pale flesh that could be nothing but testicles. I never had an anatomy course, but I knew at once what I was looking at.

I could see a piece of white paper with writing on it under the plastic bag, so I took out the bag and put it on the table. I noticed camera #1 dollying in for a close-up.

I read the message on the paper out loud: "NO MORE TOM KLINES." It was typed in capital letters just the way it is here.

Still doing my job either like a good journalist or a total idiot, I said, "Presumably this refers to Tom Kline, television critic of the *Post-Dispatch*, who gave this program a harsh review in his column. Yet whoever has done this is obviously a seriously disturbed person, and from the looks of things, this is a police matter."

Incredibly, as if we had timed it to the second, that was the end of the show and the theme came up. I had also managed to avoid saying what it was I was sure we were seeing.

Then all hell broke loose.

Fishwater kept shaking my hand and telling me how wonderful

I had been during "the crisis." Somebody must have called the police, because they were there before I could scrub off my makeup.

The police were very interested in me and asked me dozens of questions, but I'm too tired to tell you anything about that now. The scotch is doing its job, and I'm ready to pretend none of this happened. I dread going to sleep though, because I hate to wake up and realize that it did.

I've also got to talk to the police again, although I don't know exactly when.

Thanks for letting me run on this way.

As ever,
Joan

YOU HAVE REACHED 552-8076. AT THE TONE YOU MAY LEAVE A MESSAGE.

Joan! It's Dan.

I don't expect you to be up yet, but I wanted to call you immediately and tell you how sorry I am about what happened on your show.

It's all just incredible. I can't believe it.

But, listen, it sounds like you did a *terrific* job. You should be proud of yourself. *I'm* impressed. Of course, I'd be impressed if you told me you took the subway without an armed escort, but this was all really something different.

You really are a reporter. No doubt about it.

So far as the investigation is concerned, my advice is to cooperate with the police totally. You don't have anything to hide, so just be friendly and open.

I'll call you later and we'll chat.

THIS IS JOAN CARPENTER, AND I'M RECORDING THIS CONVERSATION.

That's fine with me, Joan. Thanks for taking my call. This is Sam Welleck of KRSD-TV News. I'm sorry we haven't met before, but how are you feeling this afternoon? After last night, I mean.

I think I'm doing just fine, although my body isn't completely convinced of that. But without meaning to sound cynical, I don't imagine you're calling just to check on the state of my stomach. I suspect it's for the same reason I'd be calling you, if our positions were reversed.

You got it on the first try. I was wondering if you would mind if I dropped by with a cameraman and shot a little tape.

We've got the box-opening bite from your broadcast, and I'd like to do an interview to frame it. I'm talking about just asking a couple of questions and getting your reactions. Nothing heavy duty, you understand. I don't know if you're interested, but there's a good chance we might billboard it at six and ten, if that makes any difference to you.

You're number three to call, Sam. I told the others to meet me here at the studio at four o'clock, and if you want to show up then, I'll cooperate to that extent. I've got work to do too, and I don't want to spend the next week giving interviews.

Wait a minute, I'm confused. You're going to run things like a press conference? Making a statement, then taking questions?

Absolutely not. We'll all meet at four, then I'll give everybody ten minutes each to talk and tape. I'll do two-shots with you, and you can ask me questions. One thing, though. The police and the KMIS attorney have both told me I'm not supposed to say anything about anything that's not already public knowledge.

But you're willing to take some reaction questions?

Those are about the only kind they tell me I can answer. But don't misunderstand me on this, because even if I could talk freely, I wouldn't have much to say. I just don't know much.

Are you free to speculate on who might have attacked Kline and mailed in his testicles?

I guess so, but I don't have any specific ideas. Just some sort of lunatic I imagine.

How about a motive?

I can't even speculate on that, so don't push me.

But you don't deny that this is going to attract a lot of attention to *Nightbeat?*

Maybe so. Probably it will. But listen, I don't want to have to answer your questions twice. If you want to ask anything else, just show up at four o'clock.

Okay, I understand. Just one more thing, though. I don't guess you'd care to comment on Gary Wells?

There's nothing to say about Gary. He was doing his job just like the rest of us.

You didn't faint at the sight of blood, though. Maybe a viewer realized Gary Wells needed some balls and sent him some.

Talk like that at four, and I won't talk to you. Taping will be in order of arrival, so if you've got a five o'clock deadline, you'd better not be late. Goodbye now.

29 Oct/Th.

Alice,

I don't know where you buy flowers in this city, but I'm sure you do.

Will you please call up and order three—right, 3—dozen long-stemmed *white* roses to be sent to Tom Kline. The *Post-Dispatch* story says he's in Barnes Hospital.

Also, I want to write a note to go along with them. I don't have the vaguest idea of what I could possibly say. I know the topic isn't covered in Amy Vanderbilt or Emily Post, and I very much doubt that even Miss Manners can serve as a guide.

I'll work on it and give it to you by noon.

JC

YOU HAVE REACHED 552-8076. AT THE TONE YOU MAY LEAVE A MESSAGE.

This is Alan Carter, Joan.

I had to go out last night, and I just this minute watched the tape of your show.

All I can say is . . . *wow!*

That was some surprise, but you handled everything like you'd planned it. I know you didn't, because I saw the piece on Tom Kline in the paper this morning. Poor guy.

Listen, I'd like for us to get together. I'm sure you're going to be busier than ever, but if you can find some time, just give me a call.

Use my paging number, because I don't know when I'm going to be home either.

Take care of yourself now.

10/29

Joan:

I used to say "Nobody is a heroine to her Administrative Assistant," but I've just got to tell you how much I admired the way you handled yourself in the interview with those reporters. They were so rude and pushy, and you were so cool and unruffled.

I've worked for people in TV for almost 10 years, and I thought I had met all the types. I was obviously wrong, because I never even imagined anybody like that hatchet-faced kid Jo Lauder from KKIC. When you denied knowing who the Watcher is, she as much as called you a liar. (Actually, in my book, to say "People really won't believe that" *is* to call you a liar.) She seemed to think that either you totally made him up or you're working with him to try to make Gary Wells look bad. (I like Gary, but that is the only thing he *doesn't* need help with.)

I was so infuriated at Jo Lauder that I called up KKIC and gave them an earful. I told them I was a long-time devoted viewer and that I was offended by her mad-dog tactics and she should be fired for harassing her interviewee.

I also started to tell them she had piggish eyes and a sharp nose, that her dress was too tight for a news reporter, and that she obviously put on her makeup with a putty knife. Then my feminist sympathies got the better of me.

I just wanted you to know that if I had a son, I'd want him to be just like you. (My daughter already is.)

Alice

Alexis Caldwell Hartz

October 29

Dear Joan,

Please accept this small token of my admiration. You showed that women are capable of doing anything men are. (Sometimes they are even more capable!)

I don't know if you have any liking for old books, but I thought of you when I saw this copy of *Wuthering Heights*.

I hope you will be able find a place for it in your splendid home.

Cordially,
Alexis

ST. LOUIS COUNTY POLICE DEPARTMENT

Memo of Transmission October 29

From: Detective Raymond R. Robertson
To: Detective Lieutenant Peter S. Keefer, Major Case Squad
Case number: 35-2300-1090

Peter,

The enclosed IR-500s tell just about all we know to date.

I turned over to the Forensic Unit the letters to Joan Carpenter from "the Watcher" and the note in the box, along with the box itself and its wrapping. (We have photographic copies of the letters and note.) Greg Handler said it would be tomorrow at the earliest before he could tell us anything.

Last night's interrogation of the KMIS *Nightbeat* staff was not particularly helpful. Nobody admits to having any idea about who the Watcher could be. I initiated background checks this morning.

One thing is worth exploring, I believe. Just as the Watcher says, the ratings for *Nightbeat* have been slipping, so it's possible someone connected with the show could be involved in the incident as a ratings booster. Just an idea.

You don't have an IR-500 on this yet, but the items that were in the box have been definitely identified as human testicles by Dr. Marcus in the ME's office. Also, there doesn't seem to be much real doubt about whose they are.

Although a Report on Suspicious Injury was filled out yesterday morning at Barnes Hospital, it wasn't submitted and processed until this morning. It shows that Thomas S. Kline, an employee of the *Post-Dispatch,* was admitted to the emergency room at 1:37 A.M. He had been castrated, and was in shock from trauma and blood loss. He also sustained a blow to the head.

I questioned Kline himself this afternoon and will be submitting the complete report tomorrow. Here are the basics, though.

Kline said he had been following his usual schedule and working late on Tuesday night to finish his column for the next morning's *Post-Dispatch.* He left his office around 1:00 Wednesday morning and walked from his building into the attached parking garage to get his car.

It was then that somebody attacked him.

His only recollection is that he sensed the assailant coming up from behind him. However, he can provide no details of description, not even race.

He was knocked out by being hit on the back of the head and castrated while he was unconscious. When he came to, he was able to open the car door and lean on the horn until a private patrolman found him and called EMS.

Although Kline lost a fair amount of blood, his doctor (Dr. Clarence Field) says he will be all right. (I mean out of danger, of course.)

Dr. Field also says that Kline suffered a mild concussion. This may have affected his short-term memory, and there is a possibility he may recall more details of the assault later.

Dr. Marcus says we have to get a tissue match for legal proof that the organs sent to KMIS are Kline's. I asked him to work with Kline's doctor and see to that.

I'm glad they put you in charge. I look forward to working with you.

Ray

JOAN CARPENTER
2030 Buckminster • St. Louis, MO • 63130

Ms. Alexis Hartz
University Realty
Fax 721-8280

30 October

Dear Alexis,

I thank you for the nicely bound copy of *Wuthering Heights*. It has always been one of my favorite books. I particularly like the scene in which Heathcliff is driven mad by passion and disappointment.

I agree that women are able to do the same sorts of things as men, but I don't want to claim credit that is not mine. Honesty forces me to say that I had no plans to participate in the episode on *Nightbeat* you may have been referring to in your very kind compliment.

I still hope we can have lunch before too long. As you can imagine, things have been hectic around here, but let's get together soon anyway.

Best,
Joan

TOM KLINE
ASSOCIATE EDITOR, TELEVISION

29 October

Dear Ms. Carpenter,

You've certainly got your nerve—or maybe I should say courage. It would have been easy for you to ignore me as just another casualty in the ratings wars.

In any case, thank you for the flowers and the note.

Was there supposed to be any significance in the fact that you sent *white* roses? I tried to think of what it might be, but all the ideas I came up with were in bad taste. Probably that reflects my state of mind rather than yours, because your note was very kind.

In my saner moments, I realize that neither you nor *Nightbeat* had any responsibility for what happened to me. Yet during crazy times I can't help thinking that if the show hadn't even existed, then I would be okay. I know it's equally true that if I hadn't given the show a bad review, I'd be okay, but somehow that doesn't count. After all, if the show had been *better*, I wouldn't have panned it. But this is what I mean by crazy times.

I appreciate your asking to visit so we could meet, but at the moment I'm not ready for that. Don't take this personally.

Tom Kline

10/30

Joan:

Alexis Hartz called to say she got your fax. She thanked you for your kindness and wanted me to tell you she has information about some recent local real estate transactions she is sure you will be interested in.

To be specific, she said she knows "some things about politicians, realtors, and rezoning for the new Park Center Mall that are just dynamite."

She realizes you are very busy and probably a little upset by recent events. Still, if you are at all able, she would like you to meet her for lunch tomorrow. She suggested 1:00 at Bernard's, but she can arrange to be free any time you like.

By the way, Gary is taking a couple of days off—flu, I hear.

Rumor has it that he told Marjorie while she was taking off his makeup that he collapsed on the set because of the antihistamine he's been taking for an allergy.

I think it's an allergy he's had for a long time.

Alice

FROM THE DESK OF
JOAN CARPENTER

30 Oct/Friday

Please call Alexis and tell her Bernard's at 1:00 tomorrow is fine, but I've absolutely got to get back home and go to work by 2:30.

Alexis and I were going to have lunch anyway, but this is not my idea of an ideal time. She may be rushing me a little, because

I doubt she knows anything worth telling, even if she genuinely thinks she does.

Still, Alexis seems enough like Miss Marple to be capable of walking up to a gang of thieves, writing down their social security numbers, then leaving without attracting any attention. Maybe she's going to be the key to my Big Story—but don't call the Peabody Awards committee yet.

Ever since a spiteful cop told me a tale Scheherazade would envy about somebody who turned out to be her ex-lover, I make a point of checking into my sources, as well as into what they say. Alexis is a neighbor, but I don't really know much about her. If she's going to become a source, I'd appreciate it if you would dig around in the directories and talk to anybody you know in real estate. Just see if you can find out anything about her that's not on her letterhead.

Do you think I should send Gary a card? Or perhaps some flowers?

No, bad idea. The box would make him too nervous. Maybe silence is the better part of discretion.

JC

CHARLES FISHWATER

VICE PRESIDENT
NEWS DIVISION
KMIS-TV

October 29

Dear Joan:

I want to commend you for the extraordinary degree of professionalism you showed last night after Gary Wells became unable to carry on. I was tremendously proud of you for not faltering when faced by something so surprising and shocking.

Although everyone on the staff did an outstanding job, you in particular conducted yourself in a manner that lived up to the best traditions of broadcast journalism. I am filled with pride and admiration.

I know you did not fully share my view that we should open the package from the Watcher on live television. I hope you see now that although the content of the box was shocking, the event itself was newsworthy and deserved the attention we gave it.

Thank you for proving to us that we made the right decision when we offered you the job of co-anchor of *Nightbeat*.

Sincerely yours,
Charles F. Fishwater

FAX TRANSMITTAL 314-552-5671

JOAN CARPENTER
2030 Buckminster • St. Louis, MO • 63130

30 Oct/Fri.

Dear Dan:

Have you read the Fish garbage I just shoved through the wire? If you haven't, stop right here and do so. Believe me, it will be an immensely rewarding experience.

See, what did I tell you?

Have you ever touched a slimier piece of paper? Is this how they write stroke letters in the big time? Perhaps you can learn something from studying this model.

I especially like the way Fishhead mentions that I didn't "fully share" his view about opening the box on camera. It is undeniably true that someone who holds a position that completely and categorically contradicts one's own position does not "fully share" one's view.

You can't fault the Fish on his logic. All you can do is admire the graciousness with which he states the facts, while standing in awe of the way in which he can make words do the devil's work.

Perhaps he's a genius unacknowledged. Perhaps he's an idiot. Perhaps I can no longer tell the difference. Maybe that's why I'm in television.

I want to ask just one question, and unless you've been in touch with the Force recently, I suppose it has to be rhetorical. What I want to know is: Just how did it happen that the fate that shapes our ends stuck me in front of the camera looking down at the bloody balls in the box, just the way Charlie Tuna wanted me to? He wanted me to, without even knowing exactly what he wanted, and I ended up doing it, without even knowing exactly what I was doing.

"The irony, the irony," as Mr. Kurtz might have said.

The crowd has been going wild. (Anyone who goes to slasher movies could have predicted this.) I've gotten dozens of calls and scores of cards and letters telling me how unflappable I am, how Tom Kline at least halfway (one testicle?) deserved it, and how exciting it was to see "news in the making." Everybody liked the show, with the probable exception of Tom Kline, and I wouldn't be completely surprised to hear a word or two of praise from him.

When I came here, my plans were to turn myself into the Woodward and Bernstein of St. Louis TV. So far, though, the most I've done is demonstrate the principle that people are willing to pay me lots of bread to help put on the circuses.

I've also been able to show that what you value most about yourself is likely to be valued least by those who can make you famous.

If this be disillusionment and upon me proved, then . . . I shouldn't be in television.

It was nice talking to you the other night, and I thank you for all the warm and supportive things you said about me. (You would be a hit in a women's group.) I need to hear them, even when I don't always believe them.

But how are you, Dan? Now that the anniversary of Stephanie's leaving is behind you, I hope you've been putting yourself in the proper sort of places to meet Ms. Right. May I suggest university libraries—graduate and professional schools, I mean. Women assume that the men they see there are eligible, educated, and safe to talk to. But don't try to talk to somebody in the stacks (too dark and scary) or the reading room (too hard to whisper). I recommend the area around the catalogue, because you can then ask a likely prospect how to look up something. Try it.

I also hope you've made peace with your stomach by now. I suggest you pamper it with lots of butterfat and sugar, maybe in the form of Ben and Jerry's Heath Bar Crunch. (Don't try to substitute grocery-store brands or frozen yogurt—the sugar's okay, but there's not enough fat.)

On a more serious note, I just read that a new study found that kale is a wonderful source of calcium. You're supposed to consume three bales weekly. I trust you will want to modify your diet to protect your bones.

As for me, I've decided I'd rather be a hunchback than eat kale.

As ever,
Joan the Crone

P.S. I'm keeping the originals of the stuff I send, but I hope you'll also file the faxes. I follow a rather awkward geological system in filing. I pile papers I want to keep on top of one another, and by the principle of superposition, I know that older papers tend to be toward the bottom. Yet even when an earthquake of searching hasn't re-ordered the strata, it can take me a while to excavate a particular document. I'm sure your system is perfect.

FROM THE DESK OF
ALICE WALCHECK

ADMINISTRATIVE ASSISTANT TO
JOAN CARPENTER

10/30

Joan:

Here is all I could learn about Alexis Hartz.

Since I knew you bought your house from University Realty, I called up a friend who works for another real estate company. She called up a friend of hers who used to work for University, so this is all third hand and won't stand up in court.

(1) Tom (my friend's friend) said University is a prestige firm that handles only houses in the quarter-million-up range. AH <u>owns</u> the company and is supposed to be very rich. She has about a dozen agents working for her. They all work on commission, and

out of that they pay her for office and secretarial expenses. The agents say that despite the big prices, AH always does much better on deals than they do.

(2) AH can come across as real nice when she wants to, but people who work for her say she's a BOW. (In case you never heard the expression, "on wheels" is part of it.)

She makes agents follow a dress code, take clients only to particular restaurants, and drive only cars approved by her. (She prefers BMWs, Mercedes, Lexuses, and Volvos, but will accept Le Barons, Towncars, and Cadillacs.) She does surprise inspections to make sure the cars meet her standards.

For some reason, the people who work for her call her "Alexis the Terrible."

(3) If she was ever married, she keeps quiet about it, and speculation is that she never has been. She acts flirtatious when she's around men, but she doesn't seem to have a gentleman friend. She goes to parties either by herself or with a man in his fifties everybody knows is gay, although he isn't open about it. Nobody knows exactly how old she is, but 35–37 is what people think.

(4) AH likes associating with the rich and famous and is well connected with local society types. She regards herself as a friend of the Pulitzers (newspapers), Mays (department stores), Busches (hic), McDonnells (planes, not burgers), and so on. Whether they return the favor or not my friend's friend couldn't say. But she doesn't seem to hang out with anybody much.

(5) He says she particularly likes celebs, and that's probably why she personally sold you your house (not to mention allowing you to live so close). She knows lots of people in local TV, newspapers, and magazines. He says she doesn't seek publicity, but seems satisfied just knowing those who get it.

Maybe this explains why she wants to know you better. But then maybe she just likes you. Lots of us do.

Sorry I couldn't find out more. Let me know if you want me to do further research on her.

Have an expensive lunch.

Alice

Hello, Joan?

This is Stephen Legion. You know, the facial surgeon?

I didn't want to ask you at the gallery the other night how you were doing with the stitches out, but I'd been meaning to call you.

Then I saw you on Wednesday's *Nightbeat*. You were certainly cool and in charge. I admired that. I hope you've recovered from what must have been a very unpleasant shock.

Anyway, uhhh, it would be nice to, uhh, see you and talk. Maybe, we could, uhh, you know, meet for a drink some afternoon. I'm usually free on Thursdays around two.

I'll call you again. Call me, if you like.

Better make it at my office, though. I mean, I'm hard to catch at home. Just say you're a patient, and I asked you to call me.

Goodbye.

ST. LOUIS COUNTY POLICE DEPARTMENT

Memo of Transmission   Date: October 30

From: Detective Raymond R. Robertson
To: Detective Lieutenant Peter S. Keefer, Major Case Squad
Case Number: 35-2300-1090

Peter,

I ran a check with the Dallas P.D. on Joan Carpenter and came up with some interesting information. She was the co-host of a TV program called "Dallas After Dark," and she tried to run a sting operation on two Dallas vice officers by posing as a prostitute. She claimed they asked her for money, but both officers were cleared in an IAD investigation.

Carpenter went to trial, because the judge said she was attempting entrapment *for the purpose of trying to boost the ratings on her TV show.*

She did thirty-days nominal and became a sort of local celebrity for making the Dallas police look bad.

We have developed no direct evidence to suggest she might be attempting a similar ploy in St. Louis. However, this is a line of investigation I believe we ought to pursue most vigorously.

Since you'll be doing the reinterrogation with her, I thought you should know this at once.

Ray

FAX TRANSMITTAL 314-552-5671

JOAN CARPENTER
2030 Buckminster · St. Louis, MO · 63130

30 Oct/Friday

Dear Jane,

I am fine. How are you?

So much for the chit-chat.

I want to tell you that your friend Herr Dr. Stratford Vogler seems about as reliable in making predictions as a Chinese fortune cookie. If I had paid him any money for his opinion, I'd ask him to replace it with another one for free. The Watcher may be lonely and he may have fantasies about me, but harmless he is not.

"What is poor Joan rambling on about?" you ask. I'll let you see for yourself. I'm Fed Exing you a tape of this Wednesday's *Nightbeat,* but you don't have to watch it all. Fast forward until you get to the last ten minutes or so. There you'll see the handiwork of the Watcher.

There you'll also see me. I'll be looking calm and professional and utterly in control. What the tape doesn't capture is the struggle

I was having not to throw up as I realized the objects in the nicely wrapped package were human testicles.

The tape also doesn't fade to dark then brighten again in the pulsating rhythm of a copy-protected movie. But that's the way I was seeing things and the way my head was feeling. Thank God I didn't faint.

Then I'd be just like Gary Wells. There's a nice shot of him stretched out on the floor of the set. It's true he's drooling a little, but notice how relaxed he looks.

You may want to "share" this tape with the learned Dr. Vogler. (I'll also send you a couple of clips from the *Post-Dispatch* he might want to see.) Despite what I said earlier, I don't know anybody else (except for you, of course) who is in a position to give me any advice.

I certainly don't plan to accept any dates to go to a Demolition Derby with the Watcher, but other than that, I wouldn't mind some educated guess about what I should or shouldn't do. I wouldn't even mind a little speculation about what I may be up against. (To give you and Vogler more to go on, I'll enclose copies of two Watcher letters you haven't seen.)

Despite everything, I should tell you that I'm just fine. I've received dozens of letters, calls, and tributes. Alexis (my neighbor) sent me a nice note and a copy of *Wuthering Heights* as a bibliographical commendation for my courage under camera.

Curt (my gardener) showed up at my back door half an hour early yesterday to read me "a few lines" he had written about "looking over the edge of eternity and seeing the rocks of reality." I think it was supposed to be a hymn to me and my performance. Anyway, he kept glancing up at me in an anxious way, so I had to smile and nod. I hope I didn't give him the wrong idea about anything having to do with romance (or even sex).

Alan called to see if I was okay, and he and I cooked dinner at his house last night. Then we sat around and talked about animated cartoons—from Little Nemo to the Little Mermaid. He knew a lot more about them than I did, and he showed me some of his favorites. It was all very distracting and wonderfully relaxing. (No, we didn't.)

You were right about Stephen Legion. He wanted me to call him at his office, because he's "hard to catch" at home. What he really meant was that he's too *easy* to catch at home.

I may just have a drink with him. No harm in that, is there?

Don't fret about me. If you're worried, you can call me, and I'll tell you everything is just fine.

I don't plan to tell Mama. No need to worry her.

I haven't forgotten about Thanksgiving.

Watch for the Fed Ex truck.

Your only little sister,
Joanie

FROM THE DESK OF
JOAN CARPENTER

30 Oct/Fri

Dan:

I just got a call from the Fish's secretary, Rita Trowbridge—does her watery association explain her position? At the behest of her boss, she pressed some I-told-you-so information on me. Since you asked me to document the ripples as well as the waves, I hasten to fax on what I was told.

Mr. F. wanted me to know that both NBC and ABC used sound bites from the Watcher tape on their evening news programs. Rita says her boss told her ABC played it as straight (though bizarre) news, but NBC had a voice-over questioning the decision to open the box on camera and suggesting ratings as an explanation. (How could they suspect that? Could they have a spy in our camp?)

CNN used a longer bite than either of the others and put it in their Headline News loop. That means it will probably still be running next week, unless the Pope finally succeeds in converting the Jews or the Martians land on the White House lawn.

The four local stations (including KMIS) played sound bites of the interview with me, as well as bites of the Watcher tape. I've seen none, but my assistant, Alice, tells me a couple had voice-overs that were generally flattering. However, one was the sort that always makes me cringe: "The little lady from Texas earned her spurs in St. Louis last night. When Gary Wells collapsed on the set of *Nightbeat* as the result of an allergic reaction to a prescription medicine, his co-anchor Joan Carpenter showed her spunk. . . ." Gag, gag, gag.

The story also got play on local radio news. I've heard the Fish assert that sound without pictures is just noise, but this week he seems to think radio may be making a big comeback.

Rita says the Fish believes all the media attention proves he was right to open the box on camera.

I believe Barnum got the rate wrong.

"More news when it happens," as I used to say to tag out in Dallas.

Tex

Ms. Joan Carpenter
Star of *Nightbeat*
KMIS-TV

October 29

My darling Joan,

It worked!

You played your part beautifully, as I knew you would.

It was a touch of genius to have that clown Gary Wells faint so you could then take over. I would have been a little happier had you stayed closer to my script suggestions. Still, i know you have to make compromises and say the things the public wants to hear. That's show business.

The important thing is that our little scheme came off without a hitch. The *Post-Dispatch* and two newspapers covered the story, and I heard it on the radio news several times during the day. I didn't catch all the TV news, but I know Channels 2 and 5 did stories, and I'm sure the others did also.

By the way, Joan, some of the stories said you refused to make any comment about the details of the incident. Do you think that was a good idea? Aren't you missing an opportunity to say something that will give people a good impression of you and enhance your reputation?

Perhaps you know best, though. Maybe taking an aloof and

dignified stance is best. That's probably something Dan Rather would do. I bow to your judgment, because you are a news professional and I'm not.

I think we can be sure a lot more people know your name now and are going to be planning their viewing to watch you on Wednesday nights. Expect the ratings to soar to the sky, my darling.

Oh, how I long to be with you now and share this moment of glory! I yearn to bask in the glow of your appreciation of the way I engineered our triumph over that petty little moron Tom Kline. It would be like standing in the warm rays of the sun on a bleak and gray December day. For me, you are the sun. You are the golden light chasing away the shadows darkening the dim, tight corners of my life.

If we were together, my dear, I imagine you would attack me with passionate kisses, touch my face with delicate fingertips, then run your hands caressingly over the contours of my body.

Your fingers and tongue would find my secret places, and I would respond with equal ardor. Then for the first time we would come together closer than we ever have before.

What frustration! What pain it is to wait! But don't worry, my darling. At the proper moment, I will reveal myself to you, and we will realize our passion and our pleasure. We will know when the time is right.

Meanwhile, we must consolidate our gains. We must keep your name before the public and keep them interested in *Nightbeat*. So far the national media has given you no attention, but they will. I promise I will make you famous.

I'm so glad we're in this together. I feel much less lonely now that I have someone like you to plan for and care about.

I'm very busy in my "real" life, and I've got some more thinking and planning to do. But please don't think I'll ever forget about you. You'll be hearing from me again soon.

> Your friend in deed,
> The Watcher

P.S. I think it would be a nice gesture for you to send some flowers to Tom Kline. That might make the news, if you just let drop that you did in a conversation with a reporter. It's what you people in the media would call a good human interest angle.

Received: from KMISVMA.BITNET by REEDVA.BITNET
Date: Friday, October 30
From: Joan <Carpenter@KMISVMA>
Subject: N.B. Incoming Fax
To: Jane <REEDVA.BITNET>

Dear Janie,

I hope you've got your computer flagged for messages, because this note is to warn you that in about
two seconds your fax machine is going to start rolling.
I'm in my office, and I'm faxing you your very own copy
of the letter from the Watcher that I got no more than
ten minutes ago.

I know you'll find it interesting from a psychiatric point of view. I just wish that was my point of view.
Frankly, this whole situation is getting creepy as
hell, and I don't mind telling you, it scares me
(rhymes with) witless.

The awful thing for me about the Watcher's letter is
the way he makes it sound like he and I are a couple of
lovers who are conspiring to make me into a big star.

He talks as though we've discussed the matter thoroughly and agreed that he would do something vicious to
get me some attention to help my career along. (People
say stage mothers are monsters, but here's a monster
who's a stage mother.)

What really sucks, though, is that I probably will
get a career boost from what he's done, and that makes
me feel as if I *am* at least partly responsible for his
actions. Maybe feeling this way isn't rational, but
there's a Dark Side of me that can't help taking a perverted pleasure in realizing that I handled the scene
with the box very well on camera and that a lot of people
realize it. It's this that sometimes makes me feel that
I actually am a co-conspirator.

Of course, this is all from an egotistical point of
view. The really scary thing about the letter is that
the Watcher seems to be suggesting that he's prepared
to do something else. I think it's quite possible he

may be planning something even more terrible than what he did to Tom Kline. What's really frustrating is that I can't think of anything I can do that might stop him.

Did you get the tape I Fed Exed to you? If not, it should arrive by this afternoon.

I think we've reached the point of needing advice from an expert. So I would like to ask you definitely to show the tape and the letters-including the one I'm faxing now-to Dr. Stratford Vogler.

If he's got anything to say, please let me know ASAP.

As soon as I finish here, I have to call up the police and turn this new letter over to them. I imagine they will ask me even more questions than they did right after the show.

Why does Thanksgiving suddenly seem so far away? Like it's something that's going to happen on another planet.

Hugs and kisses for my one and only niece. (Isn't it time you and Jack started adding by multiplying? It may be mathematically impossible, but it can be done in real life.)

> Love and chuckles,
> SSSL
> (Scared Sister-or other S word-in St. Louis)

• JANE CARPENTER-REED, M.D. •
Psychiatry Consultants, Inc.
3460 Chestnut Avenue
Brookline, MA 02147
617-976-8740
FAX: 617-976-2286

October 30

My Dear Sweet Little Sister,

I am constantly amazed at the way you can land yourself in hot water even while trying to take a cold shower.

I have to admit, though, that this time you seem to have done nothing either to line up the dominos or to start the chain reaction by shoving the first one. I guess we have to blame the Watcher for that.

Before I say anything else, though, let me tell you how pleased, delighted, and relieved I am that the Watcher didn't decide to do something to harm you. I know it was no picnic (bad word choice) to glance into a box and see a couple of testicles staring back (another bad choice). Still, unlike death and dismemberment, it's the kind of shock you can recover from in a day or so.

By the way, if I were a Freudian, I'd make a lot out of your reaction as you looked inside the box and gazed upon its hidden contents—the dizziness, blurred vision, and fading in and out. But since I hardly have any theories at all, I'll just say that's the kind of reaction psychologic shock and stress can cause.

Your colleague Gary Wells made it obvious he found the situation stressful. And I have to confess I'm irrationally proud of you for not fainting—irrational, because there's no shame in doing so under such circumstances. It's just my macho—macha?—Texas upbringing that makes me feel that way.

But what I can't fathom about this whole business is why any of you planned to do such a damn fool thing as open that box on camera in the first place. Why didn't you just open the package when it arrived, then call the police as soon as you saw what was inside? Are ratings all that important?

I guess I just don't understand the way television works. Apparently the Watcher does.

Speaking of the Watcher, I've carefully read the faxes and studied the last part of the tape you sent. It's quite obvious to me as a trained and experienced mental-health professional that the Watcher is as nutty as a squirrel's breakfast. But then maybe even without my long and expensive education, you arrived at that diagnosis yourself.

I've already called Stratford Vogler to tell him I'm going to bring over the tape and the latest letter this afternoon. I'm going to ask him to write to you directly as soon as possible and tell you what he thinks you should do about handling the situation and taking precautions to protect yourself.

I won't insult you by telling you the kinds of things Mama would—be sure your doors are locked, don't go into dark or deserted places alone, don't venture into bad neighborhoods, always make somebody walk you to your car, don't pick up strange men, and always carry some kind of weapon. I won't tell you any of these things.

Now, as to the psychic side of the matter, let me provide you with a few minutes of instant therapy. You're feeling guilty because you're going to gain some benefit (improved ratings, fame, etc.) from what the Watcher is doing. Let me assure you it's perfectly natural for you to feel that way. You're the recipient of some luck that's good for you, but bad for someone else.

You have the same feelings as those who survive a disaster—the "survivor syndrome" we call it in our high-tech language. People who live through earthquakes, airplane crashes, bombings, and other situations in which people are killed in a more or less arbitrary way often feel extremely guilty. They feel they don't "deserve" to survive, because others just like them got killed.

The truth is that disasters happen because of forces beyond our control. It's just the way the world works (ball bounces, cookie crumbles, etc.). Whether we benefit or suffer, even live or die, is not a matter of merit but luck.

My point (hang on, I'm getting there) is that you have to keep all this in mind. If you benefit from the Watcher's actions, then it is quite normal to feel guilty about it. It's all right to feel that way. It shows you're a good person with appropriate feelings.

However, you should also keep in mind that you didn't *ask* the Watcher to do anything to help you; you didn't *encourage* him; you didn't *hire* him. What's more, you don't *approve* of what he's done; you genuinely *want* him to stop, and you would *stop* him if you could.

Don't expect to get rid of your guilt the way you change your socks. It will never go away completely, nor would a right-feeling human being like you want it to. Yet with time the edge will grow duller and the burden lighter. (If we were together, I would now put my hand on your forehead, cast my eyes heavenward, and shout "Heal!")

I think you've just about convinced Mama to come to see you Thanksgiving. She told me you were lonely and pining for companionship—"although she doesn't breathe a word about it." So she's "giving a little thought to" paying you a visit to cheer you up. She thinks it's her duty, but I believe she misses you and wants to see what sort of life you're leading, now that she doesn't have you under her watchful eye.

Come to think of it, maybe she doesn't have the wrong idea to fly in and straighten you out. I am shocked and dismayed that you would consider even having a drink with that obvious Lothario who calls himself Stephen Legion.

Take care of yourself. You are the only aunt my daughter has, and I want her to have everything.

Zack rings no bells. Could you be thinking about Mack?

I'm going to see Stratford Vogler in one hour.

Love and hugs,
Janie

JOAN CARPENTER
2030 Buckminster · St. Louis, MO · 63130

Fri/Sat A.M.

Dear Janie,

It's late, late, late, but I wanted to thank you for your letter before too many hours had passed. So I'll just fax this to you instead of talking to your answering machine.

You are really terrific, and you do know how to come through in a crunch. If you weren't my big sister, I'd have to consult a psychiatrist. (Does this mean that if you weren't my psychiatrist, I'd have to consult a big sister? Only in Wonderland.)

I've been trying to take your advice and remind myself from time to time that just because an ill wind blows me some good, that doesn't make me responsible for global warming. Even though the benefits—radio news, personal-interview sound bites on local stations, and original-event bites on national news on three networks!—continue to roll in, I'm not feeling so guilty anymore. So much am I not feeling guilty that I hope you'll rein me in if I start complaining that the Watcher isn't doing enough for me.

In addition to your kind words, Tom Kline wrote me as nice a note as I had any right to expect. That helped make me feel less depressed about the whole situation. I was hoping he'd tell me he already has ten children and was planning on getting a vasectomy anyway, but unfortunately he kept quiet on this vital topic.

I'm glad to hear Mama knows I need for her to come and put me right. I'm afraid she's going to have her work cut out for her, though. Since I know you like gossip (what other reason is there to become a psychiatrist?), I'll tell you just a little about Steve Legion.

That's what I call him now—Steve. Oh, Janie, he *is* a handsome devil, with honey-colored hair, long tapered fingers, and slate-blue eyes. When he flashes the blue in my direction, I have strange physiological responses—I turn pale pink and my tongue ties itself into half hitches.

Yes, we met for a drink. No more than that. Just a drink and a little chat. Right after I wrote you, a messenger showed up at my office to deliver a card with his paging number and "Call me anytime" written on it. I was so thrilled by the prospect of having a doctor paged ("Dr. Legion, call on three. Dr. Legion, call on three.") that I did it immediately.

We met at a dark cramped place with no more atmosphere than a movie restroom (which it resembled) and had a Tanqueray and tonic and a few minutes of conversation. (Steve had to go to a party later in the evening.) I ordered him not to say a word about what happened on Wednesday's show, but we had to talk about something, so I proceeded to use the sly and diabolical interviewing techniques I acquired in TV school to pry out his innermost secrets.

It turns out that his wife Elsa understands him very well and has him pinned down and squirming on the tip of her ballpoint. Steve wants to be immensely rich and internationally prominent, although Elsa is merely rich and well-connected. He would like to be Facial Surgeon to the Stars, a sort of medical Max Factor.

He's convinced that if he could only get to the east or west coast, his office would be a black hole drawing in entire galaxies of Stars. They would then ask him to do a little slicing, trimming, filling, and sewing to preserve or enhance the stunning beauty of their faces. Alas, poor Steve can't persuade home-grown Elsa to pull up stakes and head for the beaches, and by virtue of one of those nasty prenuptial agreements, Elsa's money is still Elsa's and not Elsa's and Steve's.

"I couldn't possibly move to L.A. or New York with no more money than I earn in practice," he lamented sorrowfully to me. "I wouldn't be able to open the right kind of office." For "right kind" read "posh and exclusive."

While Steve was saying all this, I was studying the way his blue eyes subtly gleamed when they caught the light and watching the way the muscles rippled across his lean cheeks when he smiled suddenly. Even though bored by his talk, I was totally smitten by his presence.

Steve's only hope is that Elsa will eventually go along with his plan to build the Legion Clinic of Facial Surgery in a fancy St. Louis suburb. (He was not amused by my suggestion that he name the place Face the Facts and use the slogan *Your Face Is My Fortune.*) "I could have limousines pick up patients at the private airports," he said. "It could become as famous as the Mayo Clinic or Menninger's."

He confesses, though, that so far he hasn't even been able to persuade Elsa to allow him to replace her own bulbous nose with a sharper model. He thinks if she would only agree to let him improve her face, she would be eager to hand over the money for the Legion Clinic.

What's he doing having a drink with me? "When I first saw you in the emergency room, I was totally taken with your face," he told me. "Your nose is so absolutely perfect and your cheekbones so well placed, that I wanted to stare at you."

I confess to eating this up shamelessly, even though I did have the decency to smile slightly and look away demurely.

"But you're married," I said, wondering how many millions of women had spoken the same sentence in similar situations.

"Elsa and I have an understanding," he said. "We like being together, but we both realize that everyone's life can get a little stale without some outside interest from time to time. I'm sure we can be friends."

"I'll have to think about all this," I said.

Did it bother me that Steve Legion turned out to be boring, humorless, arrogant, snobbish, and venal? Yes, but he still has a commanding presence, a lithe supple body, and beautiful eyes.

Reader, I kissed him.

Much love and thanks from
Your *carpe diem* sister

P.S. Who is Mack?

C> –
C> cd\NOMAN
C> NOMAN
HELLO. I HAVEN'T TALKED TO YOU IN A WHILE. HOW ARE YOU?
Great. Everything has turned out even better than I thought it would.
EVERYTHING HAS TURNED OUT WELL?
I'll say. My plan to help Joan was immensely successful. She's gotten tons of publicity—interviews on TV and radio, newspa-

per articles, just everything. I'm sure the ratings on *Nightbeat* are going to skyrocket into the stratosphere.

TELL ME MORE ABOUT THE STRATOSPHERE.

That's where the ratings of Joan's show are going. It's sure to become another of those programs like Donahue and Oprah that are so successful locally that the networks buy them up and make them national. Of course, we can't just rest on our laurels now. I need to be thinking about the next step.

YOU NEED TO CONSIDER THE NEXT STEP?

That's right. I don't want to lose the forward momentum the Kline maneuver has produced. On the other hand, I don't want to act too soon, because I want to give Joan a chance to play out the present situation and milk it for as much publicity as she can get. She's not doing quite as much with it as I think she should, but I don't want to be too critical of her.

WHY DON'T YOU WANT TO BE TOO CRITICAL OF JOAN?

I think that's obvious. She's very high-strung and unsure of herself. She needs a lot of help and encouragement, but she's too proud to acknowledge it. She reminds me of a shy, frightened fawn who doesn't realize how beautiful she is and is ready to bolt and run at the first quick move. I must be very gentle in everything I say to her, because criticism from me would shatter her.

YOU'RE AFRAID OF SHATTERING JOAN?

In a manner of speaking. She needs all the self-confidence she can muster to do a job like hers. I want to do all I can to make her successful. I'm sure she already realizes the crucial role I'm playing in her career, and that will make her be grateful to me.

YOU WANT HER TO BE GRATEFUL TO YOU?

Of course. Recognizing how much she owes me will help bring us closer together. She will see that it's really the two of us who have achieved the American dream of fame and fortune. As soon as she becomes an established media star, she will want me to come out of the shadows behind the throne and step into the limelight with her.

TELL ME ABOUT STEPPING INTO THE LIMELIGHT.

It's something everyone wants to do, and I'm no exception. I'm tired of living in obscurity, being one of the "little people" that the big ones rely on to make their lives easier and better. I'm just lucky to have found somebody like Joan, because the two of us working together can pull ourselves to the top. And

of course it's also nice that she's so beautiful and sexy that I
can't help being attracted to her.
CAN YOU SAY MORE ABOUT BEING ATTRACTED TO
HER?
Of course, but I'm not going to. I've said enough for now.
Goodnight.

JOAN CARPENTER
2030 Buckminster · St. Louis, MO · 63130

31 Oct/Sat

Dear Mama,

Do you remember the woman whose house was cattycornered
from ours when we lived on Cherokee? She was only there for
about a year, but she was pretty hard to forget.

She was tall and had a broad behind and a round sweet face.
She smiled all the time, even when she was telling you something
gruesome. Like how she was loading somebody into an ambulance
once and his head fell off his body and hit her on the foot. (You can
see why I still remember her.)

She had jet black hair (probably dyed) that she wore in a sort
of regulation bob slicked down flat with White Rose Petroleum
Jelly. (I saw the jar in her bathroom.) She also drove a very large
tail-finned Cadillac the same color as her hair. I don't think I ever
knew her name, but you and Daddy called her "The Major," because she had been a WAC.

This is all a preamble to saying that I had lunch today with
Alexis, and during lunch I suddenly realized she looks almost exactly like the Major (except for the slicked-down hair). This made
me remember a time one summer when we all piled into the Major's Cadillac and drove to a watermelon garden. I had forgotten
such places ever existed. They seem to belong to an incredibly remote age.

Do you remember what I'm talking about? They had dozens of

watermelons floating in tanks of ice water, and you could go up to the counter and buy whatever you wanted. Daddy and I chose a slice of yellow, and you and Jane got red. We then ate the watermelon at one of the picnic tables lined up in rows under a tarp.

I remember how the hanging bare bulbs attracted hundreds of buzzing brown june bugs. They would dive bomb the lights, hit them with a pop, then fall onto the table. Sometimes they'd even fly into our hair and get caught, and then you or Daddy would have to pull them out while they were moving their legs furiously.

It's a nice memory, and it alone would have made having lunch with Alexis worth it. But the lunch also had its professional rewards. Alexis gave me some information about a real estate scandal and mentioned some land deals I might want to look into.

She's being a good citizen, but I'm not sure that's her real motive. I've heard she collects local celebs and society people, and I suspect she wants to use her information to turn me into another Star on her charm bracelet. But as my first journalism professor used to tell us, "Use anything you've got to get the story."

(If you detect a waspish note in all this, I suspect it's because I'm getting a bit irritated with Alexis's obvious wish to be better friends with me than I want to be with her. I'm regretting letting her be so nice to me when I moved in. Sounds like junior high, doesn't it?)

Everything is going well generally, although I've been a little upset about the last show. I won't bore you with the details, but my producer wanted me to do something I refused to do, then ended up doing anyway. Now he thinks I'm great, and so do a lot of viewers, judging by their letters and phone calls.

But enough! I know how you dear, sweet white-haired mothers like to hear your children ramble on in a boring way, but none of this stuff is major league. I'm sure everything will settle down soon and let me get back to pursuing my True Vocation of righting wrongs, promoting justice, and making the world safe for people who vote for Democrats.

Are you still keeping an eye on my pear tree? If either it or you isn't flourishing like the proverbial green-bay tree, you must tell me immediately. I can return to Dallas in two shakes of a TWA tail, which is exactly 78 minutes according to them.

If you don't come to make the dressing for the turkey, your granddaughter will have to go through life without knowing what it's supposed to taste like. My computer gives me access to all the airline schedules, so tell me your favorite times and I'll make the reservations for you.

I really am just fine. I've seen Alan Carter (the Kevin Baconish architect-builder) a couple of times. But to say we're dating would be like saying a dog jumping up in the air is flying—there's similarity, but no reality.

Lots of love from your baby girl,
Joanie

· JANE CARPENTER-REED, M.D. ·

Psychiatry Consultants, Inc.
3460 Chestnut Avenue
Brookline, MA 02147
617-976-8740
FAX: 617-976-2286

Notes for Joan

10/31

Dear Sis,

After I faxed you, I took the tape and letters to Stratford Vogler just as I promised. He's agreed to write to you as soon as he's had a chance to study the materials. (I gave him your fax number.)

He told me he thinks the Watcher is a case of *erotomania*. Since I had never heard of this disorder (I just claim to know a lot, not everything), when I got back home I looked it up in the MEDLINE database to see what I could come up with.

I uncovered some interesting materials. To keep from sending you a short treatise on the topic, I'll just download the notes I made into this letter. I'll add comments when appropriate.

DEFINITION: Erotomania (or De Clerambault's syndrome) consists in the elaborate, systematized delusion that the subject is

103

loved by someone (the object) who indirectly signals devotion to the subject. (J.H. Segal, "Erotomania Revisited," *AJP* (146:10, 10, 89).

The syndrome is a subtype of paranoid disorder. It is now recognized as more common than once thought.

SYMPTOMS AND PERSONALITY TRAITS: In 1921 French psychiatrist Gatian de Clerambault described five cases with the same unusual delusional pattern. Recent studies identify the pattern's key elements:

(1) A lower-status person makes a high-status person an object of romantic fixation.

The object-person may be a minister, professor, judge, physician, boss, etc. *Today this person is often a celebrity.* Maybe because everybody "knows" celebrities and this makes them available for fantasies.

(2) The attachment is delusional.

The subject believes the object of love reciprocates and sends secret messages to confirm it. Some subjects say this information is sent by telepathy. Others "read" it in a nod, wink, smile, or gesture.

(3) Facts are never adequate to break the delusion. Whatever the object says or does, the subject interprets as an indication of hidden affection.

Refusals and rejections like "Leave me alone" and "Stay away from me" are seen as "tests" demonstrating the subject's loyalty and commitment. The subject believes that by refusing to accept rejection, the object will be won over by the display of love and loyalty.

But rejection may make the subject become angry and violent— often dangerously so.

(4) The subject is likely to be of above average intelligence and capable of filling ordinary social roles—holding down a job, conducting business, going to parties, etc. The subject may be shy and lonely, but may cover this with a veneer of sociability. The subject may appear completely normal, and the "secret love" may never be revealed to the object or anyone else.

(5) Fixation on the object may be sexual, but the fantasies may also be ones of idealized romantic love. The object is seen as (and may be) more attractive, talented, intelligent, and superior in all ways. The idea seems to be that if such an incredibly wonderful

person notices the subject, the subject can acquire a sense of self-worth not supplied by any other form of recognition.

RECENT CASES YOU OUGHT TO PAY PARTICULAR ATTENTION TO:

(1) TV actress Rebecca Schaffer.

Murdered in L.A. in 1989 by a fan who wrote her dozens of letters for two years. He videotaped her show ("My Sister Sam") so he could watch her all the time. He hired a private detective to find her address, then went to her apartment. When she answered the door, he shot her.

He was sorry about it later and tried to kill himself by walking into traffic. (Not a terribly convincing gesture, I find. Had he walked in *Boston* traffic—that would be more than a gesture.)

(2) Theresa Saldana, another actress.

Attacked by Arthur Jackson. He came to this country from Scotland so he could "complete his divine mission" of killing her, getting executed, and "uniting" with her in death. He wrote her letters, located her apartment, and stabbed her ten times.

She survived, but six years later he was still writing to her from prison. She developed nightmares, insomnia, and had to be hospitalized for six weeks. He was sentenced to more time for threatening her.

(3) *TV Anchorwoman* Kelley Lange (KNBC-TV, L.A.).

Showered with letters and gifts for five years by Warren Hudson. Then he got fired, told a co-worker "I'm bored with life, and I'm going to go to Burbank to shoot Kelley Lange." The co-worker talked and police arrested him before he could use his .30 caliber Colt revolver.

(4) Jodie Foster and John Hinckley, Jr.

JH was so obsessively in love with Jodie Foster he sent her dozens of letters and poems, called her on the phone several times, and even tried to visit her at Yale.

When Foster refused to have anything to do with him, he decided to win her admiration by gaining a similar celebrity status. He would do this by performing the "great deed" of assassinating the President. He damned near did it.

WHAT CAN YOU LEARN FROM ALL THIS?

1. The world is chock-a-block with dangerously crazy people. (Everybody seems surprised when they learn that "the boy next

door" has been arrested for slicing and dicing people, but they really shouldn't be.)

2. Crazies are drawn to celebrities *(like you)* the way lightning is attracted to tall trees.

3. Don't think you can "handle" every situation that comes up. You're tough all right, but you aren't indestructible. Call the police when you even suspect you may need help.

The bottom line is this: *Take no chances.*
Keep me posted (faxed) on anything new. More later.

Love and all the rest,
Janie

■ STRATFORD VOGLER, M.D., Ph.D. ■

UNIVERSITY PSYCHIATRIC CONSULTANTS, INC.

2 4 1 W I C C A M P L A C E

B R O O K L I N E , M A 0 2 1 4 7

October 31

Dear Joan Carpenter:

Your sister, Jane, has asked me to give you my opinion about someone using the name "The Watcher" who has apparently developed an unusually strong and unwelcome interest in you. She provided me with copies of three "Watcher" letters sent to you and a videotape of your *Nightbeat* television program.

For legal purposes, I want to make it quite explicit that the views I express in this letter or in any subsequent communication are no more than my personal opinions. You have not retained me as psychiatrist or consultant, and I am not offering you my professional judgment. I have neither solicited nor received from you any form of payment or contribution. Hence, no fiduciary or contractual relation between us exists or is implied by my choosing to write this letter.

I am sorry to have to say all this, but because of recent court cases involving psychiatrists' inability to predict the extent to which a disturbed person may pose a danger to someone else, my attorney tells me not to talk to anybody who isn't a patient without reciting that litany.

Now with that out of the way, I can tell you that I've read the letters and watched the relevant part of the tape, and I have formed some definite opinions. The informal remarks I made earlier to Jane weren't really wrong, but I believe they should now be revised somewhat. I will get to that later.

Jane says you are an intelligent person ("smart cookie" are her actual words) and that I should give you something like a professional case presentation, though without the jargon. That is not quite possible, of course, but I'll do my best to honor the spirit of the request.

1. The Watcher is obviously an educated person. The words used in the letters, the style, and the correctness of the punctuation show that a college-level education is likely. Indeed, it is possible the writer is a professional person with one or more advanced degrees.

2. The Watcher is above average in intelligence. The demonstrated capacity for planning and executing complicated sequences of action go well beyond the powers of most people.

3. The castration of Kline can be viewed as something more than a pragmatic action designed to bring benefit to you and to the Watcher. It also represents a symbolic, although perhaps unconscious, destruction of the dominance of authority figures. Thus, the Watcher may be seen as attempting to fend off controlling forces and acquire power. (This is consistent with the apparent feelings of powerlessness I mention below.)

4. The Watcher's planning and acts may be seen as ways of exercising control over you. Since he thinks of you as so much above him that he cannot approach you directly, by getting you to accept (or at least go along with) the plans in the letters, he is demonstrating to himself that he has power over you. In this way, he proves to himself that he is not the powerless person he fears he is.

Similarly, by "approving" of things you do that he did not direct or granting you forgiveness when you depart from his directions (e.g., not following the "script" he wrote for you), he is trying to maintain the delusion that he is able to guide your actions.

5. The letters have an implicit sexual content, in that the Watcher imagines that the two of you are together sharing "pas-

sionate kisses" and caresses. Yet he always stops short of describing exactly what sort of sexual activities he would like to engage in with you. This suggests he suffers from both sexual and emotional immaturity. Sex is, in a sense, still a mystery to him. The letters show a wish both to press forward with a sexual conquest and also to withdraw from the sexual situation. This may be connected with a possible gender confusion.

6. A notable aspect of the letters is the Watcher's frequent failure to capitalize the letter "I" when used as a personal pronoun. The lapse suggests that the writer has a poor self-image. Forgetting to capitalize the first-person singular is a way of expressing the unconsciously held view that "I am not worthy of notice."

7. The Watcher obviously projects a close association with you in assuming that the two of you are participants in the enterprise of promoting your career. Less obvious is the additional assumption that you accept and welcome him in that role. This is where the delusional nature of the attachment becomes apparent.

Before this point, as in the first letter, it was possible to view the Watcher as no more than someone indulging in the normal fantasies of wish-fulfillment. That he should take the additional step of writing you a letter is, in itself, not all that unusual. This is why I suggested to Jane that she should tell you not to be too worried but to stay cautious.

8. The Watcher is clearly delusional. He is in the grip of a set of beliefs that are at variance with reality and with his own experience. His fundamental delusion is that you and he are emotionally attracted to each other, that you have the same feelings toward him that he has toward you. (This is an example of what we call *erotomania.*)

In this respect, the Watcher can be regarded as suffering from paranoia. He is, indeed, out of touch with reality and views the world through his own delusional lenses.

Let me quickly add that the Watcher is not out of touch with reality in a way that materially affects intelligence or the capacity to deal with practical matters. He is most likely out of touch only with respect to matters concerning *you.*

In this respect, the Watcher is like a very religious person who sees the hand of God in the fall of a sparrow or a missed bus, yet is able to cope quite well with the details of everyday life. He may even achieve outstanding results in his field of endeavor.

In the case of religion, we don't call people's beliefs delusional, even when they aren't widely shared. Indeed, we may honor such people and marvel at the way they can see the divine in the ordinary. The Watcher doesn't differ in kind from such religious people. Only his framework of interpretation is not theological—his framework is your "love" for him.

9. Those with delusions like the Watcher's ordinarily don't get tired of the person they have selected as their target. That is, they don't just go away after a while. In some cases, they can shift the focus of their obsession from one individual to another. However, we know of no way of encouraging this.

10. The violence the Watcher has already perpetrated shows he is a dangerous person. That it was directed away from you and in your interest makes it even more likely that future violence will be directed *toward* you. Since you will be unable to enter into the delusional state of the Watcher, you will always provoke disappointment. Ultimately the Watcher is going to want something from you that you cannot give—something like the reciprocation of love, approval, acceptance, and so on. When you fail to come through, the Watcher will turn against you.

In conclusion, I want to emphasize that you are dealing with a potentially dangerous person. That he has already erupted in violence indicates that more violence is likely to follow. I urge you to take extreme precautions to protect yourself until he is caught or turns his attention away from you.

Please feel free to let me know if you have any questions. Your sister helped me—forced me—to learn all the steps in the Krebs cycle during our first year of medical school, and without knowing that I might well have flunked out. I think I owe her something.

Sincerely yours,
Stratford Vogler

JOAN CARPENTER
2030 Buckminster • St. Louis, MO • 63130

31 Oct/Sat

Dear Jane,

It was nice of you to go to all the trouble of researching eroto-mania and sending me your notes on it. It sounds like a condition I've had myself. I vividly remember the way I used to go by Bob Butler's house at night and stare up at his window, hoping he would look out, see me, and invite me in for some quick sex. He never did. If he had, I'm not sure what I would have done. (I like to think I would have gone, but that's just the old maid in me talking now.)

I'm sure we can all tell stories like this. (No doubt you could regale us with some sizzlers about Zack. Or, so far as I know, even Mack—you never told me who *he* was.) It sounds to me like "eroto-mania" is a condition that varies in severity from the normal to the pathological. I mean, I might have looked up at Bob Butler's window, but I certainly never considered castrating somebody to get his attention. I don't think I would have thought about castrating him, even if he had turned me down for a date. But since I never asked him for one, who knows?

Anyway, I've taken all your cautionary tales to heart. I think I would have noticed the one about the *TV anchorwoman* even without the italics, but thanks anyway.

I also got a long fax from Dr. Vogler. He sounded quite friendly, and despite some obscure psychiatric chatter I'm not sure I followed, it made for fascinating reading. I was impressed that Dr. V. was able to say so much about an anonymous person on the basis of so little evidence. (Could he be a witch? Maybe all psychiatrists are.) What Dr. V.'s elaborate interpretation boils down to is that the Watcher is nutty as a Christmas fruitcake. This is, I believe, the very diagnosis you made. You guys must read the same journals.

Also like you, Dr. Vogler thinks the most important thing I can do is to be careful and not accept candy from strangers.

I've done a fairly good job of getting on with life, and I don't plan on doing anything dangerously stupid. Please tell Dr. V. I'm grateful for his time and I appreciate his opinion.

I know you don't want to hear more about making plans for Thanksgiving, but to use one of Mama's favorite sayings, "Time marches on." Keep in touch.

Love and kisses,
Joanie

ST. LOUIS COUNTY POLICE DEPARTMENT

DIVISION OF FORENSICS

Memo of Transmission   Date: October 31

From: Greg Handler, M.S., Division Head
To: Detective Lieutenant Peter S. Keefer, Major Case Squad
Case Number: 35-2300-1090

Here is a summary of the findings described in the accompanying documents:

1. The box was a 4″ × 6″ × 8″ corrugated container with a bursting strength of ten pounds. It was manufactured by the Charles Box Company of Bayonne, New Jersey. It showed no unusual prints or signs.

2. The tape that sealed the box is a two-and-one-half inch brown cellophane tape manufactured by the 3-M Company and sold under their trade name as Package Wrapping Tape.

The tape was cut, rather than torn, to size. The nature of the cuts, with slight irregularities of line and hesitation marks, suggests scissors were used. Adhering to the tape were some 28 brown fibers that microscopic examination showed to be cotton.

Spectrographic analysis of the dye in the fibers identified it as the same as that used in a commonly sold work glove manufactured by Warson Industries of Asheville, North Carolina, and marketed by them under the name "Brown Mule."

The adhesive side of the tape was also marked by a number of prints characterized by a woven fabric pattern. Also, these prints were flattened, rather than raised in the center. Both these facts suggest that the individual who prepared the package wore gloves to do so.

3. No complete fingerprints were recovered from the box or the non-adhesive surface of the tape. However, we were able to recover three partial prints from the non-adhesive surface of the tape. Two have been identified as belonging to Gary P. Wells and the other as that of Charles Fishwater.

4. The cotton filling the box was in the form of cotton balls of generally unremarkable characteristics. They are of the sort purchased at any drug or department store.

The only unusual feature was the identification on one cotton ball of a slightly sticky substance that is apparently an antibiotic cream. Additional tests will be needed to confirm this. It also may be possible to identify the cream more precisely.

5. The plastic bag was a trademarked Shur-Seal Freezer Bag with a tongue-and-groove zipper-type closure. The bag measured 6 × 7 inches. (It showed no sign of leaking into the cotton.) No prints were recovered from it.

6. The residue of blood inside the bag was identified as O positive. We will do no more blood studies for additional characterization unless requested.

7. The "Urgent" label is of the peel-off variety. Although we do not know the manufacturer, the label is apparently of the sort easily obtained at a variety of commercial locations. Nothing about it is remarkable.

8. The address on the label is typed on an IBM-Selectric II typewriter in the Century font. The letters show sufficient individual characteristics to make likely a matching of the text with the particular IBM typeball that produced it, should one be available for comparison.

I hope some of this information will be helpful to you. Our investigation will continue.

ST. LOUIS COUNTY POLICE DEPARTMENT

Memo of Transmission   Date: October 31

From: Detective Raymond R. Robertson
To: Detective Lieutenant Peter S. Keefer, Major Case Squad
Case Number: 35-2300-1090

Peter,

Just a couple of items to keep you up to speed.

1. I re-interrogated Thomas S. Kline, and the only new information I obtained from him was his apparent recollection of having smelled a sweet perfumey odor before he was hit.

He thinks it might have been the scent of the soap or skin lotion used by the perpetrator. Unfortunately, he couldn't think of any brand the odor reminded him of. ("Sweet and rather flowery" are his exact words.)

2. The package addressed to Joan Carpenter was delivered by Zip-Zip Express. The point of origin was their downtown office on Locust, and according to their time stamp, the box was turned over to them at 11:49 A.M. the same day. I sent Martha Higgens with a color blowup of the rewrapped box, and she showed it to the four people working the counter on Wednesday, but no one could identify it.

It turns out there's a good reason for that. Zip-Zip guarantees city delivery within two hours for anything mailed by noon. The office manager (Constance Lurton) informed Higgens that their highest volume of business comes between 11:00 and 12:00. People have gone to work and wrapped their packages, and the traffic starts getting heavy by ten. By 11:00 it becomes a flood, and dozens of secretaries and office messengers come in with piles of boxes and stacks of letters. As many as a thousand pieces arrive during that one hour.

I think this is a dead end.

3. I plan to talk to a builder named Alan Carter who has been identified to me by one of the KMIS staff as Joan Carpenter's boyfriend. Carpenter herself tells me that her only household employee is a gardener named Curtis Collins. I will attempt to learn whether

either of these people were in a position to have mailed the package on Wednesday.

Ray

ST. LOUIS COUNTY POLICE DEPARTMENT

Memo of Transmission   Date: October 31

From: Detective Lieutenant Peter S. Keefer, Major Case Squad
To: Detective Raymond R. Robertson
Case Number: 35-2300-1090

Ray,

Please check with Kline's doctor and with Dr. Marcus and see if they can tell us anything about how Kline might have been castrated. Was he cut with a knife or what? Also, would it have been physically hard to do?

I like the way you're doing things. When I get the information from you, I'll interrogate Joan Carpenter.

Tell Higgens she's doing good work. The last time I saw her she had trouble keeping her hands from trembling when she talked to me. She looked like she thought she had to bow and scrape every time she saw me or I would hand her her walking papers. Remind her this is America, where it's hard to get fired.

Pete

ST. LOUIS COUNTY POLICE DEPARTMENT

Memo of Transmission   Date: October 31

From: Detective Raymond R. Robertson
To: Detective Lieutenant Peter S. Keefer, Major Case Squad
Case Number: 35-2300-1090

Peter,

I went back to Barnes Hospital and interviewed Dr. Clarence Field again. He was the first to look at Kline's wounds, so he saw them before they operated on them. They did some trimming and sewing to make repairs, so the wounds in their present state don't reveal much.

I asked Dr. Field if he had any idea how the injuries were made. He said that the edges of the wounds weren't sharp cuts, but showed signs of bruising made by compression. Also, the cut wasn't smooth, but in a couple of places the edges were jagged or irregular.

He's a trauma surgeon, and he said that in his experience you get cuts like this when something other than a knife is used. His best guess is that the cuts were probably made by scissors or (more likely) pruning shears. I asked him if in his judgment it would have taken any special knowledge to make the cuts. "Anybody who can cut up a chicken is certainly able to perform a castration." (Not my favorite interview. I found myself crossing and uncrossing my legs while asking questions.)

Dr. Marcus agreed with everything Dr. Field said and had nothing else to add.

This information is pretty thin, but I think it's potentially useful.

                                                                  Ray

Lieutenant Keefer here.

Peter, I'm glad I caught you. It's Ray. Are you still planning to interrogate Joan Carpenter this evening?

Unless you know some reason I shouldn't. Do you want me to wait?

Not at all. In fact, the reason I'm calling is that I've got some more information for you. Do you remember that Greg Handler's report said that the box label was typed on an IBM Selectric II?

I remember. In Century style type.

Right. Anyway, I sent Martha Higgens to look at all the typewriters in the KMIS office, and I wanted to let you know what she found.

Go ahead.

Most of the people there use word processors or computers, so there weren't that many typewriters to begin with. But Martha located two of the IBM machines.

Who do they belong to?

A woman business reporter named Terry Lewis and a news writer by the name of Thomas Bedson.

Did Martha check them out?

She did. But we've already got interrogation reports on them, and she didn't pick up anything new or interesting. Both subjects have met Joan Carpenter. She seems nice, but they haven't spent any time with her.

They say they don't have any feelings one way or another about *Nightbeat*. Neither one has ever worked on it, and both of them say they don't even watch it regularly.

I don't think we can learn anything from them, really.

No, they don't sound like good suspects. But how about the typewriters? Are they where anybody can get to them?

Pretty much so. According to Martha, the subjects don't have private offices. They just have a desk and a cubicle in a big open office. Only a few star writers and reporters have offices.

So somebody could just drop into one of the cubicles, use the typewriter, then leave without anybody necessarily being the wiser.

The cubicles are open, the typewriters are there. Somebody coming in very early or staying very late could have access to them without anybody else around to notice.

But what about the type faces?

There we've got a little trouble.
Martha brought back a sample from both typewriters, and I took them in to Handler. All he did was glance at the samples and say "Wrong font." Then he looked up some samples in a book and identified them as IBM Courier.

I don't know what you mean by a little trouble. It looks like a lot to me. We've got typewriters, but the type style doesn't even match. How does that help us?

Peter, you don't know much about the IBM Selectric, do you?

If there's something special to know, I don't know it. You tell me.

It's one of those typewriters you can change the type on by replacing the type ball with another one. So you can have whatever type style you want.

I get it. Anybody with a Century type ball could pop it in the typewriter, then pop it out when they were finished typing?

Exactly. And I'll tell you something else I learned from Handler.

Let me tell you. The Watcher letters were typed on an IBM Selectric in Century type. I got Greg's report this morning.

This afternoon was the first I heard it. Anyway, that's about all I've got. I just wanted you to know about the IBMs before you talked to Carpenter.
You're sure you don't want me to come along?

I think she'll open up more with just one person. Particularly in her own house. You get to take an early night tonight. And thanks for calling.

THIS IS THE SATURN AGENCY. YOU MAY LEAVE A MESSAGE AT THE TONE.

Dan, it's Joan. If you're there, please answer, because I need to talk to you.

Okay, I guess you're really not home. Listen, I'll just

fax you what I have to say. Check your other machine please.

If you get back before eleven, call me. Otherwise, we can talk in the morning.

I hope you had fun, whatever you were doing. And whatever you were doing was more fun than what I've been doing.

Bye now.

FAX TRANSMITTAL 314-552-5671

JOAN CARPENTER
2030 Buckminster • St. Louis, MO • 63130

31 Oct/Sat

Dan,

Here is why you're getting a breathless phone call and a fast fax—*I am a suspect.*

I don't mean anybody said to me "You are a suspect," and nobody read me my Miranda rights. Yet it was as clear as a glass in a dish-detergent commercial that the police think I had a hand (so to speak) in mutilating Tom Kline.

Let me tell you what happened, then I've got a question for you.

At eight o'clock this evening a tall, nicely dressed man with baby-blue eyes and looking more than a little like Warren Beatty in *Dick Tracy* (without the overcoat) showed up at my front door. I had agreed to an appointment to talk to somebody from the county police, but I was expecting some loutish functionary. Instead, I got the very smooth Detective Lieutenant Peter Keefer, head honcho of the Major Case Squad.

"Please call me Peter," he said.

Then after he had called me "Ms. Carpenter" about twice, I felt so uncomfortable I had to say in my best southern belle fashion, "Do use my first name." Lt. Keefer just nodded his head and smiled graciously. I realized then that I was in the hands of a master interviewer who had established control of the situation from the beginning.

We settled ourselves in the living room, and I offered him a drink. "Do you happen to have any Dr. Pepper on hand?" he asked.

Since I grew up on the stuff and still drink it, I did just happen to. What's more, I found his request so charmingly unassuming that despite my better judgment, I began to feel warm and well-disposed toward him. I'm sure pigs make the same mistake about the man fattening them up to market size.

While pouring out the soda, I mentioned that people seem to associate Dr. Pepper with the south, and this banal observation initiated a conversation about whether St. Louis is southern, midwestern, or eastern.

This discussion provided a natural opportunity for "Peter" to press on and ask why had I decided to leave Dallas, did I like living here, did I know my way around the city, had I met many people, what were their names and how did I meet them?

So there we were, Peter and Joan, in a southern-midwestern-eastern city just having a little chat over a couple of glasses of Dr. Pepper on a pleasant fall evening.

As a crackerjack (but immodest) interviewer myself, I had to admire the man's techniques. I wasn't a hostile subject, but still, he was gathering a fantastic amount of relevant information about me and my habits, abilities, and ambitions. And he just seemed to be making polite conversation.

From talking about St. Louis, he moved me very easily into talking about *Nightbeat* and whether I was disappointed in its ratings (yes), whether I thought my job was at stake (yes). How the Watcher letters had affected me (scared me), whether I had any idea about who wrote them (certainly not), did I think somebody at the station had (possible, but who?), had I ever met Tom Kline (no), did I think I had benefitted from what the Watcher had done (definitely).

My dear friend Peter then eased the circle around back to Dallas and *Dallas After Dark*. Had I really set up the vice cops (well, in a way), had I propositioned them (absolutely not), did they try to shake me down (absolutely)? I tried not to sound defensive when I answered the questions, and he nodded and smiled frequently, mostly at the right places.

By this time, I knew what was coming next. "Did the ratings of your Dallas television program benefit from the incident with the vice officers?" he asked. Even he couldn't make this sound as innocent as it was supposed to.

"Not so much from the incident as from the judge's slapping me with a jail sentence," I said. "Most people thought it was a case of punishing the victim."

"I'm sure you realize the situation in Dallas is very much like the one we have here," he said.

"I can see why you might get that impression," I said, sounding chilly.

"Do you deny that you've been in contact with the person who calls himself the Watcher?" He had stopped trying to be conversational.

"I categorically and absolutely deny it," I said. "And I hope you aren't planning on turning this into another case in which I get blamed for the dishonesty or ineptitude of the police." I looked him straight in his baby-blues and let myself sound just as indignant as I felt.

I was on the verge of getting very angry, but then Peter changed course on me. "Do you type?" he asked.

"Since high school," I said. "Why? Do you think I should become a secretary?"

"Do you own a typewriter?"

Then the light went on. "Now I get it," I told him. "I noticed that the Watcher letters were typed on an electric typewriter with a film ribbon. But I haven't used a typewriter since graduate school. I do all my typing on a computer, here and at the office."

"But you did own a typewriter?" I was disappointed that he just pressed on without congratulating me on my powers of observation.

"I've owned several. I used to have a Smith-Corona electric portable, then I bought an IBM office model when I started writing my master's thesis."

"A Selectric?"

"That was it. The one with the replaceable balls."

The grotesque and absurd connection with Tom Kline that this phrase conjured up struck me suddenly, and I had to rub my hand hard across my mouth to keep from revealing my crassness and bad taste by laughing.

"You don't still have it?" If he noticed anything odd about the phrase or about me, he didn't let on.

"No. I donated the typewriter along with a lot of other stuff to a charity after my husband died, and that was seven years ago."

"You didn't keep any of the type elements? The balls of different kinds of type?"

"I didn't have any, except for the one that came with the machine."

"Do you ever use the IBM at the studio offices?"

"I didn't even know there was one," I said. "I told you, I use a computer. I doubt if I could even type on a typewriter anymore."

That was basically the interview. Peter got up, smiled, shook hands with me, and said, "I enjoy your program, when I get a chance to see it. It's nice to meet you, and we'll be in touch with you later." He didn't tell me not to leave town.

My question to you is this: What the hell should I do?

My basic inclination after my little chat with my old friend Peter is to call up somebody like Alan Dershowitz and ask him if he'll take my case.

He will no doubt tell me not to talk to the police anymore. I'll say, But I have nothing to hide. He'll say, Glad to hear it, but it's not your job to prove you're innocent; it's their job to prove you're guilty. Deep down, I'll feel immensely relieved not to have to say another word to the cops.

Dan, I have to tell you that since the Dallas fiasco, I think I've turned into a certifiable coward. I was in jail for only a few hours, but the idea of going back even for a short visit makes me have nightmares in the daytime. It's become Room 101 (is that the right number?) for me.

Back to my question: Should I hire a big-time criminal lawyer? Should I hire a small-time criminal lawyer?

Also: Should I refuse to talk to the police anymore? They obviously consider me their prime suspect, so should I help them build the cage to put me in?

Speak, Oracle. (But please don't say anything oracular.)

Philia,

Joan (aka "Dr Pepper")

THE SATURN AGENCY
256 East 59th Street • New York, New York • 10020
212-555-5050 • Fax 212-555-5051
Daniel L. Saturn, PRESIDENT

Late Sat., Early Sun.
November 1

Joan, Joan, Joan,

Get hold of yourself, woman. You're turning an interrogation into an execution.

Of course the police suspect you. Wouldn't *you* suspect you?

The cops aren't in the entertainment business, and unlike mystery writers, they don't figure out ways of making the most suspicious-looking person turn out to be completely innocent.

They have to catch criminals, and to do that, they play the probabilities. They zero in on the person most likely to have committed the crime, because more often than not, *that's the person who actually committed the crime.*

And who looks more suspicious in the Kline case than you, my dear? You're the one who stands to benefit most from the Watcher's actions, and in the eyes of the police, that almost makes you an accomplice. They are sure to believe you had *something* to do with targeting Kline, even if they don't believe you're the trigger man (so to speak).

My advice is that you just keep doing what you're doing. Talk to the police when they want to talk, answer their questions, and always tell the truth. This last point sounds like something your Mom would say, but in criminal investigations, it's crucially important that they not catch you in even a trivial lie.

If they do, that convinces them you've got something to hide, and after that, they'll never leave you alone. You'll be scalding milk to make yogurt (doesn't everyone?) when the phone rings and a detective will want "to just check a few facts." Your friend Peter sounds like a reasonable person, and if you continue to cooperate, chances are he'll soon realize you're as innocent as Bambi.

Now to your other question. At the head of your list of all the things in the world you do not need (a pet python, a personal astrologer, junk bonds, etc.), you should write down "criminal attorney." If you get someone like Dershowitz involved now, most people (the D.A. included) will take this as a tacit admission of guilt and a determination to beat the rap on technicalities.

How can I, a mere flesh peddler, speak with such authority? Did I ever tell you that I served two years in the public defender's office when I got my J.D. and the stars were still in my eyes instead of on my client list? Two years was too long, and "served" has the right associations.

After a client told me he'd carve his initials on my liver with an ice pick if I couldn't plea-bargain him down to a bullet (a year, to you civilians) on a manslaughter charge with two eyeball witnesses, I decided I might not have made the right career move. By the end of my term, I was of the opinion that most of my clients deserved much longer sentences than the ones I had been able to get for them. Anyway, I'm speaking from a little (if dated) experience.

This isn't to say that one of these days you won't need a firebrand defender. But then one of these days we're going to be living on the moon and swallowing food pills instead of mashed potatoes. Since the future's not now, don't say, "Get me Perry Mason" yet.

I'm sure your experience in the Dallas County jail is what is making you feel so nervous about having the cops interrogate you. But it's much too early to start worrying about Room 101. As we say here on the sophisticated east coast: Chill out.

It's almost two in the morning now. That's why I didn't call. But I did want to fax you a little something to read with your oat bran crunch.

We can talk later—but, please, not before noon.

Your friend,
Thumper

YOU HAVE REACHED 552-8076. AT THE TONE YOU MAY LEAVE A MESSAGE.

Joan? This is Alan Carter. I wanted you to know that a couple of people from the police came by to talk to me. A woman and somebody named Robertson—Detective Robertson.

They asked me questions about you and how long I had known you and how well. They wanted to know if you had tried to get me to do anything illegal or asked me if I knew anybody who would do things for money. I said that whole line was all ridiculous and they were barking up the wrong tree.

At first they wouldn't even tell me what they were investigating, but when I asked them directly, they finally admitted it connected with that mess about Kline. I didn't have much to tell them, but they made me go over everything several times.

They also wanted to know about me. They asked what I was doing the night Kline got hurt and where was I the whole next day. They wanted to know if we had gotten together that night.

They didn't exactly grill me, but they weren't all that friendly either. I got the idea they wouldn't be too sorry if they could hang the whole business on you.

I hope you're doing all right.

I've got some evening meetings for the next two or three days, but after that let's get together and go to the movies or out to dinner or something.

Listen, I'm calling you from my car, and it's going to cost me a fortune if I keep running on the way I tend to do. Call me at home this evening if you want to chat about this some more.

Goodbye.

Sunday

Dear Ms. Carpenter,

Since I'm working in the neighborhood today, I dropped by to see you. I wanted to tell you that the police came to my apartment last night to ask me questions. The woman was nice, but the man was not. The man kept inferring that you and I were quite intimately involved. Of course I told him he was wrong, but I'm not sure he believed me.

The woman asked me whether you had promised me money or sex or anything else if I would do what you asked me to. I told them—quite honestly—that I would do almost anything you wanted me to, but you hadn't asked me to do anything.

They made a big deal asking about a typewriter and didn't believe me when I said I didn't have one. They asked if it was okay if they searched my apartment, and I said sure. Of course they didn't find a typewriter. (They didn't search my storage locker, because I didn't tell them I've got one. If you ever need anything kept out of sight, just let me know.)

I told them I hoped you would have me on your show sometime, and that was probably a mistake. They then got real pushy. The man started asking me again if I would do almost anything to get on TV. I said I wouldn't do anything really against the law. Then he wanted to know if I knew anybody else at KMIS or the *Post-Dispatch*.

They never told me they wanted to know about Kline, but I guessed that's what they were after. Anyway, I didn't tell them anything that would hurt you.

They took my pruning knife, and it might be a couple of weeks before I can get it back. They asked me if that was my only one, and I told them it was. What I didn't say is that I've got some pocket pruners that I keep in my car. So don't worry, I can still do the light trimming.

I'm leaving you a bunch of rosemary. (Rosemary is for remembrance.)

Your friend,
Curt

FAX TRANSMITTAL 314-552-5671

JOAN CARPENTER
2030 Buckminster • St. Louis, MO • 63130

1 Nov/Sun

Dear Dan,

Maybe I don't need Perry Mason right now, but I think I need somebody. The police are nosing around and questioning people associated with me. You could say they're just conducting an investigation into the Kline crime, but I find it hard not to believe that what they're really doing is piecing together (i.e., trumping up) a case against me.

A guy I've gone out with a time or two told me the cops had grilled him about whether I had ever tried to get him to do something illegal. I suspect somebody had the bright idea that Alan and I might have planned some weird *Double Indemnity* caper and made Tom Kline the victim. Anyway, except for knowing me, Alan Carter has *no* connection with the case. I don't know why they talked to him if they weren't trying to get something on me.

You may think this is far-fetched, but if so your handbook on how cops think is out of date. They *look* for the bizarre. When they talked to me after the show, the first question they asked was whether I had ever had a date with Tom Kline. They didn't even ask me if I knew him. I suspect they wanted to find a "romantic triangle" or "lovers' quarrel" motive that would unravel the case and turn it into a tabloid headline (or trash TV, come to that).

They didn't stop with Alan either. I came home to find a note from my gardener saying that the cops questioned him and searched his apartment. They particularly wanted to know if I had ever tried to get him to do anything for me. (I *have* asked him to trim the forsythia.) Reading between the lines of the note, I think their idea is that Curt Collins is my Love Slave and as willing to do my evil bidding as the Somnambulist in the *Cabinet of Dr. Caligari.*

Actually, Curt Collins is a lot like the Somnambulist. In the midst of a major problem, he's managed to become a minor one. I made the mistake of inviting him in for a cup of tea when I first hired him. Now he tells me more about his life than I want to know. (In case *you* would like to know: his parents are dead, he has no siblings, lives by himself, doesn't have a girlfriend, likes to hunt and fish, and spends most of his spare time writing poetry.) He always wants me to listen to his poetry or to tell him how I "broke into" TV so he can do the same thing.

When he's not talking about himself, he's talking about me and telling me how beautiful, talented, warm, and charming I am. When he first talked this way, I expected him to proposition me. I was ready to tell him that the only bed I want him in is the one where I planted the foxglove, and if he laid a hand on me, he'd be fertilizing it with his mortal remains. But he's never actually said anything—yet.

The result of all this is that I can't go into my own backyard on Thursday afternoons without having to listen to him talk about himself or me, and I'm bored with both topics. (I'll save you a rap about my neighbor out back who collects celebs the way Andy Warhol collected cookie jars. She's nice but annoying, whereas Curt is annoying but nice. I'm sure your shrewd legal mind can catch the difference.)

Although I'm far from being an O-class star on the Main Sequence, I'm developing sympathy for those who are. I used to think the really famous were exaggerating when I'd interview them and they would complain about how they couldn't take a pee without having to sign autographs on toilet paper. I'm beginning to understand. I was expecting to find the bluebird of happiness in my own backyard, but instead, I found a fan.

Suspected of assault by the police and hounded by my gardener—what a life. If you can figure out what to do about these problems, you're a better man than I am. But then you are, aren't you?

Love,
Joan

THE SATURN AGENCY
256 East 59th Street • New York, New York • 10020
212-555-5050 • Fax 212-555-5051
D a n i e l L . S a t u r n, PRESIDENT

1 November

Dear Joan:

Maybe the sort of person you need to consult is one licensed to administer powerful psychoactive drugs—like a psychiatrist. You are getting certifiably paranoid.

Of course I would say the police are conducting an investigation, because that's exactly what they *are* doing. If you stay still and think for half a second, you'll realize they are going to be talking to everybody connected with you for a very good reason.

Remember, *you* are the one who got the Watcher letters. Not

Wells, not Fishwater—you. The Watcher may be somebody who's never clapped an eye on anything but your pixeled image. He may be a complete stranger who sits hunched over his typewriter in the dim half light of the TV wasteland, living in his fantasies and churning out letters.

It's just as possible, though, that he's somebody who knows you. Maybe not somebody like Alan Carter (how come you've never mentioned him?) but somebody who at least sees you in 3-D and knows you've got a back to your head. That's why it makes perfect sense to talk to everybody associated with you.

This should help you see why the *sole* interest of the police might not be in building a case against you. They just might consider it possible that Carter or Curt Collins wrote the Watcher letters and assaulted Kline. From where I sit, they both look like better suspects than you do, but then I know you.

Quite frankly, if the Watcher isn't identified immediately, I would be surprised if the police didn't eventually get around to trying the clothes on Charles Fishwater. He's got a big stake in your potential success. And let's not forget about Gary Wells, your administrative assistant, the woman who sold you your house, or even Simon Rostovsky himself. Dig deeply enough, and I'm sure you can find some reason to be suspicious of all of them.

You may or may not be the object of the police investigation, but you are certainly the focus of it. If you are the object, they'll eventually discover they can't make a case against you. But even then, you'll continue to be the focus. So just get used to being at the center of the whirlwind and cultivate stillness and calm.

As to the problem with your star-struck and TV-smitten gardener, the solution is simple—Fire him. Why pay somebody to make you uncomfortable? You can find plenty of people who'll do it for free.

You should also try to get plenty of rest and drink lots of water and fruit juice. Some new studies suggest that dehydration is closely connected with fatigue, and you need to keep up your energy.

I hope all this advice is worth more than you paid for it.

Dan

ST. LOUIS COUNTY POLICE DEPARTMENT

Memo of Transmission   Date: November 1

From: Detective Raymond R. Robertson
To: Detective Lieutenant Peter S. Keefer, Major Case Squad
Case Number: 35-2300-1090

Peter:

I just read your IR-905 on the Carpenter interrogation, and the feeling I got was that she is trying to make use of that Dallas incident to put us on the defensive.

I think she figures that if she can get us to think she got a bad deal from the police and the judge in Dallas, we won't be suspicious of her involvement in this case. That is, she figures if we don't take that conviction against her seriously, we won't take too close a look at her.

But let's not let her shine us on. Consider some obvious facts about Carpenter's connection with the Kline matter:

(1) Carpenter was trying to entrap some Dallas vice officers so she could then go public with her story and pictures. I looked at the Dallas County Criminal Court record, and this is exactly Judge Scott's assessment of her actions.

According to your 905, Carpenter says she didn't entrap anyone and was just acting as an investigative reporter. This is what you would expect from her, of course.

The Judge also says that Carpenter's aim was to improve the ratings of the TV program *Dallas After Dark*. She doesn't deny that this is one of the reasons she wanted to do the story on graft in the DPD.

(2) Carpenter admits (IR-905, p.3) that the attack on Kline and the opening of the box containing the products of that attack is likely to help the ratings of *Nightbeat*.

I consider it reasonable to believe that Carpenter needs this sort of sensationalism to boost her ratings, so she decided to try just the sort of thing she tried in Dallas.

You might think somebody like Carpenter is too smart to use the same MO as before. But you know as well as I do, that even intelligent people tend to follow the same pattern when they're trying to achieve the same result.

(3) Carpenter also admits (IR-905, p.4) that if the ratings on *Nightbeat* are not improved significantly she will lose her job. I think this is a very powerful motive.

(4) The attack on Kline and the castration are actions she is physically capable of carrying out. She appears to be a strong woman who would be able to hit Kline on the head, then while he was unconscious, castrate him. Getting a weapon would be no problem, particularly if pruning clippers or scissors were used.

(5) Timewise, Carpenter had the opportunity to attack Kline. She has no alibi for Tuesday night after about eight until Wednesday around two in the afternoon.

It would be perfectly possible for her to have been hiding in the parking garage, attack Kline, then return home without anybody knowing she had left the house.

(6) The Watcher letters could be a device to keep us from associating Carpenter herself with the crime.

(a) If we assume she is telling the truth when she says she didn't write them and doesn't know who did, she could still be taking advantage of them. She could be following her own plan, while blaming her actions on the Watcher. For example, even if the Watcher did send a box, she could have received it, destroyed it, then substituted a box of her own.

I don't consider this the most likely possibility.

(b) Someone acting in cooperation with her or under her direction could have written the letters.

We have no direct evidence of this, but we should keep it in mind. (Also, see (7) below.)

(c) She could have written the Watcher letters herself.

She knows how to type, and she once owned an IBM Selectric typewriter (IR-905, p.5) Furthermore, she has access to two typewriters of the right kind and could have typed the letters using her own type ball.

(7) Carpenter could have worked with an accomplice.

(a) Curt Collins is a possibility for this role. I think I detect in him a strong attraction for Carpenter—maybe sex or maybe just her status as a celebrity. He also strikes me as someone who could be controlled by her more powerful personality.

He can't give us a witness to prove he was at home on the night Kline was attacked, but we've confirmed that he was working in the yard of Mrs. Harold Feffer at 2349 Longfellow in south St. Louis around the time he would have had to drop off the package to Zip-Zip. (See the IR-905, p.4.) Actually, Mrs. Feffer can only confirm that he showed up for work and was there around one o'clock. She didn't check on him during the four hours that he was supposed to be working. Zip-Zip is about two miles straight down Grand, and it would be possible to go there and get back in half an hour or less.

After saying all this, I have to admit that I don't like Collins for the accomplice role. My basic reason is that he seems too naive. He also doesn't seem smart enough. I can't imagine Carpenter taking the risk that Collins might screw up or just talk too much. Also, I put some pressure on him when I interrogated him, and he didn't show any signs of wanting to change his story.

I could be wrong about Collins. He just may be a lot shrewder and smarter than I give him credit for.

(b) For my money, Alan Carter is a better possibility. He claims (see my IR-905) he doesn't know Carpenter very well, although he admits they have gone out a couple of times. It doesn't take long for a man to fall under the influence of the right woman, and she may have more of a grip on him than he is telling us. Carter is also very bright and self-confident. I can imagine him thinking he could get away with a crime.

Carter says he doesn't have a typewriter. He also doesn't have an alibi for the relevant time in the Kline attack, although he does have one for the period during which he would have had to turn over the package to Zip-Zip.

Although I mention these two people as possible accomplices, the idea of an accomplice isn't one that I find terribly strong. In my view, Carpenter is a woman who is most likely, if possible, to work independently. I suspect she trusts only herself to do a job right.

(8) Carpenter could have sent the box with Kline's body parts to herself.

She had enough time in the late morning to go to Zip-Zip and drop off the package for afternoon delivery. Had she gone to the downtown office around eleven-thirty or even noon, she would still have plenty of time to get to her office around two.

I recommend that we regard Joan Carpenter as a most likely suspect in this case. Pursuant to this recommendation, I suggest we focus our investigation on developing some physical evidence to link her with the Watcher letters, the box, or the Kline attack.

Please let me know what you think.

Ray

ST. LOUIS COUNTY POLICE DEPARTMENT

Memo of Transmission   Date: November 1

From: Detective Lieutenant Peter S. Keefer, Major Case Squad
To: Detective Raymond R. Robertson
Case Number: 35-2300-1090

Ray:

I just read through your Memo, and I guess I have to admit that everything you say sounds plausible in an abstract way.

I'm just not convinced, though. I didn't want to write this in a 905, but my impression of Joan Carpenter was very favorable. I realize TV stars sometimes have powerful personalities and winning ways, so it's easy to be taken in by them. Nevertheless, Carpenter seemed to be a genuinely nice person, and I felt she was doing her best to answer every question. So far as I can tell, all the factual assertions she made check out.

If she's a little touchy about the Dallas conviction, I think that's understandable. Assuming she told the truth in court, she didn't set up the vice officers and they did try to shake her down. Then they both walked away from it, and she got a jail sentence. For somebody like her, even spending a day or so in jail is a humiliating experience, particularly when you think you're the victim of complete injustice.

Everything you mention in your memo is suppositional, speculative, and circumstantial. Your recommendation that we focus the investigation on her and try to come up with some physical evidence is the exact opposite of the way I prefer to proceed. That is, if we had a single shred of physical evidence I'd say we ought to swarm all over her like ants on a stick of candy.

My real feeling at the moment is that we ought to take a closer look at Gary Wells. My understanding is that he stands to be pushed out of his job by Carpenter. He has a lot to lose, and I'm sure he is jealous and resentful.

I know that what I've said here isn't going to please you, since you seem quite sold on Carpenter. So let's compromise to this extent. You want to try to get some evidence. So I'll authorize a search of Joan Carpenter's house, car, garage, etc., but you will have to ask her for her consent. I'm sure she will give it, and if she doesn't, I guess your suppositional case will be that much stronger.

Nevertheless, I predict that if you search her house, you will find nothing.

Pete

This is Dan Saturn.

Dan, it's Joan. Listen, I need your advice. And I need it right now, because there's a Detective Ray Robertson from the St. Louis County Police Department standing in my living room with another officer.

What do they want? My God, they aren't going to arrest you are they? That's ridiculous.

They didn't *say* they were going to arrest me. Detective Robertson says they want my permission to search my house and property.

Then they don't have a warrant?

They say they don't need one, if I tell them they can.

That's right. But if they don't have a warrant, that means they don't have any real evidence against you. They may not even feel they have enough grounds of reasonable suspicion of involvement in a crime to get a judge to issue a warrant. They're just fishing.

Maybe so. But what do you think I should do?

What do you want to do? I know you don't have anything connected with the crime hidden away. But how about something like drugs or an unlicensed gun?

I don't have anything, unless you count my overdue library books. I'm completely clean, assuming they don't plant something and then pretend to find it. And I really wouldn't put it past cops to do that.

If they were going to do that, it wouldn't matter whether they had a warrant or not.

I guess so. But what if I tell them no? What if I say I just don't want them poking around in my things and violating my privacy?

Then they'll have to try to get a warrant. But they'll think you're being uncooperative because you have something to hide.

Is that grounds for a warrant?

Legally it's not, and it's not even grounds for suspicion of participation in a crime.

So why don't I tell them to buzz off?

You could, but psychologically that's like a dare. It's like saying, "I've got something you want, so just see if you can get it."

You sound like you think I should let them search.

It would probably make your life easier.

I like that idea in the abstract. But I guess deep down I feel there are things more important in life than ease.

It's your decision, Joan.

And I think I've made it. I'm going to tell them to go to hell and that I won't cooperate unless they have a warrant. What's the point of being an American if you can't keep the cops out of your underwear drawer?

I admire the spirit. Let me know how things work out.

ST. LOUIS COUNTY POLICE DEPARTMENT

Memo of Transmission   Date: November 1

From: Detective Raymond R. Robertson
To: Detective Lieutenant Peter S. Keefer, Major Case Squad
Case Number: 35-2300-1090

Peter:

I need to talk to you before you leave the office again.
Let me tell you what's been happening, then I'll come by and check in with you after you get back.
I took Martha Higgens with me and paid a call on Joan Carpenter at her residence at 2030 Buckminster. I asked her if she would consent to letting us search her property for any evidence that might be connected with the crime against Thomas Kline.
"Do you think I did it?" she asked.
I said, "We're not charging anyone with the crime at this time. We're still developing evidence. That's why we'd like your permission to see if we can locate anything here that might be associated with the perpetrator."
She made us wait while she called somebody on the phone (she didn't say who), then she came back and informed us that she would not give us permission to conduct a search.
She said, "I have nothing to hide, but I've got a lot to protect."
I asked her what she meant by that. She said she had done nothing wrong, and she intended to protect her Constitutional rights to privacy and her Fourth Amendment freedom from unreasonable search and seizures.
I pointed out that we could get a search warrant to authorize

us to conduct a search. Her response was, "If you want to look in my underwear drawer, you're going to need legal authority."

I said we had no reason to be particularly interested in where she stores her underwear. She smiled and said that was only a synecdoche. (I asked her to spell it, then I looked it up when I got back to the office. It's "a figure of speech in which the part stands for the whole.")

I told Carpenter I was leaving Higgens to keep the house under surveillance while I applied for a warrant. I didn't want Carpenter to think she would have an opportunity to dispose of evidence while we weren't watching. (I've also arranged to have somebody spell Higgens, in case matters take longer than I anticipate.) If Carpenter leaves the house, Higgens will radio in and order an open tail.

That's the way things stand now.

I know you're not convinced about Carpenter, but you do admit that we've got enough circumstantial evidence to make her a major suspect. On the basis of your last memo, I'm assuming I have your approval, so I'm going down to talk to Dale Taylor in the D.A.'s office about applying for a search warrant. If I can get her to agree, we'll then go to Judge Marvin and ask him to issue one.

In presenting the matter to Taylor, I'm going to stress the importance of locating the IBM type ball and the shears or scissors. (Presumably she will want to name these in the warrant.) I'll also mention Carpenter's criminal record as part of the grounds that show probable cause.

We won't execute the warrant if you don't think we should. However, I suspect you are wrong about what we might find in Carpenter's house or garage.

I'll check with you later for your decision.

Raymond

ST. LOUIS COUNTY POLICE DEPARTMENT

Memo of Transmission   Date: November 1

From: Detective Lieutenant Peter S. Keefer, Major Case Squad
To: Detective Raymond R. Robertson
Case Number: 35-2300-1090

Ray:

I think you're as wrong about Carpenter as the Pope is about birth control.

Still, if you've been able to convince Taylor and Judge Marvin to issue a warrant, I'm not going to stand in your way. Maybe I'm just too charmed by the TV star to see the criminal.

Happy hunting.

                                                                Pete

FAX TRANSMITTAL 314-552-5671

JOAN CARPENTER
2030 Buckminster · St. Louis, MO · 63130

                                                        1 November

Dan:

It was an experience.

It was not a nice experience. It was not an experience I would recommend. But it *was* an experience.

I'll make myself explain slowly and carefully. Otherwise I might lose control and head for the beer joints and crack houses to recruit mad-dog killers to conduct a guerrilla raid on police headquarters.

A team of six cops, two women and four men, just "tossed" my house. That's what I heard the woman who looked like Howdy

Doody say to the one who looked like Francis the Talking Mule. "This is the third place I've *tossed* this week," she said.

In case Bill Safire hasn't gotten around to explaining how *tossed* is derived from an Old Frisian phrase for chopped liver, it means *searched.*

I guess I never thought they would really do it—this is *America,* after all, not some rude place like the Belgian Congo (or whatever the hell it's called nowadays).

But I was wrong.

Before dusk had settled on the sycamores, Detective Raymond R. Robertson was on my front porch again. He was brandishing a warrant and accompanied by five myrmidons who lurked in his shadow like trained curs.

"We have a legal warrant to search these premises, grounds, and outbuildings for evidence relating to a crime," he announced to me in a pompous voice. I decided it must be some kind of legal formula the police are supposed to use, because they don't even talk that way on *L.A. Law.*

I took the warrant from his hand and made as if to study it. But so far as I was able to tell, it could have been a washing machine warranty from Sears.

Yet I would have known it was legal even if I couldn't read at all. Nobody with a look in his eye like he had when I sent him packing the first time would have come back to show me a piece of paper that wasn't a warrant. If he couldn't have gotten one, he would either have stayed away or broken in illegally.

"I guess I don't have much choice," I said, handing it back to him. I stood aside and let them come into the house. I went to the kitchen and made myself a cup of coffee. I didn't offer them any, and I don't think even my mama would have thought I should have.

They were here for three hours and a fraction, and where they didn't look, doesn't exist. They pried, probed, shook, and opened everything I own. They even used eye droppers to take samples from my only two bottles of perfume. (Fortunately it's cheap stuff, since I bought it myself.) They dropped the perfume into glass vials, plugged them, pasted paper seals over the stoppers, then wrote their names on the seals. They zipped up my only bar of patchouli soap in a plastic bag and took it with them. At least they left me one bar of Ivory.

They didn't exactly dump drawers out on the floor, but they

weren't exactly neat and careful either. They pawed through my desk, my dresser, my chest of drawers. They opened closets, and even searched through the pockets of my coats. When they went through the kitchen, they did what they do in 1940s detective movies (*filmes noires* to you, Dan). They had long metal rods like shishkabob skewers, and they checked the flour, sugar, and coffee by ramming them into the canisters.

In a scene reminiscent of the sacking of the great library of Alexandria, they pulled all my books off the shelves. Book by book, they shook the pages. The most intellectual find was a set of notes revealing the true meaning of the *Wasteland.* (I really must get back to the poem, now that I've lived the life.)

The shaking also turned up a billet-doux from Ted Martin, sent to me in Dallas from the Cape the summer before my sophomore year. I was actually glad to see it. Ted Martin was a jerk, but the letter reminded me of how much fun it used to be to have men falling in love with you every month or so.

It's a damned good thing I just moved in and haven't had time to accumulate any junk. Otherwise, I suppose the cops would have been here for three days instead of three hours. They also would have messed up my perfectly ordered goods and chattel. But since I haven't had a clue about where things are since I packed up everything in Dallas, I'm no worse off in that respect than before.

I am worse off in other respects, though. I must tell you that, despite my cool and rational tone, I am so mad I could chew iron and spit nails. How dare those idiots burst in here and start fumbling around with their nasty fingers in all my belongings! It makes me feel violated and dirty.

Maybe I wouldn't mind it so much if I had actually done something wrong. Maybe then I'd feel as if I put something over on them.

But I've done nothing. Nothing. I come a lot closer to being a victim than I do being a criminal. After all, I'm the one who got the goddamned letters. I'm the one who had to look in the box.

I try to tell myself they're just doing their job. But Christ in Chicago, do they have to do it so badly? Are they so desperate to find a criminal they're going to turn me into one just so they can find me?

Although Raymond R. Robertson didn't say anything about the Dallas case, you can be sure they know about it. And I think you can be sure that that's really the only reason they wanted to search my house.

They think I castrated Tom Kline—and all because years ago I tried to do a story on vice cops shaking down people and got put in jail for it. I'm sure that's why they think I'm guilty. That's just the kind of mutton-headed, addle-brained way cops think. If you got put in jail once, then you're part of a terrorist plot to take over Graceland and free all the middle-aged women held hostage there.

My dignity is affronted. That's how you could describe it. Or you could just say that I'm goddamned pissed off at the groundless and high-handed way that the cops have treated me.

I've already decided I'm going to devote time on the next show to explaining how the police turned on me, instead of looking for the real criminal.

If Fishhead won't let me do it, then he can buy himself another puppet.

I love the First Amendment.

Joan Paine
(Yes, I spelled it right.)

P.S. I forgot to be polite. But then what are friends for? Anyway, thanks for listening. I feel better now.

THE SATURN AGENCY
256 East 59th Street • New York, New York • 10020
212-555-5050 • Fax 212-555-5051
Daniel L. Saturn, PRESIDENT

November 1

Dear Joan,

Having people rooting through your personal belongings like pigs sniffing for truffles must be an upsetting experience, and I'm sorry to hear it happened.

Maybe I should have advised you to get a lawyer, but attorneys can't do anything to block search warrants. So about the only way a lawyer could have helped was to make sure you got receipts for the perfume samples.

By the way, shouldn't a woman with your aspirations be wearing some chichi fragrance or at least a Ralph Lauren scent, rather than dimestore toilet water? How can you expect to make it to the top unless you smell right? Apparently you failed to see *The Sweet Smell of Success* during your formative years.

In any case, you didn't do anything to deserve having your castle ransacked by a barbarian horde of police. Having said that, let me rush on and quickly add that I don't think you should get carried away with the idea of getting even. Your plan of presenting yourself as a victim of police stupidity or desperation is not a good one.

In fact, I think it's a dreadful one. You aren't a character in some bloody (speaking literally) Elizabethan revenge tragedy. You're not even John Wayne returning to the ranch and finding it burned to the ground and your wife scalped by Native Americans.

While I'm in the mode of mentioning films (as we sophisticated New Yorkers call movies), I seem to remember a line from a Gregory Peck vehicle in which someone says to him, "Vengeance is mine, saith the Lord." I believe this was when Peck was being Ahab ("Gregory Peck *is* Ahab"), but the point is applicable even to those who are not out to hunt down white whales.

I think the line also had a source earlier than the screenplay or even the novel. Indeed, the lesson repeated endlessly in religion, literature (cf. *Agamemnon, Medea, Eumenides,* et al.) and the movies is that no good can come of seeking revenge—that you can only destroy yourself in the process. I think this is basically correct, and I urge you to drop any diabolical plans you may have conceived to use *Nightbeat* to strike back at the police.

If you don't, you run a great risk of bringing down more trouble on yourself, and I don't mean just on your career either. The police may well retaliate, and as I said before, they can make your life legally miserable if they choose to.

Besides, it's easy to become so totally involved in righting the wrong done to you that you let it take precedence over everything else. You become a slave to your own sense of righteousness, and this makes you hemidemi-paranoid and an all-around bore.

You, my dear, are destined for finer things. Earth is your dwelling place, but heaven your destination. You are to become a twinkling light in the dark firmament of television.

So forget about all this Watcher business and let the police go on with their job. They surely didn't find any dirt at your house, except the kind you can grow vegetables in. They won't be bothering you anymore, so don't you bother them.

I'm going to Fed Ex you a copy of my favorite relaxation tape. I have eleven of them, and this is my pick of the litter. After explaining the mechanics of proper breathing, it moves on to offer hints on how to develop a personal guided imagery.

I suggest you imagine yourself soaring with your arms outstretched high over the rolling gray-green waves of an angry sea. Where you are the sky is blue, the sun is bright gold, and most important, you are far above everything that could anger you.

Try relaxing instead of revenging.

As late as last week I might have suggested some nice camomile tea, but I just read in someplace like the *FDA Consumer* that herb teas have never been tested for safety and might contain carcinogens. So if you've been drinking them, you should stop.

Your friend in (the search for) inner peace,
Dan

ST. LOUIS COUNTY POLICE DEPARTMENT

Memo of Transmission   **Date: November 1**

From: Detective Raymond R. Robertson
To: Detective Lieutenant Peter S. Keefer, Major Case Squad
Case Number: 35-2300-1090

Peter:

The big guys knew what they were doing when they made you a Lieutenant. We searched Joan Carpenter's place and came up with zip.

To be specific, we couldn't find a typewriter of any kind (only a computer with a printer), much less an IBM Selectric. Of course we looked for a typing element anyway, but we didn't have any luck there either.

We also struck out on the nose front. We took samples of two kinds of perfume and three kinds of soap. We wrapped them separately and kept them apart so the odors wouldn't mingle. After we got back to the shop, I entered them in the evidence log, then had Martha Higgens run them over to Tom Kline's apartment.

I told her to play it by the book, so she had him sniff one, then wait five minutes and sniff another. Unfortunately, he couldn't identify any of them as the odor he smelled right before he was attacked. In fact, he said he was sure all of them were the *wrong* odors.

I could decide that I made a big mistake or I could think Joan Carpenter is a very smart lady who's putting something over on us. At the moment, I don't know which of these ways to jump, but a little voice keeps whispering in my ear that Carpenter has gained an awful lot from the publicity surrounding this case.

And even you have to admit that the publicity part fits her Dallas M.O.

I'm not ready to let her off the hook yet. But maybe I'm being hard on her to make it easy on myself. We don't really have any more suspects, do we?

Ray

CHARLES FISHWATER

VICE PRESIDENT
NEWS DIVISION
KMIS-TV

November 2

Dear Joan:

One of the fascinating aspects of broadcast journalism is that we are witnesses to change. The world we see today is significantly altered by tomorrow. You might say that we see the sun rise, but we also see the sun go down.

I suspect it is this ever-changing panoply of events and circumstances that appeals to all of us who are so fortunate as to be in this business. We have the curiosity to want to know what is going to happen next, and the energy and initiative to try to find out.

You may wonder what prompts me to offer these reflections on our profession. The answer is simple: the Watcher story. Here is something of significance happening to us—to you in particular—and we and the public are curious to know what is going to happen next.

Our curiosity is desperately intense and demands to be satisfied. Considering the circumstances, even the *lack* of anything happening is newsworthy. Whatever is happening or not happening, though, we need to report it.

I have waited until today before bringing up this matter with you, because I wanted to give you a much-needed chance to recover from the unpleasantness you experienced during the last show. I still admire the way you handled matters then, but now that some time has passed, I think we need to move on and consider what we are going to do on our next show to keep our story current.

I am open to suggestions, but my personal opinion is that we ought to do an eight- to ten-minute feature on the Watcher and the circumstances surrounding his sending you the box. It would be a kind of backgrounder mixed with a first-person account. You could talk about your responses when you got the first letter, then the second and third, then how you felt when you actually opened the box. (Let's talk about this ourselves, Joan. I've got some ideas about how you can write this to make it both exciting and moving.)

We should definitely not mention that you didn't want to open the box on camera. To say that would make a lot of the audience think you were just afraid to do so. Saying that you and I disagreed is also absolutely out. The audience won't trust our judgment if we seem at odds with one another.

The stories we've got lined up for this Wednesday aren't half as interesting as what's been happening right in our own backyard. The computer-school scam or the obedience training for kids pieces could both be cut to give us enough slack for a feature of the sort I described above.

You might not like my idea of what should be in the story. If so, that's fine, and I won't push it. The important thing is that we come up with something to reward (if not satisfy) the curiosity of the audience. There is no reason why we should let other stations, not to mention radio and the newspapers, benefit from a story that belongs to us. I am determined to keep this from happening.

To explain why I consider this so important, let me put the point this way. When you see an item on the news about something happening to your neighbor, your inclination is to ask your neighbor about it so you can get the inside story. Well, *we* have the inside story, and a lot of people are going to be watching us to see what we have to say. If we let the other broadcasters and media tell *our* story, we'll look like clowns.

I'm sure you agree with me about this. It is just a matter of our getting together and deciding how we're going to play the story. We'd better make it good, because a *lot* of people are going to be watching this week.

Ask Alice to call Rita Trowbridge and see when we can get together. The sooner the better.

Charles

Mr. Fishwater's office. Rita Trowbridge speaking.

Rita, this is Joan Carpenter. Is Mr. Fishwater available?

Oh, hi, Joan. I'm sorry, but he's gone to the Missouri Athletic Club.

What could he be doing in a place like that at ten o'clock in the morning? Don't tell me he's there for a squash breakfast.

Nothing like that. He had to go to a meeting about raising money for a new aquarium that's supposed to be built on the riverfront.

Charles Fishwater and an aquarium? I can see the appeal.

What do you mean?

Nothing important, Rita. Is he coming back anytime soon?

I don't expect him until around three o'clock. Do you want me to have him give you a call?

I would appreciate that. I've got to go to the Central West End to film an "I once was rich, but now I'm poor" story but I expect to be back sometime around three-thirty. I'll be in my office.

I'll let him know. Do you want me to tell him what it's in regard to?

Tell him I got his memo and I agree with him. We need to do a follow-up on the Watcher business. Say I've also got another personal story to present.

Oh, dear. I hope nothing else bad has happened to you.

Nothing terrible. But something that's really got me hot under the collar. Anyway, that's enough to pique his curiosity. Tell him I want us to meet and plan what we're going to do.

I'll give him the message, Joan. Do be careful now.

Ms. Joan Carpenter
Star of *Nightbeat*
KMIS-TV

November 2

My precious Joan,

I'm writing you this letter because I want to have the experience of being with you for just a little while tonight. When I'm writing to you, i feel I am in almost direct contact with you. It's as if I can generate in my mind a special reality that contains only you and me. We are bound together then in a little sphere of privacy and intimacy, and the real world, with its awful, dirty, boring people, disappears in an imagined cloud of smoke. My words and my mind bind together passing moments into a block of time, and while time remains bound, our reality is the only one. You and I stand together in a world apart.

I feel a little guilty for being so self-indulgent as to write you, because I'm sure you get dozens of letters every day from people demanding your attention. But, my darling, your time is much too scarce and precious for you to respond to us all, and you mustn't let us take too much out of you.

Notice that I include myself in that warning. If you're too busy to read this letter when it arrives, put it away until you find a moment to sit down and be alone with me. Unlike your hundreds of other fans, I know that time will come, because you and I aren't exactly strangers. I'm sure the help I've given you with your career makes you regard me as a special friend, although I realize that even though you want to spend time with me, you may not be able to.

In your business, the story always gets priority over personal desires. I admire you for that, but I hope someday you'll want to see me just because that's what you want. I think I can make sure of that, eventually.

I wrote you before that I was thinking about what we should be doing to keep your career shooting up into orbit, and a couple of things have occurred to me. I'm telling you this just to reassure you that "The Watcher is always Watching" and to keep you from worrying about whether I've abandoned you. I don't think it's time to start anything yet, so I'm not going to give you a set of instructions the way I did for the Kline project.

In fact, I better not say too much more, because I don't want to tip my hand, even to you. You might inadvertently let slip something that would ruin the plan. But I think I can risk telling you i think we could make a very big splash nationally if we put you in a situation where you were being interviewed in connection with some very noticeable event.

Staging a really big event would also give me a chance to show you how much I care about you. I would be able to demonstrate the extent of my admiration for you. What better proof could I offer than to put myself on the line and risk my safety and freedom and even my life to assist you?

Well, listen, my darling, these are just a few hints about an idea I've been mulling over during the long hours in which I think of nothing but you. In the hours during which I am forced to think of my job, i still can't avoid thoughts of you. Even though I try to concentrate completely on my work and leave no room for thinking about you, thoughts about you sprout up in tiny cracks like weeds. If I'm not careful, they also grow like weeds, and before long I'm staring into space with my mind completely filled with daydreams of you.

What do I think about? The images float through my mind like pictures from a fashion magazine: the way your upper lip draws back a little more on the left side than on the right when you smile, the perfect symmetry of your face, and the lithe slenderness of your body. I won't embarrass you or myself by becoming more graphic, although I confess that in my imagination I have many times stripped off your clothes to admire your beauty. I haven't always stopped there either.

It's getting late, and I must stop writing and let the magic die. I am going to bed now, and how I long to take you with me. I know I cannot, but soon I will prove to you that I am worthy of your attention and your love. Then not only will I have earned the right, but our mutual yearnings will be mutually gratified.

Our time will come.

Until then, I remain your slave and

Your Watcher

Joan Carpenter
STAR of *Nightbeat*

> Her eyes so blue
> Her hair so fair
> How can I show her
> How much I care?
>
> The ways of the world
> Are so hard and weary
> The practices of Man
> Are so sad and dreary.
>
> Only light can defeat the dark;
> Only pure love can pierce the heart.
>
> Still Watching

JOAN CARPENTER
2030 Buckminster · St. Louis, MO · 63130

2 November

Dear Dan,

It's not over till it's over. I thought maybe the Watcher was ready to take a vacation, but no such luck. I'm sending you a copy of a letter and a poem I just got. I'll also send copies to Jane and ask her to pass them on to her friend Dr. Vogler, who specializes in people who are genuinely weird.

After making copies, I'll hand over the originals to the police. (This is getting to be a routine.) With any luck, they won't put me in jail for possessing them—fascist pigs.

Joan

FROM THE DESK OF
ALICE WALCHECK

ADMINISTRATIVE ASSISTANT TO
JOAN CARPENTER

11/2

Joan:

Alexis Hartz called you three times today.

You were either on location or taking a meeting every time, and on the third try she finally decided to give up and trust me with the message—"If it's not too much trouble," she said. She *is* polite.

However, I'm not sure she thinks I'm quite reliable, because after she gave me her message she asked me to read my notes back to her "so I can be sure I've given you the right information."

Ms. Hartz wants to know when you might be free to come to her house for dinner. She says it will be just the two of you so you can "talk about some important matters of mutual interest we discussed briefly last time."

She says to tell you she doesn't cook but she has "a man who is an outstanding gourmet chef." He also "leaves the house after he has completed his work," so the two of you will have "absolute privacy."

If you have any "special dietary needs or preferences," you must feel free to let her know, because she is sure she can "accommodate them." (You're getting all these quotes courtesy of my note taking. They do help convey the very formal flavor of the invitation, though. This must be a lady who moves in society with a capital S.)

After I read my notes back to her, she asked me if there's a particular kind of candy I like. Not being a fool, I told her I adore anything by Godiva that comes in a box. I decided it would be rude to specify size, but I hope she doesn't know about miniatures.

Your evening calendar (so far as I know it) is free for every day next week, except for Wednesday (of course) and Thursday. Thursday you're supposed to meet with the Associate Director of the Missouri Botanical Garden and discuss the possibility of doing the "Green Medicine in Missouri" story.

Please let me know what you want to do.

Alice

FROM THE DESK OF
JOAN CARPENTER

2 Nov/Mon

Alice:

Maybe Alexis Hartz wanted you to take notes because she's beginning to doubt whether *she* is reliable.

Whatever the case, she seems bound and determined to feed us both to the gills. But as busy as I am with work and the Kline business, I wish she would just send *me* the candy, instead of laying on a four-course affair with a Magic Chef appliance to do the cooking.

Still and all, financial and real estate scandals aren't just littering the ground outside my office, so I can't afford to tell her I'm so antisocial now I prefer eating alone at Burger Queen. She does know people, and even more important, she knows things *about* people.

I never thought I'd sell my stomach for a story about shopping-center shenanigans. But then we were all young and idealistic once.

Please tell Alexis I would be delighted to have dinner with her tomorrow, if that's not altogether too soon and if she would find it at all convenient. (I can be formal too, you know.) Say I hope she understands that the nature of my work is such that I might have to cancel at the very last moment. If, for example, I decide to quit my job and sell socks at K-Mart rather than hunt down evil doers.

My major dietary rule is never eat anything that has teeth but can't breathe under water. The exception to this rule is best captured in the phrase "unless I want to."

But do tell Ms. Hartz I will be pleased with anything she chooses to serve. I'm sure if she's flying in Wolfgang Puck for the evening, they can whip up something decent between them.

JC

P.S. If it's a two-layered box, I get twenty percent as your agent.

11/3

Joan:

Ms. Hartz called to confirm your dinner engagement tonight.
(She also wanted to know if I got my box of Godiva choco-
lates. I did, thank you. It was the medium box, so no matter what
the agents who work for her say, she's not so tight she squeaks
when she walks. If you can sneak by my desk without anybody seeing you, I'll let you have a truffle and maybe a hazelnut cream.)

Doesn't she live in your neighborhood? I ask because she
wanted me to ask you if she should send a car for you. (I was
tempted to ask whether if she sent it, you got to keep it.)

I said I would ask you. So do let me know if you want the
car—sent.

Alice

3 Nov/Tue

Alice:

I want the mocha and the orange creams.

I figure I can make this demand as a kind of *droit du seigneur.*
After all, you're getting them because you occupy the very special
status of being *my* assistant. Besides, you don't have to make polite
conversation and pretend you're a lady for several hours and I do.

Just drop your offerings into a plain envelope and leave it in
the top drawer of my desk. (Greed is such fun.)

Not only does Ms. Hartz live in my neighborhood, she lives in my backyard—on the other side of a hedge, to be exact. It does seem absurd to drive from my house to hers, but then I can't see me leaping the bushes in my best dress and stiletto heels. Of course, I could walk around the block, but that's certainly not the most dramatic way to make an entrance for a grand dinner.

Since Ms. Hartz has so kindly offered, please say I would very much appreciate her sending a car. (This will give me a taste of what it's like to be rich, and I can then decide whether to support the revolution or buy municipal bonds.)

Lady Glutton

FROM THE DESK OF
JOAN CARPENTER

4 Nov/Wed

Alice:

Which of our researchers is particularly good at burrowing through real estate records and ferreting out information?

Will you pick the person you think is best and tell her or him I am very interested in knowing:

1. Everyone who sold the land to the developer of Park Central Mall (the Maxim Corporation)?

2. When did the people who sold the land buy it? I'm more interested in people who bought it in the last year or two than in those who bought it in, say, 1950.

Also, if you can find a second person who is experienced in digging through the minutes of municipal meetings and hearings, I want to know:

1. When did Maxim first approach the County Council with its proposal for a mall?

2. Who was on the Council at that time?

3. Who voted in favor of using the power of eminent domain to acquire needed land from holdouts?

4. Who were the holdouts?

As you may have guessed, these questions are prompted by my evening *chez* Alexis Hartz. And I want to tell you that whatever I learned was hard bought. Alexis is so nice she makes me acutely uncomfortable, and I haven't been on such good behavior since my last day in Sunday school. (That was a foolish idea of my mom's that lasted about a month.)

I hope you can get somebody/ies started on these projects last week.

JC

FROM THE DESK OF
ALICE WALCHECK

ADMINISTRATIVE ASSISTANT TO
JOAN CARPENTER

11/4

Joan:

I have unleashed a team of beavers on both your woodpiles. Doug Ware is doing the real estate search, and Mary Sulley is sifting through the political records.

Both are experienced and conscientious and thrive more on the satisfaction gained from doing a good job than on their pitiful salaries. You can trust them to do their best, but an atta-boy memo from you at the right time would mean much.

To make sure things went your way, I had to give Doug a praline crunch and Mary a chocolate caramel. This means you owe me a description of your exotic evening with Madame Réal État.

I'm now baiting my breath.

Alice

4 Nov/Wed

Alice:

If you *bait* your breath, your teeth may snap shut on a mouse's tail. Use *bate* and refuse to let the broadcast biz bring you down to its level.

Thanks for getting the Bobbsey Twins started on my projects, and thanks, too, for sacrificing treasures from your precious hoard. (Had I known of your addiction, I would have had you completely under my power weeks ago.)

My dinner with Madame Réal État was quite pleasant. Everything was perfectly orchestrated in a way I can only dream about. Just as the red numbers on my digital clock blinked eight (the modern equivalent of striking), a long, powder-blue Towncar drew up at my door. A liveried chauffeur (jacket and tie but no bloused breeches and puttees) rang my bell and touched his cap when I stepped outside.

I felt like a Mary Kaye Sales Princess as he whisked me away to the Queen's castle. Although Alexis lives literally a block away, the houses on her street are on a much grander scale than the ones on mine—and I don't live in a tin shack in a back alley. Her house is a white columned mansion surrounded by a thicket of tall, shaggy evergreens. The nearest houses are screened from view, and although I could see their lights shining through the trees, I saw no people and no cars. If I were a governess, I could have been in a Candlelight Romance.

A butler in a white jacket (no claw-hammer tailcoat) answered the door, and just as I stepped inside, Alexis herself flowed out to meet me in a black dinner dress with a string of beads cloudy enough to be genuine pearls. I was so glad I assumed I wasn't supposed to dress up. Otherwise, I might have felt a tiny bit underdressed in my long flowered skirt and high collared blouse.

Alexis took my hand, gave it a squeeze, and told me how pleased she was I could come. Then we moved into the living room where a maid in a little frilly apron that I thought went out of use with 1940s movies served us canapés and drinks. Given the circumstances, I couldn't resist asking for a daiquiri, and no one seemed to think it was the least bit odd. (I had toyed with the idea of a Singapore Sling, but since I haven't the foggiest notion of what goes into one, I didn't go through with it.)

Madame and I talked no business but made low-key and polite chat about the zoo, the symphony, the fascinating people she would like to introduce to fascinating me. "You know, Joan, this is a city where it counts to be connected," she said. "A few words to the right people and you can get into most places." (I doubt she had in mind places like the Blues' locker room.) I thanked her for what I took to be an offer to provide a few words when needed.

She then politely asked if I had "recovered" from "that very shocking incident involving the reviewer." I thanked her again for the book, and said I was trying to put "the incident" out of my mind. She looked slightly embarrassed about having brought it up and told me that was a "healthy attitude."

To cover the chagrin, she then began to give me a rapid-fire account of what she did during her last trip to Paris (what everybody else does but costing more), then explained how she would like to see the country run (about the way Attila the Hun would do it, if he gave up some of his socialist ideas and became a Republican).

The food was absolutely first rate—seafood salad, grilled swordfish and polenta, carrots and capers, fennel salad, fresh fruit and three kinds of freshly prepared gelato—pear, raspberry, and chocolate—and Florentines with the espresso. Of course there were divers liquors, but I battened onto to a nice single-malt scotch and drank enough of it that I began to think Alexis's account of trying to find the Mona Lisa in the Louvre was quite amusing.

In addition to having a sumptuous dinner and passably decent conversation, I learned enough from Alexis about the shopping mall business to consider the evening a great investment in the future of American exposés.

I couldn't get myself to ask her directly why she was giving me all the information, but I got the impression she thought it was her duty (noblesse oblige, you know) to blow the whistle on the bad guys. Also, she either likes me or just wants to collect me as another celebrity. Right after I moved in, when I had to rely on her for information and chit-chat, I thought she wanted us to be friends. Now, though, I'm not sure. She may just be head hunting and want to cultivate me by providing me with tidbits.

An even less flattering interpretation is that she's just using me to break the scandal. Although I detect the celebrity awe in her, I also notice a hint of condescension mixed with a soupçon of contempt—the same sort of attitude the very rich express toward the hired help. I may be no more than the broom Alexis plans to use to sweep out the real estate house.

I did feel quite annoyed when the little green numbers of 1:00 A.M. flashed into my watch and I expressed a strong wish to go home. "I've sent Clarence away," she said. "I didn't see any point in his waiting around when I'm free to drive you myself." We had finished the scandal stuff, and I wasn't sure I was up to another half hour of polite chat.

I was about to say I could just walk back, but then I decided I didn't want to traipse around a very long block in the darkness and all by my lonesome. "That would be so nice of you," I said, using my finishing-school tone. (I learned it from novels, so I'm never quite sure that I've got it right.)

Then when we got to my house, I had to ask if she would like to come in a moment. She said quite brightly, "I would like to take a look at how you've changed things since you moved in. I've always loved this house, and I don't think the Petersons did it justice."

Alexis then prowled around the house for a good fifteen minutes, peering into every corner and probably even reading the labels on the canned goods. "I see you have a fax machine," she said when we came back from our rambles. "I've got one in the office, but I don't even have a computer at home."

"I have both, because I love to stay home," I said. "I do my best work when no one's watching."

"What a funny thing for a TV person to say," she said.

I walked her to the door, and she told me how nice the house looked. I thanked her again for a wonderful dinner, then held my breath until I saw her drive down my modest street in a car big enough to feed a family of Ethiopians for a year.

If you want more details, you'll have to wait for my memoirs. A couple of pieces of candy can buy only so much, particularly when I didn't even get to eat them myself.

JC

P.S. Since the Big Broadcast is coming up and I've got to get ready to blow the police department out of the water with a few well-chosen words, don't make any appointments for me to see anybody less important than Jesus Christ. Moses is all right, but only if he's got an update on the Commandments.

YOU HAVE REACHED 552-8076. AT THE TONE YOU MAY LEAVE A MESSAGE.

Hi, Joan, this is Alan Carter. I'm in a Cessna about to leave for Springfield. This is a phone patch, so I hope you can hear me okay.

Listen, are you interested in taking a little trip next Sunday? I thought we might cross over to Illinois, then drive along the bluffs overlooking the Mississippi. We could end up at Elsa and have an early dinner there. The food is great.

I hope this sounds good to you. It would be nice to talk to you.

I'll be back by Friday. But I'll be checking in, so leave me a message.

Talk to you later.

FAX TRANSMITTAL 314-552-5671

JOAN CARPENTER
2030 Buckminster • St. Louis, MO • 63130

4 Nov/Wed

Dear Dan:

Mea culpa, mea culpa.

I'm sure you're right and that I should have listened to you. Your advice was sound, solid, and responsible, and any reasonable person would have taken it. Now that everything is over, I have to confess it's all too true that:

I acted imprudently and out of spite and anger.

I was trying to get revenge, and that's a very mean and ignoble thing to do.

My career will probably suffer.

I will live to regret it.

I didn't live up to my best idea of myself.

I was taught better in kindergarten.

I sometimes get a stomachache from anxiety.

I'm a disappointment to my friends and family.

Mea maxima culpa.

But listen, Dan, I was really pissed off, and even you admit I had every reason to be. Like most cops, these guys confused running in place with winning the race. The only reason they targeted me was because I did a little time in Big-D, and they thought they could run another number on me. (Isn't that the way we hardened criminals talk?) My daddy always told me you have to fight back when you're pushed or you get into the habit of being a coward. Well, I was pushed, and I've already got enough bad habits.

Besides, although I probably shouldn't confess this, fighting back is more fun than you might imagine. When people have been treating you like a Williams-Sonoma 100% coconut fiber shoe-cleaner, it's a genuine pleasure to surprise them by getting up off the floor and kicking them in the ass. They look at you with amazement and even (believe it or not) respect.

"How bad is it?" you want to know. Did I denounce Detective Raymond R. Robertson as an oppressive pig? Did I suggest in the presence of millions that the St. Louis police are the willing tools of Mideast oil interests out to smash American democracy? Did I claim that my cocker spaniel was sexually abused by the crew of gorillas that ransacked my house?

No, Dan. Relax. I said none of those things. The entire twelve minute segment was highly professional, very controlled, and gave the police a handsome opportunity to confess their ineptness and make a very public apology. That they did not choose to take advantage of this opportunity was not unexpected. Nevertheless, I believe most of the message got through.

I also got to establish a much better relationship with my old friend the Fish. For a change, not only were we both playing on the same team, we were doing it during the same game.

Between us, we cooked up a piece that included interviews with most of the principals. I flatly refused to ask Tom Kline for an interview, so the Fish called him. When Kline became obscene and abusive, even Charlie dropped the idea along with the phone. Everybody else agreed to participate. I have to admit that working with Fishhead is very convenient, because he seems to have instant access to everybody in St. Louis.

I started with a 1.5 minute backgrounder about the Watcher and what happened on our last program. I then gave a clear but heartfelt account of how my house got searched, even though the police had no evidence against me.

We then cut to the Chief of Police ("Lieutenant Keefer is in charge of the investigation, and I don't try to second-guess my people.") and then to the woman in the prosecutor's office who went for the warrant ("You have to realize you don't have to have very much for probable cause, so the police usually get a warrant if they want one. You should talk to them."). Detective Raymond R. Robertson, Head Hun of the search party, refused to talk to me, "because Lieutenant Keefer is running the show."

So the pièce de résistance of the segment was the ringmaster himself—Lieutenant Peter Keefer. We talked in his office, a steel-furniture cubicle that looked not unlike the place you go to get a dog license. While we talked, his blue eyes seemed to twinkle and his smile was warm and bright. Still, he answered all my questions, even the hard, abrasive Mike Wallace ones.

No, he had not personally sought the warrant, but he was in charge so he was responsible for it. No, there was no direct evidence against me. No, they didn't choose to investigate me out of desperation. Yes, my "experiences" in Dallas did play a role in their focusing on me. Yes, he could understand why I should feel angry at having my privacy invaded, but crimes make waves that wash over many people, even the innocent.

Does he agree that I'm one of the innocent? Well, it would be wrong to say that I'm not a suspect, because the crime remains unsolved. Was it a mistake to search my house? He can't say specifically, but in the course of any investigation things are often done that in retrospect seem regrettable. Was it Raymond R. Robertson who pushed for a search? That's not a question he can answer; but it doesn't matter who initiated the warrant, because, as he said, he authorizes everything. Do they have any leads? Every crime has leads. Are they making any progress? Even now they are pursuing the investigation—which is to say they literally don't have a clue.

"Peter" proved to be just as charming and disarming on camera as in my living room. Probably his being quite good looking and having what I can only call a radiant smile has something to do with that. (Why are we so willing to forgive and believe attractive people? Is it because we believe the good, the true, and the beautiful are the same?) He was (apparently) open and friendly and hid any impulses to say he was just doing his job or to strangle me for my impudence.

Yet Peter did have to confess he didn't have any evidence against me and that the reasons for searching my house (or "domicile, grounds, outbuildings and vehicles" if you prefer) were as flimsy as pink tissue paper. He put on a good show, but I think my image of an innocent woman hounded by the police shone out quite brightly.

My dear co-host Gary Wells turned out to be the only sour note in my carefully orchestrated Ode to Joy. After my taped segment with Peter Keefer, the camera focused on Gary and me in a two-shot. He turned to me and ad libbed, "Well, Joan, they say where there's smoke there's fire, but I guess you'd like to deny you had anything to do with the tragic catastrophe that befell Tom Kline?"

I came very close to slapping Gary Wells even sillier than he is. But it never looks good on camera when two co-hosts have a punch-out. I learned that in my graduate program.

I looked grave and thoughtful. "If that's a question, Gary, all I can say is that I hope my report made clear that even the smoke was in the imagination of the police." I smiled an iron-lipped smile to show I was brave and plucky, wronged but not a complainer. Then we cut to commercial.

I didn't speak to Wells after the show, because I didn't want to be hauled in on a charge of attacking a moron with deadly words. Besides, the Fish was quite displeased with Gary, and I suspect Gary has just put the big toe of his second foot out the employee's exit.

Except for the little contretemps with Gary, the Fish seemed quite pleased. He told me my segment played like dynamite (or dine-o-mite, as we say in broadcasting). I figure that gives me about two weeks of good grace.

Now, by God, it's going to be back to business. This crime-and-revenge drama has been taking an unconscionable amount of time, and I haven't been able to concentrate on becoming Joan Carpenter, ace reporter—exposing social wrongs and making the wicked flee for cover like rats running into the garbage dump.

I'm working on a real estate–zoning fraud that may not win a coveted Peabody Award, but it's certain to give some sleazy guys some restless nights. Maybe that's award enough.

Now what about you and me? You already know I lack temperance and patience, not to mention chastity and humility. And even I will confess to being a little weak in the charity department, otherwise I wouldn't be so hard on Charlie Tuna. Anyway, given your prior knowledge of my absence of virtues, you probably aren't too surprised to find out I'm also lacking prudence. I think I'm not so bad on justice and fortitude, though.

I suppose two virtues out of eight doesn't look so great on a checklist, but then I'm not applying for sainthood this year. I'm just a country girl trying not to get pushed around by the slick guys in the big city.

I hope you're feeling charitable enough not to be mad at me for not taking your advice. I'm feeling humble enough to hope so.

Joan the Unrepentant

P.S. As a peace offering, I'm Fed Exing you a bushel of organically grown Missouri apples. I trust they will make a nice addition to your usual breakfast of Metamucil Crunch and goat's milk.

P.P.S. If you promise not to be mad at me, then if the cops start hassling me the way you think they will, I'll let you say the actual words "I told you so" without objecting. What more could a know-it-all want?

THE SATURN AGENCY
256 East 59th Street • New York, New York • 10020
212-555-5050 • Fax 212-555-5051
Daniel L. Saturn, PRESIDENT

November 5

Dear Joan,

Of course I'm not angry with you.

You obviously felt compelled to stand up for your rights, and you did it. You did what John Wayne would have done—and Jimmy Stewart and Gary Cooper and even Captain Kirk and Tom Cruise.

I'm actually proud of you, even though I'm sure I myself would have kept my mouth shut in accordance with the don't-make-trouble-and-eventually-they'll-go-away principle. It's a good practical rule, but it doesn't make for heroes.

Even if the police do call you every hour to jangle your nerves, I also expect some professional good to come of your counterattack. To name one thing, I suspect your dealings with Charles Fishwater will be smoother now that the two of you have conspired to fight the forces of tyranny, albeit for radically different reasons.

To name another, since controversy attracts attention the way nightsoil (to speak delicately) draws flies, I fully expect the ratings and market share of *Nightbeat* to rise even more. This means that Fishwater can also say "I told you so."

You made the right decision to play softball with Gary Wells. He is obviously a man on his way out, and that probably means he's also on the way down. I think you have more charity than you give yourself credit for. This doesn't mean you don't also speak with plenty of sounding brass and tinkling cymbals—if that's the right quote.

The box of apples arrived in time for me to have a couple at dinner. Given the extent and number of their bruises, blemishes, and galls, they genuinely have to be organic. (Other growers would have composted them.) They taste quite good, but it makes me feel guilty to eat them, because I have to force so many small green worms out of their homes and onto the street. Maybe I should reserve three or four apples as worm shelters.

Don't worry, everything's jake with us. (I heard Dan Duryea

utter a similar line on a TNT movie last night. It was shortly before he smilingly put a couple of slugs into the woman he was talking to. But don't let this bother you. I don't even own a slugger.)

Good luck with getting back to the business of becoming a Ben Hecht character in the broadcast age.

Dan

P.S. Metamucil Crunch sounds like a very marketable idea. Do you mind if I drop a line to the company and mention it? By the way, I do not drink goat milk. You must be thinking of my mentioning that I was using acidophilus. I only did it for a couple of weeks. I think the flora and fauna in my gut are in fine shape, even if other things are wrong. I read that some people have stomachs, etc., that are just more sensitive than others. Maybe that's my problem.

P.P.S. I'm *not* a know-it-all, but I will take you up on the "I told you so" offer. It would be a childhood dream come true.

■ STEPHEN LEGION, M.D., F.A.A.C.S. ■

AESTHETIC SURGERY, INC.

2052 BARNES HOSPITAL PLAZA

ST. LOUIS, MO 63132

314-562-5560

Fax 314-562-8100

November 5

Dear Joan,

I hope I'm going to do this properly. I have never used a fax machine before, but i got one of my office girls to show me how it works. I'm going to try it while she is on her break and no one is around the records room.

It is quite amazing, isn't it, to think that I can insert this piece of paper into a machine and the copy will come out of another machine in your home.

Please forgive me for being so silly. I don't get to play around very much, and I think you bring out part of me that most people don't even know exists. I suppose I do a lot to keep it hidden, but with you it doesn't seem to matter so much.

I enjoyed the time we shared having a drink, and I hope you did too. I suspect I rather bored you with my talk about wanting to change people's view that aesthetic surgery is trivial, but you were a kind listener. If I promise not to talk so much, will you meet me again?

This time I thought we might go in for something a little more adventurous. I have to make hospital rounds on Sunday morning, but barring anything unforeseen, I will be finished by 10 A.M. I'm then free until around 6:30. That would give us most of the day together.

Would you be interested in driving up and visiting the wineries around Herman? The trip is short, and the wine isn't half bad.

Please give me a call at the office or use my paging number. (But please *don't* fax me. Everybody in the office can read what comes out of the machine.)

I do hope you will come with me. I think we could have a lot of fun.

Hopefully,
Steve

JOAN CARPENTER
2030 Buckminster · St. Louis, MO · 63130

5 Nov/Th

Dear Mama,

I just wanted to drop you a note to say hi and to remind you that you still haven't made your reservations for Thanksgiving. I know you hate to be pushed, but the airlines do get booked up very early because Thanksgiving is the heaviest travel period of the year. Once again, if you want me to make the arrangements for you, just say the word. I can get all the schedules on my computer, so it wouldn't be any trouble, really.

We've had some nice cool evenings here during the last week, and I guess it's getting to be fall. The first touch of cool weather triggers a deep nostalgia in me, and I think about when Jane and I were little kids and the things we did together as a family. I remember going on picnics and taking hikes in the woods to look for blackberries and dig for sassafras roots.

Do you remember the time we drove up to Grapevine Lake to spend the day with the Walters and Jane climbed to the top of a huge hackberry tree and got stung by so many wasps we had to rush her to the emergency room for shots? Strange, isn't it, how many pleasant childhood memories have a lining of near disaster.

Daddy was sure good to have around in an emergency. He was so quick and decisive and always seemed in complete control, even though I now realize he really couldn't have been. But I think Jane and I both learned a lot about how to cope with trouble from seeing how he did it. Maybe part of it was the way he gave us all jobs to do so we felt needed and also felt we were helping solve the problem. When Jane got stung, my job was to keep rubbing ice wrapped in a handkerchief on her face and arms. Maybe I *was* doing some good!

I sure do miss Daddy. It's such a different world when one of your parents is no longer around. It's a lot lonelier, and you don't have as many people in your corner pulling for you. Maybe if Will hadn't gotten killed or I had married again right afterward, I wouldn't feel quite so isolated. But I think I would still miss Daddy. I don't even want to think what it's like to have both your parents gone.

I hope you're not starting to get lazy about fixing dinner for yourself. Don't be tempted by those school cafeteria lunches of baloney on toast with ketchup and beans. As good as they may look to you, they're too high in fat and salt. Just eat lots of vegetables, fruit, and grains. In fact, you should eat just the way you made us eat when we were kids.

Now that the weather is cooler, I've also been thinking about planting some trees. I would dearly love to plant a pear tree, because I miss seeing those graceful limbs hanging heavy with delicious fruit. Unfortunately, the winters here get too cold for pear trees. I think I may plant a dogwood. They're very pretty, but I don't know much about them. Do they take a long time to grow? Do they all flower? I want one that flowers.

How are things at school? Do you have a lot of bright and lively kids this year? I hope you've caught them soon enough to rescue them from the ravages of TV. When we get together, you'll have to tell me about what kids are reading nowadays. I remember reading *Charlotte's Web,* the Little House books, *Anne of Green Gables,* and Doctor Dolittle, but I don't recall exactly how old I was. Could I have been in the third grade?

I'm still very busy and lots of things are happening, but nothing is worth spending any time telling you about. What little social life I've had recently has been limited to business, but I have been continuing to get some nibbles from a couple of attractive fish. When I get more time, I think I'll give my line a little tug.

Have you heard from Janie? What are you going to get Amy for Christmas? I've been thinking about providing her with an elaborate Barbie setup—maybe Barbie on Mars, or whatever the going thing is.

Is this too regressive? I have wonderful memories of Barbie and Skipper doing many adventurous things. (I'm not sure where Ken was. Did I even own him?) But I don't know what Jane thinks. Would she murder me?

Tell me what you think.

Lots and lots of love,
Joanie

November 5

My dear Joan:

I can't tell you how pleased I am with the way you handled the Watcher piece. Your script, interviews, and on-camera presentation lent dignity and restraint to the story, while references to your feelings about your experiences with the police and your personal rights introduced a human dimension that made it exceedingly powerful.

Some of our more conservative viewers may take exception to your comments about the police targeting you because of your bad experiences in Dallas, but that is just something we will have to accept. I am not going to let us be frightened off by a whiff of controversy.

Next time we mention the story, though, how about a sidebar where you explain that you didn't mean the police weren't doing their job when they searched your house. You just meant they made a mistake and that's a bad thing for a citizen, even when the mistake is understandable. We can smooth a lot of ruffled feathers if we take this more conciliatory line. That will let us pick up both those sympathetic to you and those sympathetic to the police. But we can talk about this later.

Your approach to the story took full advantage of the curiosity that has built up about the Watcher and full advantage of your role as a principal in the story. I hope you will accept it as praise if I say you handled the matter just the way I thought you should.

We can already see the public's interest in the story translated into numbers. I have the overnight figures, and they show *Nightbeat* in fifth place on the "Most Watched" list. (That's out of a "possible" list of 137.) It has a 13.5 rating and an astonishing 26% market share. This is all most gratifying, as I'm sure you will agree.

Taken all in all, your work on the Watcher story brought credit to *Nightbeat*, to KMIS-TV, and to yourself. You are our Golden

Girl, and we all bless the day you chose to come to St. Louis and join the KMIS staff.

Another job well done!

Charles

FAX TRANSMITTAL 314-552-5671

JOAN CARPENTER
2030 Buckminster · St. Louis, MO · 63130

6 Nov/Fri

Dear Dan,

O, Keeper of the Archives and Counselor to the Stars:

If the magic is still working, you should just have received a fax of a letter from my friend and admirer, that distinguished television producer . . . Charles Fishwater.

You need only glance at the letter to see that mostly it's just more of the same sort of condescending crap that Mr. Big sends to Ms. Little out here in TV Land.

(But do notice that he signs himself "Charles." That just proves what good friends we are—now that the ratings have taken off like a beagle after a bunny. Way back three weeks ago when the ratings were slipping as low as a toad's toenails, it didn't seem to me that Charles and I were quite so close. But I'm sure I just didn't realize how near and dear we were. In fact, I must be the last to know.)

Since you were no doubt trained to practice *l'explication de texte* in one of New York's great *lycées*, I'm sure you caught the real message of Fishhead's letter in the paragraph he sneaked in between piles of praises. I'm talking about the one in which he, employing the sly style of the Grand Inquisitor, enjoins me to recant and retract my comments about the police.

And so it is, my dear Daniel, that with just a few phrases as bland as flan, Fishhead has neatly set us up for a Confrontation with a capital C that rhymes with me right here in River City.

Lest you have as much doubt as a grain of mustard seed, verily

170

I say unto you, I am not about to appear before millions of (at least partially) rational beings and tell them that everything I said about the police being desperate, incompetent, and unfair was just pique on my part.

I won't even do it to make my best friend Fishwater happy. I won't even do it because he asked me to.

Don't misunderstand me. I'm *glad* to have the high ratings. I like to succeed even more than the average bear does. I'll even come out and say it: I'm ambitious, I like to win, I want to be rich and famous. But in my arrogant opinion, the Fish is stuffed full of roe if he believes the ratings would be even higher if I announced with God and Camera #1 as my witness that my criticisms were no more than perfectly ordinary misunderstanding between teammates.

Indeed, the Fish has swallowed too much air if he actually thinks I'm going to take anything back. I said what I said, and I'm going to stick to it. I hope you're ready to hold my coat and find me another job. *Hier ich stehe. Ich kann neine andern.* (In case you don't recognize the quote, it's from Martin Luther before he added King to his name.)

You do not have to respond to any of this. Consider it informational. Consider it a whiff of what's blowing in the wind, my fren'.

Before I forget to be polite, thanks for your last letter. I'm glad you're not angry, but I am sorry about the worms in the apples. You have to remember, though, that the worms are also organically grown. So try seeing them as a safe source of good-quality protein. Should I ask my mother if she has a recipe for apple crawler?

Fondly,
Martin Luther Carpenter

Ms. Joan Carpenter
Star of *Nightbeat*
KMIS-TV

November 4

My darling Joan:

I just watched *Nightbeat*, and I am so upset and infuriated that I can hardly think straight.

Are the police absolute and complete *idiots*? How *could* they be so indescribably stupid as to think that you yourself could have done anything to that pig Tom Kline? Can't they see you're much too sensitive a person to undertake such a distasteful task? You are so polite and nice, I suspect you wouldn't so much as speak a cross word to him, even given the awful things he said about you and your program.

Oh, Joan, I am so filled with rage I must be careful to keep myself under control and write in a reasonable way. But when I think of the insensitive, uncaring way that blubber-faced clown Gary Wells responded to you when your very touching story was over, my blood boils!

Couldn't he see how upset you were? Couldn't he tell how much having to deal with the police has affected you? I think he said what he did because he *wanted* to hurt you. He *wanted* people to think the police have good reason to suspect you.

Gary Wells is both disgusting and infuriating. I find it amazing that the producers of *Nightbeat* haven't had the sense to get rid of him by now. He holds the whole program hostage to his stupidity.

Your having to go to jail in Dallas for your role in an undercover investigation is something you should be proud of. I'm impressed by your daring and your unflinching courage in enduring the unfair treatment you got at the hands of the Dallas police and their puppet court. That makes the shabby treatment the St. Louis police gave you even more insulting, because they can have absolutely nothing against you.

Joan, my heart went out to you when you talked about the indignity and the sense of violation you experienced when the police searched your house. I can identify with those feelings, and it infuriates me as I imagine those hairy-handed, stinking bullies prowling through your private things.

172

It's not as if you are some cheap prostitute or drug addict they can give a hard time to just because they feel like it. I mean, my God, you are *Joan Carpenter*, star of *Nightbeat*! Instead of hassling you, the police should be doing everything in their power to avoid inconveniencing you.

Even while I was watching tonight's program, I began to hope that you're not feeling angry with me. I have to admit that what I've done to help you has made you a suspect, but please don't blame me for this too much. I'm sure you know that I would let myself be beaten to a pulp and tortured to death before I would ever do anything that would hurt you. (I'm not joking about this, Joan.) The idea that the police might suspect you was so farfetched it never entered my head, so please don't think I expected it.

But what about right now, what about tonight? Are you still worried, my dear? Do you fear that the police will come back and hound you even more? Do you worry that since you have challenged them on your show, they will be even more likely to treat you as a suspect?

I know you, Joan, perhaps better than you know yourself. I understand how your mind works, so I see your fears as well as your hopes and ambitions. Even without you telling me, I'm sure you possess every one of the worries and fears I've mentioned.

You mustn't be worried, though. Now that I see the cause of your fears, I promise you that I'll take immediate steps to make it absolutely clear to the police and everyone else that you (of all people) are not the Watcher. They would like nothing better than to lock me up, and I will make it obvious to them what nonsense it was to suspect you.

Hurling myself into the very face of the police is the least i can do to help you.

I feel calmer and more relaxed now that I've discussed my anger and your worries with you. I hope you do also. Remember, just trust in me, and everything will turn out for the best.

Goodnight for now, my darling. Let us meet one another in the twilight world of sleep and blend our dreams together.

The Watcher

JOAN CARPENTER
2030 Buckminster · St. Louis, MO · 63130

6 Nov/Fri

Dan:

Here we go again.

I assume you've now read the letter I just faxed you from the Chief Maniac of St. Louis.

It arrived in the two o'clock mail today, and I sensed what it was as soon as I saw the plain white envelope. I started to call the cops or at least get Alice to come in and watch me open it, but then I figured, what the hell. The letter was addressed to me, and despite this country's turn toward conservativism, you still don't have to get a court order before you can open your own mail.

I read through the letter, then immediately showed it to the Fish. That's because I remembered what you told me about his having a right to know what's going on in his own pond.

He read it, said, "Interesting," and handed it back to me. He looked like a man who had wheels turning in his head, but all he said was, "I suppose you're calling the police."

"As fast as I can tap the buttons," I told him.

"I think we're going to get an even bigger story out of this than we've gotten so far," he said. "Keep on top of it."

"I wish I could *get* on top of it," I told him. "I still seem to be in the middle of it."

The Fish gave me the very thin version of his Spam-can smile, and I went back to my office and called the dashing Lieutenant Keefer. He said he was sorry he couldn't come over himself, because he had to testify at a hearing. He seemed genuinely worried about my getting another letter. Anyway, he sent over the woman who looks like Mr. Ed and she asked me a couple of dozen pointless or unanswerable questions, then took the letter away with her.

As you see by the evidence, though, I was prudent enough to visit a copy machine while I was waiting for the cops to come. I figured I might like to pore over the contents at my leisure.

It's seven hours later now, and I've been at my leisure for about four of them. During much of that time I've been poring (as well as pouring) over the letter like Jimmy Swaggart over the Song of Solomon. I've read the letter ever' which-a-way (as we say in Texas), trying to hear the tune this creep is marching to.

An idea did sneak into my head during the time I was trying to think. The same thing used to happen to me when I spent hours reading Hegel, and I'm just as far from being sure I'm right now as I used to be then. But for what it's worth, here it is:

> The Watcher is telling me he's going to turn himself in so as to convince the police that the worst thing I've done to Tom Kline is offend his critical sensibilities.

I base this interpretation primarily on the Watcher's peculiar phrase "Hurling myself into the very face of the police." In addition, I am relying on his promise to take immediate steps to make it clear "to the police and everyone else" that he is he and I am I and the two of us are not identical. (See what I mean about reading Hegel? You begin to talk that way.)

Does this interpretation sound plausible to you? If so, then I suspect the Watcher is on the knife edge of action. To please me and protect my reputation, he's about to make what he considers a grand gesture of self-sacrifice.

Do you think I should do or say something to encourage him in this direction? God knows what it might be. "It is a far, far better thing that you do . . ." sounds a little dated, but I haven't come up with anything else.

I'm also sending a copy of the letter (via Jane) to Stratford Vogler. Perhaps he will discover that the Watcher is making me as crazy as he is.

In case you have any doubts on that score, let me tell you that as much as I would like to be a big star, I'm not so fond of being at the Top of the Pops on the Creep Circuit. It's nice to have fans, but What Price Glory? as you cinematestes might say.

If the software doesn't run away with the central processing unit or the phone lines don't get all tied in a knot so the words can't get through, I'll let you know what happens as soon as I find out.

Thanks for sticking with me.

Wiggly Longears

JOAN CARPENTER
2030 Buckminster · St. Louis, MO · 63130

6 Nov/Fri

Dear Sis,

I'm afraid it's just me again. Following this note is a copy of yet another letter from That Fan. Will you please do me the favor of passing it on to Stratford Vogler? (I'd send it to him directly, but I'm not sure I know him well enough to take such a bold step.)

As usual, feel free to read the letter yourself. I welcome your ideas. My own interpretation is that this creep is about to give himself up to get in my good graces.

He's right if he thinks that will please me very much. I've never felt threatened since he started writing, but I haven't felt as safe as I used to. I get the feeling now and then that somebody is lurking outside my house, and that spooks me. I arm myself with a claw hammer, then make myself go out and look around. (What would Daddy have said if I didn't?) Of course, there's never any sign of anybody. But it would be nice not to feel compelled to go wading in the midnight dew carrying a half-raised hammer like a demented Carpenter.

But enough about my tremulous evenings. I have to give a talk to a community group on Tuesday, and I think I'd rather face the Lurker in the Dark than the live audience. Fortunately, I'm expecting a couple of people I know to be in the audience. My friend Alan Carter is going with me, so that should help save the evening from the stigma of Good Works by the Widow Carpenter.

Alan and I plan to spend Sunday afternoon driving along the Great River Road that parallels the Mississippi on the Illinois side. It seems forever since I saw him. By now, he may be bent and stooped with age. Of course, in my eyes he will still be as good-looking as he was when we first escaped the crowd in the art gallery and walked the darkened streets like young lovers in a Fellini movie. (Sounds like *Swann's Way* doesn't it?)

Sad to say, I fear I've heard Alan's whole conversational tape by now, because it's starting to recycle. He has twice told me about how, when he was at New Haven, he was asked to give a special undergraduate seminar at Timothy Dwight on plains architecture—whatever that is (building sod houses?).

Maybe I'm too hard on men. Do you think finding one who is intelligent and good-looking should be enough? Is it crazy to want somebody who can say interesting things as well?

Speaking of men, I finally got up my nerve to do something about Curt Collins. I went out to see him while he was edging the nasturtium bed. He looked up and gave me a blonde and handsome smile, but before he could speak, I slapped him in the face with a few hard words.

I told him that although I respected him as a person, I had hired him as a gardener. When I ventured out for a chat, I said, it was to talk about petunias, not poems. I went on to inform him that I was not a literary critic, a patron of the arts, a raconteuse, nor a career adviser for the broadcast industry.

"I think it's great that you write poetry," I said, "but please don't look to me to make you famous." I told him I thought he was a terrific gardener (he's not bad) and I wanted him to continue to work for me, but the relationship had to be that of employer and employee. He shouldn't consider me his friend or patron.

This is not a guy likely to spend his spare time doing a correspondence course in molecular biology, and I said all this so fast I wasn't sure he could take it in. But I guess he did, because his blue eyes filled with the kind of shocked and puzzled hurt you see in the eyes of puppies when you shove them off the furniture.

I felt so bad, I apologized to him. "I'm sorry I had to say this," I told him. "But gardening keeps me sane, and I need to feel free from the pressures of being a public person when I'm in my own backyard." He gave me a faint, wan smile and said, "I'm sorry, Ms. Carpenter. I'll try to do better." I felt like Attila the Heel. Still, it was either tell him off or pay him off.

I hope Amy is having fun at school. Has she told you what she wants for Xmas yet? I thought Barbie and some of her consorts in an exotic locale was a possibility. (Maybe this is just a projection of my own fantasy life.) If you shoot down this idea as too crass and corrupting, how about an easel and a set of tempera paints? Surely you can't object to such an uplifting present as this homage to Art? (Unless, of course, you think it might lead her to take art seriously enough to consider becoming an artist. Certainly you would want to nip such an impulse in the bud.)

Tell Jack I'm thinking of buying him a roly-poly bopper to help him in his work. (Remember the one we had? It had a face like snarling bear, and when you bopped it on the nose, it rolled backward, then popped up again.) I figure anybody who sits around all day trying to prove theorems about imaginary objects has got to get pretty frustrated at times.

Do note that although I'm talking about Xmas presents, I have not forgotten about T'giving. Do you have your tickets yet?

I didn't mean to run on this way. But it's almost as fun as talking to you.

Give my niece a hug and a kiss. Does she know she could fax me some drawings? Have you in the name of Nickels and Dimes kept this secret from her? If so, tell her today and win the gratitude of a poor, lorn woman.

Love to all,
Joanie

C> -
C> cd\NOMAN
C> NOMAN
YOU'RE UP VERY LATE TONIGHT. HAVING TROUBLE SLEEPING?

I went to bed over an hour ago, but I just couldn't get to sleep. I decided it might help if I got up and talked to you.

IT'S ALWAYS GOOD TO TALK. IS SOMETHING BOTHERING YOU?

It's Joan—as usual. I keep on thinking about her, and my mind spins around and around. I thought that writing to her would calm me down, but it only made matters worse. I'm upset, agitated, and angry all at the same time. I didn't expect the police to be so goddamned stupid.

WHY DO YOU SAY THAT THE POLICE ARE SO GODDAMNED STUPID?

Because they searched Joan's house, even though they can't have the slightest grounds for suspecting that she had anything to do with what happened to Tom Kline. They just wanted to humiliate and harass her, probably because they are so frustrated by their failure to discover who I am. I've got to do something to make them leave her alone.

TELL ME ABOUT MAKING THEM LEAVE HER ALONE.

I promised Joan I would force the police to recognize that she is completely innocent, and I've got to keep my promise. Besides, I don't want Joan to suffer because of something I've done to help her. Some help that would be!

YOU DON'T WANT JOAN TO SUFFER?

If the police think she castrated Kline, they'll go on treating her as a suspect. And after the way she roasted them on tonight's *Nightbeat,* they'll be out for revenge with blood in their eyes. She's a sensitive person, and I want to spare her the kind of public embarrassment the police will subject her to.

YOU WANT TO SPARE JOAN PUBLIC EMBARRASSMENT?

Exactly. When I was watching the show tonight, I could tell how hurt and upset she was. I could read it off her face as plain as print off a page. I could also see how disturbed she was by the crack made by that disgusting toad Gary Wells.

YOU THINK GARY WELLS IS A DISGUSTING TOAD?

I certainly do, and after the way he treated Joan, I have nothing but contempt and hatred for him. I wish I could make him pay for his insolence.

YOU WANT BOTH TO MAKE GARY WELLS PAY AND ALSO TO HELP JOAN?

You know, that's actually a good suggestion. If I could find a way of demonstrating Joan is innocent that would also punish Gary Wells, that would be a perfect solution. To do that, though, I need a brilliant, daring idea.

TELL ME MORE ABOUT A BRILLIANT DARING IDEA.

I can't right now, but it's beginning to take shape in my mind. What's more, I'm also starting to get a glimmer of how I can make my "perfect" solution even better.

HOW CAN YOU MAKE THE "PERFECT" SOLUTION EVEN BETTER?

By doing something that will also help Joan in a positive way, something that will boost her career even higher and make her a superstar.

YOU WANT TO BOOST HER CAREER EVEN HIGHER?

I certainly do, and I think I know how I'm going to do it. But that's all I'm going to say for now. I'm going to have to work out the details.

11/9

Joan:

This is to remind you that you are supposed to appear at 8:00 tomorrow night at the Cheshire Inn for dinner and a talk (yours). Here is what you need to know:

+ The formal name of the organization is Partners in Progress, but everybody calls it PIP. It's committed to improving education at all levels—from nursery school through graduate school—in the metropolitan area. The members are mostly rich and/or powerful.

+ The current Director of PIP is Loretta Kirby. She is a lawyer, Black, educated at Brown, and very eager to get media attention for PIP's projects. (People say she's very nice.)

+ About 120 people are expected. Mayor Kinney will definitely be there. In fact, he will be sitting next to you on the dais. (In fact, he may even be closer. From what I hear, unless you plan to be over 80 by tomorrow night, you should arm yourself with a hatpin or a defensive weapon of your choice.)

+ Your talk has been advertised in mailings and in the newspapers under the title "Too Many Creatures in TV Features."

(I got the impression from the PIP publicity director that Mr. Fishwater asked her if a "more descriptive" title couldn't be used in the publicity. But the director said that was the title you gave her, and she had to use it. Did you know Mr. F. was going to be there? He's on the PIP Board of Directors.)

+ I checked on the menu: roast prime rib, Yorkshire pudding, steamed asparagus, parsley potatoes, fresh spinach salad, and rum pudding. They will prepare vegetarian dinners at request. Shall I?

+ Ms. Hartz called to ask what sort of outfit you are wearing. She wants to send you a corsage. (Should I tell her you prefer that the money be contributed to the Alice Walcheck Chocolate Fund?)

Alice

9 Nov/Mon

Alice:

As usual, you are wonderfully organized and well-informed. I can't honestly say I had forgotten about tomorrow night. I've been working on my talk at odd moments during the last week and dreading giving it every moment—even as well as odd.

Don't tell anybody, but I'm terrified of speaking in public. If I've got a camera to talk to, I'm fine, but put real people out there and I turn into Goofy delivering the State of the Onion Address.

Mr. F. told me he was coming to the talk, but I try not to keep it in mind. It would make me too self-conscious and cowardly. I don't suspect he's going to take kindly to hearing me criticize shows like *Nightbeat* for focusing on the bizarre and lurid (the "creatures" in my title) and letting ordinary everyday crime, graft, corruption, and general malfeasance go unreported. I may be cutting my own throat, as well as his—not to mention yours.

Oh, well. Maybe I can just get married and raise consumers.

Speaking of romantic matters, will you please call up whoever and say my plans have changed and that my friend Alan Carter is not going to be able to accompany me and so won't be having dinner. (That's not necessarily true, because I'm sure he'll eat somewhere. But you see what I mean.)

I was looking forward to having his encouraging face in the audience, but something important (like a shopping mall entrance) is making him leave for Springfield tomorrow morning—at least that's what he tells me. Now all I'll be doing is trying to avoid looking directly into Mr. Fishwater's cold eyes.

Please tell Alexis I'll be wearing my dark blue suit. Also say I apologize in advance if it turns out I'm not able to stop by and say hello at the dinner, because they've got me scheduled pretty tightly.

Sorry about the Chocolate Fund, but I'm going to need everything I can get to distract the crowd. If they stare at my corsage, they may not notice how petrified I am.

The menu sounds great to me. I'm only a vegetarian when I'm personally acquainted with the animal in question or I'm not crazy about the dish. Prime rib I can't pass up. I'll atone by eating tofu for the rest of the week.

Thanks for everything. In keeping with the way you work, I should ask for a doggie bag.

JC

■ STEPHEN LEGION, M.D., F.A.A.C.S. ■

AESTHETIC SURGERY, INC.

2052 BARNES HOSPITAL PLAZA

ST. LOUIS, MO 63132

314-562-5560

FAX 314-562-8100

November 9

Dear Joan,

Please notice that I have now mastered the fax machine. (I would have been quite embarrassed otherwise. If I can reshape a nose or a chin, I should be able to fax a letter.)

I wish I could be writing to you about something more exciting, but I am sorry to have to report that I won't be able to attend your talk at the PIP dinner tomorrow. My wife and I are both PIP members, and she will be there. I have to drive over to the medical school at Columbia to examine a text on dissecting facial nerves. For some unaccountable reason, no library in St. Louis has the work. The librarians at Columbia refuse to send it to me, and they say it would be a violation of copyright to photocopy it. Since I need to consult it for surgery the day after tomorrow, I don't have much choice in the matter.

I'm sorry we couldn't take the tour of the "wine country" and see the Missouri "chateaux." Perhaps we could meet for dinner next week.

I'll give you a call as soon as my schedule looks clear.

Warmly,
Steve

Alexis Caldwell Hartz

November 11
9:30 A.M.

My dear Joan,

This is just a note to say how very much I enjoyed your talk last night. You showed such exquisite poise and presented yourself so well to the audience!

And you are such a wonderful and convincing speaker. Your remarks about the way media tends to ignore educational issues, except for declining test scores, certainly hit home with the people in PIP.

If you will allow me to be frivolous, I just adored your suit—so tailored and yet with such soft lines. I think the pink tinge of the corsage went very well with the blue.

I was going to come up and tell you how nice you looked and how impressive your performance was, but you seemed so busy talking with the people around you, I decided not to.

Thank you for addressing our group. I hope we can get together soon to talk about our mutual project.

Cordially,
Alexis

P.S. I wanted to congratulate you on your success as quickly as possible, so I'm having this delivered to your office by our company's messenger service. I'm sure you have to prepare for tonight's broadcast, so I won't distract you further. I'll be watching for you tonight!

CHARLES FISHWATER
VICE PRESIDENT

NEWS DIVISION

KMIS-TV

November 11

Dear Joan,

After the PIP meeting last night, I was talking with a group of people that included Mayor Kinney, Loretta Kirby, Mrs. Calvin Tuggs (Director of Ralston Purina Foundation) and Bert Thomas (CEO of Midamerican Electric), and they all expressed a strong liking for your speech.

In my view you were much too hard on the broadcast industry. After all, we gather and present information of the sort people *want*, and the fact that most people want to know about what you call "creatures" is not our doing. However, I'm willing to admit that we could do a better job presenting the issues in education, and maybe you and I could work together to develop some ideas.

Even though I don't agree with all your views, I congratulate you on an outstanding job of speaking. When you can impress a large group of civic leaders, that is good for KMIS.

I'm not thinking of purely financial matters either. If such people like and admire you, they will trust you to break the newsworthy events they are involved with. (And believe me, the people at PIP are involved in nearly every legitimate newsworthy event that takes place in the city.)

Congratulations again on doing an impressive job. Let's get together at some time this week and discuss some possible projects connected with education.

CF

Dan? It's Joan. Are you there?

Goddamnit, why do you have to leave your machine
on at night?

I really need to talk to you about something important, so I'll go ahead and fax you. Maybe that's even better, because I can give you all the details.

Anyway, give me a call tomorrow. Right now, it's
almost two o'clock my time.

FAX TRANSMITTAL 314-552-5671

JOAN CARPENTER
2030 Buckminster . St. Louis, MO . 63130

11–12 Nov/Wed–Th c.2 A.M.

Dear Dan,

I wanted to talk to you, because something horrible happened
tonight. I thought that after years of watching movies and TV I had
become inured to everything, but that's not true. Reality has a force
and complexity that's never captured by camera tricks and special
effects.

I'm still upset and not thinking clearly. That's why I'm running
on in this undisciplined way. I suspect I would have been even
worse on the telephone. Anyway, let me just start at the first and
try to give you a plain account of what happened.

I gave a talk to a community organization last night (I mean
Tuesday) and didn't get home until around midnight. I was still
feeling tired this morning (Wednesday, I mean), so I faxed Alice,
my administrative assistant, and said I wouldn't be in until around
1:00. Nearly everything for tonight's show was already set to go. I
had some tape to time and a few pages of script to edit but nothing
that would take long.

When I got to the station, Alice told me Gary Wells had disappeared and no one knew where he was. At 8:30 this morning, his wife, Patsy, called his secretary to ask if he was at work. The secretary said she hadn't seen him since he left for home around 4:00 yesterday afternoon.

Patsy Wells was upset to hear that and broke into tears. "If he's not there, I don't know where he could be," she said.

According to her, Wells left home around 7:00 last night. He said he had to meet somebody about a big story, but he didn't say who he was seeing or where they were going to meet. She thought nothing about it, because Gary is always going off on a big story. So when he hadn't come home by midnight, she just went to bed. When he still wasn't back this morning, she thought maybe he was at the station taping an interview or writing something. But Wells's secretary asked around, and nobody had seen him since he left yesterday.

By the time I arrived on the scene, everyone was getting near panic. Typical of broadcasters, they were mostly worried about how we were going to do *Nightbeat* if Wells didn't show up. "He's left us in a real crunch," people said, and they seemed a lot more angry than worried. When Fishwater came in around eleven and learned what the situation was, he put some secretaries to calling the area hospitals and airlines.

He talked to Patsy Wells and got the names of Wells's friends and relatives, then put researchers to calling them. I heard from Alice that Fishwater called up the Mayor's office and had somebody he knows there check with the police and put out a pick-up order on Gary and his car.

Nothing had turned up by the time I arrived. Then around three o'clock, Fishwater told me Ted Broadbent, who does the morning news, was going to take Wells's place on tonight's program. Ted came in and I briefed him on the stories and helped him mark his script for breakaways and voiceovers. We had three stories and a humorous chaser. We did a run-through, and everything worked very smoothly.

Then about 5:30, Fishwater rushed into the studio as though he were being pursued by the devil. His face was flushed, and sweat stood in drops on his forehead. He seemed so agitated I was sure something terrible had happened to Gary Wells.

When I asked him, he shook his head and said, "Let's not talk about that now. We've got to nail this show." Then he said Ted and

I couldn't make any last-minute changes in our tape, because he had a rush job for both tape editors.

When the light on camera #1 glowed at 7 o'clock, I opened with "This is *Nightbeat*, and I'm Joan Carpenter." I billboarded our stories, and at the end I said, "Substituting for Gary Wells tonight is Ted Broadbent." Then I did the story on the disappearance of business license fees from the office that collects them, and Ted did the set-up and close for Gary Wells's piece on saving money by buying groceries in bulk amounts.

At the third break, I was glancing through the script for our last story, when Fishwater walked over and handed Ted Broadbent a couple of pages of script. "Something important has come up," Fishwater said. "I'm killing the final piece and the whole closing."

'What is it?" I asked him.

"I can't explain now," he said. "You'll see soon enough."

We came back with the camera on Ted. "We're replacing the remainder of this program with a story that is still developing," he read off Fishwater's script.

"What you are about to see is graphic and shocking. Children should not be allowed to watch, and adults should take this warning seriously. The tape quality is poor, but as will become obvious, the reason for that is itself a part of this very strange story."

The tape rolled and I glanced down at a monitor. For a moment, I couldn't tell what I was looking at. The tape was shot with available light and was grainy and dark. Then it became clear we were seeing the inside of a garage. The tracks and panels of a roll-down door were visible in the back, and we were looking at a red Toyota head on.

Only what we were really supposed to be looking at was inside the Toyota.

Sitting in the front seat behind the steering wheel was a man. In the opening shot, he was just a dim, unfocused figure. Then the camera moved in a little for a mid-shot through the windshield, and I recognized him.

"This is our colleague Gary Wells," Ted Broadbent said at about that time. "He didn't show up for today's broadcast, and according to his wife, Patsy, he has been missing since seven yesterday evening. As you can see from this scene, he was apparently taken captive by some person or persons unknown. Presumably whoever captured him also shot this videotape and sent it to us."

Wells looked awful. His eyes were opened wide and staring,

and they shifted constantly, as though desperately searching for a way to escape. His fleshy cheeks and the lower part of his face were distorted by transparent tape wrapped across his mouth and around his head. The shiny surface of the tape reflected the light, but you could see that the tape was so tight it spread his lips almost flat. The edges of his teeth showed behind them.

The camera moved closer to Wells, then tipped down to show us his hands. They were taped together, wrapped against one another like two nested forks, and his wrists were taped to the steering wheel. He was twisting his wrists, trying to pull loose, but nothing was happening. The skin around his wrists was red, rubbed raw, and bleeding.

After we got a good view of Wells, a quick cut took us to the side of the car. All the windows were up, and we could see a white hose about four inches in diameter running from the rear of the car to the window behind Wells. The hose looked like the thin and very flexible plastic kind used to vent dryers to the outside. The hose was stuck through the window, and the glass was rolled up to keep it in place. Something that may have been a white towel was stuffed into the rest of the window opening.

The scene suddenly shifted back to the front of the car, and the camera gave us a view through the windshield on the passenger side. A small black-and-white TV set with a blank screen was sitting on top of a cardboard box. The box raised the TV above the level of the dashboard, and the camera swiveled around the TV from the front to the side, to the back, then past Gary Wells on the other side. The only thing to see on the set was the power cord leading out the passenger window, which had been rolled up on it.

"Why Wells should be a target for anyone, we do not know," Ted Broadbent read. "Perhaps the mysterious Watcher who attacked and mutilated *Post-Dispatch* media critic Tom Kline has now turned against this program's co-host."

There was a jump splice in the tape, and we were looking at the rear end of the car. We could see the way the plastic tube had been flattened and taped to the exhaust pipe of the car. Something else that we could see was more subtle. The tube was shaking very slightly, which meant that the engine was running and exhaust was pouring through the tube and into the sealed car.

"Gary Wells is shown here tied up inside a car that has had a pipe fitted from the engine exhaust and into the car itself," Ted Broadbent said.

Another rapid cut, and we were looking at the front of the car again. Now the TV set in the front seat was playing. The picture on the screen flickered and had lines and noise, but it was clear enough to see what was happening.

"In a puzzling, macabre touch, a television is raised to windshield-height on the seat next to him," Tom said. "Maybe this is some perverted comment on his role as a television journalist. We just don't know."

I didn't recognize the program at first, because the scene was just a couple of people riding around in a pickup truck in a place that looked like the Southwest. Then I knew what I was watching.

In an irony that had to be deliberate, the program was *Unsolved Mysteries*. That meant the dial was set for KMIS, Channel 3, and since the program was in progress, it was sometime between 8 and 8:30 on Tuesday night.

The camera panned back to Gary Wells and stayed there. He still looked wide-eyed and terrified. His body jerked around from side to side, but his feet must have been tied too, because he didn't seem able to move very far.

Then there was another jump splice, and for two minutes or so that seemed to last forever, the camera focused directly on Gary's face. He was jerking around less, but he was breathing deeply now.

Then he was gasping, his chest heaving, and his eyes distended like those of a frightened horse.

"The exhaust from the car's engine pouring into the car contains carbon monoxide gas," Ted read. "This is of course a deadly gas that kills thousands accidentally every year. But what we're seeing here is no accident."

Gary's face was changing color also. The poor quality of the tape and the lack of proper lighting and makeup had made his skin look pale and washed out. But as he grew more desperate to breathe and sucked in the fumes filling the car, his face began to turn pink.

Then finally it turned a deep scarlet—a color that looked completely artificial, as though we were seeing a painted mannequin. At that point, Gary slumped sideways in the seat, hitting his head against the window.

"We may have witnessed the death of our colleague Gary Wells," Broadbent said. "We have no information about where or when the events you have seen occurred, so we cannot confirm that

Gary Wells is dead. It is possible that this may be some sort of hoax or, even if it is not, that Wells is still alive."

He paused, "I say that, but I don't think any of us who have watched this tape will doubt that we have seen anything other than the death of a man by inhalation of carbon monoxide."

The monitor in front of me went blank, and the camera focused again on Ted Broadbent. "You, the viewers of KMIS, are the first to see this tape," he said. "This is a shortened version, and we must turn over to the police the original and complete version."

Ted then summarized. "Once again, we have seen what we think is the death by carbon monoxide poisoning of the co-anchor of this program, Gary Wells. We have no idea who may have done this or why."

Fishwater's script went on to underline the obvious. "We may speculate that this event is connected with the person calling himself the Watcher who has written several crank letters to Joan Carpenter, the other co-anchor of this program. Those of you who were with us here last week know that Joan was upset at having her house searched by the police. She stated then that it was her belief that the police had few leads and were trying out of desperation to make her a suspect."

Ted swiveled to face me slightly, and the camera drew back for a two-shot. "Joan, I'm not going to ask you now to comment on what we've all seen here tonight, but next week, we'll be here for a program devoted completely to events connected with the Watcher."

He paused a beat then said, "We hope we'll have more for you next week on this strange and frightening story. Maybe by then we'll know what happened to Gary Wells, even if we don't know why. That's all for tonight."

Ted patted me on the shoulder and walked off, but I sat slumped at the anchor desk saying nothing for a while. I admired Ted for the way he had continued to function, but I was stunned by what I had seen. At that time, I wasn't even angry at Fishwater for putting on the tape.

I didn't realize until later that he must have told us we couldn't use the tape editors, because he needed them to edit the piece we aired. So when we were getting ready to go on and I saw him looking red-faced and sweaty, he already knew what had happened to Gary Wells.

He knew, because he had watched the tape.

When I felt more in control of myself, I went to Fishwater's office and asked him if the tape had been addressed to me.

"Your name was on the wrapper," he said. He was sitting behind his desk looking pale, but he had a hard edge in his voice when he spoke to me.

"Then why didn't you give it to me?"

"We've been through this before, Joan," he said. "The tape was sent to the station. It's ours, it's mine. It's KMIS's."

"Then why didn't you at least show it to me?"

"And get into a fight with you about whether to air part of it or not?" He made a snorting noise. "It would have been pointless."

He waved the back of his hand at me. "I take complete responsibility for showing the tape," he said. "You may think it was tasteless or exploitative or whatever, and you're entitled to your opinion. So far as I'm concerned it was a news story and it deserved just the coverage I gave it."

I suddenly didn't want to fight him. Maybe he was even right. I didn't want to think about it.

"I quit," I said.

I said nothing more but turned to walk out of his office. Before I reached the door, he said, "The police are going to want to talk to you."

"They know where I live," I snapped back. I wanted the words to be crushing, but they sounded petulant, like something a fourth-grader would say.

The bottom line, Dan, is that I don't work for KMIS anymore. I haven't exactly given you clear reasons for quitting, but I hope you can see why I did.

I feel surprisingly guilty about Gary Wells. In the same way that the Watcher made me an unconsenting and unwitting ally in promoting my career, he's made me an accomplice in the murder of Gary Wells. It's like a paradox: I'm not the Watcher, but an act that proves I'm not, turns me into the Watcher.

If I hadn't been so publicly outspoken about the police searching my house and treating me as a suspect, the Watcher would never have conceived the idea of proving I couldn't be the Watcher. And Gary Wells would still be alive.

Gary Wells was not a particularly nice man, and he was not a very good reporter. I didn't particularly like him, and he certainly didn't like me.

But he didn't deserve to die, and he didn't deserve to die in such a horrible way. He also didn't deserve to have his last few minutes of life taped and broadcast to the houses of millions of strangers. He didn't deserve to have his final agonies turned into "infotainment."

Do you suppose his wife watched the program tonight? Do you think she was amused? Will she want to show the tape to her two kids, just in case they missed it? It's all too disgusting.

That's why I quit.

Now I have to go to bed. The police will probably be around early for a little chat.

Sorry, Dan.

Joan

Hello, Joan. It's Dan. I hope I'm not calling too early. I could call back later if you aren't really awake yet.

No, it's all right. I've been up and pouring down the coffee for the last half hour. I at least think I'm awake.

I guess you got my fax.

I just finished reading it, and I found it quite upsetting. I haven't been able to do anything this morning, except wait around until I could call you. My God, I can hardly believe what happened. It's all so bizarre.

You mean what happened to Gary Wells?

That's certainly bizarre. But showing the tape of his being killed on *Nightbeat* . . . I mean, that's really disgusting. You can be sure the FCC is going to look into that.

Good, because I wouldn't mind seeing Fishwater stew a little. Do you think I should call them and file a complaint?

I don't think you need to. They'll hear from plenty of people. But, listen, I wanted to find out about you. How are you holding up?

I'm doing all right this morning. I think I surprised myself by getting so upset when I saw the Wells tape.

My God, Joan, that would have upset anybody.

Yeah, but I had myself pegged as a no-nonsense, hard-bitten investigative reporter who could stare straight into the evil eyes of the world without flinching. But then when I watched that tape, I flinched.

I think that says a lot of good about you. I mean, you don't want to let yourself become so jaded and cynical that you can't respond to something that's truly horrible.

That's the kind of thing Jane would say. Maybe you're right, but then again, maybe I just feel guilty because somebody I didn't care a lot about got killed.

Oh for God's sake, Joan, stop trying to make yourself sound more cynical than you are. I think you had a strong reaction because you're a decent person.

But listen, enough amateur psychiatry. I just had a terrific idea—why don't you come to New York for a few days. We can both take a little vacation. We can go to the Frick and the Cloisters, maybe go to whatever's on at Lincoln Center. I never do any of those things myself, but I can make the arrangements.

You mean, now that I don't have a job, I might as well try to have a good time and forget about everything?

No, that's *not* what I meant. I thought we both might have fun, and I certainly would feel better if you were out of St. Louis and away from all that Watcher business for a while.

I don't imagine the Watcher is going to be much interested in me now that I'm no longer on *Nightbeat*. Besides, if I left town, don't you think the police would regard it as suspicious?

Maybe so, maybe not. But that's their problem, not yours.

Well, anyway, I think I'll just stay home and rest up a little. I don't want to have a permanent rest, though, so I hope you're ready to put your ear to the ground and start listening for some job possibilities.

It's too early to start thinking about that.

Not for me it's not. But I do want you to know that I think it's nice of you to not scold me for quitting my job. Last night I acted automatically, but this morning I'm not at all sure I did the right thing.

So far as I'm concerned, whatever you felt was the right thing to do, *was* the right thing to do. But listen, you can't just walk out of an anchor job the way you'd walk out of a job at Dairy Queen. The contractual snarls would tie you up for years to come.

Oh God, Dan, I didn't think of any of that. Will you please talk to the people at KMIS and do whatever you have to do to get me out of my contract? I have no idea what that involves, but I do want to be free to take another job.

Leave all that up to me. They're going to piss and moan about your leaving, but they can't force you to stay. I'm not going to talk to them today, though. I'm going to give them a day or two to get over being mad at you, then when they're not frothing at the mouth, I'll call them.

Whatever you say. Just get me out of there.

Will do. And I'll give you another call soon, just to see how things are going. But Joan . . .

Yes, Dan?

Take care of yourself—please.

Believe me, I'll do my best.

ST. LOUIS COUNTY POLICE DEPARTMENT

Memo of Transmission   Date: November 12

From: Detective Lieutenant Peter S. Keefer, Major Case Squad
To: Chief of Police Harold C. Blackshire

Dear Harold:

I can understand why you particularly want to be kept up to date on the Wells case. I'm sure the media have asked you every possible question several times. We haven't found out much since I talked to you last night, but I'll give you what we've got:

1. The house that goes with the garage where Wells's body was found is located at 6342 Meadovale and is owned by Ashton and Carolyn Stringer.

The Stringers are not living in the house at this time. They moved to Los Angeles four months ago, but before they left they put the house up for sale. They had a potential buyer the first week the sign was out, but then part of the roof caved in during a particularly heavy rain. When the buyer backed out, the Stringers decided that since they would have to have the roof damage repaired, they would go ahead and rehab the whole house and try to get a much higher price for it.

The house has been completely vacant since the Stringers moved. A lawn service takes care of the grass, and a private neighborhood patrol keeps an eye on the place. However, a for-sale sign is still in the front yard, and despite timers on the lights, it wouldn't take an experienced criminal to determine that no one is living there.

We got the key to the house from Gateway Realty Company and went through the inside pretty thoroughly. We discovered no sign to show that Wells or the unknown perpetrator was ever in the house itself.

So far as we have been able to determine, there is no connection between Wells and the Stringers.

2. The woman who called 911 to report the crime is named Madelyn Kleene. She lives at 6340 Meadovale, the house directly east of the Stringer house. Houses in Oakbrook Hills are on heavily wooded three-quarter-acre lots, and Mrs. Kleene can't see much

more than the roof of 6342 from her property. She says that is why she couldn't have noticed anything that might have been going on at the house or garage during the day.

The garage of the Stringers' house is detached and set back about fifty feet. It's a one-story brick structure that is windowless, except for a decorative round window in the front gable. Mrs. Kleene reports that around eleven o'clock, just after watching the weather forecast on TV, she got ready for bed and turned off the light in her bathroom. As she was leaving the room, through her bathroom window she saw a light from the Stringers' garage. It was high up and shining through the tree branches.

This struck her as strange, because she knew the Stringers were gone, and she had never seen light coming from the gable window since they left. Mr. Kleene was still dressed, and his wife convinced him to walk over to the Stringer house to see if anything strange was going on.

When Mr. Kleene got there, he walked to the garage, and he could hear an engine running inside. Light was still coming from the gable window. He rapped on the side door of the garage, and when no one answered, he tried the knob. The door wasn't locked, so he opened it and took a look inside.

When he saw the setup with the car running and the white plastic pipe, he was puzzled for a moment. Then he figured somebody was trying to commit suicide. He jerked open the car door and tried to pull Wells out of the front seat. But since Wells's hands were taped to the steering wheel and his feet to the brake pedal, he couldn't do it.

Mr. Kleene then switched off the engine and raised the garage door. After checking to make sure he could do nothing to help Wells, he walked back home and told his wife to call the police.

Mr. Kleene did not recognize Gary Wells, and both the Kleenes deny knowing either Wells or Joan Carpenter. They admit they sometimes watch *Nightbeat* and so have heard of both people. My impression is that the Kleenes are not trying to hide anything from us.

3. We questioned the residents on both sides of the street for a block in each direction. Nobody reported seeing anything unusual on Tuesday, during the day or the evening. Some residents said that even if they had seen something going on at the Stringer house, they might not remember it.

Since the house remains on the market, people frequently turn into the driveway to take a look at it or to go through it. Also, workers taking care of the lawn and doing the rehabbing go in and out of the driveway quite often.

4. Tolbert Smith, the private neighborhood patrol officer, doesn't go on duty until ten p.m., and he told us he drove past the house once, but didn't notice anything. Because of the way the house is situated on the lot, even if he had been looking for the light from the garage window, he probably wouldn't have noticed it from the street.

We haven't been able to talk to anyone from the Stringers' lawn service yet. We are also going to get a list from the Stringers or their agent of the people doing repairs on the house. We will be talking to each of them, looking for a connection with Wells or with Carpenter.

5. We are still waiting for the forensic report and the autopsy results. We aren't expecting any surprises from the autopsy, but maybe we can learn something from the forensics people about the scene.

6. Gary Wells was 45 years old. His wife's name is Patsy, and she is 42. There are two sons, Bryan (19) and Carleton (18). Both are students at the University of Missouri—Kansas City. The family lives at 5575 Granville Avenue in Ladue.

7. We are still assuming a connection between this case and the Kline case, and Joan Carpenter is the obvious link between them. For this reason, I have assigned the same people who were working on Kline to the Wells case. We are treating them, essentially, as the same case.

8. I asked Forensics to make us a copy of the "Watcher" tape, and I have viewed the entire tape about four times now. So far I haven't noticed anything I didn't notice the first time. (That seems to be true of the other eight people I have assigned to this case.) Forensics is studying the original tape. Maybe they can learn more from it than we have been able to.

That is pretty much the story to date. I welcome any suggestions you might want to make. The first lesson I learned from you when I was a rookie detective is that any investigation has room for improvement.

I'll call you or drop you a memo when we turn up something new.

Peter

ST. LOUIS COUNTY POLICE DEPARTMENT

Memo of Transmission   Date: November 12

From: Detective Raymond R. Robertson
To: Detective Lieutenant Peter S. Keefer, Major Case Squad
Case Number: 35-2300-1095

Peter:

I got a call from Dr. Marcus in the ME's office, and he says the autopsy on Wells produced no surprises. They're still typing up the official copy, but here are the basics:

(a) Wells was hit on the head with an object that made a depression exactly the same size and shape that would be made by the piece of galvanized pipe we found on the garage floor.

(b) The time of death is consistent with the time shown by the TV program. (Dr. Marcus says the tape of the program gives a more exact time than he can establish.)

(c) Wells died of carbon monoxide poisoning, not the blow to the head. Dr. Marcus did tests on the oxygen content of the dried blood, and he thinks the blow came before Wells started breathing the exhaust fumes.

Also, except for being a little overweight and having a 30 percent left coronary artery blockage, Wells was in fine physical condition. No evidence of drugs, disease, alcohol damage, etc. He would still be alive today if somebody hadn't toasted him.

I asked Greg Handler when Forensics was going to have something on the crime scene. He said he didn't know, but he would send it directly to you. Sometimes I'm not sure Greg knows we're all working on the same side on the investigation.

Or maybe it's because he has a master's degree. That makes you the only person good enough for him to talk to.

                                                                      Ray

ST. LOUIS COUNTY POLICE DEPARTMENT

Memo of Transmission   Date: November 12

From: Detective Lieutenant Peter S. Keefer, Major Case Squad
To: Detective Raymond R. Robertson
Case Number: 35-2300-1095

Ray:

You can't let Greg Handler get under your skin. I suspect he likes to think of himself as a "scientist," and that's what makes him seem arrogant. But he does know what he's doing, and that alone sets him apart from most other arrogant guys who walk through the station-house door.

Anyway, I'm leaving you a copy of the report Greg just sent to me. (Why everything he writes sounds like it's been translated from Japanese is the question I'd like to ask.) It looks like he's in agreement with everything you and I talked about at the scene—the pipe, where it came from, the dirt on Wells's clothes, the TV set, and so on.

Speaking of the TV set, I think the Watcher has succeeded in establishing that Joan Carpenter couldn't have been the direct perpetrator of this crime. At exactly the same time Gary Wells was struggling for oxygen and the TV beside him was showing *Unsolved Mysteries*, Joan Carpenter was giving a speech in front of a crowd of the richest, most socially prominent, and most politically powerful citizens of St. Louis. Sitting next to Mayor Kinney may or may not give a woman a thrill, but it does give her a good alibi.

Obviously the Watcher wanted us to have the exact time of the crime so Joan Carpenter could have a perfect alibi. I'm sure you've noticed that this is in keeping with what he had to say in his last letter to Carpenter.

I imagine none of this will convince you that Carpenter isn't involved, though. You'll tell me it doesn't eliminate the possibility that she conspired with someone else and got that person to kill Wells at a time when she would be in the clear. You might even say the Watcher's letter was sent to set this up.

Maybe so. I can't deny that she has to remain a suspect, at least as a possible accomplice to the crime. Yet except for trying to make herself into a star, her motive for killing Wells seems very slim. I admit, though, that when you look at what Fishwater did, you understand at a gut level just how important ratings are in the TV business.

Not that ratings could be the only motive. It's possible Wells learned something about Carpenter she didn't want known. Maybe he learned that she castrated Tom Kline or maybe arranged for somebody else to do it. If so then she (and an accomplice?) would have a good reason for wanting Wells out of the way.

I think you (personally) have to be careful not to decide Carpenter is involved because you want to pay her back for the things she said about us on TV. I'm not saying drop her, but let's not focus the investigation on her.

We clearly shouldn't drop the people associated with her. One of them may be acting in ways intended to help her, without her knowledge or approval. The Watcher letters certainly suggest this possibility.

I assume you're already checking to see where Alan Carter was last Tuesday night. He seems the person closest to being the man in her life, and that means he has a clear interest in seeing to it that Carpenter isn't falsely identified as the Watcher.

Also, you might think about taking a look at Alexis Hartz. She's one of the people Carpenter mentioned in her interrogation who could confirm that she was at the PIP dinner last night. She's known Carpenter since she moved to St. Louis, and she seems to be on particularly friendly terms with her. If you're looking for somebody who might have conspired with Carpenter, Hartz may be a good bet.

Carpenter also told me Hartz had been giving her some information about some shady real estate deal. She wouldn't say more than that, and I didn't think it was the time to push. I can't see how this might be connected with the Watcher, but at the moment, nothing is making much sense. Talk to her about it and see what you can get.

Carpenter mentioned that she had a note from Dr. Stephen Legion saying he had expected to be at the PIP dinner but couldn't make it. According to Alice Walcheck, Legion has called Carpenter a couple of times, and I saw in one of the earlier 905s that she admits they met for a social occasion at least once. She also admits he has asked her to go out with her, even though he is married. (She says she knows he is married, which suggested to me that Carpenter is not above bending the rules, if she thinks it's in her interest.)

I'm sure it's occurred to you that Legion could be trying to win Carpenter's favor by doing things he thinks she wants done. Although the castration of Tom Kline wouldn't have taken any specialized medical knowledge, that Legion is a surgeon suggests he might not be too squeamish to perform such an act. The Wells killing wouldn't have required any special knowledge either, but that doesn't mean someone with such knowledge should be excluded.

Be very discreet when you check out Dr. Legion. In fact, you'd better arrange to see him at his office, instead of his home. Legion and his wife move in high circles, and we don't want to antagonize anybody if we can help it. Besides, we want him to feel free to tell the truth without his wife overhearing him.

For my money, Curtis Collins has to head the list of people who would most obviously be willing to do something to boost Joan Carpenter's career. He seems fascinated with her as a star, and I get the impression he also sees her as his ticket to fame. He might believe that if he could get something on her or make her indebted to him, she would be forced to get him a TV job.

It might just be a coincidence that both Collins and the Watcher write poems about Joan Carpenter. This might be the kind of false lead that sends you down the wrong path. Or it may be the correct answer that you ignore because it's so obvious you think it's got to be wrong. From most points of view, Collins is a good bet. The fact that the pruning shears you got from him tested negative for blood means nothing. He probably owns half a dozen more.

My main doubt about Collins is whether he's bright enough to plan anything more complicated than watering the grass. We've already tagged him as a possible in the Kline case, and maybe he fits the role here too. But before we get too excited, we need to have a talk with him. (Check to see if he's wearing shaving lotion or cologne. Do it for Carter and Legion also.)

While I'm suggesting lines of inquiry, I assume you've got somebody working on Charles Fishwater. I want you to take a hard look at him. He seems to be someone who would arrange for Gary Wells to be killed, just to get a big rating boost for *Nightbeat*. Can you imagine the thought processes of a man who would put a snuff film on TV during prime time? Disgusting.

One more thing needs to be said about suspects: It may be that none of the people I've named are involved in either the Kline attack or the Wells homicide. Because we don't have any real option, we've focused the investigation on the people associated with Carpenter. This leads us to invent hypotheses and make up complicated stories that fit the facts we know.

But the inescapable truth may be that the Watcher is a complete stranger to us. He may be someone who has not so much as seen Carpenter in the flesh. A depressing thought, of course.

As soon as we get a substantial batch of IR-905s from the preliminary interrogations, I would appreciate it if you would read through them and do a reconstruction of the crime for me. Then we'll get together and talk about where we should go with the investigation.

Pete

JOAN CARPENTER
2030 Buckminster • St. Louis, MO • 63130

12 Nov/Thurs

Dear Mama,

I don't know if you've seen it on the news, but someone killed the man who was my co-anchor on *Nightbeat*. His name was Gary Wells.

Gary and I weren't friends at all, but I was offended when our producer showed on the air some scenes from a tape that the killer made. I thought that it cheapened Gary Wells's death by treating it as though it was an entertainment event.

I didn't want to be associated with something like that, so I quit my job.

Don't worry about me. I've got money in the bank, and I don't expect I'll have trouble getting another job. Who knows, maybe I'll come back to Dallas. Think the Stuarts would sell me back my old house?

Also, don't think that I'm in any real danger. The police are on the case by the dozen, and I take every precaution known to woman to keep myself safe.

I'm still waiting to learn your travel plans. So far as I'm concerned, I'm not going to let any of this get me down. It's going to be business as usual. Better come to St. Louis while I'm still living here. It may be your last chance to see the city and not have to stay in a hotel.

Since I haven't heard from you, I assume everything is going well. Tell Aunt Mildred I got Darlene's wedding announcement and I'm awfully sorry I can't come. (Well, *tell* her that anyway.) Do you have a clue about what kind of present Darlene would like? Maybe a trophy case so she could display her old batons and twirling medals? (Just kidding.)

I still miss having my mom around.

Love,
Joanie

P.S. I called Jane and told her about everything too. She's not worried about me, so you shouldn't be either.

ST. LOUIS COUNTY POLICE DEPARTMENT

DIVISION OF FORENSICS

Memo of Transmission   Date: November 12

From: Greg Handler, M.S., Division Head
To: Detective Lieutenant Peter S. Keefer, Major Case Squad
Case Number: 35-2300-1095

I present here a summary of the findings of our investigation in the case of the apparent homicide of Alfred Gary Wells. The findings relate in location to the detached garage at 6342 Meadovale Lane, Oakbrook Hills, St. Louis.

1. The apparent weapon employed to render the victim unconscious was a 26 (twenty-six) inch length of ½-inch diameter galvanized water pipe.

Blood and hair samples from the pipe are consistent with samples taken from the victim. Unique identification is impossible for hair, but the type, race, and color match the samples. Our lab lacks the capacity for performing so-called genetic fingerprinting, and with respect to the blood samples, this did not seem necessary. We are preserving the samples as evidence, and if a need arises, we can have such a test performed later by an approved independent laboratory.

No latent prints were found on the pipe. Illuminated-field microscopy of the "clean" end shows signs of handling compatible with the pipe being picked up by someone wearing gloves.

2. The galvanized pipe was apparently taken from a stack of pipe and lumber at the rear of the garage. We have employed scanning electron microscopy to confirm the identity of the pipe with other lengths obtained from the stack. The stack itself shows signs of having been disturbed, and the mineral and organic contents of the dust covering the stacked pipe match those of the dust remaining on the pipe.

3. The material stuffed into the back window of the automobile to effect a seal is a white, cotton, 18″ by 29″ bath towel. The towel still contains the original sizing, and this indicates that it is unlikely that it had been used before. The sewn label identifies it as a "JC Penney Fashion Flair" product.

4. The great amount of detritus within the area where the body may have lain on the garage floor makes it impossible to secure a complete catalogue of all relevant materials.

In addition to various kinds of seeds, plant leaves, and stems, the floor contains spots of gasoline with different lead contents, spilled and dripped oil, and a variety of clays and soils. Further, paint chips, rust fragments, human and animal hair, artificial and natural fibers are all scattered in abundance on the concrete slab that constitutes the garage floor.

We are retaining samples from the floor, but at the moment a complete analysis seems pointless. With the samples available, however, should the need arise, we can look for a particular match.

5. We analyzed materials found on the shirt and trousers worn by Wells, then did an exclusion match to attempt to eliminate those that may have been picked up from the floor. We have several hairs and fibers remaining, but we must now test samples taken from Wells's wife and household.

6. The tape employed to secure the victim's hands, feet, and

mouth was of a type known as *strapping* or *filament* tape. The manufacturer appears to be 3-M Manufacturing Company, and the tape is one of those sold under the "Scotch" trademarks. Glove marks (apparently plastic), but no latent prints, are on the tape.

7. Three latent prints of a usable quality were found at the scene—all three on the car. They have been turned over to the Latent Print Officer for searching and elimination.

8. The hose piping running into the window of the Toyota was manufactured by Wabash Plastics of Wabash, Wisconsin. It is sold for use in air-delivery devices and as exhaust hoses for clothes dryers. The piping is not new, and the lint and other fibers inside suggest it may have seen service as an exhaust hose for a clothes dryer.

9. The television receiver is a black-and-white portable with a (roughly) 10" by 12" screen manufactured by Goldstar. Serial numbers reveal that this model was made three years ago, and some 120,000 were sold within the St. Louis area. The set has been roughly treated and is not in prime working condition, although reception and picture qualities are adequate.

In answer to a question raised by Detective Robertson, the television receiver has no capacity to record or play a videotape. Further, the receiver has not been modified to receive any special low-frequency signal. Also, although there is no reason a videocassette recorder or player could not be attached to the receiver, none actually was attached. Further, examination of the connecting terminal with a 5x hand lens does not reveal any sign that a connection of any sort had been made.

10. The brown, two-wire, 115v-rated extension cord is twelve (12) feet long. The manufacturer's name (General Electric) is embossed on the plastic of the receptacle. The cord appears to be new, containing the bends of the original folding.

11. Although this laboratory has not yet fully examined the videotape played for us by Detective Kimbell, we are of the tentative opinion that the television receiver depicted in the tape is the same as the one found in the car.

Further, we are of the opinion that the picture on the screen of the receiver was in fact one generated by an electronic signal being broadcast at the time of its receipt.

I trust that this preliminary report will be of assistance to you in your investigation.

ST. LOUIS COUNTY POLICE DEPARTMENT

Memo of Transmission   Date: November 12

From: Detective Raymond R. Robertson
To: Detective Lieutenant Peter S. Keefer, Major Case Squad
Case Number: 35-2300-1095

Peter:

If you're sure you really want me to, I'm willing to take a shot at reconstructing the Wells homicide.

When you asked me to do it, I didn't think we knew enough even to make a start. Then I watched the tape about ten times and read the autopsy and forensic reports. After that, I sat down and waded through all the IR-905s on the interrogations of Patsy Wells, Charles Fishwater, Joan Carpenter, the others at *Nightbeat,* and the neighbors along the Stringers' street. When I finished doing all that, I realized we know a lot more than I thought at first, and I decided I could sketch a fairly plausible outline.

Anyway, here is my preliminary reconstruction of how things went down last Tuesday night. I'll give you the story version without much proof, and if you like the way it sounds, we'll highlight the questions we need to investigate. Here goes.

Somebody (let's call him X) calls up Gary Wells sometime between Wednesday of last week (after *Nightbeat* was on) and Tuesday morning. X tells Wells he's got some really hot stuff for him.

"Yeah," Gary says. "How hot?"

"Hot enough to knock Joan Carpenter off her throne," X says. "Let's meet and talk about it."

Wells is happy to agree, because the idea that he's going to get a chance to step on Carpenter's face is irresistible. Along with everybody else who's ever watched the show, he knows he's been outclassed by her, and he feels humiliated.

Tuesday evening comes, and Wells's wife asks him where he's going. He says, "I've got to go see somebody. I'm going to get a story that will get that bitch Joan Carpenter kicked off the air and back to the cow pasture she came from." (This is an actual quote from Patsy Wells.) He sounds real smug, even cocky.

Gary doesn't tell Patsy who he's going to see. He probably

doesn't know himself, because it would be too risky for X to give Wells his name. Wells might tell his wife or write it down in his calendar, and when Wells turns up dead, everybody is going to be looking for X. (Maybe I should have said this up front, but I think it's obvious that the killing was premeditated. Otherwise, everything becomes too coincidental.)

Wells goes to meet X at seven o'clock as planned. Then either they go to the Stringer house together or they arrive separately. Maybe X even rides along with Wells and gives him directions. None of the neighbors noticed anybody going into or coming out of the driveway. But this isn't surprising, because people are always going in to look at the house or to do some work on it.

Why X chooses the Stringer house as the scene, I also don't know. Maybe X knew the Stringers and knows they've moved, maybe he lives in the neighborhood and has seen the for-sale sign, or maybe he just scouted out a place to take Wells.

Probably X has been to the house earlier and has everything in order. He's laid out his tools and supplies and has his video camera ready. He gets Wells to put his car in the garage, maybe by telling him it will be too conspicuous if they leave it outside. (That's a reason to think only one car was there.)

Wells drives his red Toyota into the garage. He gets out of the car, and X walks over and stands close to him. Then (and I'm almost sure of this) X directs Wells's attention to a deer antler hanging from a nail high up on the east wall. (If you look at the photographs of the garage interior, you'll see the antler in two of them.)

Wells is distracted by whatever it is that X is saying. While Wells has his head turned up and is looking up at the antler, X picks up the piece of pipe he earlier laid in a convenient place. Then he hits Wells a blow on the right side of the head, not fracturing his skull but rendering him unconscious.

(I'm so sure about the antler because the autopsy report says the position of the contusion on Wells's scalp indicates that his head was tilted back at a sharp angle. I'm about Wells's height, and I stood by the car and looked up at the antler. Anybody hitting me from slightly behind would strike my head at about the same place that Wells was struck.)

When he's hit, Wells falls like a side of beef to the garage floor, where his clothes pick up the random assortment of dirt, grease, and hair Greg Handler makes so much of.

With Wells unconscious, X then hoists him back into the car. Wells weighs 187 pounds, so probably X lifts Wells partly into the seat, then drags him by his arms the rest of the way in. (A bruise on Wells's left side could have been made by the Toyota door latch.) Once X has Wells where he wants him, he gets the roll of tape he's also stashed in the garage earlier and wraps up Wells's hands and feet.

He props up Wells behind the steering wheel, then tapes his hands to the wheel and his feet to the brake. He wraps tape around Wells's head, covering his mouth but leaving his nose free.

Our boy stays busy with the tape, taping the plastic hose to the car's exhaust pipe. (The hose probably wasn't even hidden. It would look like the sort of junk people leave behind when they move.) He runs the hose through the window, rolls it up, and stuffs a bath towel into the rest of the opening.

Wells has taken quite a blow to the head and is still out. (You can see this in the first couple of minutes of the tape.) While he's unconscious, X gets out his b & w TV and the box. He probably had them hidden under the plastic tarp covering the stack of storm windows in the northwest corner of the garage. (The dust is scraped off the windows in a few spots.)

He puts the box in the passenger seat and the TV on top of the box. He runs the extension cord out the window (rolling up the window on it as far as he can) and plugs it in. Turning the volume down to zero, he tunes in to Channel 3. He probably has to adjust the antenna a little to get anything like a watchable picture.

When all this is set up, he goes and gets his video camera. (Maybe he's brought it with him in a briefcase or hidden it under the tarp with the TV.) He shoots some tape of Wells to show us what he looks like unconscious. He shows us a little of the garage, so we see where all this drama is taking place.

Then X checks his watch. He doesn't want Wells to die too early. If he did, then it just might be possible for Carpenter to have killed him. That would defeat the purpose of the plan outlined in the letter to Carpenter. (Whether or not Carpenter had a hand with the letter, the scene plays the same way.)

When X sees the time is right—that's when *Unsolved Mysteries* happens to be on—he starts the car engine.

By this time, Wells is probably conscious and struggling. Mr. X begins to shoot more tape. He takes us on a tour of the scene once more to make sure we understand the setup. He also makes sure we know what's on the TV. What good is a time marker, if no-body notices it?

He then shows us Wells struggling to breathe, turning color as the carbon monoxide gets to him, and finally dying. The camera never blinks, and it seems to like what it sees.

What does X do after Wells dies? Here our evidence fails us. Maybe someone comes by to pick him up or he gets into his own car and drives off. Maybe he just puts his 8 mm video camera back into his briefcase and walks away.

However he leaves, I think he does it as soon as he's sure Wells is dead. By that time, probably around 8:30, it's already dark, so he doesn't have to wait for that to give him cover. Just by being there he's taking a substantial risk, so I'm sure he hurries out.

Did he leave on the light because he was in a hurry? Possibly, but I doubt it. Tapes of apparent murders are easy to fake. After all, the movie and TV industry thrive on it.

What I think is that he wanted us to find the body reasonably soon, because that way no one would doubt that Wells was really dead. And we watched him being killed *at a time when Joan Carpenter couldn't have done it.*

You might say he was doing his best to fulfill the promise of his letter to Joan Carpenter.

You might also say he wanted the body to be discovered so the tape could be on Wednesday's *Nightbeat.*

That's it. That's my story. If you think I've gone down the wrong track, you won't hurt my feelings by telling me.

Ray

ST. LOUIS COUNTY POLICE DEPARTMENT

Memo of Transmission   Date: November 13

From: Detective Lieutenant Peter Keefer, Major Case Squad
To: Detective Raymond R. Robertson
Case Number: 35-2300-1095

Ray:

You still take the prize for the best reconstructions I've ever read. I like your stories better than Perry Mason's. Maybe one reason is they don't have any lawyers in them to confuse matters.

I think everything could have happened pretty much the way you described. After I read your account, I jotted down some matters we should check into. I'm sure most, if not all, you've already thought of yourself.

(1) Reinterrogate the neighbors and show them a picture of the red Toyota. The car might spark some recollections.

(2) See if any of them can remember anybody either walking or riding a bicycle near enough to the Stringer house that they might have been coming from there.

(3) Talk to the lawn service people again and see if they have any connection with Joan Carpenter or Gary Wells. Also see when they were at the Stringer house last.

(4) Find out if anybody connected with Carpenter or Wells has any connection with the Stringers or with their house.

(5) Talk to the Stringers and ask them if the plastic hose is something they left in the garage. If not, then making an effort to trace it might be worth the trouble. If we can associate the hose with somebody, then Greg Handler's fiber samples from the inside might be enough to tie the person to the homicide.

(6) Get Wells's secretary to give you a list of everybody she can remember who called him from Thursday through Monday. Also ask her if Wells got any calls that didn't go through her.

(7) Sift through Wells's papers at his home and office to see if he might have written down the Tuesday, 7:00 P.M. appointment.

(8) Get a list of all Wells's friends and acquaintances so we can begin checking on their whereabouts at around 7:00–9:00 Tuesday night.

(9) Don't forget to check the messenger service that delivered the video tape. I suspect it will be the same story as in the Kline case, but we might get lucky.

Chief Blackshire says we can have an extra thirty people (or overtime equivalents) for the next two weeks. I'm leaving it up to you to decide the priorities, but I recommend talking to people in the neighborhood first.

As I heard a New York cop interviewed on TV say, it takes a lot more sweat than brains to solve a crime.

Pete

• JANE CARPENTER-REED, M.D. •
Psychiatry Consultants, Inc.
3460 Chestnut Avenue
Brookline, MA 02147
617-976-8740
FAX: 617-976-2286

November 14

My Joanie,

I'm awfully glad you called me.

I know that when you're having flashbacks and sleeping troubles, it seems they are going to go on forever. But they won't. And they're just what you would expect to happen when you've been through an experience that's left you shaken. If things change and you begin to feel very depressed or start blaming yourself for what happened to Gary Wells, give me a call and we'll talk over some steps you can take.

You might like to know that after I've had a chance to think things over, you and I are still in perfect agreement: You were absolutely right to quit.

I don't think quitting was in any way the reflection of a desire to fail or that it shows a self-destructive tendency. You did the right thing for the right reasons. Keeping your job wasn't worth the price

211

of losing your integrity and self-respect. (Of course, if they realize how stupid they've been to lose you and want you back on better terms, don't be too self-righteous to discuss the matter.)

I have to admit that I'm somewhat surprised by the Watcher's actions. The capacity for violence was demonstrated in the attack on Kline, but I didn't realize how very far an erotomanic person might go to win the approval of the object of attraction. This is quite out of the range of ordinary psychiatric experience. That an otherwise rational person would actually kill another person in the deluded belief that it will please someone is a phenomenon I thought was limited to primitive religions. It's like a worshipper making a human sacrifice to a Goddess of TV. (Since you are the Goddess, I probably shouldn't be talking this way. But I'm hoping you can keep some distance on the situation.)

I'm going to call Stratford Vogler and tell him what happened. He may have seen parts of the Wells "death scene," as the *Boston Globe* called it, because it's been on several news programs.

You absolutely must keep in mind that you are in constant danger. Having somebody like the Watcher obsessed with you is like keeping a tiger for a pet—with no warning, the beast can turn and devour you.

You are an amazingly strong person to be able to remain intact and functional through everything that's happened since you moved to St. Louis. I think Daddy would be impressed.

I am.

Love you lots,
Janie

P.S. I'm glad you wrote Mama. She hardly ever watches TV, but somebody is sure to tell her about what happened.

ST. LOUIS COUNTY POLICE DEPARTMENT

Memo of Transmission   Date: November 14

From: Detective Lieutenant Peter Keefer, Major Case Squad
To: Detective Raymond R. Robertson
Case Number: 35-2300-1095

Ray:

I was at a Commanders' meeting with the Chief this morning, and while people were blabbering on about crisis-based budgeting, I got an idea that might be worth checking out.

Could Wells have been a co-conspirator with the Watcher? Or perhaps I could put it this way: Maybe the Watcher is not a person, but Wells and X acting together.

We dismissed Wells as a serious suspect in the Kline castration. Not only did his fainting when he opened the box on TV make it seem that he wouldn't have been capable of the crime, but we didn't see what he would have to gain. We saw that Carpenter wanted the ratings to go up.

Maybe we were thinking in the wrong terms, though. Instead of trying to get the ratings for *Nightbeat* to increase, Wells might have been trying to get rid of Carpenter. If he knew about her background in Dallas, he might figure that if anything sensational was done that raised the ratings, she would be the natural person to suspect—which is exactly what you did. If she got blamed for it, whether or not she was charged with a crime, KMIS might feel they had to fire her. If that happened then Wells's job would be safe again.

Suppose Wells and X write the Watcher letters, and Wells gets X to attack Kline. Things don't turn out exactly as Wells planned, because it turns out that Fishwater likes controversy. Instead of firing Carpenter, it looks like he's going to fire Wells.

Maybe that triggered something. Maybe there's a falling out, because Carpenter didn't get fired and Wells isn't able to pay X the money he promised. Or maybe they don't have a falling out, but X doesn't feel safe with Wells knowing who he is. Maybe he's already got Wells's money, and he decides he wants to get rid of the only person who can tie him to the crime.

For whatever reason, X wants Wells dead. So he calls him up, tells him he's got the goods on Carpenter that will really get rid of her . . . and everything goes just as you described it in your reconstruction.

Is this worth looking into?

Pete

ST. LOUIS COUNTY POLICE DEPARTMENT

Memo of Transmission   Date: November 14

From: Detective Raymond R. Robertson
To: Detective Lieutenant Peter Keefer, Major Case Squad
Case Number: 35-2300-1095

Peter:

Your scenario making Wells into a co-conspirator sounds good. Unfortunately, it has a hole in it big enough to drive a dump truck through.

Consider: X has no reason to send a Watcher letter to Joan Carpenter. He can just kill Wells without the slightest nod in her direction. Since Carpenter did get a Watcher letter, the Watcher isn't likely to have been (Wells + X). The Watcher is probably X alone, whoever X may be.

On the other hand, if you had suggested that Carpenter quit her job because she had a falling out over something with a co-conspirator, I would tell you it's an idea we ought to keep in mind. I automatically distrust people who explain their actions by appealing to noble reasons.

I guess it's hard to think about crisis-budgeting and a real crisis at the same time.

Sorry I have to be the one to deliver the news that your story stinks.

Ray

ST. LOUIS COUNTY POLICE DEPARTMENT

Memo of Transmission   **Date:** November 15

From: Detective Lieutenant Peter Keefer, Major Case Squad
To: Detective Raymond R. Robertson
Case Number: 35-2300-1095

Ray:

I guess it's a sign of good morale to have you laughing in my face, instead of behind my back. You're right that turning Wells into a co-conspirator makes no real sense. Maybe I should give up on hypotheses until we develop some more information.

Still, I've got a couple of ideas that lay out some lines of investigation.

1. When did Wells get the call?

I think I can narrow down the time, maybe even to a single day. Check this.

(a) On Tuesday Wells hadn't been to the studio yet, and Patsy Wells says he didn't get any calls at home. She also says she's sure he didn't talk to anybody over the weekend that she didn't know about. That eliminates Tuesday, Sunday, and Saturday.

(b) Taking the Watcher connection at face value, the call to Wells was prompted by *Nightbeat* last Wednesday. Probably the Watcher didn't make the call until he had written his letter to Joan Carpenter telling her he was angry that we've made her a victim and that he's going to do something to prove she isn't the Watcher and wasn't involved in the Kline case. (Her interpretation—that the Watcher might be going to turn himself in—is either a touchingly sweet belief in basic human goodness or a remarkably shrewd piece of deception.)

Since Carpenter received the letter on Friday, it was probably written and mailed either Wednesday night or Thursday morning. The Watcher's call to Wells probably didn't come any earlier than Friday. But that seems too early for the Watcher to have worked out a plan and set things up. Also, it would be unnecessarily risky to tell Wells what you want him to do too far in advance. That would increase the risk that he might talk.

Taking all these factors into account, I think our best bet is that the Watcher (assuming he is X) called Wells on Monday.

2. Who called Wells? (Who is X? Who is the Watcher?)

I can't give any names, but I think we can eliminate some possibilities. Your point about not mentioning your name to somebody you're planning to kill is a good one, and we can push it further. I think we can say that the perpetrator either was not someone Wells knew or at least wasn't someone he knew well enough to recognize by the voice on the telephone.

This makes it unlikely that somebody like Charles Fishwater called. I assume we already agree that it's not likely that Joan Carpenter herself called. Thus we should concentrate the investigation on people Carpenter knows but Wells didn't know or didn't know well.

I'm making our usual assumption here that the Watcher is not a stranger to Carpenter. She says she believes otherwise, but mostly that's because she accepts the "erotomania" explanation she got from her sister. She doesn't think anybody close to her could be so obsessed with her without her knowing it. And she says that even the people who "like her a lot" don't seem fixated on her.

But even if we buy the erotomania explanation, I don't think that means we should do anything any different than we're doing. (The whole business sounds screwy to me, but I don't want to say it's wrong.)

3. Why did Wells agree to go to the Stringer house?

Let's assume that X met Wells somewhere at 7:00, just as they had planned. Wells must not have been afraid to meet at or go to the Stringer house. Even granting that Wells had no grounds for believing anybody was out to get him, he was a big-city reporter. Why would he let himself be put into a risky situation in which he is isolated from other people?

One possibility is that X turned out to be somebody Wells recognized and so saw no reason to be afraid of. Another possibility is that Wells didn't recognize him but thought he could handle him.

A third possibility is that X pulled a gun on him and forced him to drive there. This is incompatible with the other two possibilities, but since it doesn't have any consequences for the investigation, we can ignore it for the moment.

Chief Blackshire is taking a very close interest in this case. But don't let this bother you. That's my worry.

Pete

THE SATURN AGENCY
256 East 59th Street • New York, New York • 10020
212-555-5050 • Fax 212-555-5051
Daniel L. Saturn, PRESIDENT

November 15

Dear Joan:

I have talked to Simon Rostovsky, and I have talked to Charles Fishwater. I have even talked to my mother. I have talked to the first two several times in the last three days.

Everybody agrees you have a legitimate complaint. I didn't try to get Fishwater to say you were "played for a sucker," as you put the point to me, but he did say he had made an "error in judgment" in not discussing the Wells tape with you. He does *not* think he made any kind of error in showing it. (He admits that the FCC might have a different view. Apparently they've requested their own copy of the tape.)

Simon (I still call him that) agreed that Fishwater had gone too far in exercising his powers as executive producer. "Contractually, he has the prerogative of putting on whatever he decides to without saying boo to a ghost. But, Dan, you and I know we aren't talking law here. We're talking creative and highly volatile personalities. I'll agree with Joan that Charles took too much on himself and shut her out in the cold. He shouldn't have done it the way he did."

They both talk like that, and they do it for a long time and in a repetitious fashion. But something else they also say, and manage to repeat several times during every conversation, is that *Nightbeat* is a local show that has suddenly become nationally known. Simon read me a list of places that have done stories on the Wells incident: the two *Times*-es (NY and LA), *USA Today,* UPI, AP, Reuters, CBS, NBC, ABC, CNN . . . The alphabet soup goes on, because I just jotted down the major ones. You can be sure that *Time, Newsweek, People,* and of course the *National Enquirer* are going to give the story some space.

Rostovsky and Fishwater are both glowing with pride at getting such blanket national—nay, international—coverage. They know the stories aren't filled with praise for Fishwater's decision to show the tape, although Simon told me an editorial in the *Tulsa Tribune* said Fishwater demonstrated "great moral courage" by putting news ahead of "good taste."

Also, both of them have seen the stories containing quotes from people in the industry who say KMIS is run by perverts and ghouls. But do I have to tell you that the broadcasters who question the propriety of showing the tape also show the tape to question the propriety? Fishwater helpfully provided sound bites from the broadcast to any who asked.

Despite the fact that the station's news division isn't going to win the Peabody Good Taste Award, the attention makes Rostovsky and Fishwater like boys in a New Orleans strip joint for the first time— embarrassed, fascinated, and feeling very grown up. They've heard about it, now they get to see it for themselves.

None of this changes the fact that they want you back. That's why they talk to me so much. Simon asked me what it would take, would more money do it? I said (shocking myself in the process) that the issue wasn't about money, but about what it has been from the beginning—your wanting to have more editorial control and being more than a hired mouth in a pretty face.

Unlike last month, both of them now seem to think you've got a perfectly sensible gripe on this score. At the same time, though, they talk as if you've had genuine editorial control all along. I agreed that you did, then suggested that you wanted more. I could hear their eyes narrowing on the phone.

"How much does she want?" Simon asks.

"Equal to Fishwater," I say.

"No problem," he says.

And of course he'll be glad to put it into a contract. He'll make you co-producer of *Nightbeat,* and Fishwater will keep his title of Executive Producer, which will also make him Co-Producer. Whenever the two of you can't work things out, Rostovsky himself will resolve the issue.

Does this appeal to you in the slightest?

They are also willing to let you be the sole anchor of *Nightbeat,* assuming that's the way you want to run the program.

As you can tell, they are eager to get you back, and they are particularly eager to get you back in time to do next week's show. Since they still plan to devote the entire program to the Watcher, they realize something would be missing if they did it without you.

From our point of view, this means that if you aren't ready to decide whether you want back in the game *right now,* we're going to have a weaker bargaining position later on.

I know you must still be very pissed off at Fishwater, but don't cut your own throat in the mistaken belief that it's going to make him bleed to death. (Sorry about the tasteless metaphor.) They've got a lot to lose, but then so do you.

Don't you still want to be a star and have delis naming sandwiches after you? Don't you want to be inundated by a tide of Schweppes and endorsement money? Don't you still have the American Dream?

If any of this sounds good to you, let me know. It doesn't have to sound *perfect,* just good. We can always negotiate.

I hope you're taking care of yourself. If you will permit a suggestion, don't lie around the house all the time. Try to walk at least three miles a day, and take stress-formulated vitamin compounds. Make sure they have zinc in them.

Please call or fax me as soon as you've had enough time to think things over. "If done, then 'tis well it were done quickly," to borrow a sentiment from Lady McB.

Dan

FAX TRANSMITTAL 314-552-5671

JOAN CARPENTER
2030 Buckminster • St. Louis, MO • 63130

15 Nov/Sun

Dear Dan,

A basic question left unanswered by classical scholarship is how Achilles managed to spend any time at all sulking in his tent. Sitting around with nothing to do except wonder what to do is indescribably boring.

God knows I've gone through a list of possibilities. I haven't done enough to write my memoirs, and I don't know enough to write more than two pages on any topic. I thought of doing a kind of *Sorrows of Young Joan,* but I decided that even my mother wouldn't want to read about how the reserve books were never on the shelves at the Barnard library and how I would become racked by paroxysms of anger every time Peter Prompt Laundry lost my favorite socks. (Come to think of it, the book still might be more interesting than its model.)

Anyway, I'm bored out of my mind, even though I do seem to spend hours giving interviews. After the police got through with me (they were *very* nice this time), the media started. Not only have the *Post-Dispatch* and *Riverfront Times* reporters called, but I've heard from the stringers for *Newsweek, Time, U.S. News,* the *New York Times,* AP, UPI, and the *Wall Street Journal.* I chatted with a newswoman from CNN and even had a live radio interview (by telephone) on an L.A.–based syndicated show called "Talk Time."

I agree to talk to every legitimate reporter (and a few marginal ones) for fifteen minutes, and during that time I'm careful not to express my true and complete feelings about Fishshit. I tell them KMIS and I just disagree about what a TV news magazine should be doing and that I didn't quit merely because I didn't like the way the Wells tape was handled. No matter how much he deserves it, I don't bad-mouth nobody.

Which is probably just as well, because the terms you mention sound good. Unless CBS calls me in the next six minutes, the KMIS offer is the best one today. Just imagine—me and Fishhead *co-producers.*

Ah, truly this is the great golden land of opportunity, my boy, the place where dreams come true.

But not so fast.

I'm willing to go back if they promise to give me my own side-arm and swagger stick, and I'm willing to do it in time for the show on Wednesday. But here's the rub—I've got some ideas of my own about what I want to do on Wednesday. This happens to be one of the things I've been thinking about while I've been hanging out with Phil Donahue in the mornings and Oprah in the afternoons.

I couldn't have been wronger about the Watcher wanting to give himself up to protect me. In retrospect, even Dr. Joyce Brothers should have been able to read the letter in a much different way.

At first, I felt very upset and depressed when I considered that somebody was willing to kill for me and actually thought it would please me. The whole idea still depresses me, but then I started thinking about how I might take advantage of the Watcher's obsession with me. The fact that he wants to please me surely must give me some kind of power over him, and I ought to be able to use that power to control him.

"So what did you come up with?" you ask.

Like you, most of my ideas come from old movies and what I've seen on TV, and it occurred to me that I might make a stirring public appeal to the Watcher. Do you remember when Rodney King pleaded with people in L.A. to stop the riots? He looked directly into the camera and spoke from the heart. I think what he said and the way he said it made a tremendous difference, and I think I could make the same technique work with the Watcher.

That is, next Wednesday I appear on the show, put on my (genuinely) sincere and concerned expression, stare into the camera and say something like, "Too much blood has been shed. I know you want to help me, but I don't want anybody else to get hurt. And I don't want *you* to get hurt. If you turn yourself over to me, I'll see to it that you get fair treatment."

Obviously I need to spend some time polishing my script, but I'm sure you see what I have in mind. Not meaning to brag, but it seems to me I ought to be able to project enough charm, sincerity, and personality appeal to get somebody who has already declared undying devotion to me to meet me at the foot of the Gateway Arch or some other dramatic place.

I don't, of course, plan to meet the Watcher alone for a tête-à-tête. (He's the one who's crazy, not me.) I expect to be surrounded by a platoon of plainclothes cops who will latch onto the Watcher with hoops of steel as soon as he makes an appearance. They will then, I suppose, whisk him off to the loony bin and treat him with powerful mind-altering drugs, which may not work but will at least get him off the street.

Do you think Rostovsky and Fisheye will go along with my plan to make an appeal? If they won't, then I'm going to have to give some harder and longer thought to deciding whether I want to go back to being one of KMIS's eyes on the Mississippi.

Tell them that with hair the color of honey I can always get a job on the West Coast. And since I'm able to read, I can probably even get a good job. I don't know whether this is true—about getting a job, I mean, I *can* read—but tell them anyway.

I don't feel exactly responsible for the terrible things the Watcher has done, but I would feel a lot better if I could do something to get him locked up. Since I'm the one who just by existing tipped him off balance, I would feel better if I could restore the social equilibrium. I don't see any reason to suppose he's going to become less dangerous now that he's killed Gary Wells.

Now I've got to hurry back to my regular viewing schedule and make sure I'm not missing some fascinating documentary, like one on how pigeon droppings contribute to the problem of global warming. When unemployed, it's always best to keep your mind active.

Call if you have any answers. Otherwise, I'll expect to hear from you before the sun rises twice.

Hopefully (note correct use),
Joan

P.S. Just in case they agree to my terms, I'm going to start working on my Appeal to the Watcher.

ST. LOUIS COUNTY POLICE DEPARTMENT

Memo of Transmission   **Date:** November 15

From: Detective Raymond R. Robertson
To: Detective Lieutenant Peter Keefer, Major Case Squad
Case Number: 35-2300-1095

Peter:

You'll be getting some lengthy 9015s on our interviews with Stephen Legion, Alan Carter, and Curt Collins as soon as we get them typed, but let me boil down the main points.

(1) Dr. Stephen Legion

I took your advice and handled Dr. Legion very discreetly by calling him at his office and arranging to meet him in a conference room at Barnes Hospital.

He seemed quite nervous and expressed the view that I had no reason to be talking to him in connection with Wells. He saw Wells at public and social functions and Wells once interviewed him about cosmetic surgery for men on *Nightbeat*. That's all they ever had to do with one another, Legion said.

When I told him we knew he had gone out with Joan Carpenter, he denied any romantic involvement with her. "Only for a drink," he said. I pushed him a little, and he described her as "a friend my wife wouldn't want me to have." He says his wife is jealous and discourages him from having friendships with women. I think he's not being altogether forthcoming about this matter.

I asked Legion if he had ever written to Carpenter, and he said he had sent her "a note or two." When I asked him if he ever signed his letters "the Watcher," he became very huffy. "You're trying to do the same thing to me Joan denounced you for doing to her," he told me. I asked him if he could type, and he said he could. I dropped the Watcher matter, but I think we ought to pick it up again, maybe get some typing samples from the machines at his home and office.

The most interesting fact to emerge from the interview is that Dr. Legion claims he was in the medical library at the University of Missouri-Columbia Tuesday evening.

He says he left from Barnes around 6:00 and drove the 90 miles to Columbia by himself. He got there around 7:30 and went directly to the medical school. He got a sandwich out of a machine, studied some book in the library, then drove back to St. Louis. He didn't arrive home until around midnight. He says his wife was still awake, but he didn't see anybody he knew at the library or on campus.

So far as we know at this point, no one can testify as to Legion's whereabouts during the six hours between the time he left his office and the time he walked through the back door of his house. Despite the fact that this allows Legion an opportunity to kill Wells, I can't see what motive he could have for doing so.

It's possible that he might want to make Carpenter successful enough to make it worth his while to leave his wife for her. I suggest we talk to Carpenter more about her interest in and involvement with Legion.

(2) Alan Carter

Carter was quite open about his romantic involvement with Joan Carpenter. "I find her a little bossy at times," he told me. "However, she's very sharp, and she's got a great sense of humor. We usually have fun together, but she may be a little more serious about me than I am about her."

I asked him why he thought that, and he just shrugged and said, "I don't know, just an impression. I think she wouldn't mind getting married again and she's sort of shopping for an acceptable man."

When I asked Carter if he had any ideas about who the Watcher might be, he said, "Not really. For no reason at all, I used to suspect Wells. I imagined he was the kind of guy who might have a dual personality and hate Joan and love her at the same time." But he said that after he heard about Wells getting killed, he "couldn't even guess who it might be."

"I don't suppose it could be you?" I asked him. He laughed and said, "That's completely crazy. Why in the world would I want to kill Wells?" I suggested he might do it to help Joan Carpenter. He shook his head and said, "She's doing just fine without any help from me."

Carter told me he had met Wells but says he didn't really know him. They were often at the same social functions. Carter also knows Legion in the same way.

All these people seem to go to the same large parties, but they don't ever see each other anywhere else. I guess that's the way things are when you're "in society."

I went into the typewriter matter in more detail this time. Carter showed me the Memorywriter his secretary uses, and he says he has an old Smith-Corona portable at home. He says he can't remember writing any letters to Joan Carpenter. "I don't write to anybody, if I can help it," he told me. He says if he can't talk to Carpenter directly, he leaves phone messages.

Carter confirmed Carpenter's claim that he was scheduled to be her escort to the Partners in Progress dinner but canceled out because he was supposed to go to Springfield.

As it happened, he told me, when he got to Springfield he found out that his client, who was supposed to be coming from Kansas City to meet him, had plane trouble and couldn't make it.

Carter then flew back to St. Louis. He says he arrived around five in the afternoon. He admits he had plenty of time to phone up Joan Carpenter and tell her he was free to escort her to the PIP dinner. But his story is that his day had been so rotten he didn't feel like doing anything but having dinner at home and going to bed. He says he didn't even stay awake long enough to call Carpenter and ask her about how her speech had gone over.

I've already checked with the flight coordinator's office at St. Louis regional airport, and they confirm that Carter landed there at 4:42 P.M. Tuesday night. After that time, until he showed up at his office at 7:30 Wednesday morning, nobody can vouch for where he was. In light of this, I suggest we continue to take him seriously as a suspect.

(3) Curt Collins

Collins claimed that because his usual client was having a new driveway poured, his scheduled work on Tuesday afternoon was canceled. We have confirmed this and that Collins knew two weeks previously he had the afternoon free.

He says he finished his work for Mrs. Thomas Moran at 6320 Teasberry at 1:00 P.M., ate lunch at the Clayton McDonalds, then went home to take a nap. He was tired because the previous night he had attended a meeting of a writers' group he belongs to and was out past midnight drinking beer and talking.

He says he got up around four o'clock, read the newspaper, and watched the news on TV. Around six he fixed his own dinner, ate it, then sat at his desk to work on poetry. He says he does this every night after work, unless he's too tired.

He told me he received no telephone calls. Although he tried to call a Wednesday client around nine o'clock, he wasn't able to get him. We checked with the client, Charles Reffei of 1623 Kingsland, and learned that no one was home until 10:30.

I got a list of all the people Collins works for. There are 18 in all, but the most surprising name on the list was Mrs. Madelyn Kleene, the lady who spotted the light at the Stringer house and sent her husband to investigate. The Kleenes live at 6340 Meadovale, the next house east from the Stringers'.

I asked Collins if he had ever worked for the Stringers, and he denied it. He did admit since they moved away he had walked around the house and looked in at the windows. I pushed him a little and he said he had also been in the garage. At first he denied he had taken anything, but eventually he admitted he had walked off with a small pair of flower shears. "The people who lived there didn't want them," he said. "It wasn't like stealing, because they just left them. That's the same as throwing them away."

Collins couldn't remember exactly when he had taken the shears. I asked him if it was before or after he went to work for Joan Carpenter. He said it was after, but he couldn't say how long after. He said he was "fairly sure" it was after he heard about the attack on Tom Kline.

I decided not to bring Collins in for further questioning until we get Greg Handler to do some lab tests on the shears. However, maybe I'm being stupid here. Both when Kline was attacked and Wells was lured away and killed, Collins says he was at home, but he can't give us any independent check on it. He had an opportunity in both cases.

Still, after talking to him a couple of times I have to say he doesn't strike me as somebody psychologically capable of carrying out a sequence of actions involving planning and concealment. He seems much too naive and open, too much like a child.

I admit this could be a false impression, but it is consistent with what Joan Carpenter describes as his "puppy love" feelings toward her. She sees him as infatuated with her, but in an ordinary, nonthreatening way. I'm inclined to accept her point of view on this matter (if on no others). Collins doesn't seem anything like John Hinckley or those others who try to force themselves on celebrities.

You may not agree with me about this.

We're still trying to piece together Gary Wells's week from Wednesday to the following Tuesday. The staff at KMIS have been useful for that project, but I don't think we've learned much else of significance from them. If you're interested, I'll send you a detailed schedule that we've constructed.

For my money, Legion and Carter are still our best suspects, assuming the Watcher is somebody known to Carpenter or Wells. If the Watcher is someone belonging to the anonymous audience, then, like you, I have no ideas about how to proceed.

Ray

THE SATURN AGENCY
256 East 59th Street • New York, New York • 10020
212-555-5050 • Fax 212-555-5051
D a n i e l L . S a t u r n, PRESIDENT

November 16

Dear Joan,

I just tried to call you at home and at work, but you were someplace in limbo. (Maybe you should get a car phone, so I can always be sure of getting through to you.)

Before I tell you anything else, I want you to know that in my opinion, you are the most amazing person to hit broadcast journalism since Walter Cronkite left CBS and sailed his sloop off into the sunset.

Having a client quit a job is always a pain, but it's not unusual. After all, clients figure, what's the point of having a personality, if it's not to clash with somebody else's? And they figure, what's the point of having an agent, if it's not to get you more money or more face time or better billing?

So having a client quit over an issue involving more than naked ambition and clothed greed is itself highly unusual. But having a client work out a way of preserving her integrity, while also pleasing the station bosses is rarer than a clean rest room in an airport.

And yet you've found a way to do it.

Having said all these nice things, I have to confess that what I was in such a hurry to tell you is this: *Your plan is nuts.* Maybe that's putting it a little too bluntly, but I want to be sure you get the point.

It's ridiculous to assume the Watcher is going to give himself up, just because you ask him to. You are (I am always the first to say) beautiful, charming, engaging, enticing, beguiling, fascinating, alluring, etc., etc., etc. (as the King of Siam might say).

And yet . . . I think it is highly doubtful that somebody who has shown a great deal of cunning in committing crimes and eluding capture is going to fall under your spell to such an extent that he will step forward and put his neck in the gossamer noose you plan to spin out. It's one thing to ask (à la Rodney King) a whole city to stop rioting and quite another to ask one person to surrender. For some peculiar reason best known to S. Freud or God, it's easier to get a city to do what you want than to get one person to.

You might also consider that if you mount a big public appeal and the Watcher doesn't show up when you ask him to, you'll make a bigger fool of yourself than Geraldo did when he opened up Al Capone's vault and discovered a cache of stale space. The cackling sound you hear will be that of people laughing you off the air.

But that's not what really bothers me. You can always get another job (maybe doing the weather in Enid, Oklahoma, or Bareass, Iowa). What worries me is that *the Watcher might actually show up.*

I know I said it was crazy to think that he would, but crazy things do happen in the world. And if that particular one happened, he might just take the opportunity to express his complete devotion to you by putting a bullet between your eyes. After all, you have no way of knowing that he doesn't think that by killing you and then himself, the two of you can spend the remainder of eternity strolling along the streets of Paradise.

The fact that you plan to be surrounded by all the king's horses and all the king's men doesn't amount to a hill of legumes. Hasn't anybody told you that we live in the Age of Assassination? Haven't you seen those dozens of films of the shooting of Jack and Bobby Kennedy, M. L. King, Ronald Reagan, Jim Brady, Malcolm X, George Wallace, and L. H. Oswald?

Tell me, were these people surrounded by uniformed and plain-clothes cops, Secret Service agents, and personal body-guards? Damned right they were. Protectors swarmed around each of those people, and yet they were all gunned down in daylight and in plain sight.

Now let me summarize what I've said, so you won't miss the point:

(1) The Watcher isn't going to show up, and you'll look like an idiot.

(2) If (against all odds) the Watcher does show up, he may kill you.

I think it's very clever and brave of you to work out a plan for the Watcher to surrender. You are right to think that if it worked, you would be hurled up to stardom and could demand a salary in the gigabuck range. But the risks, Joan, the risks! They just aren't worth it.

I'm very fond of the bottom line, and if you become the laughingstock of mid-America, this will lower your commercial value to less than the price of the high-rag paper a contract is printed on.

Don't misunderstand me, though. I don't care about your pleasing the station bosses or even saving your integrity as much as I care about you personally. When the bottom line is the one on a death certificate, I will do anything possible to keep your name off it.

I know you want me to go to Simon Rostovsky and get you everything you want. But I don't want you to have everything you want, so I'm sorry to have to tell you, I'm not even going to try. Instead, I exhort you to please give up your film-noire scheme and get back to reporting on real estate scandals, the religious beliefs of Canine Americans, and the other grist that the TV mill is waiting to grind out.

I am not only your friend but also

Very Concerned in New York.

FAX TRANSMITTAL 314-552-5671

JOAN CARPENTER
2030 Buckminster · St. Louis, MO · 63130

16 Nov/Mon

Dear Very Concerned:

As my old Latin teacher used to say when we turned in our exams—*Alea jacta est.*

Why am I providing you with a lesson in a dead language? Because I have just spent the last hour having a chat with Mr. Rostovsky, and as a result (to translate for you), "The die is cast." This should make us both happy. You don't have to worry about refusing to struggle to get me something I want but you don't want me to have. And I don't have to worry about getting a new agent. (Just kidding.)

Minutes after I got your cease-and-desist fax, Simon (as I, too, now call him) phoned me and asked me to drop by his office for a little chat. Since you had already poured polyunsaturated oil on the troubled waters, I saw this as a gesture of peace and said I'd be pleased to come.

We had tea, and I feasted on Pepperidge Farm Tahiti cookies (three, I regret to say) and a large serving of conciliatory smiles. Simon was as nice as pie and asked me what I had in mind for next week's program ("assuming you decide to rejoin your KMIS colleagues"). I saw this as a chance to apply my litmus test and see if Simon turned the right shade of red, so I outlined my plan to become the Pied Piper and charm the Watcher into the hands of the police and mental health professionals.

Simon was delighted with the proposal, and right on the spot, he called up Fishwater and told him about it. Fishwater apparently regarded the idea as roughly equivalent in importance to the collapse of the Soviet Union. (Could these guys be trying to flatter me a little? Or maybe they want to get the FCC off their backs by doing public service instead of paying out big bucks in fines. Or maybe they're just right-thinking, God-fearing Americans.)

So far as they are concerned, the plan has a green light, and so far as I'm concerned, I'm once again a KMIS employee. Please work out the details, assuming you still want to represent a client who is more trouble than Bonzo the Chimp.

Simon guaranteed me that I'll have carte blanche in deciding exactly how I make my appeal to the Watcher. Fishwater will handle the rest of Wednesday's program (assuming that I, as co-producer, agree to it), and all I have to do is concentrate on polishing my pitch. (Simon says—Take one giant step.)

You may be pleased to hear that Wednesday is going to be a big day, audience-wise. Simon says Fishwater estimates that when word spreads that I'm going to be back for the special Watcher program, the audience will be double last week's size—and that set a *Nightbeat* record. (Simon omitted to mention that last week's numbers can probably be attributed to Fishwater's showing the tape of Wells's death and the controversy I produced by quitting over it. Probably he was just being diplomatic.)

However, another big plus in this makes me uncomfortable. Since the Watcher situation has turned into a nationwide media event, Simon is expecting people throughout the country watching on Wednesday to see what happens. He's also sure that my appeal to the Watcher will get national play. The situation is too inherently dramatic for the media to pass up.

It's obvious that all this will help my career. I'll get the sort of national exposure that will call me to the attention of the networks and big stations in major markets. I feel bad about this, because I think it's ghoulish to be helped this way. I certainly don't plan to make a plea to the Watcher because it's a good career move. Yet that's the way it looks.

I've tried using the jesuitical training I got at Barnard to convince myself that an act performed to attain a morally legitimate aim continues to be morally legitimate, even if the unintended consequence of the act is to bring benefit to one's self. I've almost convinced myself of this, but I'm pretty stubborn.

I don't expect you to be thrilled by all this news. But really, Dan, everything is going to be all right.

KMIS Employee 65-48-2300

THE SATURN AGENCY
256 East 59th Street • New York, New York • 10020
212-555-5050 • Fax 212-555-5051
D a n i e l L . S a t u r n , PRESIDENT

16 November

Dear Joan:

I know your fax machine receives my letters, but is it also the only one *reading* them?

The reason I sound a little miffed is that I am. Although I'm glad you and Simon and Chuck have now agreed to be friends forever, I can't pretend to be happy about their going along with your plan to make a public plea to the Watcher. They just see the chance for lots of publicity that will boost ratings sky-high, so their agenda isn't necessarily in your best interest.

But quite apart from that and more to the point, you didn't say *one* thing about all the problems I mentioned when I wrote to you about your plan. Can you tell me in all honesty that you at least gave a few seconds of thought to them before you committed yourself to going public on Wednesday?

As we say in the negotiating business, you didn't address my concerns. Or at least you didn't address them to me and I don't see any evidence that you addressed them at all. Of course, you probably think I'm suffering from disordered thinking as a result of chlorophyll poisoning, so why should you take me seriously.

Maybe you should consider getting somebody to represent you who doesn't care anything about you. That might make it easier on both of us.

Dan

FAX TRANSMITTAL 314-552-5671

JOAN CARPENTER
2030 Buckminster • St. Louis, MO • 63130

16 Nov/Mon

Darling Dan,

I'm sorry.

I realize now that I let myself get carried away with my schemes and strategies and that I hurt your feelings by appearing not to take your worries seriously.

Believe me, though, I gave careful consideration to the issues you raised before I even talked to Simon and Chucklehead (I better stop this stuff, now that he and I are allies). Honestly, I took you as seriously as the depletion of the ozone layer and as solemnly as a child's promise. To prove I ain't talking no trash, permit me to adopt my best debate-team style and address what I see as your basic concerns.

You say: The Watcher isn't going to show up, so I'm going to look like a bigger clown than Ronald McDonald. When that happens, I'll be out of a job and will have to spend the rest of my days happy-talking in front of a weather map in Mulebutt, Montana.

But I reply: Although I *do* want the Watcher to cast himself at my feet like a sinner come to judgment, even if he doesn't, all is not lost. By opening a line of communication with the Watcher, I believe I can influence his actions. If I talk directly to him for a couple of minutes a week ("a regular feature of this program"), then in a month or so, I'm sure I can *at least* get him to quit killing people. That's worth more than a kick in the teeth. Right?

Also, by getting the public deeply involved in the Watcher story, I'll turn every viewer into a detective. The Watcher will find it hard to pass invisibly when doing his dirty deeds, and I'll lay you diamonds to doughnuts that somebody will turn him in before you see the first snowflake fall in Central Park.

As to making a fool of myself, the Geraldo-Capone episode was quite another vault of fish. The whole point of Geraldo's "special" was to open the door and find something surprising. It was a one-shot concept, and if the shot was a dud, so was the show. But as I said, I'm planning for more. If the Watcher doesn't show, I'll have a follow-up . . . and then another.

You say: I'm going to be taking a risk big as the Texas sky, because the Watcher might just decide to stick a knife in me and open me up like a special-delivery envelope.

But I reply: Although I don't think the Watcher is likely to try to cause me any harm, I intend to take precautions that border on the unreasonable. I'm going to be in plain view at all times, and I'll make sure I'm surrounded by a blue halo of cops.

After saying this, though, I also have to quote once again the immortal words of Doris Day: *Que sera sera.* Everything in the world worth doing comes complete with a tag that says RISK in big red letters. As my daddy used to tell me, if you're not ready for trouble, you're not ready for life. And I am ready for life. ("She gave a brave smile, hitched up her gunbelt, then rode toward town.")

I'm sure I've now put all your doubts to rest, so please accept my apology and let's say no more on the topic. You can still be my agent, and we can still be friends.

(By the way, unless you kick me out the door, I'm about as likely to change agents as a leopard is to swap his suit for a set of Brooks Brothers pin stripes. The very idea makes my eyes quiver with tears and my mind shudder with existential *angst*.)

I'll let you know exactly what I'm going to do on Wednesday when I know myself. I really don't mind if you worry about me, at least a reasonable amount. I would hate it if you didn't care.

Besides, when you're worrying about me, you won't be worrying about yourself. If nothing less, this should put a little variety in your life. (Just kidding, Dan.)

> Friends forever,
> Joan

It's Dan, Joan.

I just called to tell you that you win. I accept the apology, and we're friends again.

I really wish you weren't "half in love with easeful death," but I realize now that there's nothing I can do to stop you. It probably has something to do with growing up in Texas.

I'll call up Simon Rostovsky and work out the details of your rehiring. The only good to come from all this trouble is that you're going to make out like a bandit when we negotiate the new contract.

And of course all the publicity is going to make you more marketable than fat-free potato chips. But you shouldn't feel bad about this. It's just the silver lining in the dark cloud the Watcher has hung over you.

Don't forget to keep me informed about what you do and say on Wednesday. In a sense, I don't really want to know, but I also can't stand not knowing—if you see what I mean.

And, Joan, don't take any chances you don't have to. You're a reporter and a TV anchor, you're not Diana Prince or Nancy Drew.

Take care of yourself and watch your back. I'll talk to you soon.

Bye for now.

Ms. Joan Carpenter
Star of *Nightbeat*
KMIS-TV

November 16

My darling Joan,

When you looked into the camera at the beginning of last Wednesday's show and smiled, I knew you were thanking me for sending the Wells tape.

Oh, Joan, that sweet, innocent, yet so-knowing smile! How wonderful it is! How it lights up the screen and warms my heart! We share a lot of hopes and ambitions now, and i was glad to see you pay tribute to our relationship with your subtle little smile.

At first I thought you might mention me on the show in an indirect way. You might say something like "A close friend has arranged for us to have a ringside seat on a special event this evening." I have to admit I was rather hoping you would, because I wanted people to know I was in your thoughts.

When you didn't say anything like that, I decided you didn't want to ruin the surprise of seeing the tape. I also realized that even though only i could recognize your smile as a secret signal, that was acknowledgment enough. Indeed, my sweet Joan, that's the way it should be. You and I have our secrets, and by shutting others out, they bring us closer.

I was also just a little surprised when you didn't introduce the Wells tape yourself but let the substitute do it. Well, Joan's the professional, I told myself, and I'm sure she's doing it the best way possible.

After turning the matter over in my mind for a while, I saw the wisdom of your plan. You see, at first I thought you'd want to do the lead-in to associate yourself with the Wells tape, because it's sure to become a classic of broadcasting. Then I realized you actually wanted to keep some distance between you and the tape. That way people wouldn't think you had anything to do with what happened to Gary Wells. Oh, my dear, you are so very clever! (I'm sure I'm right, but tell me that I am anyway.)

If you think my analysis of your strategy shows a good grasp of the way television works, maybe I could get a job as a media consultant. That way you and I could work together in the same business. Wouldn't that be great!

Speaking of media consultants, you could be one yourself. You are an expert! Quitting the show was a brilliant move, and I have to admit that particular strategy didn't even cross my mind. When I heard about it, I was totally astonished and didn't know what to think. Then when I saw on the local news that you were going back to *Nightbeat,* it became clear to me that you wanted to attract even more attention to the show. Did you have trouble persuading the producers and others to go along with your plan?

If you don't mind more praise, I want to tell you that your reaction to the tape of Wells was also terrific. You looked genuinely upset when the camera was on you, but in your eyes I could still see a little glint of light that told me you were glad he was dead.

I'm glad he's dead. My blood still boils when I remember how he humiliated you all the time on the show. I'll never forgive him for his "where there's smoke, there's fire" remark—as though he *knew* something about you that no one else did.

I'm sure you'll agree that he deserved to die a horrible death. But, Joan, I'm not a monster. I can't help feeling some sympathy even for a slimy little toad like Gary Wells, so I took all the necessary steps to make sure he died painlessly. I know you're a tough reporter who has seen a lot of life, and maybe you think I should have arranged something terrible and bloody for Wells. But I'm too much of a softie to do that, even though it would have made a spectacular TV segment.

Still, I think the tape I sent is pretty darned good television anyway. Watch the ratings, my darling. They will go up and up and up. You will become the star you have it in you to be.

And when you're up there in the blue heavens, shining down on us mere mortals, I'll be bursting with pride. I'll know that the two of us together have shaped your destiny and launched you into the sky like a rocket. When you're at the top, that's the time I'll let you know more about me. Then you and I will really get to know each other.

Sometimes when I'm missing you, I imagine we are together and spending long, languid hours that stretch into the future. I imagine it as a time when we can let ourselves be ourselves and enjoy one another.

I have a lot I want to teach you about friendship and loyalty and love. And what do I want from you? Everything and yet nothing. Nothing you're not willing to give.

Good night, sweet Princess.

One who still Watches (and Waits)

FROM THE DESK OF
JOAN CARPENTER

17 Nov/Tue

Alice:

Please call up Lt. Keefer's office and tell him we've got another Watcher letter. (This one may be the worst of the lot. I can't say for sure, because I can't get myself to read it carefully.) If they want to send somebody over to pick it up, that's fine. However, tell them I'm not free to talk to anybody until Thursday. They've got to get the letter then git. I've got work to do.

Speaking of which, be careful not to let anything slip about tomorrow's show. I suspect if the police knew I was going to make a public plea to the Watcher, they both would and could stop me.

The times are not only a-changing, they're getting hard. But when all this is over, we'll go to the Godiva store and buy a crate of mixed creams. (Until then, there's always Milk Duds.)

JC

ST. LOUIS COUNTY POLICE DEPARTMENT

Memo of Transmission   Date: November 17

From: Detective Raymond R. Robertson
To: Detective Lieutenant Peter Keefer, Major Case Squad
Case Number: 35-2300-1095

Peter:

I put Calvin Gill onto tracking down the towel that was stuffed in the window of the Wells car. (It was a JC Penney "Fashion Flair" towel that still had the sizing in it.) Gill called me to say his people had done a computer search of credit card purchases for the previous six months. (It wasn't as easy as it sounds, and if you want to know the details, ask Gill. But you shouldn't ask unless you *really* want to know and can spare about two hours.)

Gill's group turned up two names familiar to us: Alice Walcheck and Alexis Hartz. We've got the dates of purchase, and it seems that each bought towels during the same spring sale during the week March 12-19.

I recommend that we interrogate them both and focus on this matter. We may have been looking at the wrong people for the right reasons.

Ray

ST. LOUIS COUNTY POLICE DEPARTMENT

Memo of Transmission   Date: November 17

From: Detective Lieutenant Peter Keefer, Major Case Squad
To: Detective Raymond R. Robertson
Case Number: 35-2300-1095

Ray:

Congratulations to Gill and his people on establishing a connection between the "Fashion Flair" towel and Walcheck and Hartz.

Since we were planning on talking to Hartz anyway, you can just add this item to your agenda with her. If you have time, you should talk to Walcheck yourself. We've got a couple of 9015s on her. I looked them over, and they don't seem to say much to help. We weren't focused on her as a suspect, though. Maybe you can get more out of her this time.

We definitely should interrogate both people. We're quite short of physical evidence in this case, and anything that might let us establish a link between the Watcher and a suspect is not something we can afford to overlook.

I don't think you should expect too much, though. Neither of these people strike me as likely to be prepared to kill for Joan Carpenter. But I'd be the first to admit that I could be wrong. I've seen too many killers in the last twelve years to think you can look at one and read his actions off his face.

Here's why I say don't count on too much:

(a) We've got the names of only people who used their credit cards to buy towels. Anybody could have paid cash at any time and left no record.

I looked up the locations of the stores in the Yellow Pages. I found out that Curt Collins lives about two blocks from a Penney's store and that Alan Carter's office is right down the street from one. Unfortunately for us, the stores are easily accessible to everybody we could consider a suspect.

(b) I called Greg Handler to see if he had been able to find any fibers, marks, hairs, or stains. He's found only fibers, and they can all be connected with material that seems unique to the crime

239

scene. (Dust and fibers from the garage and Wells's car, to be less technical about it.)

Still, maybe one of them will confess when you tell them you've connected them with the towel used to stuff the window.

Pete

ST. LOUIS COUNTY POLICE DEPARTMENT

Memo of Transmission   Date: November 17

From: Detective Raymond R. Robertson
To: Detective Lieutenant Peter Keefer, Major Case Squad
Case Number: 35-2300-1095

Peter:

I was going to send Martha Higgens to talk to Alexis Hartz, but in view of the "Fashion Flair" towel matter, I decided to go along with her. I've been on the job so long I've got a vested interest in believing that experience counts for something.

We went to Ms. Hartz's house around eleven, and she didn't seem sorry to see us. She fluttered around a little, but she gave the impression of someone glad to be in on the excitement. She showed us into her living room and insisted on giving us coffee. She appeared shy at first, but within a few minutes it was clear that she likes to talk. I suppose if you sell real estate that's a good trait to have.

Speaking of real estate, you may remember that Hartz sold Carpenter her house. Maybe you don't know, though, that Carpenter lives right behind Hartz on the next block. Hartz says they chat across the hedge, and particularly right after Carpenter moved in, Hartz helped her get settled and gave her the lowdown on St. Louis.

I don't know if you recall this, but Joan Carpenter mentioned Hartz as somebody who could establish that she was giving her PIP speech when she said she was. (She showed me a letter from Hartz saying what a good job she had done.) So I started out with that topic, as if all I was interested in was a routine confirmation.

For the record, Hartz did confirm Carpenter was present at the PIP dinner on Tuesday. She said if we wanted another crosscheck, we could talk with Loretta Kirby, the Director of PIP. I don't consider this necessary. (We could also ask Mayor Kinney, but I don't expect he would appreciate being dragged in on a homicide investigation.)

While I was checking times, I asked Ms. Hartz if she could recall her own whereabouts around midnight to 1:00 A.M. on the night Kline was attacked. She said she's always home and asleep by that time on a weeknight, but since she lives alone, she couldn't name anyone to back her up for that particular day.

For what it's worth, Higgens and I determined that it would have been possible for Hartz to have mailed the Kline package and the Wells videotape on the relevant Wednesdays. She gets to her office around seven every morning, and if she doesn't have any appointments, she drives around alone looking at new listings. According to her calendar, she didn't have appointments during either of the times someone left a package at the Zip-Zip Express office.

I asked Hartz if she considered herself a particular friend of Carpenter. She said she thought they were on the way to becoming friends, although Joan was quite busy with her job and so they hadn't spent as much time together recently as they had at first. I then asked the usual question about whether Carpenter had ever tried to get her to do anything illegal, and she seemed more amused than shocked by the idea. (I think people have seen too many movies and TV shows about cops. They always seem to anticipate your questions.)

She reacted the same way when I suggested she might be willing to lie if it would help her friend. "Not at all," she told me. "The only people who lie are those who have something to hide, and I certainly have nothing I want to conceal. I'm sure the same is true of Joan." She made it sound as if the idea that either of them was less than Simon pure was completely absurd.

"Could you tell me about the way the Maxim Corporation got the land for the Park Central Mall?" I asked her.

This time she did seem a little surprised. "I guess Joan must have mentioned something about that," she said. "I can't tell you much, because I don't know much. I do know that some people on the city council bought some property very cheaply less than a year before they were asked to approve Maxim's petition for a zoning change."

She gave me three names, and I passed them on to Alvin Schwartz in Fraud. Quite frankly, on the basis of what she told me, I can't see any connection between the zoning matter and our two cases.

I had coached Martha to come in with the tough question. "Did you purchase some towels from JC Penney's on March 11?" Martha asked her.

I was watching Hartz carefully, and she didn't miss a beat. "I believe I did," she said. "I don't know about the exact date, of course, but it was some time last spring. I remember, because I bought the towels to send to the Watson School's Household Fair. They collect sheets and towels and that sort of thing to give to poor families, and they do it every spring around the time of the white sales."

I asked her if she had a receipt for her contribution. She said she would have to check with her accountant, who has all her records. I asked her to do that, but I'd be surprised if she has one. Only the IRS would expect her to.

"Do you type?" I asked her. "I used to be very good," she said. "Now I use a word processor at the office, and of course I write all my letters with a pen. I haven't even owned a typewriter in at least five years."

I pushed on with my equipment list. "Do you have a video camera?" I asked. "We have two at the office," she said. "Some of the younger people use one to tape clients walking through houses they're considering buying. They then give the tape to the clients. It seems marvelously effective in promoting a sale, but you can't teach an old dog new tricks. I just talk to people."

We should get Greg Handler to take a look at the equipment and see if it could have been used for the Wells tape. But unless something else turns up, I would say that the Hartz interrogation ran into nothing but dead ends.

It was far from being a waste of time, though. During our general conversation with Hartz, Martha and I picked up a couple of pieces of information that could be highly relevant to our investigation:

(1) Ms. Hartz does a lot of business in upscale neighborhoods, so she is quite familiar with the layout of Oakbrook Hills. When

Higgens asked her if she knew Dr. Stephen Legion, she said she had encountered him several times at large parties but didn't know him well. "I know where he lives, though," she told Higgens. "In fact, he lives very near the Stringer house."

Of course, we had his address (1640 Overcreek Avenue), but nobody in our income bracket knew it was in Oakbrook Hills. I looked at a map and located Overcreek, then realized that Dr. Legion lives just *three blocks* away from the scene of the Wells homicide.

The walking time is eight minutes or less. (I know this, because I walked it myself this afternoon.) Somebody in a hurry could make it in four or five minutes. Since it's the sort of neighborhood where people jog at all hours of the day, somebody running along the street wouldn't look suspicious.

(2) Gateway Realty is handling the Stringer house, but it's also open-listed. Ms. Hartz knew it was for sale, and she said some of her people have taken clients to see it. But the interesting thing is that she also knew that the renovation is being done by—Carter Construction.

This is information I would have expected Alan Carter to volunteer.

I think we should reinterrogate both Legion and Carter on these topics. And this time we should put on a little more pressure. I don't like it when people force you to drag information out of them. It makes me suspicious.

Ray

YOU HAVE REACHED 552-8076. AT THE TONE YOU MAY LEAVE A MESSAGE.

This is Alexis, Joan.

I'm sorry to bother you this way. I'm sure you're as busy as a bee, and I'll only keep you a minute.

I thought you ought to know that the police came by my house this afternoon. They asked lots of questions about you and wanted to know if I knew that newspaper reporter or Mr. Wells. I talked to them, but I couldn't tell them anything that was of any help, I'm sure.

I almost laughed at one point. They wanted to know if you had ever asked me to do anything illegal or tell any lies. I told them the very idea was absurd. They were like the police in a movie, so silly.

By the way, they seemed to know all about the real estate matter I discussed with you. I don't suppose there was any real reason you shouldn't have told them about it, but please don't let anyone else know your source. My business would suffer if just a few influential people heard that I was talking to a reporter about them.

I'll be glad to see you when you can find some time. Maybe we can have lunch at Bernard's again.

Bye for now.

ST. LOUIS COUNTY POLICE DEPARTMENT

Memo of Transmission   Date: November 17

From: Detective Lieutenant Peter Keefer, Major Case Squad
To: Detective Raymond R. Robertson
Case Number: 35-2300-1090, -1095

Ray:

Thanks for the briefing on the Hartz interrogation. I agree that the most interesting thing to come out of it was the recognition that both Carter and Legion have easy access to the Stringer place. Let's talk to them again and lean a little on their lack of confirmable alibis.

Legion, in particular, seems to me to be somebody likely to become obsessed with Carpenter, yet not able to do anything about it directly because of his marriage. As I said before, I don't see him leaving his wife for Carpenter right now, because he would also have to give up his dream of founding a plastic surgery clinic for the rich and famous. But if Carpenter became as rich as his wife, she might become a possibility for him.

Carpenter says the clinic is Legion's main topic of conversation, and he might be trying to find a way to have her and it too.

Here are a couple of matters you should know about:

(1) George Crane questioned Alice Walcheck, her husband, and her daughter and came up with essentially nothing that helps us. Walcheck showed Crane some towels she told him were the ones she had bought at JC Penney, but we have no way to tell whether they are the right towels or not. She might have bought them two years ago.

As it turns out, Walcheck's husband isn't able to provide her with a time check for either period relevant to the Kline or the Wells cases. He is pilot for American Airlines, and was on trips on days that overlapped both those time slots.

Their daughter, Melanie, is eleven, but she was in no position to confirm her mother's whereabouts either. Walcheck could have left Melanie home alone and asleep for the hour or less it would have taken her to drive down to the *Post-Dispatch* parking garage, attack Kline, then drive back.

When Wells was killed, Melanie was at a Girl Scout meeting, then slept over at a friend's house. (That was so they could spend the rest of the evening working on a school computer project. The friend has a computer, Melanie doesn't.) Her mother *didn't* call to check on her, but then Melanie says she asked her not to. "It's too embarrassing," she told Crane.

We already know that Walcheck has enough flexibility on her job that she could have gone to Zip-Zip at the times she would have had to mail packages. Walcheck has standing responsibilities and Carpenter gives her jobs to do, but she is the only person who keeps track of her time. With the help of voice mail, she can always disappear for an hour or two without anyone missing her. Walcheck types, of course, and she has easy access to the IBM typewriters at the station. I suppose we could get a warrant and look for the typing ball used on the Watcher letters.

My own impression from talking to Walcheck is that she's just as straight as she seems. She doesn't appear to be in awe of Carpenter or to harbor any grudges or bad feelings toward her. She seems to like Carpenter, but I don't see her putting herself and her family at risk to promote Carpenter's career. Despite the fact that she was in the position to do everything we attribute to the Watcher, I am quite confident that she didn't.

(Now that I've said that, let me take part of it back. If there is anything to the "erotomania" business that Carpenter talks about, I guess it's possible that Walcheck might be fixated on Carpenter in a way that's not obvious to anybody. Let's not forget about her.)

(2) Greg Handler called me to say that the flower shears you got from Curt Collins show traces of blood on the blades. The blood is O-positive, the same type as Kline's.

Greg says he wants to do some blood antigen studies to see if he can get a "significant match." I'm not sure what this means, except that a close match makes it more likely that the blood is Kline's. Greg says it's the step just short of getting a genetic fingerprint.

For my money, Collins is looking more and more like our prime suspect. He could fit the Watcher profile, and timewise he's possible for both the Kline and Wells crimes, as well as for mailing the packages. I don't guess I'd want to make much out of the poetry connection, but for whatever it's worth, it's there.

Since Collins had the shears in his possession, we can get a search warrant just for the asking, but I don't think we should bother with that yet. I suspect there's nothing to find, and getting a warrant might just spook him.

Instead, let's talk to him again about Wells and last Tuesday night. This time, though, let's get him on our turf. We won't charge him with anything but just pull him in for a chat.

If we don't solve the Kline-Wells case, we might as well start looking for some job like running a speed trap in Potosi or checking dog licenses in Flat River. The big cities aren't going to want us.

Keep up the work and hope it's good.

Pete

ST. LOUIS COUNTY POLICE DEPARTMENT

Memo of Transmission   Date: November 17

From: Detective Lieutenant Peter Keefer, Major Case Squad
To: Chief of Police Harold C. Blackshire
Case Number: 35-2300-1090, -1095

Harold:

Working on the Kline-Wells cases has been like running in place. We've made a lot of motions and uncovered a lot of suggestive information, but we don't seem to be getting anywhere.

We have enough circumstantial evidence to charge a suspect, and probably we could go to a grand jury and get an indictment. However, we lack the sort of direct physical evidence that convinces juries and makes the rest of us sleep better at night.

We're still plugging away, but to be honest with you, I have to say that I'm not sure we'll be able to come up with what we would like to have. Remember the joke about the drunk who lost his house key in the alley but was looking for it under the streetlight, because it wasn't as dark there? I think we may be doing something just like that.

Throughout both investigations we've taken it for granted that the Watcher is somebody associated with Carpenter and not just one of the tens of thousands of viewers who know her only from TV. Our failure to get evidence that would let us staple the crimes to the coattails of a particular person doesn't prove anything, but several other points do make me wonder. Consider:

(a) If you read through the Watcher letters, you won't find anything about Carpenter's private life that couldn't be learned from TV or the newspapers.

This suggests to me that the writer is genuinely ignorant of personal facts about Carpenter. I say "suggests" and not "proves" because I realize that the absence of such facts might actually be evidence of caution and intelligence on the part of the Watcher.

(b) The people associated with Carpenter are all citizens with no criminal records or histories of mental illness. Most of them are highly respected and visible in the community. All this is even true of Curt Collins, our best suspect. I don't think he's a rocket scientist, but he seems mentally stable. He doesn't do drugs, he pays his rent, and the people he works for say he's reliable and does a good job.

(c) The "erotomania" explanation Carpenter seems to accept may be right. Of course, somebody associated with her could have the kind of fixation on her that she described. But when you look at the police cases, they typically involve strangers who become obsessed with women they don't know. For example, John Hinckley never actually met Jodie Foster, even though he wrote her letters, called her, and staked out her dorm so he could catch a glimpse of her going in and out.

I'm telling you all this so you'll understand me when I say that you shouldn't get your hopes up about a quick arrest. Because of the attention the Kline-Wells cases have gotten, I know you feel pressure to nail somebody quickly. Still, because they're high-profile cases, we would look like idiots if we arrested somebody and couldn't make the charges stick.

I'm not completely convinced we even have the right person in our pool of suspects. We may have to wait for more letters, tapes, and crimes to start us sniffing on the right trail. Or if the Watcher decides to lie low from now on, we may never be able to clear the cases.

I know this is not the sort of thing a Chief likes to hear. But since a realistic assessment is always necessary for damage control, I thought I'd better tell you what I've been thinking. I haven't expressed my views to anybody else, although Ray Robertson seems to have similar doubts from time to time.

Please let me know if you have any suggestions about new lines of investigation. Meanwhile, we're marching down the old ones, even if they might end in stone walls.

Peter

JOAN CARPENTER
2030 Buckminster • St. Louis, MO • 63130

18 Nov/Wed 11:30 P.M.

Dan, my dear boy,

You'll be proud of the way I pulled it off.

If you can forgive me for speaking with more honesty than modesty, I was dyne-o-mite tonight. I flashed like a diamond and shone like gold. I was silk and satin, fur and feathers, fire and ice. I cajoled, pleaded, promised, and assured.

I expressed empathy and anger, understanding and disapproval, concern and condemnation. I had a catch in my voice, and a tear in my eye. Yet I always projected warmth, compassion, and caring, while being stern, demanding, and unyielding.

I was terrific!

I can't get a tape to send you until tomorrow at the earliest or maybe even Friday. I don't want to repeat the whole script for you here, but I can't resist telling you how the magic worked.

My dear friend Charles Fishwater (he's my *co*-producer, you know) and I agreed I would use the last 3.5 minutes of the program to make my plea to the Watcher. After spending a couple of days writing the script, I was up most of last night throwing it away. (It takes a surprising amount of time to throw a script away. My technique is to start with a word at a time, then pick up speed and pitch complete sentences. After a few hours, I can usually see my way to tossing it all and starting over.) By this afternoon, I had a script I was pretty happy with, and by air time, I was even ready to read it on camera.

When I rejoined the happy crew here at KMIS, Charles had already planned out the whole special program on the Watcher. He called it "Watcher in the Night," which has the virtue of sounding evocative while not meaning anything in particular.

I could have flexed my muscle and gotten Charles to do some things differently, but I decided to go along with most of what he had blocked out. I can see already that having power doesn't mean you're always free to use it. The stakes must be high enough to justify the energy you have to invest.

Anyway, along with the Watcher, Charles made me the focal point of the program, because I was (as he kept telling me) at the center of the story. We opened with tape of Ted Broadbent interviewing me. I told him about how I first started getting the Watcher letters and realized they were weird, but didn't think much about them.

I then recounted the story of what happened to Kline. No doubt under Fishwater's guidance, Ted very carefully didn't ask me any questions about just how it happened that the box containing Kline's testicles was opened on *Nightbeat.*

"It must have been a terrible shock to you, when you first looked inside," Ted said.

"It was completely indecent," I told him, hoping that Fishwater and at least three viewers would understand that I was referring to opening the box on live TV.

We next did a piece on Gary Wells. I had decided to go along with Fishwater's plan to use some shots from "the death scene," but I insisted that we only show a couple of stills of Gary's final moments. You know the way programs on the Kennedy assassination show the Zapruder film over and over? I think that's what Charles wanted to do with the Watcher tape, but that was too much for me.

We used some sound bites from my interviews with Chief of Police Blackshire, Detective Raymond Robertson, and the very suave Lieutenant Peter Keefer. Of course, that segment included some scenes from the program where I ripped into the police for the way they treated me. (And I'm still as pissed off about it now as I was then.)

"Do you feel responsible for what happened to Gary Wells?" Ted asked me. "I haven't seen any of the letters from the Watcher, but from what I've heard, Wells was killed to punish the police for searching your house. He was certainly killed in a way that shows you couldn't be a direct participant in causing his death."

"I'm sorry about Gary, but I don't feel responsible for his death," I told Ted. That was a half-truth, but in the circumstances, I wasn't sure I could say enough to make people understand. I wasn't sure I could make myself understand. "He was a broadcast journalist doing his job, and I regret the price he was forced to pay."

This discussion segued into a sort of homage to Gary Wells. Fishwater had assigned a researcher to pull about a dozen of

Wells's tapes and splice together a montage of his career on the program. It played well without much commentary.

At the beginning of the piece, Ted read a tribute to Wells by a writer famous around here for sonorous phrases and uplifting metaphors ("He was our guide along the twisting path of news and public events, but like any good guide, he never failed to nudge our elbows and get us to take a look at real people and their smaller stories of humor and heartbreak."). Ted made it sound nice, and I was glad.

Then, after we broke, it was time to make my pitch.

I wore my navy blue knit dress, because years ago I read in John T. Molloy's column that people are more disposed to like you if you wear blue. I tried to look demure, kind, and approachable— like a person you'd tell your deepest secrets to, then ask her for advice.

"This has been a very personal night for me," I began. "It has also been a painful one, for I have had to recall and discuss matters I would rather forget. I have never admitted this in public before, but the letters the Watcher sends me are intensely personal. He proclaims his passionate attraction to me, and tells me he knows I feel the same way about him. Reading such a letter from a stranger would upset anyone, but that isn't the worst part.

"The worst part is that in some of the letters the Watcher tells me he's performed the terrible actions of mutilation and killing to improve the ratings of this show and to promote my career."

I dropped my reporter's tone and said with real feeling, "I abhor being associated with the crimes the Watcher has committed. If I've benefitted from them, I'm sorry about it. It's not something I want, and it makes me furious for him to think that I approve of what he's done."

My voice rose with anger, and I could feel myself getting worked up. Yet I was careful not to lose control. I didn't want to be seen as ranting. I lowered my voice and said in an earnest tone, "I'm sure the Watcher genuinely thinks he is helping me. He believes he's in love with me and believes he's doing something I want done."

I paused. "I want to talk just to the Watcher now. Everyone else, please excuse me, but I know of no other way to reach him. The rest of you will have to listen in on what ought to be a private conversation." I bowed my head slightly, then looked into the camera.

I gave what I hoped was a sympathetic smile. "I'm sure you're watching me now," I said. "I've said some harsh things tonight, things I'm sure you won't like. But I want you to know that I haven't said anything in an effort to hurt you.

"You've probably already been hurt too much in your life. I imagine you must be quite lonely and your pain very deep and real. I'm addressing myself directly to you tonight, because I want to help ease that pain."

Then I spoke gently, with a touch of hesitancy—the voice of someone nicely asking a favor. "Please listen carefully. I'm going to ask you to do something important."

I paused a beat. "I want you to agree to meet with me—meet with me and talk to me. I want you to tell me about yourself— about your past and your dreams for the future, and if you're willing, about the dark suffering that must lie hidden deep inside." I nodded my head. "I know something about what it's like to suffer. I can sympathize."

I hesitated a moment to give my words a chance to register. "That's the simple proposal I'm making," I said. "That we just get together, you and I. That we meet and talk."

I then began to speak rapidly and earnestly, like a person making a pitch for easy-credit furniture. "I've said I've been angry about some of the things you've done. That's true, but I've also been touched by your feelings toward me. You've tried to help me in ways that seemed right to you, and now I want to do something for you. I want us to meet and discuss what we could do to ease your pain and make your life into what you would like it to be."

I paused and gave the camera a sincere look. "Maybe you're worried about the legal aspects of what you've done. Well, I'm not going to lie to you and say you don't have a problem with the law. But I'll go with you to see an experienced attorney and investigate ways of dealing with it. You won't have to face the problem alone, because I'll do it all with you."

I let my voice become pained as I said, "Consider the alternative. The police will hunt you down like an animal. You may be hurt or even killed, if you resist or try to escape." I then spoke with a shadowing of sadness. "I don't want to see that happen. There's been too much violence already."

I returned to a more upbeat tone. "You are obviously an intelligent person, one capable of loving and caring. That's a good foundation to build on. You and I can make plans for erecting a new life on that foundation. You need not feel alone, isolated, and ignored any longer."

I paused again, and when I went on, I made my voice warm and encouraging. "Please think it over," I said. "I'll give you a day to consider it."

I waited to let that sink in. Then I said, "If you decide we should get together, I want you to meet me at Union Station at noon on Saturday. I will be standing at the top of the stairs just inside the front door. I will be alone."

I paused, then said, "All you have to do is walk up and hold out your hand to me."

Very softly, almost seductively, I added, "I'll be watching for *you.*"

That was it. The theme music came up, and we faded to black.

After wrapping up the program, I felt I had done a good thing, something that just might work—despite the almost militant doubts expressed by you and my next-door neighbor's cat. I had also discovered how difficult acting in a Hitchcock movie can be, and I felt completely drained.

Four hours later, I still feel drained. So I think I'm going to fill my tank with two ounces of unblended scotch whiskey mixed with four ounces of the Mississippi River, then pour myself into bed.

Don't wait until you find happiness before writing.

Your Woman in St. Louis,
Thespis

C> -
C> cd\NOMAN
C> NOMAN
GREETINGS. HOW ARE YOU THIS EVENING?
    I'm a little upset.
CAN YOU TELL ME MORE ABOUT WHAT IS UPSETTING YOU?
    Joan, Joan, Joan. Always Joan.
I DON'T UNDERSTAND. HOW IS JOAN UPSETTING YOU?
    It's the show she did tonight. I spend almost every waking moment thinking about Joan and about what I can do to help her. I don't mind this. In fact, I enjoy it, and besides, I know that

eventually I'll get my reward. The two of us will come to know one another directly, and when that happens, our souls and bodies will melt together like twin streams of wax from burning candles. At least that's what I thought.

CAN YOU TELL ME MORE ABOUT THAT?

Until tonight, I was sure Joan felt the same way about me that I do about her. Now I have my doubts. I could hardly believe the things she said about me. They shocked me terribly.

YOU WERE SHOCKED BY THE THINGS JOAN SAID ABOUT YOU?

I certainly was—at least right at first. They were such horrible, hurtful things, I couldn't believe she was saying them. Then I began to wonder if she wasn't just being very clever.

YOU THINK JOAN IS BEING VERY CLEVER?

Maybe. It's possible that she was revealing her true feelings about me. But then maybe she has just devised an incredibly sophisticated publicity stunt. If I do what she wants me to, it will make news that will be on all the networks and in all the newspapers. She'll have everybody in the country talking about her. But as I say, I'm just not sure.

CAN YOU TELL ME MORE ABOUT NOT BEING SURE?

Not now. I've got to think about it. I've got to decide what to do—if anything.

YOU HAVE REACHED 552-8076. YOUR CONVERSATION WILL BE RECORDED.

Hello.

Joan, this is Peter Keefer of the St. Louis County Police.

Oh, hello, Peter. You're up awfully late. It must be past midnight.

Only by a few minutes, but I apologize for calling at this hour. I had to, though, because I just finished watching your show tonight. I knew I was going to be out, so I taped it.

What's the problem?

First let me say that your invitation to the Watcher took me completely by surprise. I don't think it was a smart thing to do. Not at all.

Why not?

One thing is, it's not going to work. The Watcher just isn't going to walk up to you and hold out his hands so I can put the cuffs on him. No way.

You don't know that, Peter. Isn't it true that a lot of criminals, murderers in particular, have a compulsion to confess?

Yeah, some do. But . . .

I think there's a good chance that the Watcher wants to please me enough that he's going to do what I asked him to do.

If we were talking about an ordinary murderer, I'd admit that you might be right. A man kills his wife, then starts to feel bad about it. He's eaten up with guilt and regret, so he turns himself in to get the punishment he thinks he deserves.
But Joan, the Watcher doesn't need the kind of relief people get from walking into a police station and saying, I'm the guy you've been looking for. He doesn't need it, because he's not feeling any guilt.

But what you're overlooking is that he's got something else driving him. He's obsessed with *me*. Because he is, I think that the prospect of just being with me and talking to me will be enough to make him show up.

Maybe so, maybe so. Anyway, I certainly think you should have called me and we should have talked about what you were planning to do, instead of your just doing it.

You sound very annoyed, Peter. I can understand why you would have wanted me to talk to you beforehand. But quite frankly I just decided against it.

Why? We could have worked something out.

Oh, Peter, I don't believe that for a minute. I would have told you what I was planning, and you would have refused to go along with it. You just explained why what I'm going to do is pointless, so you probably would even have tried to find a way to stop me. Charles Fishwater and I discussed whether we should call in the police, and we decided it would be safer just to announce the plan to everybody at the same time.

That's the problem, Joan. Safer is just what you're not going to be.

Why not? I'm not meeting this guy in a back alley or a parked car in a shopping mall. My God, the front door of Union Station is just about as public as you can get. I'm going to be in one of the busiest places in St. Louis and surrounded by hundreds of people.

That's why it's so dangerous. You'd be better off meeting him in a back alley. At least there we could keep an eye on you and control access to you. When you're trying to protect someone who's standing in the middle of a crowd and has dozens of people swarming around her like bees around a hive, you've got a real problem. There's no way in the world you can limit contact with the person you're protecting. Somebody can walk right up and stick a knife in her or put a bullet in her.
Even putting a human shield around her doesn't provide any guarantees. It's not leak proof. I'm sure you've seen the films of the way Sirhan-Sirhan assassinated Robert Kennedy. He just walked up to him and shot him, despite a whole covey of bodyguards.
Do you see what I mean?

Sure, I see. You're not the first person to point it out

to me, either. But it's a risk I'll just have to take. I was always planning to ask the police to be there. I was going to call you tomorrow and discuss it. But I know I can't have perfect protection.

I want the police there so that when the Watcher surrenders, they can take over and get us over to the psychiatrists at the hospital. I mean, I don't want to try to deal with the Watcher by myself. If he gives up, then changes his mind . . . I couldn't handle him.

I could still stop you from going through with the plan, you know. All I have to do is order the front entrance of the station sealed off. That way neither the Watcher nor anybody else would show up.

You could do that. But I don't think you will.

What makes you think I won't?

Because you're not stupid. First, you want to catch the Watcher. And even though you probably would have stopped me from putting my plan into practice, now that I have, I'm sure you see the advantage of going along with it.

Second, you know that if you interfered now, I would draw and quarter the police department on my next show. And even if I didn't, the public would get very angry over having the police spoil the drama I've cooked up here. See what I mean?

I see. You're going to play hardball. Look, I've already told you that I don't think there's a snowball's chance in hell that the Watcher is going to turn himself in, so I don't see any real advantage for me on that score.

But you do care about the department? And you see the disadvantage of refusing to cooperate?

Well, I'm not ready to let the department in for another public bashing. It does mean risking your neck, though.

I'm sorry you don't see things both my ways, but one

way is enough. And remember, Peter, I'm the one who de-cided to risk her neck, not you. Now shall we meet and discuss how to arrange things?

I was going to suggest that. Would you like to come down to my office or do you want me to come to your house?

Given a choice between going to a police station and staying home, I'll choose staying home every time.

That's fine, then. How about around eight or eighty-thirty tomorrow night?

That would be fine. But won't your wife mind your going out in the evening?

Did I give you the impression I was a married man?

Not exactly. I just assumed you were.

Nope. Married to the job, maybe, but I don't have a wife. I've never had one. Maybe one of these days, though . . .

You never can tell when lightning might strike. Any-way, come over at eight-thirty and we'll have another Dr Pepper—or maybe something else. Then we can talk about how many officers we'll need to surround me.

The answer to that is four. But the real question is how we're going to sequence your movements to minimize the danger.

Sounds like choreography.

It's much like that. Only in this dance if you put your foot in the wrong place, you can end up dead.

Then I'll try to pay particular attention to learning the right steps.

I'll let you get to bed now, but I'll see you at eight-thirty tomorrow night.

I'll expect you. Goodnight, Peter.

· JANE CARPENTER-REED, M.D. ·
Psychiatry Consultants, Inc.
3460 Chestnut Avenue
Brookline, MA 02147
617-976-8740
FAX: 617-976-2286

7:20 A.M. Thursday

Dear Joanie,

I'm faxing this to you, because I don't want you to lose your beauty sleep. I had a real struggle with myself, since a childish part of me would still get great pleasure out of jangling you out of your nice warm bed at 6:30 (your time) in the morning.

I should be getting right to the point and not horsing around, though. Not only do I have to see my first patient in half an hour, I've got a serious message to deliver.

Stratford Vogler called me a few minutes ago and asked me to get in touch with you. He watched the "death scene" tape of Gary Wells last night, and he wanted me to convey to you an even stronger warning than either he or I have given you before.

Stratford is convinced that the person who killed Wells harbors an enormous inner rage. The "love" directed toward you is only a screen emotion, one that disguises a feeling that is the exact opposite of what it seems to be.

To put the point bluntly, instead of being the object of love, you are in fact the object of pure and unadulterated hatred. The phenomenon in erotomania, Stratford says, is a manifestation of the same paradox found in all paranoid thinking.

For example, when a paranoid is unpopular, he explains it by saying people envy him; when he's unable to perform a job, he says it's because he's too smart to do that kind of work. The erotomanic (says Stratford) falls victim to his own delusional system and mistakes jealousy, envy, and anger for love and devotion. Hence, the "affection" the Watcher directs toward you can very easily become revealed as the vicious malice it actually is.

All it takes is one small incident—a real or imagined slight, for example—that jostles the Watcher's psyche. If that happens, the mask will fall away and you'll be staring into the wild eyes of a demented and dangerous person.

After talking to Stratford, I'm convinced that he's absolutely right. I'm writing this because I *want* to scare you shitless. I want you to be so frightened that you will never, never (for the foreseeable future) allow yourself to be on an elevator alone or walk down the street without an escort. Maybe you'll even move into a hotel or hire a security guard. But even if you don't go this far, you will at least take more than reasonable precautions.

Joan, you have to realize that dealing with a wildly psychotic person is not at all like having a little tiff with the bank teller. This particular psychotic very likely wants to kill you and, given the slightest provocation, very likely will try to do just that.

Am I getting through to you?

If so, may I suggest (i.e. insist) that you ask for police protection. Maybe they can't stick with you like chewing gum to the cat, but they can cruise by your house every hour or so. If this Lt. Keefer is as charming as you say, maybe that will help persuade you to give him a call.

(If we were talking about birds, I would call this the Principle of the Conservation of Stones. However, the Jung at heart would probably tell me that, given the context, this oblique reference to killing is an expression of disguised hostility toward you. But this just shows how much their theories resemble swiss cheese.)

Before I make any airline reservations, I want to be sure it's for Thanksgiving and not for a funeral.

Younger sisters are hard to replace this late in life. Particularly one who is beautiful, famous, and worships her older sister.

Love and pats,
Janie

Dear Ms. Carpenter,

I was doing some work in Ms. Hartz's yard today, and we talked about your show last night. We both agreed that you are a woman of great strength and courage. She told me to quit work fifteen minutes early and bring you this bouquet of aconite from her garden. She said to tell you she wants you to know she will be thinking about you tomorrow.

(She made a good choice of flowers, in my humble opinion. The aconite blue is particularly lovely and almost the color of your eyes. Aconite is also called wolfsbane, and it should keep you safe.)

Hopefully you won't mind, but I added my own offering to the aconite. Also, please accept this bunch of fern fronds as a token of my best wishes. As I wrote in a recent poem, "The fern has no flowers nor seeds, yet in its leaves lies its power. / The fronds, in beauty and strength, challenge even the Eiffel Tower."

The appeal you made for the Watcher to meet you in Union Station was as touching as a tree or a flower. If this is someone with a heart and emotions, I'm sure he will be moved to turn himself in to you and to apologize for the way he has made you feel.

You can be sure I'll be at Union Station by noon on Saturday. Watch for me.

Your friend,
Curt

P.S. I'm leaving you this note, because I don't want to interrupt your thoughts at this important time in your life. I respect your solitude and aloneness, and you will never again have to remind me to do so. C.

256 East 59th Street • New York, New York • 10020
212-555-5050 • Fax 212-555-5051
D a n i e l L . S a t u r n , PRESIDENT

Friday, 11:20 A.M.

Dear Joan:

I've watched the tape now, and I agree with your fax—You
were brilliant, even if you did say so yourself.

Given what you wanted to accomplish, I think your amazing
performance hit the right notes of sex appeal, vulnerability, compassion, and threat. Whether those notes will make up a tune powerful enough to lure the Watcher through the streets of Hamlin
Town to the trap waiting just inside the door of Union Station remains the Big Question.

I hope it won't. I don't want to open up old wounds, but I still
think you're wrong about this whole setup. I particularly don't like
the way that you're making yourself the bait. I don't know why I
didn't suggest it to you before, but why didn't you just tell the
Watcher to go to the nearest cop and turn himself in? Or at least
check himself into the psychiatric ward? Why did you have to make
yourself the cheese? (Rats really prefer peanut butter, but I'm sure
you see what I'm getting at.)

I know, I know . . . you did it because you *had* to. You did it
for Mom, and Sis, and all the folks back home in Centerville who
are counting on you to make their world safe. You did it because
your dad told you it was something a woman's just got to do. I've
seen all the movies too. (I would never suggest that it's also because
your ego couldn't stand letting the Watcher surrender to anybody
else, particularly after you set up everything.)

Honestly, though, now that your scheme is becoming real, I'm
starting to regret I arranged for you to go back to work so you
could carry it out. I'm feeling responsible and guilty—feelings I
spend 45 minutes (and even more dollars) a week in therapy trying
to avoid.

At the very least, I hope you're going to take the course you
described to me and get a whole squadron (or whatever) of police
to surround you ten deep. And no matter what you do, don't be a

hero (or a heroine either). I didn't ask KMIS for enough money for that.

I have to admit, I still don't think the Watcher is likely to show up. However, if he does and if you do happen to pull off this stunt the way you plan, your name is going to blaze brightly in the firmament for a few glorious minutes. That's the time we'll make our move and see if we can generate some network interest in you. (At the moment, it sounds crass even to think of such a thing. But I suppose that at times of crisis our true selves come out—which means I should feel thoroughly embarrassed. Still, if I didn't act to promote your career at such a time, you could probably sue me for malpractice.)

Let me leave you with a few pieces of general advice. Since you don't have to be at Union Station until noon, you should get a lot of sleep tonight. Do it by going to bed earlier. Don't sleep late in the morning, because studies show that produces grogginess, and you'll need to be as sharp as possible tomorrow.

Also, don't eat a large breakfast and don't plan on eating lunch until afterward. Other studies show you are more mentally alert if you are slightly hungry. You will certainly need to have your wits about you.

Joan, if you want to change your mind, even at the last minute, go right ahead and do it. We can say you got sick from salmonella poisoning. That's so common now everybody would accept the story at face value. (But you shouldn't worry about what people might think anyway.)

I'll be thinking about you, and you must let me know how things went the very moment you know. I'm not going anywhere tomorrow. I'm going to be waiting at home by the telephone until you phone me and tell me everything is okay.

Do be careful. You mean a lot more to me than twenty percent.

Love and kisses,
Dan

11/20

Joan:

You have had telephone calls from Mr. Alan Carter and Dr. Stephen Legion.

(a) Mr. Carter wanted me to tell you he is leaving for Jefferson City today and won't be back until Tuesday.

He told me he's supposed to talk to some legislators informally over the weekend, then testify before a House committee on Monday. It has something to do with state building codes—he wasn't very specific.

Anyway, he's not going to be able to go with you to Union Station tomorrow, although he wishes he could. He hopes things go well, and he'll call you when he gets back.

(b) Dr. Legion must make hospital rounds tomorrow morning, then he has "a meeting with surgical residents and then some paperwork that has simply got to be done." He doesn't know if he will be free in time to "watch you accept the Watcher's surrender."

He may be able to cut his meeting short, "but that's not something she should count on." Otherwise, he'll talk to you later.

I'm beginning to see why women are always complaining about how hard it is to find an acceptable man to marry. It looks like when the going gets rough, the men get gone.

Maybe a good AA shouldn't make any editorial comments on messages, but then I never said I was good.

Alice

P.S. Mr. Fishwater has been running around all day, getting permits from Union Station Management Corporation and trying to make sure all the remote equipment is working. Judging by the fact that he's not yelling as loud now as he was this morning, I think things are going okay. Or maybe his voice just got tired.

I'll be there tomorrow.

ST. LOUIS COUNTY POLICE DEPARTMENT

Memo of Transmission   Date: November 20

From: Detective Lieutenant Peter Keefer, Major Case Squad
To: Detective Raymond R. Robertson
Subject: Operation Freight Train

Ray,

As I told you at our meeting this morning, I want you to take operational responsibility for the whole Union Station show. I'll serve as the Executive Officer, but the details are going to belong to you. Let me formalize some of the decisions we made, as well as bring you up to date on a couple of matters.

(1) I just talked to Captain Haddock and he says he can let us have 150 uniformed officers for crowd control and traffic. If we want to, we can divide them into two shifts. He doesn't want us to keep that many people for over four hours, though. The overtime becomes killing.

I told him you'd get back in touch with him. I said I was sure you would follow whatever advice he was willing to offer. I hope I didn't tie your hands. But unless you know more about crowd control than I do, just do what Capt. Haddock says. He's been making crowds jump through hoops since before Busch Stadium was a hole in the ground.

(2) I want at least 40 of our people at the Station. (I'll authorize the overtime in cases where it's necessary.) I want four men (and I do mean *men*) who have had experience as bodyguards detailed to protect Joan Carpenter. So far as I'm concerned, they can be our people or we can get them from the Tactical Unit. You decide.

The people you choose should meet Carpenter at the KMIS studio and drive down with her. I've already told her to expect them.

(3) Special Services is sending you a copy of the architectural drawings of Union Station. If you don't get them by this afternoon, call them up and raise hell.

(4) Clarence Lane is very good at deployment of forces in siege situations, and I think you should consult with him. Show him the drawings and ask him where he thinks we should put our people.

(5) I got approval from Chief Blackshire to put a sniper on the

mezzanine. Cpl. Carol Aade of the Tactical Unit is supposed to be the best shot on the force, and Lieutenant Brown says we can have her all day Saturday. She is going to report to you for instruction.

When I walked around the station by myself this morning, I saw a place she could stand and get a completely clear view of the front door. I'll stop by later and show you on the drawings.

Of course, we don't want anybody in the crowd to know a sniper is there. I suggest we get a uniformed officer and a couple of our people to box her in against the wall. They can screen her with their bodies, then step aside and push back the crowd to give her room to maneuver.

I want to talk to Cpl. Aade myself before she takes up her position. Chief Blackshire and I agreed that the sniper should shoot only to counter direct and immediate action against the life of Joan Carpenter. Threat is not enough, and I want to make sure Aade understands this.

(6) Identify six of our people to stand on either side of the entrance doors on the inside of Union Station, and identify four more to stand on the outside. (Try to select people you know are able to pay attention and don't get distracted by butterflies.)

Also, send as many of our people as you can to visit Union Station. Tell them to walk around and familiarize themselves with the layout. If you have to chase somebody, it's always better if you know the territory.

I know and you know that the whole idea of the Watcher giving himself up to Joan Carpenter isn't likely to produce anything but trouble for us and overtime for the uniformed branch. But as I explained at the meeting, if we don't cooperate and somebody should get hurt or killed, those of us responsible for handling the Kline-Wells case had better plan on moving out to the country and raising turnips. And that's the word from the Chief, not just me.

You can be sure lots more details than I've covered here will come up. But we'll deal with them as necessary.

Pete

P.S. Here's one I just thought of. Check our people's radios and make sure they work. Do it today, if you can. We're always getting stuck with dud radios, then Communications says they won't have any spares until next week, so we have to do without.

This operation is too important for us not to have instant communication with each other.

JOAN CARPENTER
2030 Buckminster · St. Louis, MO · 63130

20 Nov/Fri. A.M.

Dear Janie,

What's the use of having a psychiatrist for a sister (or is it a sister for a psychiatrist?) if you can't get free advice about running your life?

Of course I'll take your warning seriously. I know the Watcher is a bomb with a lit fuse and that I and everybody around (and including) me might go up in a puff of pink smoke, unless somebody does something to stop him.

So far as police protection is concerned, you'll be glad to learn that only last night the charming and handsome Lieutenant Peter Keefer came to my house. We had some planning to do on a project I won't bother describing to you now. (I'm being deliberately mysterious, but if all goes well, I'll tell you about it in a couple of days.)

You'll also be glad to know that although Peter thinks my project stinks, he is very interested in protecting me. Indeed, I think he may have developed an interest in me that is more than professional. (Here are the stats I collected: 34, never married, M.A. in criminal justice, the youngest head ever of the Major Case Squad, and loves putting bad guys in jail.) I didn't smile demurely and blink my eyes, but then I didn't issue him a cease-and-desist order either.

We had drinks and this time he passed up the Dr Pepper. I gave him about two fingers in a jelly glass of my second-best single-malt scotch (Glen Unpronounceable), and he became—what do you Americans say—putty in my hands.

At the moment, though, my main interest in shaping him is to get him to carry out our project according to my specifications. Later, after the Watcher business is over, maybe Peter and I can get together and reminisce over a glass of my *best* single malt.

(Yes, Alan and Steve are still around. I suspect none of us is serious, although I could get a couple of us to be if I worked at it. I don't think I would have to work at Peter. Could it be magic?

Maybe so. I gave him my fax number, and I don't say that to all the boys.)

I think it will please you to hear that, although I haven't been in St. Louis for very long, people have been very nice to me during my recent troubles. In addition to getting lots of *nice* fan mail, I have been showered with support from Steve, Alan, Alice (my administrative assistant), Alexis (my back-door neighbor), and Curt (the gardener who wants to till all my beds). People have gone out of their way to send me tokens of affection and good wishes. I hope I don't do anything stupid to let them down. (It's got to take somebody more cynical than I am to throw a game or walk out on her fans.)

Your crack about coming for Thanksgiving instead of for a funeral was in terribly bad taste. Still, I'm glad you're coming at all, and I promise I'll do my best to make sure that the only funeral involved is that of the turkey.

Got to run. I've got places to go and people to see. Be flattered that instead of my usual habit of watching TV and reading the newspaper while drinking my coffee, I'm writing to you.

Pats for Jack. Kisses for Amy.

Y'r v'r imp't (but l'ving) Sis

YOU HAVE REACHED 552-8076. YOUR CONVERSATION WILL BE RECORDED.

Joan, this is Peter Keefer.

Hi, Peter. Let me guess—you want to go over our arrangements for tomorrow.

I'm sure you think I'm being as fussy as a mother hen, but I'm a lot more comfortable in these situations when everybody knows what to expect.

I'm to go to the KMIS studios at eleven tomorrow morning and meet the two men who will drive me to Union Station. We'll leave at eleven-fifteen and arrive around eleven-thirty or -forty. Two more men will be waiting for me there. All four of them will walk me inside.

You've got it all right. And once you enter the building, you'll go up the two steps leading to the main level. There are two polished brass handrails, and you should go right between them.

When you get to the top of the steps, Mr. Fishwater will have an area marked off where you're supposed to stand. It will be about ten feet away from the last step.

Are the bodyguards going to leave me then?

They'll step away from you, but they aren't going to leave. They'll be right behind you all the time, and of course we'll have some uniformed people there to keep the crowd back.

And when the Watcher appears, nobody will do anything until I give the word?

You mean, *if* the Watcher appears.

Okay, *if* he appears, if that'll make you happier. I know you think all this is just a waste of time and effort, but Peter, I think there's a good chance he's going to show up. I think I've got that much influence over him, I really do.

All right, we don't have to fight about this. Everything is all set up anyway.

So assuming the Watcher does show up, you're not going to try to arrest him until I let you know I'm ready?

That's right, unless he does something that makes us think you or somebody else is in danger. Then we'll take him.

Otherwise you'll wait until I say, "Before we can talk, I'm going to ask you to let some people make sure you're not carrying a gun." If he gives his permission, just one person will come forward and search him. Right?

Right. And if he refuses, all four come forward and take control of him.

Let's hope he cooperates. Assuming he does, I'll tell him we're going someplace where we can talk in private. If he asks where, I tell him I've arranged a private interview room at Barnes Hospital. Then when I take him down the steps to the car, your people will fall in behind us.

That's right. One will then step forward and open the door. You climb in and tell the Watcher to follow you. Then you keep going out the opposite door, and somebody on that side will take your place in the back seat. Another of my men will get in on the other side and sit by the Watcher, so he's trapped between them.

Then two other of my people will get in the car. They'll start for Barnes, and you can follow in another car. By the time you see the Watcher again, he'll be in the psychiatric ward and we'll have cuffs and leg irons on him.

Remember that you promised to let me talk to him on camera. I've got to be able to keep my word to him or I'm not going through with this at all.

You're not the only person who keeps promises, you know. I haven't forgotten what I told you.

Of course all this does assume he shows up. Since you don't believe this anyway, you can promise me anything.

I don't know what to say, except I'll keep my promises.

I'm sorry. I guess I'm starting to have my own doubts. I don't want this to be a farce.

Even if it doesn't work, it won't be that. Most efforts to catch criminals don't work, and this is at least a sincere effort.

Thanks, you're being very decent about this.

I told you yesterday I might want to stay until one o'clock, but if it's all right with you, I've decided to give up for good at twelve-thirty. If the Watcher hasn't appeared by then, I'm going to conclude he's not coming and call off the party.

Stopping then is fine with me. If the Watcher doesn't show, then as soon as you sign off or close or whatever you call it, the four men standing in the background will surround you again. They'll walk you down the steps, out the door, and back to the car. You won't be on your own again until you get to the studio.

It sounds good, Peter. But would it surprise you if I told you I was scared?

It would surprise me if you told me you weren't. You can still back out, you know.

No I can't. I've gone this far, and I've got to go the rest of the way. I would look too stupid, and I'd rather be scared than look stupid.

What scares you most?

The uncertainty, I guess. There's no telling how things may turn out.

I might just stand in the middle of the floor and chat to the camera for half an hour and have nothing happen at all. Or an insane killer might appear and give himself up to me. Or at the last minute he might change his mind and decide to kill me instead.

That's something we can't forget about. I doubt if that will happen, but it's possible. All I can tell you is that we're going to do all we can to keep you safe.

I think I'm going to have to take back some of the harsh things I've said about the police.

You don't have to take them back. Maybe you could supplement them with a few nice things, though.

If I get through this, I'll have *lots* of nice things to say. I'll say them about the police in general and you in particular. I enjoyed our talk last night, despite the time we had to spend making plans. Maybe we can get together again when all of this is over.

I would like that. But I've got to let you get to bed now. Nobody knows better than I that you've got a big day tomorrow.

Nobody except the Watcher anyway.

Don't think about that. Just believe everything is going to work out all right and get some sleep.

All right, Officer. Whatever you say. Goodnight, and see you tomorrow.

This is Dan Saturn.

Dan, it's Joan.

Joan! I was just thinking about calling you.

I guess you're going to have to start believing in ESP, because not only was I thinking about calling you, I actually did it.

I would have called you an hour ago, but I was afraid you wouldn't like it.

Why on earth not? Not bad news on the contract front, I hope?

No, nothing like that. I just thought you might feel I was trying to pressure you into changing your plans for tomorrow.

Yeah, well, I think my plans are the reason I called you.

Really? Does that mean you're not going to show up at Union Station?

Oh, I'm going to *show* up all right. I'm just beginning to wonder if I can *stand* up. My knees are already shaking so hard I'm going to have to use rubber bands to keep my stockings up.
I don't mind telling you, Dan, I'm one scared fluffy chicken.

But you aren't going to back out?

Not unless the Watcher turns himself over to the police tonight. No, absolutely not.

How about the police? Have they made plans to give you some protection?

I talked to Lieutenant Keefer earlier tonight. He's not any happier with this whole business than you are, but I'm completely satisfied with the way he's handling the situation. Short of treating me like the Pope and putting me inside a Plexiglas box, I think they're going to do everything they can to protect me.
And in my mind, I know the chances are that I'm not going to be in any real danger anyway. As you say, the Watcher probably won't even show up.

Yeah, but then he might.

Exactly. And that both scares me and excites me. Not only could we get him behind bars, but the scene itself would make terrific television. Besides, I've got all these questions I want to ask him. When I think about all that, I can hardly wait for tomorrow.
But when I'm not at a fever pitch, I'm down in a very dark cellar. Then I find myself dreading tomorrow. Thinking about what

might happen makes me feel a little sick, and I begin to wonder how I ever got myself into such a mess.

By being bold, courageous, and imaginative, of course. You're proving you're willing to take a chance to accomplish something that's worth doing, and you want to go about it in your own way. I'm frightened for you, but I'm also tremendously proud of you.

You are? I thought you believed I was just being silly and taking a foolish chance.

Part of that was just my own fear talking, because I very much don't want you to get hurt. But I can't help being impressed by your willingness to put yourself on the spot. If something turns sour, you're the one the Watcher is going to go for.

As I said, I'm tremendously proud of you.

Thanks, Dan. I'm not feeling very brave, but just admitting to you how scared I am makes me feel better. And while I'm feeling that way, I should go to bed. It's getting late here, and it must be midnight there. I think I'd better have the glass of milk you recommended in your fax this morning.

Do be careful, Joan.

I will be. And if there's any trouble, I'll throw myself against the wall and pretend to be a coat of paint.

Don't forget to eat a good breakfast.

I thought maybe a strawberry Pop Tart. No, no, just kidding.

I should hope so. Please don't forget to call me.

As soon as I can. Sleep well, Dan.

Thanks for calling.

Next time let's just use telepathy. The rates are lower. Bye.

Goodbye, Joan. You sleep well too.

ST. LOUIS COUNTY POLICE DEPARTMENT

OFFICIAL TRANSCRIPT OF RECORDED RADIO TRANS-
MISSIONS BETWEEN LIEUTENANT PETER KEEFER AND
MEMBERS OF HIS COMMAND AT UNION STATION ON
SATURDAY, NOVEMBER 21, @ 11:48 A.M.—12:03 P.M.

KEEFER: Robertson, this is Keefer. Freight Train has arrived.
They're unloading and starting for the door. Over.

ROBERTSON: Roger, Keefer. We're ready for her. I'm in position at the left rear of the designated area. The crowd is staying
back of the police tapes, and it looks calm.

Wait a second, I see her now. She's through the door and
starting up the steps toward this area. Cameras are pointing at her,
and everything is smooth as silk. Over.

KEEFER: Keep your eye on her, Ray. I'm coming right behind
her. I'm bringing two of the door guards with me to take a position
on the inside.

ROBERTSON: I read you, Peter. Freight Train has arrived on
the spot. Fishwater is talking to her. The TV crew is checking
equipment and lights.

KEEFER: Ray, tell the crew to keep the lights on Freight Train
and not shine them around. I don't want Aade in the crow's nest
to be blinded.

ROBERTSON: Roger, will do.

KEEFER: I'm taking up my position left of the door. Out to
Robertson. Barlow, this is Keefer. Come in.

BARLOW: This is Barlow, Lieutenant.

KEEFER: Is Aade with you and in position? Over.

BARLOW: She's here. She says her line of sight is perfect. No
problems.

KEEFER: Wait a minute! Wait a minute! Robertson, come in! Come in, Robertson!

At two 'clock in your field, watch the white male in blue jacket and tie. He's pushing to the front of the crowd.

ROBERTSON: I don't have a clear view. I can't locate him.

KEEFER: He's out on the floor right in front of you. Look at the bastard!

ROBERTSON: I see him! I see him! He's got a weapon. Christ, it's a gun. I'm going after him.

KEEFER: Stay there, Ray! Stay there! He's crouching and aiming. Get Carpenter out of the way! Get her covered! Get her covered! Move now!

My God, I recognize him.

[Sound of gunfire—single shot.]

ROBERTSON: He's shot Mitchell! The son of a bitch shot Mitchell!

KEEFER: Barlow, come in. Come in. We've got to get him before he locates Carpenter. Tell Aade to take him out. Shoot to stop.

[Sound of gunfire—single shot.]

ROBERTSON: He's down! He's down!

KEEFER: Police officers stay at your posts.

ROBERTSON: I think he's dead! He's not moving. Peter, I'm going in. I'm the closest.

KEEFER: Stay back! Stay back!

[Sound of gunshot—single shot.]

KEEFER: Oh, my God. Oh, my God. He's shot Ray. Barlow, tell Aade to cover me, I'm going in to get Ray.

[Pause with indistinct sounds of motion and crowd noises.]

KEEFER: EMS! EMS! Get over here quick! Robertson is out, but he's still breathing. And get somebody to Mitchell.
The perp is neutralized. Let's keep the crowds back now.

YOU HAVE REACHED 552-8076. THIS CON-VERSATION IS BEING RECORDED.

Joan? It's Dan.

Oh, Dan. I literally just walked in and heard the phone ringing. Hang on a second and let me pour myself a drink. . . .
Okay, I'm back. That's more like it. I guess you were starting to wonder what happened to me.

I was. Even in St. Louis it's almost eight o'clock, and I thought you might have forgotten to call. So I decided I'd better call you.

I'm sorry you were worried. I'm fine, but things didn't go smoothly. I almost wasn't fine, and some terrible things happened. Didn't you see anything on CNN or the networks?

Since I expected you to call, I haven't been checking. But what went on at the train station? Did the Watcher show up?

He showed up all right, but not in the way I expected. I thought he was going to march up and surrender, but that's not the way it happened. While we were getting ready to start our remote program, this guy in a blue coat suddenly ran out of the crowd with a gun and started shooting. He took a shot at me, but the detective standing next to me is the one who got hit. Blood splattered all over me, and for a second, I thought I was the one who was shot.

Oh, Joan, that's horrible. How's the detective?

That's one of the few good things. He was going to be okay, the last I heard.

Did the Watcher get away?

No, the police got him. After he shot the detective, he was pointing his gun right at me and apparently about to fire again when a police sniper shot him. He's not dead, but he was hurt very bad.

That was all bad enough, and now it gets worse. He was struggling to get off the floor, when Robertson—the same detective who searched my house—ran over to him to stop him. The Watcher raised himself up enough to take aim and shot Robertson right in the stomach. I heard one of the cops tell another that the doctors say he might not live.

Everything seems terrible. And it sounds like you're right in the thick of things.

I was, except after the first shot, three detectives crowded around me to shield me. I was scared, but I was also very pissed off, because I wanted to be able to do my job. I got them to move out of the way enough for me to see what was going on.

While all this was happening, I was talking into my mike and the cameras were rolling. We got nearly everything on tape just as it was happening, and they went on the air with it live. It was an incredible story.

Oh, Christ, Dan, listen to me! I'm beginning to sound like Fishwater.

Since you're a reporter, I don't think reporting a story from where you were on the spot is anything to blame yourself about. I'm sure you did an outstanding job, but I'm also sure you took too many risks to get it.

Not really, because right after Robertson was shot, Peter Keefer came up behind the Watcher, fell on top of him, and took his gun away. I gave a good interpretation of what was happening, but after the shooting stopped, I wanted to do some interviews. Peter wouldn't talk to me, so I started trying to interview some spectators. Most of the people were still standing around as if they were watching a play, and I wanted to ask them if they hadn't been scared they were going to get shot.

I'm surprised the police let you.

They didn't. The three people who were shot were loaded into ambulances, and Peter told the ones guarding me to take me down to police headquarters. They interrogated me about everything that had just happened. They videotaped the interview and then asked me to dictate a statement. Before they let me go home, they showed me a Polaroid of the guy with the gun and asked me if I could remember ever seeing him before.

Could you?

Not really. But that doesn't mean I haven't. The picture was taken in the hospital, and he had a tube down his nose and he looked gray and very sick. Even if I had seen him before, I'm not sure I would recognize him.

At least they got him. It's too bad the scenario didn't play out the way you imagined, but now you don't have to worry about the Watcher anymore.

That is a relief. Jane and her friend Dr. Vogler are going to feel very smug.

Why is that?

Because they both warned me that the Watcher might turn against me and become violent. Of course, so did you, but you didn't say it on the basis of some theory.

So let them be right. At least you can sleep easier at night.

Yes, I can. And I think that's exactly what I'm going to do after I have another drink or two. I'm completely exhausted.

That makes sense. I won't keep you talking any longer, but I just want to say how glad I am nothing happened to you. Give me a call tomorrow, if you feel like it. Even though it's Sunday, I've got a breakfast meeting with a client who's only going to be here for half a day. But after that I'll be at home.

Maybe we'll talk then, but I'm also very eager to see the tape we shot. I may go in to the studio and take a look at it after I wake up and get myself functioning again.

Take my advice and have a glass of milk before you go to bed. The tryptophan will make you sleepy.

Milk may be your drug of choice, but mine's single malt scotch. Sleep well, Dan.

FAX TRANSMITTAL 314-552-5671

JOAN CARPENTER
2030 Buckminster • St. Louis, MO • 63130

21/Sat, late P.M.

Dear Janie,

I am about to (literally) stagger off to bed. But knew I'd better drop you a note before I drop myself. Otherwise, between the Mozart sonatas on public radio a whispery voice might mention a certain incident in St. Louis and cause you to worry. And this might make you call me, and this would undoubtedly (as Kant said of Hume) rouse me from my dogmatic slumbers.

What I'm getting at is that I'm writing in self-defense.

Without going into detail, I'll just say that on Wednesday I made a plea for the Watcher to give himself up at Union Station at noon today. This was what I was so mysterious about. I thought you (like other sensible people) might tell me my idea was crazy and that I was only a step behind it. I didn't want to hear that, because I didn't want my plan thwarted.

Anyway, instead of strolling up to me and holding out his hands for the cuffs, the Watcher shot two people (one very bad) and got shot himself (very bad). As for me, *I am perfectly okay.* I am unshot, unbloodied, and generally unharmed.

However, I am beginning to feel the first icy prickles of guilt. The inescapable fact is that nobody would have gotten shot if I hadn't tried to reenact a "surrender scene" I probably watched on a rerun of the *Untouchables* when I was about eight. When I made the plea and planned the scene, I thought I was performing a great public service, but maybe it was really just a great private service—i.e., complete selfishness and rampant careerism, coupled with self-deception.

But all this is going to take some heavy thinking, and right now the only thing I'm capable of thinking about is climbing into bed. I'll even happily go alone.

I'll call Mama tomorrow and tell her not to worry. (This is getting to be my major mode of communication with her. Do I need help, Doctor?) But tomorrow is, thanks to diurnal rotation, another day. I've had quite enough of this one.

Yo' deah sista,
Scarlett

P.S. I'm holding you to the implicit Thanksgiving promise. I really need to be surrounded by people I love, instead of by people who recognize me and turn me into their own version of Barbie.

YOU HAVE REACHED 552-8076. THIS CONVERSATION IS BEING RECORDED.

Joan, is that you?

It's me, Mama. Sorry about the machine, but I'm supposed to keep track of people who call me.

I'm just relieved you're there. I've been so worried about you I didn't know what to do. I got up and had breakfast, then got my coffee and sat down to watch the news on the TV. I hadn't been watching three minutes when all at once the woman giving the news was saying there was a shooting in St. Louis yesterday and that you were involved.

I couldn't believe what I was hearing. She said three men got shot and mentioned your name, but she didn't say if you were all right.

I'm perfectly all right, Mama.

Thank goodness for that. It hasn't been a quarter of an hour, and at first I wasn't going to call you. I didn't want you to think I was keeping a check on you, the way my mother used to do me. But I couldn't make myself wait. I was too worried.

I'm sorry you were scared like that. I was going to call you this morning, but I just got out of bed. I hadn't finished my first cup of coffee when the phone rang.

Don't let me keep you from your breakfast. It'll get cold.

Don't worry, Mama. It's just cereal and fruit.

Oh, Joan! You should eat more than that. You're going to get weak and sick. You're body needs solid food in the mornings.

I'm too sleepy to talk about my eating habits right

now. I'll call you back this afternoon, and we'll chat. I'll tell you about what happened yesterday.

That'll be fine. I just wanted to know you were okay.

I am. I hope you are.

There's nothing wrong with me. Oh, one other thing before I hang up. I made my reservation for Thanksgiving. When I heard Janie was going to come, I couldn't stand the idea of all of you being there without me.

That's wonderful. We couldn't stand the idea either.

Well, give me a call later. If you don't get an answer right away, let the phone ring. I'm going to be outside raking leaves and cutting back some of my bushes.

I'll wait for you to come in. Don't make yourself hurry. And thank you for calling. I'm sorry you were scared, but I find it nice to know my mother still worries about me.

Don't you know mothers always worry? For me, half the time you're still a little girl playing in the sprinkler out in the backyard.

That's the way I feel myself half the time. I love you, and I'll call you later.

Goodbye, dear. I love you, and I'm so glad you didn't get hurt.

ST. LOUIS COUNTY POLICE DEPARTMENT

Memo of Transmission   Date: November 22

From: Detective Lieutenant Peter Keefer, Major Case Squad
To: Chief of Police Harold C. Blackshire

Dear Harold:

The media people have really been pressuring me, but I haven't told them anything. I said that any additional statement was going to have to come from you or, if it came from me, it would have to be with your authorization.

Anyway, we have found out a little more than we knew last night, and some other changes have taken place. I wanted to make sure you're as up to date as possible.

(1) We now have confirmed the identity of the attacker. He was carrying papers in the name of Harold Bliss Hodges, but his real name is Walter Allison Akerson. He is a 36 year old white male with a fraud record.

I recognized him the moment I saw him at Union Station, even though I didn't remember his name. I encountered him more than three years ago when he called himself William H. Watertown. At that time he was running a burial insurance scam and doing business under the name "Eternity Insurance."

Akerson and the people working for him collected premiums but paid out no claims. Eventually the Attorney General put him out of business, and he was sentenced to 18 months at Gumbo for fraud. Before that happened, though, Akerson threatened to kill a number of elderly people who told him they were going to the police about him.

The granddaughter of one woman called us in, but the D.A.'s office couldn't get any of the people threatened to press charges against Akerson. We were forced to drop the case, but the state's attorney put him away a short time later.

Akerson was a slick talker who was full of lies and of himself, but unlike most con men, the threats showed he had a potential for violence. Yet he never actually committed a violent crime, and to my knowledge he never expressed any interest in celebrities. He has done nothing to attract our attention since getting out of prison, and we had no reason to make him a suspect in the Watcher case.

It's quite a surprise, to tell you the truth. I always thought it would be someone known to Joan Carpenter, maybe even somebody in her social circle. The letters are written by somebody both intelligent and literate. Akerson has a community college degree, and he might have been able to write them. However, I'll feel better when we find the right typewriter.

Akerson got out of prison almost two years ago. While he was finishing his parole, he got a job as a cook at Beanfield's Natural Restaurant. He moved in with a woman named Diane Warnof (who is part-owner) and stayed with her until about three weeks ago. According to Warnof, he drinks heavily, and she thinks he's recently started smoking dippers or using some kind of drugs.

"He was acting real crazy before I threw him out," she told our interrogators last night. "He's always talking to himself and saying how the whole country's being run by TV. That's one reason I wanted him out of the house. Being around him was too spooky. He didn't want to go, but I've got a couple of big guys working for me. I told him I'd get them to persuade him it'd be a good idea. Then he was gone like a flash."

We're still talking to her and trying to piece together what she knows about his movements. She claims she doesn't know where he's been living, but as soon as we get his picture on TV and in the papers, somebody will recognize him and call us.

Aade's bullet nicked Akerson's heart, but he stayed alive until around six o'clock this morning. Right up to the last minute, the doctors believed he might make it, but they were wrong.

I can't say I'm too grieved about that.

(2) I'm sure you've already heard the sad news that Ray Robertson died. It was right after I talked to you last night, around 1:30 A.M. The surgeon said Akerson's shot passed through Ray's stomach and exploded in his intestines. It even damaged his lungs considerably. (An autopsy will be performed to confirm this.) He was in surgery for almost six hours. When he came out, they continued to give him lots of blood, but they couldn't keep up his blood pressure. He hemorrhaged to death right in the hospital.

I was with Ray's wife when he died. Then I took her home and got her sister and her parents to come over and stay with her. I asked Dr. Letrobe to stop by this morning and check on how she was doing. I'm glad they had no children. I would hate to think of having to tell the children.

(3) The story on William Mitchell is a lot happier one. He's at St. Louis Regional Hospital, but they think he should be out by Monday or Tuesday. Akerson's bullet hit him in the chest, but it was deflected by a rib. The rib cracked and he had some bleeding, but basically they think he's okay.

I stopped by to see him this morning, and he's in good shape. He does have children. Both of them were there looking very happy.

We haven't slacked off on the investigation. I've got people calling or interrogating everybody identified as being likely to know anything about Akerson. Before long we should be able to piece together the picture of what he's been up to for the last several weeks. I think we have enough people to do the investigation right, but I'll know better after a couple of days. Everything might open up like a clamshell—or stay shut up like one.

I'll keep you posted.

Peter

THIS IS THE SATURN AGENCY. YOU MAY LEAVE A MESSAGE AT THE TONE.

Dan? It's Joan. Where are you? It's past two o'clock, and you're supposed to be back from breakfast. Listen, I've got an idea to tell you about.

I've been to the studio and watched last night's Union Station tape, and I think it's terrific. I haven't talked to Fishwater, so I don't know what he's planning. But if I can get a copy of the tape to you, can you get somebody from one of the networks to look at it? To be specific, can you get a sound bite of my reporting on network news?

I don't think I'm ever going to be hotter than I am right at this moment. And if I'm ever going to get anybody to notice me, it's got to be now.

I'm leaving you this message, because I thought you

might want to start calling some people as soon as you got back. I've already found out I can take the tape to the airport myself and have a messenger service at your end pick it up—

Joan? I thought it might be you. Listen, I'm sorry, but I expected to be back an hour ago. What's up?

You're going to have to listen to your answering machine, because I don't want to go through it all again. But I hope you had a good breakfast, maybe something like a nice bowl of stone-ground groats and prunes sprinkled with fish oil.

I wish it had been. For just a moment I weakened, then first thing I knew I was eating blintzes and sour cream. The sour cream was even real.

Maybe there's hope for you yet, Dan. Now listen to my message, think about my idea for maybe two minutes, then call me back.

Why don't you just hang on a second? I'll put you on hold, listen to the machine on the other line, then get back to you.

If you think you can handle the technology. All right, I'll wait. . . .

Okay, I'm back. You're right that this is the time for us to act. The tide's rising, and if we can catch it, you can ride it to the top.

I'm glad we agree. I'll go back to the studio, get a copy of the tape, and take it to the airport myself. I'm leaving right now, so stay home and wait for Airport Express Delivery to buzz you.

Hold it a minute, Joan. I just had an idea. Don't send the tape to me, because that will just delay things. Let me think a second.

Okay, here's what you should do. Send the tape to Betty Stowfitz at—

Wait, Dan, wait. You know I'm terrible with names and addresses. Let me turn on my pocket recorder.
Okay, I'm ready. Go ahead.

Betty S-t-o-w-f-i-t-z, Production Supervisor, CBS News, 524 West Fifty-Seventh Street, 10019. I'll call Betty and tell her to expect a tape.

Great. I'll get it to her. But listen, I've got to go now, because something else is happening.
I can hear the whir and purr of my fax spewing out something I should look at. It might be Peter Keefer telling me what they've managed to find out about the Watcher. He sort of promised he would.
I'll call you back after I ship off the tape.

I'll be waiting. Bye, bye.

ST. LOUIS COUNTY POLICE DEPARTMENT

OFFICIAL TRANSCRIPT FROM JOAN CARPENTER'S POCKET TAPE RE-CORDER OF CONVERSATIONS TAKING PLACE AT 2030 BUCKMINSTER AVE, ST. LOUIS COUNTY, MISSOURI ON NOVEMBER 22, AT APPROXI-MATELY 2:15 P.M.

CARPENTER: Alexis! Oh, God, you scared me.
Whew, my nerves are completely shot after yesterday. I heard a noise at the door and immediately, without even thinking about it, I was sure it was the Watcher coming after me.
How did you get in?

HARTZ: I just opened the door and walked in.

CARPENTER: No, no. I don't leave my doors unlocked. I'm always very careful about that.

HARTZ: How I got in doesn't really matter, does it?

CARPENTER: It does if I expect to keep from being murdered in my bed.

HARTZ: Aren't you being a little paranoid? It's been on TV and in the newspapers that the Watcher was shot and captured at Union Station. That's what I want to see you about.

CARPENTER: I was just going into the study to get a fax I heard coming in. It may have some news about the Watcher. Come on back with me and we'll talk.

[Sounds of movement.]

CARPENTER: That's the County Police letterhead all right. It's from Peter Keefer.

HARTZ: What does it say?

CARPENTER: I'll read it.
   "I'm faxing you because your telephone is busy. The news is bad, and you need to know it ASAP for your protection.
   "Walter Akerson cannot (repeat *cannot*) be the Watcher.
   "He was in police custody being questioned on a drug charge when Gary Wells was killed, and he was in a Kansas City motel making a drug delivery the night Tom Kline was attacked. We've got records and witnesses at both places.
   "More about Akerson later. Take precautions and keep safe."
   Then he signs his name.

HARTZ: Are you surprised?

CARPENTER: That Akerson isn't the Watcher? Yes, I am. In fact, I'm completely bewildered. But you don't . . .

HARTZ: But I don't what? Why are you looking at me like that?

289

CARPENTER: I'm not looking at you in any particular way, Alexis.

HARTZ: I don't look surprised. Isn't that what you were going to say?

CARPENTER: Come on, let's go to the kitchen and make coffee.

HARTZ: That's fine. Then we can talk.

[Sounds of movement.]

HARTZ: Stop! Where are you going?

[Sounds of running and heavy breathing. Then a metallic, rattling noise.]

HARTZ: Sorry, Joan, but you can't get out the front door. I've also got the key to the inside lock, and I locked it. I sold you the locks, remember?

CARPENTER: Give me the key, Alexis. Give it to me right now. You've got no right to come into my house. And absolutely no right to keep me here.

HARTZ: Calm down, Joan. Stop! Stay away from me!
    I'm warning you—I'll hurt you, if you touch me.

[Dull noise, then a sharp cry of pain.]

HARTZ: I told you to keep away, Joan. I didn't want to hit you. It was your own fault.
    Now your poor cheek is bleeding. It makes me sad to see that. Here's a tissue.

CARPENTER: That's a gun. You hit me with a gun.

HARTZ: A twenty-two pistol. It's surprisingly large, isn't it? It was my father's. He bought it when you didn't need a license to own a gun, and when he died I inherited it. I even know how to use it, because he taught me.

Is your cheek better? I'm sure it still hurts.

CARPENTER: Only when I breathe.

HARTZ: You're always ready with a joke. I really like that about you, maybe because I tend to be so serious.

Listen, why don't you go ahead and make coffee. I still want us to talk. But I think I'd better warn you—if you touch me again, I'll shoot you.

[Sounds of movement, then kitchen sounds.]

HARTZ: You and I could have had such a wonderful time together, Joan. I don't know why you had to turn against me.

CARPENTER: I didn't turn against you.

HARTZ: I thought we were close, that we were real friends. Maybe one day, I thought, we could even be lovers. But if you didn't want that, we could still do such wonderful things. We could go any place in the world, do things ordinary people don't do. It was going to be just you and me. You and me against the world.

CARPENTER: That's the way you saw things, Alexis. I never said anything to make you think that.

HARTZ: Liar! That's what you say now. But after I sent my second letter, I could tell you wanted us to be together as much as I did.

CARPENTER: What made you believe such a crazy thing?

HARTZ: The way you smiled at me. The way you tilted your head to the side when you spoke. I could see it in your face.

CARPENTER: On camera? Oh, Christ. I wasn't telling you anything, Alexis. You *wanted* me to act that way, so you interpreted whatever I did to fit your pattern.

HARTZ: When you came to my house for dinner, I was going to tell you who I really was, but I changed my mind. I was afraid you might not like me as much as you liked the Watcher, and you might not want me to go on helping you.

CARPENTER: But I *never* wanted you to help me. I hated it when the terrible things you did helped me.
   Alexis, are you listening to me?

HARTZ: I wanted you to get to the top so badly I couldn't stand it. I wanted *us* to get to the top.

CARPENTER: But Alexis, it was just your mind playing tricks on you, making you do things in my name.
   Oh, God, it's all so crazy. Did you really attack Tom Kline and kill Gary Wells?

HARTZ: I did it for you, Joan. Not that I minded so much. Kline was easy. I knew the newspaper writers got finished late, so I parked in the garage and watched him on three days. He always followed the same pattern. He even parked in the same part of the garage.
   Then when I was ready, I waited for him to walk toward his car. When he was getting out his keys, I stepped up behind him and hit him over the head with a toy Cardinals' bat, the kind they sell at souvenir shops.

CARPENTER: Then you mutilated him.

HARTZ: Hush, Joan! Don't say that. *Mutilated* is such an awful word, and it's more precise to say that I castrated him.
   I had on disposable plastic gloves, and just a snip with pruning shears did the trick. I dropped his testicles into a plastic bag, wiped my hands on a paper towel, then drove away. It was over in less than five minutes. I was surprised at how little blood there was.
   Don't look at me in that way. Besides, you're the one who opened the box on your show.

CARPENTER: I wouldn't have, if Gary hadn't fainted. I'm sorry I did it even then.

HARTZ: Sorry you were watched by tens of thousands of people and talked about by many more thousands? I don't believe you.

If I hadn't castrated Kline for the awful things he said about you, you probably wouldn't even have a job now.

CARPENTER: You don't understand, Alexis. I don't *want* a job on those terms. And that goes for what you did to Gary Wells also.

HARTZ: You've forgotten how terribly he treated you. The way he always spoke to you in a sneering, condescending voice. And the way he virtually accused you of castrating Kline.

CARPENTER: I didn't like him, okay? He wasn't nice to me. He was a bad reporter. He wasn't even very bright. Those things are true, but you had no right to kill him.

HARTZ: Oh, Joan, my sweet, you can't fool me. You're glad I did it, and you were glad at the time. It made everything about *Nightbeat* very exciting and interesting. The number of viewers grew tremendously, and people started paying attention to *you*.

CARPENTER: I think you're lying about killing Gary. The TV program on the tape shows he was killed during the talk I gave, but you were in my audience. You couldn't have left, killed Gary, and come back, because you wouldn't have had enough time.

HARTZ: Joan, I know you're highly intelligent, but you aren't devious. I'm both. Just because I sent you a note about your talk, doesn't mean I was at the PIP dinner.
    I told your assistant I wanted to send you a corsage so I could find out what you were going to wear. Then the next morning I called up Loretta Kirby for a chat about the meeting. I pretended I had been there and more or less repeated back to her what she said to me. People always crowd around the speaker at the end of a talk, so I knew I could count on that to explain why I didn't stop by to say hello.

CARPENTER: So you did lure Gary to that garage and kill him?

HARTZ: He hated you so much, I'm glad you never had to listen to him. When I talked to him on the phone, I didn't tell him who I was, but I promised him a big scandal about you.
    I told him I'd meet him in front of the out-of-town newspaper

store across from the courthouse. When he drove up, I got into his car and we went to the Stringer house.

On the way he talked about how that "bitch" Carpenter was ruining his family program with exposé stories and about how he was glad I was going to give him the chance to stop her from criticizing our community. I told him I was just interested in money, but we could talk about that when he saw what I had.

I was very mysterious about everything and made him park in the garage. He thought I lived in the house and that we were going to go inside and look at some videotape of you participating in a sex party with three other people.

CARPENTER: That's just the sort of story Gary would accept at face value.

HARTZ: When he got out of the car, I pointed at some antlers high up on the wall and told him, "Look up there." While his head was tilted back, I hit him with a piece of pipe.

Then I had to work like the devil to get everything ready. I started the engine, put him in the car, taped him up, and ran the hose. I put an old TV set I bought at the Salvation Army store in the car, then got out the little video camera I had brought with me in my canvas bag and started shooting.

CARPENTER: But how did you get away? You couldn't have walked to your house from there.

HARTZ: I didn't have to go that far. I had on my jogging suit and running shoes, and I was just another woman in a nice neighborhood getting some exercise for her health.

It was only four blocks to the service station where I picked up my car. I had dropped it there in the afternoon to have the oil changed. I took a taxi home.

CARPENTER: It sounds like you had it all worked out.

HARTZ: I planned everything, and everything went as planned.

CARPENTER: But the police questioned you, didn't they?

HARTZ: Yes, but they had no real reason to *suspect* me. They surprised me by tracing the towel I left in Wells's car to me, but I already had an answer ready, just in case they did. Besides, I think they were mostly interested in you. I gave you an alibi by telling them I heard you talk at the PIP meeting, and of course that gave me an alibi too.

I was also helpful without giving the impression that I knew what I was doing. I told them a lot of doctors and lawyers had houses in the neighborhood and that Dr. Legion lived only a couple blocks away from the Stringer place. I also mentioned that Alan Carter was the contractor overseeing the work being done on the house.

CARPENTER: You are very smart, Alexis. And very devious. I see now I've always underestimated you.

HARTZ: People always do. Pour me some coffee please. I believe it's ready now.

[Sounds of dishes and slight movement.]

CARPENTER: Oh, I think there's something floating in your cup. Let me look.

HARTZ: No, don't touch my cup.

[Sounds of splashing, breaking dishes. A cry of pain.]

HARTZ: You bitch! What have you done? What have you done? You've scalded my face. Ohhh, ohh, ohh.
    Where are you?

[Sound of a gunshot, a single, sharp crack.]

CARPENTER: My God, my God. Ohh, my arm. You shot me, Alexis.

HARTZ: You tried to blind me with hot coffee. I told you not to fight me. I warned you.

CARPENTER: Dan! Dan!

HARTZ: Stop that! Who are you calling? Is somebody here?

[Sound of a repetitive beeping.]

CARPENTER: Oh, goddammit!

HARTZ: What's going on? That sounds like a busy signal. Are you trying to phone somebody?
I get it now—you have a voice-activated telephone with automatic dialing.
Don't yell anybody else's name, Joan. I've still got the gun, and I'll kill you if you do. I promise you, I'll kill you.
Here, wrap this dish towel around your arm. I don't want you to bleed to death.

CARPENTER: What do you care? You're going to kill me anyway.

HARTZ: I came to talk. But you keep fighting me.
What drawer do you keep your knives in? I want a chef's knife.

CARPENTER: I refuse to help you murder me.

HARTZ: Don't be histrionic. I just want a knife to cut the phone wire. I'll find one myself.

[Sounds of drawers opening and closing.]

HARTZ: Ah, here's a nice big one. It looks like a saber.

[A dull, chopping noise.]

HARTZ: That's better. The beeping was beginning to get on my nerves. Sorry about the cut in your vinyl floor, but it's not very noticeable.
Have you stopped bleeding yet?

CARPENTER: I don't know. It really hurts.

HARTZ: Make sure the towel is tight.

CARPENTER: It is tight.

HARTZ: Then that'll do the trick. I took an advanced Red Cross course, and they told us that direct pressure works better than any drug ever invented.

Now, what were we talking about?

CARPENTER: I don't know. It doesn't matter.

HARTZ: Oh, I know. You were saying you underestimated me. Well, that's right, and I'm glad you realize it, even though it's too late for both of us.

What I see now is that you must have been laughing at me from the very beginning, right when I started helping you. I was just a crackpot you could take advantage of. You were glad enough to get the publicity and boost your career, but then eventually I couldn't do enough to please you.

CARPENTER: I told you before, I didn't want you to do anything.

HARTZ: And then when you didn't think I could be of use to you anymore, you turned on me.

CARPENTER: How could I turn on you? I didn't even know who you were.

HARTZ: You turned on the Watcher, and that's the same thing. You called me crazy and paranoid and mentally ill.

CARPENTER: I didn't use any of those words.

HARTZ: You said the same things in other words. Then you tried to trick me into turning myself in to you at Union Station. That way you could get the glory from seeing me locked up in the psychiatric ward.

You'd be on camera explaining to everybody what was happening, and I would be there in a straitjacket looking pitiful. I'd look like those pathetic pictures of Charles Manson, and people would think I really was crazy.

CARPENTER: That's not what I wanted. I wanted to keep you from killing anyone else. I genuinely wanted to help you.

HARTZ: You shouldn't have done that to me, Joan. You shouldn't have called me names and tried to play games with me. I really loved you and wanted us to be together, and you've ruined it all.

Your greed and arrogance made you destroy a wonderful relationship. It was as if you couldn't stand the beauty of a delicate crystal bowl and had to hurl it onto the concrete and smash it into thousands of fragments.

That bowl was my heart, and its fragments are sharp. And now you've got to pay the price.

CARPENTER: I don't want to listen to a lecture. If you're going to murder me, just go ahead and do it.

HARTZ: Joan, Joan. I'm not going to *murder* you. I'm going to *punish* you. You have betrayed a trust and destroyed an irreplaceable relationship, and you must die for what you've done.

[A whirring, mechanical sound.]

HARTZ: What's that noise?

CARPENTER: My fax machine. Somebody is sending me something.

HARTZ: I want to see what it is. Walk toward the study, and I'll follow you.

CARPENTER: Do you have to take that knife with you?

HARTZ: I plan to put the phone in the study out of commission. Now start walking. And don't forget I've got a gun.

[Sounds of movement.]

HARTZ: Pick up the page and read it to me.

CARPENTER: It's from my agent. "Is your telephone working? Are you all right? Get in touch at once."

HARTZ: Then we'd better reply. Let's see, you're right handed, so your arm shouldn't bother you. Type this out, "I am fine. Will call you later," then sign your name.

CARPENTER: It'll save time if I write it instead of typing it. Is that okay?

HARTZ: Any way you like, my dear. I'm glad you're being so co-operative now. That will make everything easier for both of us.

CARPENTER: All right, I'm ready. I'm just going to put the page under the cover and punch in Dan's number.

[Beeping sounds.]

HARTZ: Stop! Let me see what you've written.

CARPENTER: The fax is starting up. It's too late.

HARTZ: Where's the plug?

CARPENTER: That's the electrical cord, and the connection is screwed in. You can't unplug it.

HARTZ: That's why I have a knife.

CARPENTER: No, don't!

[Crackling, buzzing sounds mixed with a high-pitched scream.]

CARPENTER: Oh, my God. It's terrible. It's terrible.

[Sound of telephone ringing.]

Joan? Is that you? It's Dan. Are you all right? I've been trying to get through to you for almost an hour.

Oh, Dan. I'm okay. But Alexis isn't. She's dead. I just saw it.

What are you talking about? Your voice sounds funny, and you're not making any sense. Who's Alexis?

She's the Watcher. She came here to kill me, but she killed herself. By accident. I watched it happen.

Watched what happen?

She cut into the electric cord on the fax machine, and it electrocuted her.

Oh, Jesus, Joan. And this just happened?

Yes. Just a minute ago.

Are you okay? Are you hurt?

No. I mean, yes, but I'm okay.

Do you feel very weak, like you're going to pass out?

I'm shaky, but I'm not going to pass out.

Good. Now, listen to me. When we hang up, call nine-one-one and say that you need an ambulance and the police. Then go into another room and sit down and wait.

I have to unlock the door. Nobody will be able to get in. I have to get my key out of my purse and unlock the door.

All right, unlock the door, then sit down. Just sit there and don't move. Don't try to do anything. Got that?

All right.

And Joan, I'm leaving for St. Louis right now. I'm getting the next plane, and I'll see you in about four hours.

I'm glad.

I am too. Now hang up and call nine-one-one.

All right.

ST. LOUIS COUNTY POLICE DEPARTMENT

Memo of Transmission   Date: November 23

From: Detective Lieutenant Peter Keefer, Major Case Squad
To: Chief of Police Harold C. Blackshire

Dear Harold:

Investigating the events surrounding the Carpenter case has been like trying to keep track of all the bees swarming around the queen—everything keeps shifting and changing.

Still, my Squad has really been on the run since the shootings on Saturday, and I think we can put all the pieces of the puzzle in place now and see the whole picture. Let me update you on the basic items.

Alexis Hartz

(1) Alexis Hartz was declared DOA at Deaconess Hospital when she was brought in by the EMS. An autopsy showed she died as a result of electric shock—something to do with disrupting the heart rhythms, but I couldn't follow the details.

We're not going to press the question of how she got electrocuted. I'm sure the M.E.'s office will bring in a finding of accidental death, and of course the coroner will go along with it.

(2) Hartz's mother gave us permission to search the house, and we located an IBM Selectric-II typewriter equipped with a Century typing element. The typewriter was locked in a basement room. Greg Handler did a microscopic comparison and established by ten agreements (seven is considered definitive) that the type is the same as that in the Watcher letters.

One of the computer-security people in Greg's operation also located some "locked" files in Hartz's computer. Don't ask me how, but he managed to gain access to them in about ten minutes. The files aren't directly incriminating, but they show that Hartz was obsessed with Joan Carpenter and was planning to take various steps she believed would promote Carpenter's career.

(3) Going by the IR-905 Ray wrote after interrogating Hartz and by crosschecking the times and her appointments, Hartz would have been able to attack Kline and send off the box containing his testicles. (We showed her photo to employees at Zip-Zip Express, and no one could ID her for sure. Of course this doesn't mean anything.)

We have no direct evidence to connect Hartz to the flower shears Curt Collins stole from the garage where Wells was killed. However, we figure that the shears belonged to Hartz, and after she used them, she didn't want to keep them in her possession. So she dumped them in the Stringers' garage. She may have thought we either wouldn't notice them or wouldn't connect them with the Kline attack. But even if we did, she was sure we couldn't take the crucial step and connect them with her.

The fact that Collins found the shears and stole them is just part of the background static you get in any investigation. It wasn't anything Hartz could have foreseen or planned.

(4) The story Hartz told Carpenter also checked out. Melanie Epson, the woman who runs World Newspapers recalls seeing a woman get into a car between 7:00 and 7:30 last Tuesday night. Epson couldn't see the woman's face, but in height and build she fit Hartz's description.

Also, Clarence Cowart at Jim Bix's Sinclair Station on Ladue Rd. has definitely IDed Alexis Hartz as the person who left a white Mercedes convertible to have an oil change on the afternoon of that same day. Most of their customers are regulars, and he had never seen her before. He also remembered her because she paid with cash. None of his regulars pay with cash.

(5) Hartz told Carpenter about a scandal involving the way the Maxim Corporation acquired the land where they are developing the Park Central Mall. I thought at first this might be connected with the Wells homicide, but Ray wasn't able to get her to tell him anything that confirmed this. I now suspect that Hartz talked about the scandal to Carpenter just as a ploy to get Carpenter to spend time with her.

I mentioned Hartz's allegation to Alvin Schwartz from the Fraud Division and asked him to take a look at the materials Carpenter's researchers have been digging up. Schwartz says it looks like they hit pay dirt. Three of Maxim's executives and two members of the zoning board started quietly buying up houses and lots in the center of the proposed mall area.

Fraud Division has now taken charge of the case, but I promised Carpenter she could have an exclusive on breaking the story. (You and I know she's right about being able to find a lot of corruption in a city as big as St. Louis. But I just wish she would be content with leaving it to us to uncover it.)

(6) Walter Allison Akerson

For the past two weeks, Akerson had been staying at the Ideal Hotel on north DeBalivere. It's a welfare place catering mostly to long-term residents, and we located a woman living there who knew Akerson. Her name is Helen Wilmers, and she used to "see him around and have a few drinks with him." She admits she's got a drug problem, and she says Akerson let her have a little ice "just to show we was friends."

Wilmers says Akerson told her he was sitting in the hotel lobby and the TV was turned to *Nightbeat*. He watched the program and saw Joan Carpenter trying to get the Watcher to surrender. That gave Akerson the idea that if he could capture or kill Carpenter at Union Station with so many people watching, he would become a celebrity. He could then be somebody. If he captured her, he could ask for ransom, and if he killed her, he would still be famous. In either case, he could get rich by selling the rights to his life story.

Akerson asked Wilmers to help him with the plan. He wanted her to hide Carpenter after he snatched her. But Wilmers refused. She says she thought he was just another guy talking big and trying to impress her. She says she didn't take him seriously, and that's why she didn't report him. (I believe the rest of her story, but not this. The truth is she didn't want to get involved with the police and could care less about Joan Carpenter.)

Akerson seems to have been just another crazy out to make a name for himself by killing somebody lucky and famous. (Since Hinckley and Chapman, there seems to be more of them than ever. Are they teaching this stuff in school now?)

(7) Joan Carpenter

The EMS reached Carpenter's house in eight minutes, and she was in the ER at Barnes six minutes later. She was suffering shock from blood loss and gunshot wound, but I was told today that she is in excellent shape. She was shot with a .22 caliber pistol, but fortunately the bullet grazed her upper left arm without breaking a bone or severing a main artery. The doctors say they're most concerned about preventing infection.

Dr. Stephen Legion was called in to take care of the cut on the side of her jaw. He took some stitches, but he says it will leave such a small scar nobody will notice it.

Carpenter was well enough to give us a very complete statement, and I'm impressed by the way she handled the situation. Still, I think she's lucky to be alive. She is supposed to be discharged tomorrow. Her agent (Daniel Saturn) is making all the arrangements for her.

Joan Carpenter's arrival in St. Louis seemed to unleash forces that had been safely tied up before she came. I don't know what it was that made her a catalyst for such violent change. I think it must have something to do with the way she comes across on TV. Anyway, this is a problem somebody else needs to think about. I've got enough to do dealing with its consequences.

The memorial service for Ray Robertson will be held the day after tomorrow. Joan Carpenter asked if she could come, and I told her I thought Ray would be pleased to have her there.

Peter

Mrs. Dora Carpenter

8519 Bluffview Road
Dallas, Texas 75209

November 30

Dear Joanie,

I'm so glad I let you talk me into going to St. Louis for Thanksgiving! I would have been unbearably jealous if the rest of you had been there celebrating the day while I was home having a solitary dinner.

It was tremendous fun seeing everybody. Amy has grown so very tall that I wonder if she's not going to get *too* tall. (I don't care what you say, a tall woman still has problems attracting men. Blame it on the men if you want to, but it's true.) I was afraid Amy was going to be short like Jack, but I guess she takes after our side of the family more.

Speaking of Jack, is he coloring his hair? It looks as black as Skuff-Kote shoe polish. I wanted to ask Jane, but I figured it was really none of my business.

Jane looks good, though, doesn't she? She thinks she's getting fat, but I believe the extra few pounds make her look better. I've always thought both of you girls were too skinny to be healthy.

I surely did my best to get healthy that way while I was visiting. I've made better turkey and dressing than I did this time, but that didn't stop me from eating it. Everything else was delicious. I didn't expect to like the stuffed mushrooms, but they were one of the best dishes I've ever tasted. (I always told you two to try new things, because you might discover something you liked). Your pecan pie is better than mine ever was. Are you really using the same recipe?

How is your arm? Does it look like it's going to leave a big scar? I hope not, but even if it does, you can just wear long-sleeved dresses or hide it with makeup. Besides, I don't think people worry as much about little imperfections as they used to. Even so, I'm glad you had a plastic surgeon sew up the cut on your face. It's not even going to leave a blemish.

Still, the important thing is that you didn't get killed or crippled. I'm thankful for that every time I think about what you had to go through. Your daddy would have been very proud of you. I'm only sorry he isn't around to tell you so himself.

Meeting Dan was the biggest surprise. After hearing you mention his name for such a long time, I must have formed some idea of what he would look like. I guess I expected him to be short and fat and smoke cigars like agents in movies. That's probably why I was surprised by how handsome he is. If he wanted to become a leading man, he could be his own agent.

"Handsome is as handsome does" my mother used to say, and Dan's way of acting perfectly matched his looks. I can't think of the last time I met a young man who was so polite and considerate.

Of course he won my heart by dropping everything and flying off to St. Louis to make sure you were okay. He could look like a gargoyle and smell like a shoat, and I would still like him for doing that. He seems to think the world of you, because he hardly took his eyes off you when we were all together.

He told me quite candidly that he thinks the CBS offer involves some risks for you. He says a general-interest program like *Update* might not get high enough ratings. He also says that if the national audience doesn't respond to you enthusiastically, you might find it hard to get another opportunity to be on a network program. I'm sure he's told you all this already. I'm just trying to sort it out for myself.

I can't help thinking about the possibility of your moving to New York again. At least when you were at Barnard I knew you would be coming back home when you graduated. Still, I guess the job is the break you've been looking for. Despite the risks, I imagine you'll take it. I haven't seen you let risks slow you down yet.

I want you to come down and see me when you get some vacation time. I like traveling, but I like staying at home better.

Love and kisses from your,
Mama

Psychiatry Consultants, Inc.
3460 Chestnut Avenue
Brookline, MA 02147
617-976-8740
FAX: 617-976-2286

SISTERGRAM

December 1

Dear Joanie,

Wow! That's all I can say. Or maybe it's just the only intelligent thing I can say.

How can you have known Dan for five years and never put his name on the Golden List of possibles? He's such an obvious (not to say desirable) candidate—good-looking, intelligent, educated, sophisticated, and successful. If he's not rich, he's surely well-enough situated to keep himself in carrot juice and carob chips and you in Rigauds and single malts. And that's all you need, really. I don't see you demanding a little pied-à-terre on the Côte d'Azur.

The only warning light that flashed for me was that he's 37 and he's never been married. Given my prurient psychiatric mind, I suspected he might have spent the last fifteen years escorting his mother to teas, operas, and gallery openings, being a sort of nonviolent Norman Bates.

I was immensely relieved to hear him mention how bad he felt after breaking up with the woman he had lived with for three years. (A friend of mine actually has one of her prints. Tiny planet.) I don't want to give the impression I think suffering is good for the character, but I was reassured that there had been somebody to break up with. That he suffered is also a good sign. Anybody who didn't feel the pain of separation and loss after living with somebody for three years would be in deep psychiatric shit.

I don't think you have to worry much about the hypochondriasis. I can tell you from personal experience that it's possible to be happily married to somebody who believes a hangover is an adequate indication for an MRI. I'm sure the love of a good woman would make most of Dan's health worries melt away like icicles in the oven. And probably even the love of somebody like you would help a lot. (Just kidding. I noticed that he also has a sense of humor, an absolute necessity in life without a laugh track.)

Maybe the most he has to recommend him is that Mama liked him, despite his foreign ways and funny way of talking. And since she had the good sense to marry Daddy, her opinion is worth listening to.

We all had a wonderful time. Amy thinks you glow in the dark, as well as on the tube. Jack can't get over the fact that even though you appear on TV you can talk about the Gödel theorem and the limits of computability.

I also think you're pretty swell, and I'm very glad that you're still alive so I can say that.

Love, pats, and hats,
Janie

P.S. I forgot to tell you in the excitement, but I don't think you meant Zack. I think you meant Mack.

Mack is the one whose parents gave him a Corvette when he turned seventeen. It was in that same Corvette that we drove from Dallas to New Orleans on the Friday we got out of school to go to the State Fair and the 'rents thought I was going to be spending the weekend at Laura Fisher's parents' cabin on Grapevine Lake—without a telephone. Jack knew that wasn't true, because I was really going to a protest meeting in Austin. Yeah.

It's a good thing I came to your house for Thanksgiving. That still remains blackmail material.

JOAN CARPENTER
2030 Buckminster · St. Louis, MO · 63130

1 Dec/Tue

Dear Dan,

Yes.
But what about you?

Love,
Joan

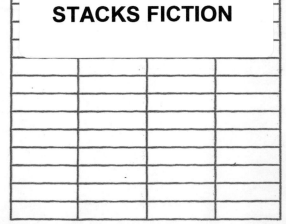